TURKEY DAY SUSPECTS

Hayley stepped out onto the porch and waved good-bye as she made her way back to her car. As she drove away, her thoughts lingered on the conversation she had just had. The Sweets might have had every reason to be frustrated with Tom, but they did not strike her as people who would resort to violence.

But that still left the question: *if not the Sweets, then who?*

Hayley's mind drifted back to the other suspects—the Murdocks, with their wealth and ambition, Reid Norton, with his temper and love of firearms, and Lori Gunning, the reclusive therapist who was difficult to read. Each of them had their reasons for wanting Tom out of the way, but the truth still felt elusive.

One thing, however, was clear.

Someone in Bar Harbor had decided that Tom Farley's stubbornness was a problem that needed solving . . .

DEATH
of a
TOM TURKEY

LEE HOLLIS

Kensington Publishing Corp.
kensingtonbooks.com

DEATH
of a
TOM TURKEY

Chapter 1

The annual turkey shoot hosted by the Bar Harbor Volunteer Fire Department was the highlight of the town's pre-Thanksgiving festivities. This year, like every other, the event promised a large turnout. Crisp autumn air filled with the scent of pine and distant woodsmoke greeted the attendees as they gathered at the fire department's open field, a sea of plaid flannel and bright orange hunting vests.

Hayley Powell adjusted her woolen scarf, glancing at her husband Bruce Linney, who was practically vibrating with excitement. Bruce, a crime reporter for the local paper, the *Island Times*, had been bragging about his shooting skills for days.

"You'll see, Hayley," Bruce said, patting the stock of his gleaming rifle. "First prize is as good as ours. I'm a natural marksman."

Hayley, a food columnist at the *Island Times* and

owner of the popular local restaurant Hayley's Kitchen, chuckled at her husband's overconfidence.

"Yes, dear, I'm sure you are," she replied with a wink.

She had only come along for the fun, not expecting to participate seriously.

The event was well underway, and the field was buzzing with activity. Hayley watched as families gathered around picnic tables, sharing hot apple cider and homemade pastries from the local bakery, Morning Glory. The smell of roasting chestnuts mingled with the crisp air, creating a cozy atmosphere that was quintessentially Bar Harbor post-tourist season.

Bruce took his turn at the firing line, his bravado on full display. He puffed his chest out as he raised his rifle. A few spectators gathered around, curious to see if he was as good at shooting as he boasted.

Bruce squinted, aimed, and fired.

His shot was good, but not great—certainly not the bullseye he had predicted.

A few scattered cheers and polite applause followed his attempt.

"Not bad, honey," Hayley teased, patting his shoulder. "You've got this."

Although he had not scored a bullseye, he still had scored the closest shot over the other entrants in this contest so far.

Bruce grumbled good-naturedly, stepping aside as Hayley took her place. She had not planned on competing, but the gleam in Bruce's eye spurred her on. With a deep breath, she raised the rifle, aimed, and squeezed the trigger.

The shot rang out, and the crowd fell silent for a moment before erupting into cheers.

Hayley had hit the bullseye.

Bruce stared; his mouth open in disbelief. "Well, I'll be damned," he muttered, shaking his head. "Looks like Randy's not going to have to go foraging at the Shop 'n Save for a good turkey. We can just drop off your first prize."

Randy, Hayley's brother, was hosting Thanksgiving dinner this year. Hayley's two grown children, Gemma and Dustin, were celebrating the holiday in New York and Los Angeles respectively, and so Randy had invited Hayley's whole gang, including besties Liddy and Mona, to join him and his husband Sergio, the chief of police, at their sprawling seaside home.

As Hayley collected her prize—a plump turkey that was so big she suspected it would feed half the town, she could not help but feel a swell of pride. She held up the turkey for Bruce to see, a wide grin on her face.

"I guess I'm the sharpshooter in the family," she said, winking at him. "Maybe I missed my calling. I should've become a Delta Force assassin, or a spy, oh I love that, Jane Bond! When Liddy, Mona and I played *Charlie's Angels* when we were kids I was always the one pretending to have the gun."

Hayley struck the iconic *Charlie's Angels* silhouette pose, her fingers forming into the shape of a pistol.

Bruce feigned a scowl, but she could tell he was proud of his wife for slaying the competition, himself included.

"Okay, Annie Oakley, let's get that turkey over to Randy's freezer," Bruce said.

Their playful banter was interrupted by a sudden commotion nearby. Raised voices and the sound of a scuffle drew the attention of everyone around them.

"What's going on over there?" Hayley asked, craning her neck to see.

Local crank Tom Farley, known for his smelly and nasty turkey farm that his neighbors were constantly complaining about, was in a heated argument with one of those neighbors. Retired Army Major Reid Norton, whose property lay to the north of Tom's farm, was red-faced and shouting.

"Oh, boy. Not this again," Bruce sighed, recognizing the familiar scene.

Tom's turkeys had a habit of crossing over onto Reid's property, wreaking havoc on his garden. This past summer, the birds had destroyed Reid's meticulously tended vegetable patch, and it seemed Reid had finally had enough.

"You've got to be kidding me," Reid yelled, his face inches from Tom's. "Those damn birds ruined my garden! You need to keep them contained, Farley!"

Tom dismissed Reid's fury with a dismissive wave of his bony hand. "Oh, give it a rest, Norton. It's November, your garden is just mulch now anyway. Why don't you take up an indoor hobby like needlepoint or crocheting, something a little more your speed."

Reid's nostrils flared.

Hayley closed her eyes.

She knew what was coming.

It was the last straw.

Reid swung a fist, and the fight erupted. The crowd

gasped, some stepping back while others moved forward to get a better look.

Before Bruce could make a move to stop them, Hayley's best friend, Mona Barnes, a tough-talking, gruff bruiser of a lobster woman and a close friend of Reid's, charged forward. With her strong arms from a life hauling heavy lobster traps, and her typical no-nonsense attitude, Mona physically intervened, yanking the two men apart with ease.

"Break it up, you two!" Mona barked, standing between them like a human barricade. "This is supposed to be a community event, not a boxing match! Who do you think you are, Oleksandr Usyk and Tyson Fury? They could be your grandsons! Chill out!"

Neither man budged.

Mona ripped off her Maine Guide wool cap and hurled it to the ground, fists raised, ready to take them both on, if necessary.

Tom and Reid glared at each other but reluctantly stepped back, muttering under their breaths. The tension in the air was palpable, but Mona's presence kept the situation from escalating any further.

Hayley, still holding her prize turkey, exchanged a concerned glance with Bruce. "Why does this always happen? Those two are natural born enemies. I wish they could just find a way to bury the hatchet. Life is too short to be at each other's throats all the time."

Bruce shook his head. "It's not just Reid. None of Tom's neighbors appreciate his smelly turkeys and lack of landscaping. Can you imagine living next to his property? The town dump has more charm. I feel bad for all of them."

"Well, the more they complain about him, the more defensive and intractable he gets," Hayley said. "They should all just try to get along."

"I think they're way past that," Mona interjected, brushing herself off, having successfully sent the two feuding men to their respective corners. "I heard the Murdocks, his neighbors to the south, tried to sue him to clean up his property, and lost. If the Murdocks, with all their power and money and influence, can't win in court, then Tom and his turkeys are untouchable, in my opinion."

Bruce observed Tom and Reid still glaring at each other, Tom firing off a smattering of four-letter words loud enough to be heard, as military-trained Reid, with his imposing physique and buzz cut, his face red with rage and his contempt flagrant, shook his head in disgust.

"Sergio should keep an eye on those two," Bruce acknowledged. "Something tells me this isn't over."

As the turkey shoot continued and the commotion died down, Hayley could not shake the feeling that Bruce was right, and the events of the day were just the beginning of something much bigger.

And more dangerous.

Little did she know, the annual turkey shoot might have been a highlight of Bar Harbor's calendar, but this year, it marked the start of a disturbing chain of events that would change everything.

Permanently.

Chapter 2

The crisp November air was now filled with the aroma of fried dough and maple syrup as Hayley made her way back to the booth where Bruce was nursing a thermos of coffee. The volunteer fire department's Thanksgiving turkey shoot was still in full swing, with laughter and cheers punctuating the otherwise serene Maine morning. Hayley's thoughts drifted back to the scuffle between Tom Farley and Reid Norton. The tensions between the two men were simmering just as hot as the turkey fryer on the other side of the field.

Hayley's musings were interrupted by the unmistakable voice of her other BFF, Liddy Crawford, who arrived with a large wicker basket. Liddy's usual polished look was even more dazzling today, thanks to the extra effort she had put in to impress the influential Murdock family, her latest real estate clients, who would no doubt be attending the turkey shoot at some point today.

"Hayley!" Liddy's voice carried over the crowd as she waved. "Good lord, woman, you are the hardest person to find. Where have you been hiding yourself?"

"No one's hiding, Liddy. I'm standing right here in plain view." Hayley laughed.

"She just beat the pants off me in the turkey shoot," Bruce piped in. "She won a twenty-five pounder!"

"Oh, I'm sorry, Bruce. I know what a number that must have done on your fragile male ego!" Liddy cackled before quickly pivoting back toward Hayley. "Did you get my text?"

"No, what's wrong?"

"Nothing's wrong. I just need your help today, talking me up, telling everyone what an incredibly talented and award-winning real estate genius I am, loud enough for everyone who might happen to be within earshot to hear."

"Okay, what do you want me to say?"

"Just what I told you. Talented. Award winning. Genius. In your own words, of course. But don't go overboard."

"You don't think genius is a little overboard?" Bruce cracked.

Liddy chose to ignore him and raised her basket. "Look what I've brought for everyone!"

Liddy unveiled a batch of homemade blueberry pancakes, their golden edges and plump blueberries making all their mouths water instantly. Liddy's culinary skills had come a long way from the days when she could barely boil water.

"I see someone's been practicing," Hayley teased, nudging Liddy.

Liddy beamed, but Hayley knew her friend well enough to see the ulterior motive beneath that bright smile. Sure, she was here to serve the firemen and their families, but Liddy was also here to curry favor with the Murdocks, whose mansion purchase she was overseeing. A hefty commission was on the line, and Liddy was determined to seal the deal.

"Where are they?" Hayley asked, scanning the crowd for the Murdocks.

"Over by the shooting range, of course," Liddy said, rolling her eyes. "Lester's probably making a scene about something trivial as usual. He's not the easiest client I've ever had to deal with. Not by a long shot."

Bruce hung back to chat with some buddies as Hayley and Liddy made their way to the shooting range, where they found Lester Murdock gesticulating wildly, his face red with annoyance. His wife Melody, already clutching a plastic cup filled with a suspiciously pink liquid, swayed slightly as she laughed at something only she found amusing. Their two sons, both in their late teens, Alan and Bo, stood nearby, looking bored and entitled.

As they approached, Lester's bluster became clearer. "I'm telling you, this range isn't regulation! How am I supposed to practice my aim with all these distractions?"

The two firemen in charge of the range just stared blankly at Lester, unsure what they could do about it.

Hayley bit her tongue, but Liddy stepped forward with her best professional smile. "Lester, Melody, boys!

So glad you all could make it. I brought some of my famous blueberry pancakes."

Lester's eyes lit up, not with appreciation, but with the same calculating look he always had. "Ah, Liddy! Always thinking ahead. Maybe these pancakes will bring some luck to my aim today."

He winked, making Liddy's skin crawl.

Hayley could not help but notice the way Melody's gaze sharpened at the mention of luck, her drunken haze lifting momentarily. "Luck? Lester, darling, you need more than luck," she slurred. "You need a miracle to hit anything today." She burst into peals of laughter, almost spilling her drink.

"Thank you, dear," Lester seethed. "I can always count on you as an unwavering pillar of support."

Melody snorted into her cup then downed the rest of her drink in one gulp. She pouted as she turned the cup upside down to indicate it was empty.

Lester sighed and turned to his son Alan. "Go get your mother another Rose Kennedy, would you, son?"

"Dad!" Alan whined. "That's like pouring gasoline on a brush fire."

"It's better than having to deal with her sober, or worse, hung over," Lester muttered as Alan, resigned, trotted off toward the family's truck.

Liddy handed out plates of pancakes to the remaining Murdocks, trying to ignore Lester's lingering touch on her arm. She caught Hayley's eye and subtly rolled her eyes, signaling her discomfort.

Hayley gave her a sympathetic smile, wishing there was something she could do to help her friend endure Lester's unwanted attentions.

Liddy's efforts paid off, though. The Murdocks were too busy enjoying the pancakes to cause more trouble for the moment. But then came the next shooting competition, and the peace was short-lived.

Liddy also turned out to be a crack shot, much to everyone's surprise, including Hayley's.

Bruce, slack-jawed, just shook his head. This was the second time today he had been reminded that his shooting skills were not as sharp as he had convinced himself they were.

When the dust settled, Liddy was declared the winner of the round and was awarded a large, succulent ham. The crowd cheered, but the victory did not sit well with everyone.

Bo Murdock, his face twisted into a sneer, approached Liddy. "Nice shooting, Ms. Crawford. But maybe next time, it might be in your best interest not to do so well. My dad likes to win, and he doesn't take kindly to being shown up."

Hayley bristled at the veiled threat, but Liddy remained unfazed. "Thank you for the advice, Bo. I'll be sure to keep that in mind."

Hayley and Liddy exchanged a knowing look. It was clear that the Murdocks were a force to be reckoned with, but Liddy was not one to back down from a challenge. As they walked away from the range, the tension lingering in the air, Hayley could not shake the feeling that this Thanksgiving turkey shoot was just the beginning of an intense drama about to cast a shadow over Bar Harbor.

Chapter 3

Hayley's fork clattered against her plate as she pushed her half-eaten pancakes away. Her appetite had vanished, and the once-appealing stack of golden-brown blueberry flapjacks now seemed like an insurmountable challenge.

"I can't finish these," she muttered, putting a hand to her mouth.

Liddy was at her side in a flash. "Why? What's wrong with them? Did I add too much salt?"

"No."

"Sugar?"

"No."

"Baking powder?"

"No, Liddy. They're perfect. I'm just stuffed," Hayley moaned, preparing to scrape them into the garbage bin.

"Hold on, Hayley," Liddy said, catching her just in

time. "Use the green bin on the other side of the food tent. We use the leftover scraps to feed the pigs on the farm next door. Chief Grady appreciates the extra slop for his hungry hogs."

Hayley nodded, grateful for the redirection. She carried her plate to the designated bin, trying not to think too much about the sour turn her morning had taken. The turkey shoot was supposed to be a fun event, but something about it felt off to her today, especially after the unpleasant altercation between Tom Farley and Reid Norton.

As she scraped her pancakes into the green bin, Hayley's younger brother Randy's voice boomed across the field, capturing everyone's attention. She turned to see him approaching with a broad smile, a couple trailing behind him.

"Hey, everyone!" Randy called out, his tone as lively as ever. "I want you all to meet Daniel Sweet and his lovely wife, Hannah. They're new in town, and Daniel's just joined us at Drinks Like A Fish."

Hayley found herself smiling at the young couple. Daniel looked to be in his mid-twenties, tall and lanky, with a friendly demeanor that matched his bright eyes. His wife, Hannah, stood beside him, her hands resting on a small but noticeable baby bump.

"Nice to meet you," Hayley said, extending her hand. "Welcome to Bar Harbor!"

"Thank you," Hannah replied with a warm smile. "We're excited to be here and thrilled to be starting our family soon."

Hayley sized up Hannah's tummy. "Congratulations. When are you due?"

"Early January," Hannah replied.

"A New Year's baby!" Randy gushed.

Bruce introduced himself to Daniel, shaking his hand. "Where did you folks move here from?"

"North Conway, New Hampshire. That's where I was born and raised. Hannah and I met when she moved there senior year and we've been together ever since."

"I told him I wanted to raise our family near the ocean and so Bar Harbor was a natural choice," Hannah said.

Randy clapped Daniel on the back. "Daniel here has been a godsend. My bar manager Michelle went off to Florida indefinitely with her boyfriend, so Daniel's taken her place and he's doing a bang-up job."

"That's great to hear," Bruce said. "Whereabouts are you living?"

"Tom Farley's neighbors to the west," Daniel said, nodding. "A double-wide on a small strip of property. It's all we could afford for now, but we're hoping to save enough to buy a bigger place to raise our family."

"It's a start," Hayley said encouragingly. "And you'll make it work."

"I sure hope so," Hannah said, her eyes sparkling with optimism. "We had no idea how expensive Bar Harbor would be, but Daniel's job at the bar is a big help."

"And we're excited to make new friends," Daniel added.

"Well, you've come to the right place. Just about everyone in town shows up at the annual turkey shoot," Hayley said, smiling.

"Speaking of which," Daniel said, glancing at his

watch, "I've got to head to the firing line. My turn's coming up. Nice meeting you all!"

As Daniel jogged off toward the line of shooters, Hannah stayed behind, striking up a conversation with Hayley. They talked about the town, the upcoming baby, and the adjustments of moving to a new place. The exchange was light and pleasant, a welcome distraction from Hayley's earlier unease.

But their conversation was abruptly interrupted by a sudden commotion. A collective gasp rose from the crowd, followed by screams and shouts. The head of the fire department's voice cut through the chaos, urgent and commanding.

"Cease fire! Cease fire!"

Everyone who was lined up at the firing line immediately stopped shooting, their attention snapping to the source of the disturbance. All eyes fell on Tom Farley, lying face down on the ground, moaning in pain. Blood was pooling beneath him, staining the grass.

"Oh my God!" Hayley cried, her hands flying to her mouth.

"Tom!" someone shouted, rushing to his side.

Bruce quickly pulled out his phone and dialed 911, his voice steady despite the panic around them.

Hayley rushed over as a man inspected Tom then cranked his head around to address the onlookers. "He's been shot!"

"What?" Hayley gasped.

By a real bullet?

Impossible.

All the guns were loaded with bean bags.

Sock-shaped pouches filled with lead.

They're specifically designed not to penetrate skin.

Within minutes, the distant wail of an ambulance siren could be heard, growing louder as it approached. The police were not far behind.

As the ambulance arrived, paramedics jumped out and sprinted over to Tom, barking orders and pushing through the gathering crowd.

Police Chief Sergio, Randy's husband and Hayley's brother-in-law, strode onto the scene, his presence commanding immediate attention. At his side were two of his most loyal officers, Lieutenant Donnie and Sergeant Earl.

"Alright, everyone, stay where you are!" Chief Sergio ordered, his voice carrying over the crowd. "No one leaves until I've had a chance to question everybody."

Donnie and Earl fanned out to gather up all the guns on the scene and to corral the still stunned crowd, plucking them one by one and escorting them over to where Chief Sergio was waiting.

The paramedics worked swiftly, assessing Tom's injury and preparing him for transport.

The crowd watched in stunned silence as they loaded him onto a stretcher and rushed him towards the waiting ambulance. The vehicle sped away, leaving a trail of anxious murmurs in its wake.

Once Tom was whisked off to the hospital, the atmosphere shifted from shock to a tense silence. Hayley, Bruce, and Randy gathered near the food tent, their minds racing with questions.

"This is bad," Randy muttered, rubbing the back of his neck. "How on earth did this happen?"

Bruce shook his head, his jaw clenched. "I don't know. But this wasn't an accident."

"Who would do something like this?" Hayley whispered, her hands still trembling.

Randy raised an eyebrow. "Are you kidding me, sis? Tom's a cantankerous old coot with a ton of enemies. He's never once tried to be friendly to anyone, especially to his neighbors. He rubs everybody the wrong way. Half the town could be suspects in his shooting."

Hayley shook her head in disbelief. "But why now? Here, in broad daylight, in front of all these people?"

Randy's usually jovial face was set in a serious expression. "This is going to be a serious mess."

"Someone must have had a reason," Bruce said, his eyes narrowing. "We just have to figure out who and why."

As Chief Sergio began questioning the witnesses, Hayley felt a knot of dread tighten in her stomach because she knew what everyone was thinking.

There was a would-be assassin loose in Bar Harbor.

The turkey shoot had suddenly taken an even darker turn, and the ripple effects were just beginning to spread through their tight-knit community.

Chapter 4

The police were doing their rounds, but the tension in the air was thick. Chief Sergio, Lieutenant Donnie, and Sergeant Earl methodically checked the rifles that had been gathered, the sunlight glinting off the metal barrels as they were examined one by one.

Hayley watched the scene unfold, her sharp eyes missing nothing. She noticed how Sergeant Earl seemed particularly distracted today. As Earl half-heartedly listened to the testimony of a few witnesses on the scene, his gaze kept drifting over to where Mona was standing, nervously shifting from one foot to the other. Their recent romantic relationship was not exactly a secret in town, and Mona despised any sort of gossip about her private life. This moment was awkward for everyone, but especially for Earl, who was clearly struggling to maintain his focus. Mona could plainly see a group of women huddled together obviously chattering about her dating a man nearly half her age.

Mona, visibly frustrated, approached Hayley. "Can you believe it, Hayley? Look at those busybodies over there! I know they're talking about me. Why can't they just stay out of my personal business? Earl and I have been trying to keep things low-key, so the last thing we need is a few town gossips running their mouths off!"

Before Hayley could respond, Liddy appeared, a mischievous grin on her face. "Low-key? Oh, Mona, that's so adorable. Hate to break it to you, but it's not just a few town gossips. The whole town knows."

Mona's eyes widened in shock. "What? Are you serious?" She paused, anger flashing across her face as she pounded her fist into the palm of her hand. "Who spilled the beans? Only my family and a few friends, namely you two, knew about this. I swore everyone to secrecy."

"Don't look at me," Liddy sniffed. "I have more compelling topics to discuss than your sordid love life, Mona Barnes!"

Hayley threw up her hands. "It wasn't me!"

"What about Bruce?" Mona grilled Hayley.

"Oh, please. He can barely remember to put on his socks, let alone keep track of who you might be dating at any given moment," Hayley laughed.

"Well, if I find out who spread the rumor, they're dead meat!" Mona bellowed. "I can't handle people clucking on and on about me behind my back!"

Liddy chuckled, clearly enjoying the moment. "Oh, Mona, come on. The Butlers have been the talk of the town for years. Remember when your Uncle Frank got into that feud with the Millers over the lobster traps and set fire to their boat?"

"That was never proven!" Mona protested.

"Or when your cousin Emily ran off with that drifter and ended up in in jail down in Portland after the guy tried robbing a convenience store with a toy gun?"

"She was young and stupid! She's redeemed herself now and is a registered nurse in Waterville!"

"And let's not forget about your Aunt Clara, who was better known as 'the Black Widow' because she buried three husbands under mysterious circumstances."

"Aunt Clara was no murderer! She was just a horrible nag who henpecked all her husbands to early graves. There was never any concrete proof of foul play!"

"Well, my point is, your family is practically the backbone of Bar Harbor gossip! They have been for generations."

Mona groaned, her frustration mounting. "I know, but this is different. It's about me and Earl. *My* private life, not Aunt Clara's, may she rest in peace."

Hayley grabbed Mona's arm gently. "Liddy's right, Mona. People will always talk, but what matters is how you and Earl feel about each other."

Mona took a deep breath, nodding slowly. "You're right, Hayley. They can't get to me if they have nothing to talk about. I'm going to go ahead and dump Earl right now."

She took a step toward Earl who was busy questioning one of the turkey-shoot registrants, but Hayley yanked her back by the sleeve of her sweatshirt. "No! That is not the takeaway. You can't break it off with

Earl. You like him. He likes you. Stay strong. Don't let a few hens on the fence ruin something good."

Mona sighed, rubbing her eyes. "Okay, fine. I won't toss him to the curb. At least not yet. I do like hanging out with him. He makes me laugh. But sometimes he chews with his mouth open, which is just gross, and he has this weird habit of talking back to the television, like the people on the screen are actually in the room with us having a conversation. So he's far from perfect."

"Ha! Who is?" Hayley smiled.

"I don't know, I believe I'm pretty close to perfect," Liddy announced with not even a shred of irony as she drifted off.

Mona turned back to Hayley and gently nudged her in the rib, pointing at the gossips who were still chattering with each other and throwing judgmental looks over in Mona's direction. "I'm going to go over there and barge into their conversation and see how nervous they suddenly get."

As Hayley watched Mona shuffle off, determined to shake things up, she felt a presence sidle up next to her. It was Bruce, with his typical nose for news. He leaned in and whispered, "Sergio started with Reid Norton's gun. Everyone's been buzzing about the fist fight he had with Tom earlier today."

Hayley nodded, her curiosity piqued. "And?"

Bruce shrugged, "Well, it's loaded with bean bags, just like the rest."

Sergio's voice cut through the murmurs of the gathered crowd. "Alright, folks," he said, holding up his hands for attention. "We've inspected all the firearms here.

Every single one is accounted for and loaded with bean bags. No live ammunition. No loaded gun with real bullets has been recovered from this scene."

The crowd murmured with confusion and concern. It was a wide-open space, and all registered shooters had been in plain view at the time of the incident. There was no place for a sniper to hide, no treetops offering concealment.

Hayley glanced over at Bruce, who looked just as puzzled as she felt. "So how did Tom Farley get shot with a real bullet?" she asked, more to herself than to anyone else.

"It's a mystery," Bruce replied, echoing her thoughts.

Sergio approached them, his brow furrowed. "I'm totally stubbed over this one."

Bruce cocked an eyebrow. "Stubbed? Like you stubbed your toe?"

"No! You know, baffled, bewildered," Sergio explained. "Stubbed. I'm stubbed."

"Oh, you mean stumped!" Bruce smiled.

English was Sergio's second language.

His first was Portuguese as he was born in Brazil.

"Stumped? Like a tree stump? How does that make sense?"

Hayley nodded. "We know what you mean, Sergio. And we understand. It doesn't make any sense."

Sergio sighed, rubbing his temples. "I know. But until we figure out where that bullet came from, we can't rule out any possibilities."

As the sun dipped lower in the sky, casting long shadows across the field, Hayley couldn't stop thinking that they were missing something crucial. The answer had to be right in front of them, but what was it?

"Bruce," Hayley said, a sudden idea forming. "Let's take a closer look at the area where Tom was standing. Maybe there's something we overlooked."

Bruce nodded, following her as they made their way to the spot where Tom had fallen. The ground was trampled, and the grass was stained with dried blood. Hayley scanned the area, searching for anything out of the ordinary.

"Hayley, over here," Bruce called, pointing to a small, shiny object partially buried in the dirt.

Hayley knelt down and carefully picked it up. It was a spent bullet casing. Her heart raced as she examined it. This was the proof they needed—a real bullet had been fired.

She looked up at Bruce, her eyes wide. "This changes everything."

Bruce nodded, his expression serious. "We need to show this to Sergio. Maybe this can lead us to the shooter."

As they headed back to the chief, Hayley felt a sense of urgency. Time was running out, and they needed to solve this mystery before anyone else got hurt.

Chapter 5

Later that afternoon, Bruce left to file his story on the shooting at the *Island Times* newspaper where he worked as a crime reporter. Hayley watched him go, her mind still buzzing with questions. The day had been a whirlwind of drama and confusion, and she needed a break to clear her head.

"Come on, ladies," Hayley said, turning to Liddy and Mona. "Let's head over to Drinks Like A Fish and wind down a bit."

Liddy grinned. "I could definitely use a Cosmo or two after today. Randy's bar it is."

Mona, still stewing over the town gossip and her complicated feelings for Earl, simply nodded.

Drinks Like A Fish was a cozy, inviting place with a warm, rustic charm that seemed to draw in locals and tourists alike. It had become a central hub for socializing in Bar Harbor. As they entered, the familiar scent of wood polish and the faint tang of seawater greeted them.

The bar was packed, and it seemed like everyone was buzzing about what had happened to Tom Farley at the turkey shoot earlier that day. Snatches of conversation reached Hayley's ears, each one speculating wildly about the shooting.

"I heard Tom was in a nasty argument with old Mrs. Harkins who lives a mile down the road over her dog who likes to wander and explore the area, always on his property chasing his turkeys," one patron said. "He even threatened to feed it rat poison if it came around again. Well, you can imagine how upset she was over that threat!"

"That's nothing. Last summer, he threatened to sue a family of tourists who were just passing by because their kids were playing too close to his property line," another suggested.

"I heard he fired a rifle over their heads but later denied it when the cops showed up, told 'em the kids were just making up stories," someone added.

"And don't forget the time he came to blows with Jerry Sanborn over that fishing spot," a third chimed in. "Jerry claims Tom tried to drown him. He never got over it. He was always here at the bar saying one day Tom would get his."

Liddy leaned in, amused. "Looks like Tom had a beef with just about everyone in town. No wonder there are so many wild theories flying around."

With their usual stools at the bar already occupied, Hayley, Liddy, and Mona found a table near the back, away from the main hubbub but close enough to hear the chatter.

Randy, spotting his sister, came over with a smile.

"Hey, sis. Crazy day, huh?" he said, setting down their usual order, a Jack and Coke for Hayley, a Cosmo for Liddy, and a Bud draft for Mona.

"You could say that," Hayley replied, taking a grateful sip of her cocktail. "How are you holding up?"

Randy shrugged. "Busy as ever. Everyone's got their own theory about Tom. And poor Daniel. Everyone knows he and Hannah are Tom's neighbors, so they've been pumping the poor guy for information all evening."

Hayley looked over to the bar where a young man was diligently wiping down the counter. She had already met Daniel and his pregnant wife, Hannah, who lived in a double-wide trailer next to Tom Farley. He noticed their gazes and gave a polite nod.

Hayley called to him, waving him over. "Daniel, let me introduce you to my friends, this is Liddy and Mona."

"Nice to meet you," Daniel said with a friendly smile.

"Nice to meet you, too," Liddy replied, while Mona just grunted and nodded.

"Randy says you've been the most popular guy in the bar tonight given the fact you're one of the lucky few who live next to Tom Farley," Hayley said, trying not to push too hard, but curious as to what he had to say.

Daniel's expression tightened slightly. "Yeah, it's been pretty intense. But I'm new to town and don't want to say anything that might get me in trouble with my new neighbor."

Hayley sensed there was more to it. "Come on, Daniel. We're just curious. Off the record."

He sighed, glancing around the bar before leaning in. "Look, Tom hasn't exactly been friendly to me and Hannah since we moved in. He's complained about our trailer, the noise, even my wife's cooking smells. He must have a really sensitive nose because our trailer is about a quarter mile from his house. But listen, I'd rather not stir up any more trouble."

Hayley nodded, understanding his reluctance. "Thanks, Daniel. We appreciate it."

Just then, the door swung open, and Sergeant Earl strolled in, looking slightly weary but relieved to be off duty. His eyes scanned the bar and landed on Mona. He made his way over, a small smile on his face.

"Hey, Mona."

Mona slammed her mug of beer down on the table. "Earl, what the hell are you doing here? Are you stalking me?"

Earl's eyes popped open. "What? No! I figured if you weren't out on your lobster boat, you'd be here with your drinking buddies."

Mona pursed her lips. "Okay, I guess that's a fair assessment."

The semi-retired Mona had handed over the reins of her lobster business to her grown sons and mostly worked in the shop these days, but she could not resist joining them out on the boat on occasion, missing the days when she hauled her own lobster traps.

Earl stood awkwardly at the table. "Um, do you mind if I sat down and joined you?"

Mona flicked her eyes back and forth, considering.

Liddy sipped her Cosmo. "Good lord, Mona, the man has been on his feet all day working a crime scene. Give him a break!"

"Fine! Whatever! Go ahead, Earl. Take a load off. We need to talk anyway."

Earl sat down.

"What can I get you, Earl?" Daniel asked.

"Light beer would be great, thanks, Daniel."

Daniel took his leave.

Mona gulped some more of her beer down, wiping the foam off her mouth on the sleeve of her sweatshirt. "So what do you want, Earl? Why did you follow me here?"

"I thought we could hang out tonight," Earl said.

Liddy sighed, annoyed. "Mona, why do you always have to be so grouchy? Can't you see he just wants to spend time with you?" She turned to Earl. "On behalf of Mona, I sincerely apologize for her rude behavior."

"Oh, no worries, Ms. Crawford, Mona always acts like this right before she breaks up with me."

Hayley sat up in her chair. "*What*?"

Earl nodded. "Yeah, she basically breaks up with me every day."

"Speaking of which, Earl, we need to talk," Mona said somberly.

Earl smiled slightly. "See, here it comes."

Mona took a deep breath. "I think we should break up."

"Mona!" Liddy gasped.

"No, it's okay," Earl said, before turning to Mona. "Okay, Mona, whatever you say."

Daniel brought his beer and Earl took a sip, not going anywhere. Then he gave Hayley and Liddy a sly wink. "She doesn't really mean it. It just makes her feel better."

Hayley watched the exchange, feeling a pang of sympathy for both of them.

Mona sighed, her anger giving way to resignation. "I just need some space. I don't have room in my life for anyone else right now."

Earl nodded. "Understood."

There was a pause.

Then Earl spoke again. "Want to grab some dinner after this? How about Thai? Siam Orchid is open until eight."

"Sounds good," Mona mumbled.

Liddy, already bored by the subject of their relationship and never one to miss an opportunity, jumped in. "Earl, what's the deal with this magic bullet? How did it just appear out of nowhere? Everyone here is mystified."

Earl shook his head, his professional demeanor returning. "I can't discuss an active investigation, Ms. Crawford. But I'm sure Hayley here will start poking her nose into it soon enough. Maybe she'll come up with the answer."

Hayley laughed, trying to deflect the attention. "Oh, come on, Earl. I promise I'm not getting involved this time. I just want to check on Tom in the hospital and cheer him up."

The entire bar burst into laughter, clearly not buying

it. Hayley's reputation as an amateur sleuth was well-known, and no one seriously believed she would stay out of anything.

"Alright, alright," she conceded, grinning. "Maybe I'll ask a few questions while I'm there."

Mona and Liddy exchanged knowing looks.

Hayley Powell was on the case, whether she admitted it publicly or not.

As the evening wore on, the conversations in the bar continued to swirl around Tom Farley and the mysterious shooting. Hayley listened to the various theories, storing away details that might prove useful later. She could not help but think about Daniel's reluctance to speak, and the many stories of Tom's nastiness that seemed to link everyone in town to him in some unfortunate way.

Finally, long after Mona and Earl headed off to dinner and as the bar began to empty out and the night grew late, Hayley stood up. "I think it's time to head home, Liddy."

Liddy agreed, and they said their goodbyes to Randy and Daniel before stepping out into the cool night air where Liddy sped off in her Mercedes.

As she walked home, Hayley's mind raced with possibilities. The shooting at the turkey shoot had left too many unanswered questions, and she was determined to get to the bottom of it. Her first stop would be the hospital to talk to Tom Farley himself.

Whatever secrets lay hidden in this quaint coastal town, Hayley Powell was ready to uncover them.

ISLAND FOOD & SPIRITS
By
Hayley Powell

Thanksgiving is hands down my husband Bruce's favorite holiday. He says, "What other day can you stuff yourself with forbidden carbs and desserts, wash it down with beer, watch a parade in the morning, football in the afternoon, and just when you think you're done, you get hungry again and feast on leftovers?"

I love Thanksgiving too, but for a whole different reason. For me, it's a chance to show my love through food, whipping up old favorites and trying new recipes for my nearest and dearest.

Our first Thanksgiving as a married couple? Well, let's just say it was unforgettable—and not just because Bruce wanted to contribute.

After some sweet hemming and hawing, he proudly declared he would take charge of the turkey. I nearly spit out my drink. But who was I to crush his newfound culinary ambition?

Cut to the night before Thanksgiving. I'm sitting on the porch, sipping a fruity margarita, when Bruce rolls up in his truck. But instead of the Butterball I was dreaming of, there's a screeching, gobbling live turkey in the back of his truck! Turns out, Bruce had ordered a "fresh" turkey from local farmer Tom Farley, not realizing "fresh" meant still flapping its wings.

And that's how I found myself watching Bruce, my brother Randy, and my brother-in-law Sergio chasing a runaway turkey down the street. Bruce even wielded an axe at one point, which made our neighbors scatter like it was the French Revolution! As for that turkey? It escaped to the safety of Acadia National Park, where it still makes occasional appearances to mock Bruce from a distance.

So, no turkey for us that year—ham saved the day. And now, every Thanksgiving, I prepare this delicious ham and pasta casserole, a perfect dish for day-after leftovers when the fridge is still brimming with holiday bounty. Just don't ask Bruce about the turkey that got away! Of course, let's start off with one of Liddy's absolute fave cocktail recipes!

LIDDY'S FRUITY MARGARITA

INGREDIENTS:
2 ounces apple cider
2 ounces pear juice
2 ounces gold tequila
1-½ ounce orange liqueur
Salt for rimming glass
Lime wedge
Ice

Pour some salt on a small plate and rim your margarita glass with some lime and dip into salt. Add ice a little over halfway into your glass and squeeze the rest of your lime wedge into the glass.

Combine all of your liquid ingredients into a cocktail shaker filled with ice and shake until combined.

HAYLEY'S HAM AND PASTA CASSEROLE

INGREDIENTS:
1 onion, thinly sliced
2 tbsp olive oil
2 cups leftover ham, cut into bite-size pieces
¼ cup chicken broth
2 cups shredded Swiss cheese
½ cup heavy cream
1½ cups steamed broccoli
10 oz shell macaroni (cooked al dente)

Preheat oven to 400°F.

Heat olive oil in an ovenproof skillet. Add onions and cook until caramelized, about 15 minutes.

Stir in ham and chicken broth, heating for 5 minutes.

Add cooked pasta, half the cheese, cream, and broccoli. Stir to combine.

Top with remaining cheese. Cover and bake for 10 minutes, then uncover and bake for an additional 10 minutes. Serve hot and enjoy!

Happy Thanksgiving, everyone! Don't forget to make your holiday memorable—with or without a runaway turkey.

Chapter 6

Hayley stepped off the elevator in the Bar Harbor Hospital, balancing a bouquet of flowers and a box of chocolates from the gift shop. She instantly heard shouting coming from down the hallway. She knew exactly where Tom Farley's hospital room must be located.

As she approached the door, she had to duck as a bedpan flew past her head and clattered against the wall. Inside the room, Nurse Tilly stood, her face flushed with anger.

"That's it, Tom! I've had enough of your tantrums!" she snapped. "Either you start behaving or—"

"Or what? You gonna kick me out? I don't think so! My insurance company is paying you people a fortune to take care of me so maybe you ought to start showing me some respect!"

"This is a hospital not the Ritz Carlton! And keep your voice down. There are other patients on this floor!"

Tom mumbled something to himself about Tilly being an incompetent boob, but she decided to ignore him.

Tom gestured toward his half-eaten food tray. "Go on. Get this out of my face. I can't eat this. It's totally inedible. I wouldn't feed this slop to my turkeys!"

Tilly bit her tongue then marched over, scooped up the tray and stormed out, nearly colliding with Hayley in the doorway as she flew past. "Good luck with him," she muttered as she passed.

Hayley took a deep breath and stepped into the room. "I see you're making lots of new friends during your stay here, Tom," she cracked, placing the flowers on the bedside table. "Tilly's a very good nurse. She's beloved here. You really should give her a break."

"She's an idiot," Tom spat out, eyeing the chocolates. "Are those for me?"

She dangled the box in front of him. "Maybe. If you stop terrorizing the entire staff. I saw Nurse Kelly crying in the hallway as I came in."

"Oh her," he sniffed. "I asked her to turn on the TV for me so I could watch the Fishing Channel, and all she could find was some boring cooking shows and CNN and a bunch of chattering old bitties talking about current events. How could they not have the Fishing Channel here?"

"Nurse Kelly is not responsible for the cable TV line

up, Tom. I think you're just looking for things to complain about."

"Oh, really? Is that what you think, Hayley? Is that why you came by? To give a dying man a hard time?"

"You're not dying, Tom. You're very lucky. The bullet didn't hit any vital organs. But you need to rest."

Tom glared at her, his face a mix of pain and stubborn determination. "Rest? How can I rest when someone's trying to kill me?"

Hayley sat down in the chair beside his bed. "That's one of the reasons I stopped by today. Do you have any idea who might have had a reason to take a potshot at you . . . besides poor Nurse Tilly . . . and the rest of the hospital staff here?"

Tom's eyes darted around the room, as if he expected an assailant to jump out from the shadows, then leaned forward, wincing in pain from his bullet wound, whispering. "My neighbors. It had to be one of them."

"Why?"

"I'm sure you've read in the *Island Times* about those big-time developers wanting to buy up all our places to build that fancy hotel?"

"Yes, I heard something about it."

"Well, they need all five properties, and I'm the only one who won't agree to sell. They all hate me because of it."

Hayley frowned. "You really think one of them would try to kill you over this?"

Tom nodded vehemently. "I came into this world on that piece of land, and I'm going to go out on it! They all know that. It's the perfect motive."

Hayley sighed. "Okay then. Let's go over them. The Murdocks—they're wealthy, ready to move to a larger estate. Lester Murdock has a reputation as a ruthless businessman. You think he'd stoop to this?"

Tom grunted. "Wouldn't put it past him. He'll do anything to close a deal."

"And then there's Daniel and Hannah Sweet," Hayley continued. "They're a young pregnant couple, saving to move to a larger place. A big sale would mean a lot to them, especially with a baby on the way. Daniel works for my brother Randy at Drinks Like A Fish. I met them at the turkey shoot. They seem really sweet."

Tom's face softened slightly. "Yeah, I'll give you that. They're nice kids, but desperate people do desperate things."

"How about Reid Norton?" Hayley asked. "He's a retired veteran and gun lover. You had that brawl with him at the turkey shoot over your turkeys crossing onto his property."

Tom's eyes narrowed. "I don't even want to hear that man's name. He's always had a nasty, mean temper. A day doesn't go by when he's not picking a fight with me, trying to stir up trouble. I know he wants to move to Florida, but he can't until he sells his property and I'm standing in the way of that."

"Who's the fourth neighbor to the east?"

"Lori Gunning."

"Lori Gunning? Well, it can't be her."

Tom arched an eyebrow. "Why not?"

"Because she's agoraphobic. She runs her therapy practice online, so she never has to leave the house. I can't picture her loading a gun and driving to the turkey shoot when she won't even go outside to get her mail. I just don't see her doing something like this."

Tom shrugged. "People are full of surprises, Hayley. Could be any one of them."

Hayley looked at Tom's bandaged body and the fear in his eyes. He might be a cranky old man, but he did not deserve this. "I'll see what I can find out," she said, standing up. "But promise me you'll try to keep calm. You're no good to anyone if you have a heart attack in here."

"They'd all love that, wouldn't they? I survive a gun-shot wound but keel over from too much stress on the heart," Tom cackled. He looked at Hayley, his expression softening slightly. "Thanks, Hayley. You're a good girl."

As she left the hospital room, Hayley felt a mix of determination and dread. Tom's accusations were serious, and if they were true, someone in their small town was capable of murder. She needed to talk to the police, dig into the neighbors' backgrounds, and find out who had the most to gain from Tom's death.

Outside the hospital, the late autumn chill bit at her cheeks. Bar Harbor's streets were decorated with Thanksgiving banners, and the scent of wood smoke hung in the air. It should have been a time of celebration, but a dark cloud loomed over the town.

Hayley decided to start with Daniel and Rachel Sweet. Their house was closest to Tom's, and she hoped to quickly cross them off Tom's list of most likely suspects. They just did not strike her as capable of attempted murder.

As she got in her car and drove out toward the connecting properties to speak with all the neighbors, she had a sinking feeling that Tom might be right, and that one of them was willing to kill to get what they wanted.

And Hayley was about to put herself in the middle of it all.

Chapter 7

Hayley pulled up to the Sweets' double-wide trailer, her car crunching over the gravel driveway. The small home was modest but tidy, with flowerpots lining the steps and a couple of worn but comfortable-looking chairs on the small wooden porch attached to the front of the trailer. The late morning sun cast a soft light over the scene, giving everything a calm, almost serene feel—a stark contrast to the tension Hayley felt building within her. Something about Daniel and Hannah's situation nagged at her, and she needed to get to the bottom of it.

She stepped out of the car and made her way to the front door. As she reached the porch, she noticed the curtains in the front window twitch, and a moment later, Hannah Sweet opened the door, her face lighting up with a welcoming smile.

"Hayley! Come on in," Hannah said, stepping aside

to let her enter. "Daniel's at the bar, but I'd love some company."

"Thanks, Hannah," Hayley replied, stepping inside and taking in the cozy, if somewhat cluttered, interior. The living room was filled with baby books, a couple of small baby clothes, and what looked like a half-assembled crib pushed against one wall. The air was warm and smelled faintly of vanilla, likely from a candle burning on the coffee table.

"Sorry about the mess," Hannah said, gesturing to the scattered items. "I've been a bit overwhelmed lately, trying to get everything ready."

Hayley smiled. "I remember those days all too well. You should've seen my place when I was pregnant with my oldest, Gemma—looked like a baby store exploded. It just got worse, like the aftermath of a category five hurricane, when Dustin was on the way."

Hannah chuckled and led her over to the sofa. "I've been reading every book I can find, trying to prepare, but it's so much. I'm constantly second-guessing myself, and Daniel—well, he's so excited, and I don't want to let him down."

"You're not going to let anyone down," Hayley assured her, taking a seat. "Honestly, all those books are great, but at the end of the day, you have to expect the unexpected. Babies have a way of surprising you no matter how prepared you think you are."

Hannah nodded, but her brow furrowed with concern. "I didn't plan on getting pregnant so young. I mean, we're still trying to save up for a bigger place, and now with the baby coming . . . I was hesitant at first, but Daniel was over the moon. His excitement kind of pulled me in, but I'm still scared, Hayley. What if I'm not up to the task?"

Hayley reached over and took Hannah's hand, squeezing it gently. "You're going to be a great mother, Hannah. It's normal to feel scared—every mother does. But trust me, once that baby arrives, you'll know what to do. It won't be easy, but you'll figure it out together, you and Daniel."

Hannah's eyes glistened as she smiled, visibly comforted by Hayley's words. "Thanks, Hayley. That really means a lot."

After a moment of silence, Hayley decided it was time to broach the subject that had brought her there. She leaned back on the couch and asked casually, "So, with everything going on, I'm surprised you and Daniel didn't mention anything about the developers wanting to buy up the land around here. That could be a huge windfall for you two."

Hannah's smile faltered slightly, and she shifted uncomfortably in her seat. "Yeah, we were really excited at first. I mean, the thought of having that kind of money—enough to buy a nice place, start fresh—it sounded like a dream come true. But when we heard Tom was dead set against selling, we just figured it wasn't going to happen."

"He's as stubborn as they come, I'll give him that," Hayley said, shaking her head.

"Honestly, we didn't want to get our hopes up for something that would most likely never come through."

Hayley nodded, understanding the sentiment but still curious. "So, you just let it go? No big deal?"

Hannah sighed, leaning forward with her hands resting on her knees. "It's not that simple, Hayley. Daniel and I, well, we've both had pretty tough lives before we met. We learned not to rely on things that seem too good to be true. We've had to earn everything we have, and we're used to things not going our way. The idea of a huge payday was nice, but we couldn't let ourselves believe it was real. So, we decided to focus on what we can control, working hard and building a life for our baby."

Hayley felt a pang of sympathy for the young couple. They had already endured so much and were trying to prepare for their future in the only way they knew how. It made sense that they would not get swept up in fantasies of easy money. They had too much to lose by letting their guard down.

"I understand," Hayley said softly. "It must be hard, juggling all of this with a baby on the way."

Hannah nodded, her eyes downcast. "It is, but we're determined to make it work. We've always found a way, and we will this time too."

Hayley felt a wave of admiration for the young woman sitting across from her. Despite her fears and uncertainties, Hannah was strong and resilient, qualities that would no doubt make her a great mother. She also felt a growing conviction that Hannah and Daniel had nothing to do with Tom Farley's shooting. They were too focused on their future together, too grounded in reality, to get involved in something so reckless and dangerous.

As Hayley got up to leave, Hannah walked her to the door. "Thanks for coming by, Hayley. I feel so much better now."

"Anytime," Hayley replied, giving her a warm smile. "And if you ever need someone to talk to, you know where to find me."

Hannah returned the smile, a hint of relief in her eyes. "I'll keep that in mind."

Hayley stepped out onto the porch and waved goodbye as she made her way back to her car. As she drove away, her thoughts lingered on the conversation she had just had. The Sweets might have had every reason to be frustrated with Tom, but they did not strike her as people who would resort to violence, even if it meant securing a better future. They had learned to rely on themselves, not on luck or easy money, and that mindset was what convinced her of their innocence.

But that still left the question: if not the Sweets, then who?

Hayley's mind drifted back to the other suspects—the Murdocks with their wealth and ambition, Reid Norton with his temper and love of firearms, and Lori Gunning, the reclusive therapist who was difficult to read. Each of them had their reasons for wanting Tom out of the way, but the truth still felt elusive.

One thing, however, was clear.

Someone in Bar Harbor had decided that Tom Farley's stubbornness was a problem that needed solving.

Chapter 8

Hayley guided her car along the narrow, winding roads just outside Bar Harbor, the dense woods opening up occasionally to reveal glimpses of the rocky coastline in the distance. The Murdock property was situated close to Acadia National Park, not on the water but close enough to feel the pull of the sea. The farmhouse itself sat on a rise, surrounded by sprawling fields and thick woods that bordered Tom Farley's land.

As she approached, Hayley noticed the state of the property—the once-proud fences were sagging, and the barn's red paint was peeling away in large flakes. The main house, though still grand, had noticeable wear and tear. The Murdocks were clearly struggling to keep up with the maintenance probably using the bulk of their money for the purchase of their new home, not on the upkeep of their old one.

She made a mental note of it. The money from the sale to the developers, which Tom was holding up as the lone dissenter, would likely erase any financial difficulties the Murdocks were facing. It would also pay for the expansive new property Liddy was trying to secure for them—a place far more majestic than this aging farm.

Hayley parked her car in the driveway and stepped out, taking in the crisp autumn air. As she approached the front door, she could hear the muffled sounds of a heated argument coming from inside.

The voices were unmistakably those of Lester Murdock and his son, Alan.

". . . always favoring Bo over me!" Alan's voice was tight with frustration. "It's like nothing I do matters, but the minute Bo wants something, you're all over it. You just bought him that new boat, and what do I get? Nothing!"

"I gave you a car last year!"

"A used ten-year-old Toyota! Do you know how humiliating it is driving around in a junk heap like that?"

"What were you expecting, a Porsche? You don't deserve a nice car, not the way you act most of the time, like an entitled spoiled brat!" Lester's voice shot back, sharp and dismissive.

"What makes Bo so different from me?"

"Bo's got potential, and I'm not about to let him waste it. You should be grateful for what you have instead of whining all the time."

Hayley hesitated, not wanting to intrude, but she was here for a reason. She knocked on the door, her knuckles tapping against the weathered wood. The argument inside immediately ceased, replaced by a tense, uncomfortable silence. A moment later, the door swung open, and Lester Murdock stood before her, his broad shoulders filling the doorway.

"Well, if it isn't Hayley Powell, Bar Harbor's finest chef and amateur sleuth," Lester greeted her, his voice suddenly warm and welcoming. "What brings you out here today, doll? Looking for some farm-fresh ingredients for tonight's special at Hayley's Kitchen?"

Hayley smiled politely, though she could feel the tension lingering in the air. "Good afternoon, Lester. Actually, I'm here to ask a few questions about what happened to Tom Farley. I'm sure you've heard he's recovering in the hospital."

Lester's expression darkened briefly before he forced another smile. "A terrible thing. Tom's always been a stubborn old coot, but I never wanted to see him hurt like that. But what's this really about, Hayley? You don't think I had anything to do with him getting shot, do you?"

"I'm just trying to get a clearer picture of what happened," Hayley replied, keeping her voice calm. "I understand Tom was holding up the sale of this property, which has been causing some complications."

Lester chuckled bitterly. "Complications is putting it mildly. Tom's been a thorn in our side for years, always making things difficult. But trust me, Hayley, this sale is going through one way or another. Tom Farley isn't going to stop progress."

Before Hayley could respond, Alan appeared behind his father, his face still flushed from their earlier argument. He looked from Lester to Hayley, then back again, trying to summon some of the determination that had fueled his words moments ago.

"Dad's just trying to do what's best for the family," Alan said, his voice wavering slightly as he attempted to stand up for his father. "Tom's been making things harder for all of us."

Lester shot him a look that could have frozen fire. "Stay out of this, Alan," he growled. "You don't know what you're talking about."

Alan's face fell, his attempt to win his father's approval met with sharp rejection. He looked down at the floor, his shoulders slumping in defeat.

At that moment, Melody Murdock appeared in the hallway, her cocktail glass swaying unsteadily in her hand. Her eyes were glazed, and the ice clinked against the glass as she took an uncertain step forward. "Lester, don't be so hard on him," she slurred, her voice thick with alcohol. "Alan's just trying to help . . ."

"Go back to the living room, Melody," Lester snapped, his tone full of disdain. "You're drunk, and you're embarrassing yourself. Let me handle this."

Melody's face crumpled, and without another word, she turned and stumbled back toward the living room, leaving Alan standing there, looking more lost than ever.

Hayley watched the exchange in silence, the tension in the room almost suffocating. This was a family on the brink, held together by little more than fraying threads of obligation and control. She felt a pang of sympathy for Alan, who was clearly desperate for his father's approval, and for Melody, whose dependence on alcohol was as plain as day.

"I'm just doing my job, Lester," Hayley said finally, turning her attention back to him.

"Job? How is coming around here making veiled accusations your job?" Lester snapped.

"And I'm not accusing anyone—yet. But I need to follow up on every lead, and right now, you're one of them."

Lester's smile faded, his eyes narrowing as he studied her. "You're out of your depth, Hayley. You're a chef and a cooking columnist, not a real detective. So I advise you to stop playing Mrs. Columbo and leave the investigating to the professionals."

It sounded like a threat.

But she was not about to back down.

Not for blustery, full-of-himself Lester Murdock.

"Maybe," Hayley replied, her tone steady. "But sometimes an outsider can see things that others might miss. And right now, there are a lot of questions that still need answers."

Lester did not respond immediately, but the tension between them crackled in the air.

Finally, he nodded, though the gesture was more dismissive than anything else. "Well, then if you want to waste your time running around town investigating, I won't stop you. But I've got work to do. You know the way out."

Hayley nodded and turned to leave, casting one last glance at Alan, who stood silent and forlorn by the door. As she stepped off the porch and made her way back to her car, the weight of the Murdock family's dysfunction hung heavy on her mind.

As she drove away from the Murdock property, Hayley could not shake the feeling that something was off.

And Lester.

There was something about him that did not sit right with her. He was too controlled, too calculated. The way he switched from anger to charm the moment he saw her—like flipping a switch—made her skin crawl.

The drive back through the winding roads gave her time to reflect. Lester's quick dismissal of her questions was troubling, as was his insistence that he had nothing to do with Tom's shooting. The way he treated his family was even more disturbing—especially his casual cruelty toward Alan and Melody.

As she left the sprawling property behind in the distance, Hayley knew one thing for certain: Lester Murdock was hiding something, and she was determined to find out what it was.

Chapter 9

Hayley's shoes crunched over the frosty ground as she made her way to the eastern edge of Tom Farley's property, a chill in the late November air that seeped through her jacket. The tall pines that bordered his land cast long shadows over her path, their boughs gently swaying with the breeze. Hayley pulled her scarf tighter around her neck, a sense of unease prickling at her as she approached the neat, modest home that belonged to Lori Gunning.

Lori's house, a single-story cottage with a weathered wooden exterior, was as unassuming as the woman herself. It sat nestled among the trees; its shutters closed tight as if the house were holding its breath. Hayley hesitated before knocking on the door, her mind spinning with thoughts of Tom Farley's boorish behavior and the many grudges he had likely cultivated over the years.

She raised her hand to knock when the door swung open abruptly. Lori stood in the doorway, her pale face half-hidden behind a curtain of long, dark hair.

"Hayley," Lori said, her voice flat but not unfriendly. "I thought you might come by."

Hayley reacted with surprise. "You did? Why?"

"Once I heard about what happened at the turkey shoot, I figured it was only a matter of time before our local Nancy Drew showed up on my doorstep."

"Guilty as charged!" Hayley sighed. "Lori, I'm so sorry to intrude, but I wanted to ask you . . .

Lori finished her sentence. "A few questions about Tom."

"Yes, that is if you don't mind." Hayley kept her tone gentle, sensing the fragility in Lori's demeanor.

Lori stepped aside, wordlessly inviting Hayley inside. As Hayley crossed the threshold, a pungent odor hit her nose, making her eyes water. She stifled a cough, glancing around the small living room. The space was cluttered with books and old magazines, the walls lined with framed diplomas and certifications from various psychology associations. A laptop sat open on a small desk in the corner, the screen filled with notes from Lori's latest session, no doubt.

"It's those nasty, smelly turkeys," Lori said, noticing Hayley's reaction. She closed the door behind her, leaning against it as if the effort of standing was too much. "When the wind blows a certain way, it's all I can smell. It's disgusting!"

Hayley nodded, though she was fairly certain the smell inside her house was not from the turkeys. She glanced at Lori's gaunt figure, the dark circles under her eyes, and the lines of tension etched into her face. Lori had always been a bit of a recluse, even when she had had her practice in town, but it seemed that her agoraphobia had worsened in recent years.

"I heard about what happened to Tom," Lori said, folding her arms across her chest. "I won't lie—I didn't shed a tear. He was a terrible neighbor, always causing trouble."

"You didn't go to the turkey shoot," Hayley said, stating the obvious. "Did someone call and tell you what happened?"

"You would think so," Lori said with a bitter laugh. "This town loves its gossip. But no. I was on my computer working when I got a notification from the *Island Times*. I just saw the headline. 'Local Man Shot at Turkey Shoot'. I clicked on the article and saw that it was Tom. That's when I stopped reading. I could care less about Tom Farley's fate. He was always making my life miserable."

Hayley raised an eyebrow, sensing there was more to Lori's disdain than just a neighborly feud. "What did he do to you?"

Lori waved a hand dismissively. "It's nothing, really."

"Obviously it's not nothing," Hayley said, Lori's deep bitterness evident. "He hurt you deeply in some way."

Lori sighed, brushing a strand of hair behind her ear as she moved to sit on the edge of the worn-out sofa. "He and I . . . Well, oh I hate to admit it, but we had a thing once. A long time ago, when I first bought this house. It didn't last long, though. Tom turned out to be a real jerk. After that, we barely spoke, but he'd find little ways to torment me."

"Torment you how?" Hayley asked, curiosity piqued.

"Blasting music from his truck late at night, driving past my house on purpose," Lori said, her voice thick with old resentment. "One time, I woke up to find half a dozen of his turkeys marauding through my house. They left droppings everywhere, ruined my rugs, my furniture . . . I knew Tom had let them in. He still had a key from when we were together. He was always like that—finding ways to get under my skin."

Hayley felt a pang of sympathy for Lori. She could only imagine how lonely and frightening it must have been to live next to someone who took pleasure in making your life miserable. "Why didn't you change the locks?"

Lori shrugged. "I did eventually, but that didn't stop him. He'd still find other ways to bother me. I just got used to it. Although I'd still dream about a number of ways he could die a painful, violent death." A smile creeped across her face before she realized how she must sound. "But they were only dreams. It's not like I would ever act upon them. He was just doing a real number on me. The worst part was, he seemed to take great pleasure in it."

Hayley frowned, trying to reconcile the image of Tom as a cranky local turkey farmer with this more sinister side that Lori described. "Did you ever think about moving?"

"Of course I did," Lori said, her eyes flashing with frustration. "But where would I go? My practice was here, and I liked my house. Besides, after a while, I figured it was better the devil you know, right? At least I knew what to expect with Tom."

Hayley nodded, understanding all too well the way people sometimes settled for less just to avoid the unknown. Especially someone with her condition. "I'm sorry you had to go through that, Lori. It sounds awful."

Lori shrugged indifferently, though her eyes betrayed a glimmer of emotion. "It's in the past. I don't have to worry about it anymore, do I? Not with Tom out of the picture."

"Um, Lori, the thing is, he's not. Tom is alive. He survived the shooting."

Lori rolled her eyes. "Of course he did. What is it they say, only the good die young? Like I said, I didn't finish reading the article."

Hayley studied Lori for a moment, wondering if she could detect any hint of guilt or relief in her expression. But Lori's face was a carefully crafted mask, betraying nothing.

"Do you think he had any enemies?" Hayley asked, steering the conversation back to the present. "Anyone who might've wanted to hurt him? I mean, besides you?"

Lori let out a short, humorless laugh. "I'm sure there were plenty of people who didn't like Tom. He wasn't exactly Mr. Congeniality. But who actually pulled the trigger? I have no idea. And honestly, Hayley, I don't care."

There was a hardness in Lori's voice that made Hayley pause. For someone who claimed to be indifferent to Tom's fate, Lori seemed awfully defensive.

"Lori," Hayley said carefully, "you're sure you didn't hear anything unusual the day of the turkey shoot? See anyone around Tom's property?"

"I didn't see or hear anything," Lori said firmly. "I was home all day, working. Like I always am."

Hayley believed her—at least, she believed that Lori had not left her house. But there was something about Lori's demeanor that still bothered her, something that did not quite add up.

"How do you feel about Tom holding up the plans of the developer buying up all your properties to build a new resort? Were you angry about it?"

Another shrug. "I don't care one way or the other. If they pull up with a Brinks truck full of money, I'll probably sell, I mean, why not? But I'm not a big fan of change, it gives me anxiety."

Of that, Hayley had no doubt.

"Well, if you think of anything, or if you just want to talk . . ." Hayley let her offer hang in the air, hoping Lori would take the hint.

But Lori only shook her head. "I appreciate the offer, Hayley, but I'm fine. Really."

Hayley did not press further. She knew when to back off, especially with someone as skittish as Lori. Instead, she forced a smile and tried a different approach. "You know, Thanksgiving's just around the corner. Why don't you come to dinner at my brother Randy's place? It'll be just family, a few friends, nothing fancy."

Lori's eyes flickered with something—surprise, perhaps, or maybe even longing—but she quickly masked it with a polite smile. "Thank you, Hayley, but I'll pass. I'm not much for social gatherings."

Hayley expected that response but felt a pang of disappointment, nonetheless. Lori's isolation worried her, especially now that she knew the depth of Lori's past with Tom.

"If you change your mind, the invitation's open," Hayley said warmly. "It might do you good to get out of the house for a bit."

Lori nodded, though Hayley could tell she had no intention of leaving her sanctuary. "Okay, thanks, I'll let you know."

As Hayley turned to leave, she cast one last glance at Lori's weary face. There was so much more to this woman than met the eye, and Hayley could not shake the feeling that Lori knew more about Tom's shooting than she was letting on. But for now, there was nothing more to be gained from pushing.

"I'll see myself out," Hayley said softly, and Lori gave a small, almost imperceptible nod.

Her reaction to the smell when she had entered the house must have landed because she could hear Lori spraying a can of air freshener around the room as she left.

The cold air hit Hayley like a slap when she stepped outside, the door clicking shut behind her. As she walked back toward her car, the scent of the turkeys seemed to linger in the air.

Hayley glanced back at Lori's house, her mind buzzing with unanswered questions. She had a feeling that Lori Gunning was more than just a bitter ex or a troubled neighbor. There was a story there, one that might hold the key to unraveling the mystery of who shot Tom Farley—and why. But that would have to wait. Thanksgiving was coming, and Hayley had a column to write, a restaurant to run, and another one of Tom Farley's neighbors to visit.

Chapter 10

Reid Norton's house was a stone's throw from Lori Gunning's place, a modest Cape Cod style nestled between tall evergreens that lined the narrow, winding road. From the outside, everything appeared calm, but Hayley knew better. As she approached the front door, she could hear the muffled sound of something crashing inside, followed by a string of curses. She hesitated for a moment, wondering if this was the best time to pay him a visit. But then again, if Reid was already in a rage, it might be the perfect opportunity to see what he might let slip.

She barely had time to knock before the door flew open, revealing Reid hovering in the doorway. His face was flushed, eyes wild with anger. "Hayley," he barked, his voice taut with tension. "What are you doing here?"

"Um, I was, uh, just checking in," Hayley replied calmly. "You were pretty upset after your altercation with Tom at the turkey shoot and I just wanted to make sure you're doing okay."

"Did Mona send you?"

"No, I, uh, came on my own."

"Mona's always worrying about me. She must have called ten times to make sure I wasn't going to fly off the handle and do something stupid."

Like physically attack your neighbor in front of half the town?

She decided not to ask that particular question out loud.

"You wanna hear something rich?" Reid's voice rose, a mix of outrage and disbelief.

"Shoot," Hayley said, instantly regretting her choice of words. "I mean, sure, go on, I'm all ears."

He waved a stack of papers in her face. "Tom's suing me! Can you believe that? After everything that's happened, he's going to drag me into court over a little harmless scuffle?"

Hayley would hardly classify the fight with Tom as "a little harmless scuffle." Reid had clearly been out for blood.

Hayley calmly glanced at the paperwork Reid was thrusting at her, noting the official seal of the court. It was a summons, plain as day. "That's not good, Reid," she said, keeping her voice steady. "But getting all worked up isn't going to help."

"Getting worked up?" Reid exploded; his fists clenched tightly at his sides. "The man's been torment-ing me for years, and now this? I should have knocked him out cold when I had the chance. Maybe then he wouldn't now be lying in a hospital bed, and I wouldn't be getting sued!"

Hayley stepped inside, careful to avoid the shattered pieces of a ceramic mug on the floor. "Reid, you need to calm down. You know there's an active investigation going on. Saying things like that could just make matters worse for you."

Reid's expression darkened, but he drew in a deep breath, as if trying to regain control. "Mona keeps telling me I need to learn to keep my temper in check," he muttered, almost as if speaking to himself.

Hayley raised an eyebrow, unable to suppress a grin. "Mona Barnes? The woman with the shortest fuse in all of Bar Harbor? There are support groups for people who have crossed Mona. Lord help the woman who cut in front of her in line at the Shop 'n Save last Sunday. I hear she's still in recovery."

Reid almost smiled at that. "Yeah, well, Mona's got a point. I know I've got a temper that scares people. But it's hard, Hayley. Tom's been a pain in the ass for years. Always stirring the pot, always looking for trouble. And now he's suing *me*? It's enough to make a man snap."

Hayley nodded, trying to tread carefully. "I get it, Reid. But you've got to be smart about this. The police will figure out who shot Tom. You don't want to give them any reason to think it was you."

Although she suspected he was already on their radar.

Reid grunted, pacing the small living room. "I'm not some pushover, Hayley. I didn't spend years in the Army just to let some jerk like Tom push me around."

Hayley nodded again, remembering how everyone in town knew about Reid's impressive military service. He had never been one to hide his past, but now, in his anger, he seemed to cling to it like a badge of honor.

Reid shook his head. "It's funny."

"What's funny?"

"Not funny, funny. Just funny, like weird funny."

"What?"

"You know I was a sniper, right?" Reid said, almost proudly, as he stopped pacing. "I could hit a target from a mile away without blinking or breaking a sweat."

Hayley's pulse quickened. She knew Reid had been in the Army, but the fact that he was a trained sharp-shooter was news to her. "I didn't realize you were a sniper."

"Deadeye Norton, that's what they called me," Reid said, his voice tinged with pride. "I won that turkey at the shoot today, didn't I?" He gestured toward the kitchen, where Hayley now caught the unmistakable aroma of a turkey roasting in the oven. "Just proves I haven't lost my touch."

Hayley swallowed hard, forcing a smile. Reid was dangerous—she knew that much now. A man with his temper and military-trained skills was not someone to take lightly, especially with everything that was going on. "It's a good thing your rifle was cleared by the police, then."

"Yeah, the cops were all over it when they showed up at the range, but they didn't find anything because there was nothing to find," Reid said, though there was an edge to his voice. "But I'm telling you, Hayley, if Tom keeps this up, things are going to get ugly."

Hayley nodded, though her mind raced. Reid's rifle might have been cleared, but that did not mean he had not stashed a second gun somewhere. He had the skill, the motive, and the opportunity. But without the weapon, there was no proof. And if he was hiding something, she would have to be very careful not to push him too far.

"Just promise me you'll try and keep your cool," Hayley said softly. "Let the police handle this."

Reid grunted in agreement, though he did not seem convinced. "Yeah, yeah. But mark my words. If Tom comes after me again, I won't be responsible for what happens next." He raised the stack of papers. "And as for this?" He tore them in half and hurled them to the floor. "Let 'em come get me."

"Reid, do you want me to send Mona over here?" Hayley warned.

He finally cracked a slight, barely perceptible smile. But Hayley caught it.

"Please, don't," he begged.

"Then don't do anything foolish. Enjoy your turkey."

"Thanks, Hayley."

As she left Reid's house and walked back to her car, Hayley could not shake the feeling that she was dancing on the edge of something very dangerous. Reid had the motive, the means, and the skills to take the shot at Tom.

But if his rifle was in the clear, then where was the weapon?

How could it have just vanished into thin air?

ISLAND FOOD & SPIRITS
By
Hayley Powell

Okay, everyone, let's talk about my BFF Liddy, who, once upon a time, couldn't even boil water without an emergency call to our brave local fire department. (Yes, she had them on speed dial.) But, oh, how far she's come! Her blueberry pancakes were the talk of the Turkey Shoot this year, and believe me, that's a major achievement.

Now, Liddy has made incredible progress with her cooking, but things weren't always so smooth. She's given me permission to share this little "Friendsgiving" tale as inspiration for anyone who feels they're hopeless in the kitchen. In her words, she hopes her journey encourages others to keep working toward their cooking dreams. And, well, let's just say her story definitely adds some flavor to that journey.

After weeks of planning, Liddy felt ready to host her very first Friendsgiving. She invited a small crew to her big debut: me, Bruce, Mona, Randy, Sergio, and her latest beau. Liddy even practiced carving rotisserie chickens on Friday nights, serving them to Mona and me during our weekly margarita-fueled gossip sessions.

Friendsgiving day arrived, and Liddy was up

early, brining, seasoning, and stuffing her turkey to perfection. When she finally took it out of the oven, it looked and smelled like something out of a magazine. Beaming with pride, Liddy set the turkey on the table and, with her shiny new carving knife, began to slice.

But then—oh, Liddy!—she met some unexpected resistance. With a determined shove, something popped out of the turkey and landed on the platter. Liddy's eyes went wide. She dropped the knife and gasped, "Oh my God, there's a baby turkey inside!"

Complete silence. Then, Randy started chuckling, and Bruce followed, and soon the entire table erupted into laughter. Poor Liddy looked like she was going to cry. But then Randy reached over, picked up the "baby turkey," and explained that it was the bag of gizzards she'd forgotten to remove. Once the realization hit, Liddy started laughing along with the rest of us. The turkey turned out delicious, and we've all got a story to tell for years to come.

In honor of Liddy's Friendsgiving triumph (baby turkey and all), here's a recipe for a light margarita that's a staple for any gathering—and a comforting leftover casserole for when the holiday dust settles.

LIDDY'S SKINNY MARGARITA

INGREDIENTS:
2 ounces tequila
1 ounces fresh lime juice
1 ounces Cointreau
½ ounce agave nectar
Fresh cranberries and lime wedges for garnish
Margarita salt for rimming glass
Ice

Rub a lime wedge around the rim of your glass, then dip it in margarita salt. In a cocktail shaker, combine tequila, lime juice, Cointreau, and agave nectar; shake well.

Pour into a salt-rimmed glass filled with ice, garnish with fresh cranberries and a lime wedge, and enjoy!

HAYLEY'S LEFTOVER TURKEY CASSEROLE

INGREDIENTS:
3 cups diced turkey
2 cups mixed veggies (your favorites!)
1 can cream of mushroom soup
1 cup milk
1 cup shredded cheddar cheese
2 cups cooked rice
1 tsp garlic powder
1 tsp onion powder
1 tsp pepper
1 cup crushed Ritz crackers for topping
2 tbsp melted butter

Preheat oven to 350°F. In a large bowl, combine turkey, veggies, soup, milk, half the cheese, spices, and rice. Spread mixture in a greased 13x9 baking dish.

Mix the crushed crackers with melted butter, sprinkle over the top, and finish with the remaining cheese.

Bake for 30-35 minutes until bubbly and golden. Let it cool for a few minutes, then dig in.

Here's to culinary mishaps and the friends who make them memorable. Cheers, and happy Friendsgiving!

Chapter 11

Hayley stood at the edge of the turkey shoot field, the brisk November wind nipping at her cheeks. She pulled her scarf tighter around her neck and glanced at Bruce, who was beside her, staring intently at the expanse of grass where Tom Farley had been shot just days ago.

"This is the spot where it happened," Hayley said, more to herself than to Bruce. The memory of the chaotic scene after the gunshot rang out was still fresh in her mind. The screams, the confusion, the sudden realization that Tom had been hit.

Bruce nodded, his brow furrowed in concentration. "It doesn't make sense, Hayley. This place is too open. There's nowhere to hide, let alone conceal a rifle."

"I've been thinking the same thing," Hayley agreed, her eyes scanning the field. "But we have to figure out where the shooter hid the gun. It's the key to finding out who did this. I thought maybe taking one more look at the crime scene might jog a memory or some kind of clue."

She knew it was a long shot.

But a fresh look could not hurt, in Hayley's opinion.

They walked the perimeter of the field, retracing their steps from the day of the shoot. Hayley could almost see the crowd of locals, all gathered to test their skills and have some fun. It had been a typical Bar Harbor event.

Until it was not.

"The shot came from somewhere behind the food tent, right?" Bruce asked, pointing to where the tent had been set up.

"Presumably. But the police didn't find anything back there," Hayley said, frustration creeping into her voice. "They searched the area thoroughly."

Bruce paused, a thoughtful look crossing his face. "The food tent . . . everyone was too busy stuffing their faces with eggs, ham, sausage, and Liddy's blueberry pancakes to notice anything out of the ordinary. What if the gun was hidden somewhere close by, but not in plain sight?"

Hayley's eyes lit up. "The garbage bins! What about those?"

Bruce shook his head. "Sergeant Earl checked them all. I remember watching him. They were empty, except for the usual trash—paper plates, napkins, plastic forks."

Hayley's mind raced as she tried to think of something the police might have missed.

Then it hit her.

"What about the green bin?"

Bruce looked at her quizzically. "The green bin?"

"Yes, the one set apart from the others. It was loaded with food scraps. I remember I was too full to finish Liddy's blueberry pancakes and was about to dump them into the regular bins, but she stopped me and told me to use the green bin because the leftovers were to be fed to the pigs at Chief Grady's farm!"

Bruce's eyes widened as the realization dawned on him. "Maybe the police missed it. Or maybe it was taken away before they could check it."

Hayley's pulse quickened. "We have to get over there right now!"

Without wasting another second, they hurried to Bruce's truck and sped down the road to Fire Chief Grady's farm. The drive was short, but it felt like an eternity as Hayley's mind raced with possibilities. If they found something, it could be the breakthrough they desperately needed.

When they arrived at the farm, Chief Grady, a burly man with a thick mustache, greeted them with a curious look. "What brings you two all the way out here?"

Hayley quickly explained their theory, and Chief Grady agreed to let them search the pig pen. "But I'm warning you," he said with a chuckle, "those pigs don't like being disturbed, especially when they're eating."

Hayley grimaced and turned to Bruce. "Looks like you're up, partner."

Bruce stared at her, incredulous. "*Me*? You want me to dig through pig slop?"

"Well, it's not going to be me," Hayley said with a laugh. "I just got these boots from LL Bean, they're practically brand new, and there's no way I'm ruining them by slogging through all that mud and gunk."

Bruce folded his arms, a smirk playing on his lips. "You could always take them off and do it old school, with your bare feet, like Lucy stomping the grapes."

"And ruin my pedicure? I don't think so!"

"Hayley, we've been married for how many years now? Never once have you ever mentioned getting a pedicure."

"You don't believe your own wife?" Hayley gasped incredulously.

He adamantly shook his head. "No. But luckily I just happen to have an extra pair of old boots in the back of my truck you can wear."

Check.

Hayley was slowly starting to panic.

He was dangerously close to checkmate.

Hayley worked hard to come up with something else. "What about my hands?"

"What about them? I'm sure Chief Grady has a pair of gloves you can borrow."

Hayley shook her head. "I've got a new manicure too. Wearing some ratty old gloves will scrape off the polish. Do you know how hard it is to keep these nails looking good in this cold weather?"

"Funny, I don't remember you ever registering any concern about your nails before. In fact, I don't even recall you ever wearing nail polish."

"That's on you, Bruce. It shows a lack of interest in me, something I would definitely feel compelled to bring up if we ever saw a marriage counselor."

Bruce raised an eyebrow. "Really?" He was not buying any of this. "I have a shovel in the back of my truck too so there's no need to get your hands dirty!"

"I've seen that shovel. It's very heavy and I have delicate arms." She paused before adding, "And you're so big and strong."

"Seriously, my wife the feminist is now playing the dainty damsel in distress card? You've sunk to a whole new low." He groaned, realizing she was not going to budge. "Fine. I'm never going to win this one, am I?"

Hayley's grin widened and she shook her head. "No, but here's the thing, Bruce. I'm just an amateur sleuth. You're the official investigative reporter, so it's kind of your job to do the professional investigating."

Bruce sighed, knowing he was defeated. "Fine. But you're buying me a drink at your brother's bar after this."

"Deal," Hayley said, her eyes twinkling with amusement.

"More than one!"

"Fine."

With a look of disgust plastered on his face, Bruce climbed into the pen, the pigs immediately surrounding him, grunting and squealing as they jostled for space. Hayley leaned against the fence, watching with a mix of sympathy and barely suppressed laughter.

"Just think of it as a fun treasure hunt," she called out, trying to keep the mood light.

Bruce shot her a glare but dutifully began sifting through the slop with his hands. The pigs did not make it easy, constantly nosing around, trying to get at the food scraps.

"Careful, Bruce, the one behind you looks kind of mean," Hayley warned.

Bruce spun around.

An angry looking pig snorted.

Bruce sidestepped him, staying out of his way.

But he backed into another pig that squealed with rage and began nipping at his butt, surprising Bruce, who suddenly lost his balance and fell face forward into the mud. The pigs calmed down and continued eating.

Hayley covered her mouth and stared at the ground, trying desperately not to laugh out loud.

Bruce slowly hauled himself up, cursing four letter words for the better half of a minute before continuing his search.

Minutes passed, and Hayley's initial amusement began to fade. What if they were wrong? What if the gun was not here, and they were wasting their time? She was about to suggest giving up when Bruce suddenly froze.

"Hayley," he said, his voice tinged with excitement, "I think I found something."

Hayley's heart skipped a beat as she watched Bruce pull out a small, mud-covered object. He wiped it on his shirt, revealing a metal piece. It was part of a rifle.

"There's more," Bruce said, digging further. One by one, he pulled out several more pieces, all of which fit together to form a complete, albeit dismantled, rifle.

Hayley stared at the weapon in Bruce's hands, her mind racing. "Somebody broke the rifle down after the shooting and dumped it in the bin, thinking no one would ever find it here in all this pig slop."

Bruce nodded, his expression serious. "And if we can find out who had access to this bin, we might just have our shooter."

Hayley's thoughts turned to the people who had been at the turkey shoot. The Murdocks, Reid Norton, Daniel and Hannah, all the neighbors with the exception of Lori Gunning, and then there was everyone else who despised Tom, including Chief Grady who once suspected Tom of starting a fire in his barn for the insurance money, which was never proven.

Everyone had a motive.

But who?

And why?

Anyone of the dozens of people at the turkey shoot could have hidden those gun parts among the food scraps in the green bin.

But one thing was certain.

Whoever it was, they had gone to great lengths to cover their tracks. But now, thanks to a little bit of luck and a lot of persistence, Hayley and Bruce had uncovered a crucial piece of the puzzle.

Chapter 12

Hayley carefully balanced the weighty, blanket-wrapped bundle in her arms as she and Bruce stepped into Bar Harbor's police station. The rifle pieces hidden inside clinked faintly, still slick from their recent recovery from the pig slop at Chief Grady's farm. Bruce, always the vigilant crime reporter, cast a watchful eye around the station, his nerves tempered by a determination to see this through. No one was manning the reception desk, so Hayley and Bruce headed straight down the hall to Chief Sergio's office.

Sergio looked up from his desk, his expression shifting from routine boredom to surprise as he saw the couple approach. "Hayley, Bruce, what's going on?" he asked, his tone friendly but tinged with curiosity.

Hayley set the blanket-wrapped bundle down on the desk with deliberate care. "We found something," she said, her voice carrying the gravity of their discovery.

Sergio's brow furrowed as he slowly unfolded the blanket. The fractured rifle parts, dulled by age and exposure, gleamed under the station's fluorescent lights. The stock was cracked, and the barrel had been roughly separated from the receiver. Though the weapon was disassembled, its identity as a rifle was unmistakable.

Sergio glanced up at them, surprised. "Is this—?"

Hayley nodded. "Yes. We believe it's the weapon used to shoot Tom Farley at the turkey shoot."

Hayley could see Sergio's mind reeling. He slowly shook his head in utter disbelief. "But how? Where did you—?"

Bruce leaned in, his instincts as a reporter kicking in. "We think the shooter broke down the gun after they shot Tom Farley and hid the pieces in the green bin of food waste at the turkey shoot. That bin was meant to be taken to Chief Grady's farm for his pigs, which is why you never found the weapon at the scene. The bin was probably taken away by some volunteers before the police even arrived."

Sergio examined the broken firearm, his face thoughtful. "It's a clever move," he mused. "Most people wouldn't think to look there. Who on earth would want to go searching through all that nasty, gross pig slop?"

Bruce shot Hayley a sharp look.

She suppressed a self-satisfied smile.

Sergio scratched the stubble on his chin. "I was really beginning to think we were never going to find the weapon used to shoot Tom. I have to say, I'm impressed. You two really knocked it out the shark."

Hayley and Bruce exchanged confused looks.

"Shark?" Hayley asked.

Sergio nodded. "Yes. Shark. You got the shark to spit out the answer. It's a well-known phase. You haven't heard it before?"

Phase?

Of course he meant phrase or saying.

Still, Hayley had learned not to constantly correct her brother-in-law's many malapropisms.

As a proud Brazilian, English was Sergio's second language.

Bruce was not as sensitive as Hayley, however.

"I think you mean we knocked it out of the park," Bruce said gently.

"Knocked what out of the park?"

"It's a baseball reference. You must have misheard the phase, I mean phrase. The saying is, you hit the ball out of the *park*. For a homerun. Like, you know, Fenway Park. The Red Sox."

Sergio stared at him blankly. "I never heard that before. I don't know baseball. I know sharks. In Brazil, we have sharks."

Bruce tried again. "It means a job well done, hats off to you, you crushed it. Way to go, team!"

Sergio was starting to lose patience. "That's what I was saying. You knocked it out of the shark. Is that so hard for you to understand?"

Bruce opened his mouth to speak but Hayley squeezed his hand tightly, signaling him to put a merciful end to this "Who's on first?" routine. "Thank you, Sergio. We appreciate the compliment. So anyway, about the gun . . ."

Sergio instantly focused on the matter at hand. If anything, he was a professional. He examined the pieces of the rifle. "Yes, let's see if this gun can tell us anything more."

He put on some gloves he retrieved from a desk drawer and turned the pieces over in his hands, eyes narrowing as he spotted something on the receiver. "Looks like someone tried to scratch off the serial number," he noted, reaching for a magnifying glass from his desk drawer. "But they didn't do a very good job. I can still make out the numbers."

The room grew quiet as Sergio typed the serial number into his computer, the tension mounting with each keystroke. The seconds stretched into what felt like hours until the computer beeped softly.

Sergio's face hardened as he read the results. He looked up at Hayley and Bruce, his expression grim. "The rifle is registered to Alan Murdock."

Hayley's heart skipped a beat. Alan Murdock—the eldest son of Lester and Melody Murdock, their well-to-do neighbors who had been bitterly feuding with Tom Farley for years.

The revelation seemed almost too easy, too obvious.

But sometimes, the truth was exactly that.

"We need to head over to the Murdock house," Bruce suggested. "If Alan's involved, there's no time to waste."

Sergio nodded, already in motion. He grabbed his jacket and holstered his service weapon. "Let's go."

Pulling up behind Sergio's squad car which had rolled to a stop in front of the Murdock family's aging mansion, Hayley and Bruce hopped out of their car and joined Sergio as they marched toward the home's entrance, an ornately carved door that gleamed under the evening light. Although the property was in disrepair from the harsh Maine winters and lack of care, the main house was still mighty impressive.

Sergio took the lead, knocking firmly on the door. The sound echoed through the quiet air, a prelude to the tension that was about to unfold. After a brief moment, the door opened, revealing Lester Murdock, his imposing figure filling the doorway. His eyes were sharp, filled with suspicion and anger.

"What's this about, Chief?" Lester demanded, his voice gruff. "We were just ready to sit down for dinner."

"We need to speak with Alan," Sergio said, his tone calm but authoritative. "Is he home?"

Lester hesitated, his eyes flicking between Sergio, Hayley, and Bruce. After a moment, he stepped aside, his jaw clenched in frustration. "He's in the living room," Lester muttered, waving them in with an impatient gesture.

The interior of the Murdock home was as grand as its exterior, with rich tapestries lining the walls and antique furniture filling the spacious rooms, although everything seemed rather old and dusty. The air was thick with unease as they made their way to the living room, where Alan Murdock sat casually on a velvet armchair, scrolling on his phone.

Alan looked up as they entered, his expression shifting from boredom to confusion. "What's going on?" he asked, though his voice betrayed a hint of anxiety.

"Alan Murdock," Sergio began, his voice firm, "I'm placing you under arrest for the attempted murder of Tom Farley."

Alan's mouth fell open, his eyes wide, in shock. He seemed about to say something, but before he could utter a word, Lester's voice cut through the room like a knife.

"Keep your mouth shut, Alan!" Lester barked, stepping forward to place himself between his son and Sergio. "Don't say another word until I get our lawyer here."

Melody Murdock, perched on a plush settee with a cocktail in hand, let out a soft whimper. Her hand shook as she took another sip, clearly overwhelmed by the situation. The tension in the room ratcheted up several notches as Lester turned his fury toward Hayley and Bruce.

"This is your doing," he spat, his face flushed with anger. "You two have been sticking your noses where they don't belong, meddling in things you don't understand. I warned you to stay out of this!"

Hayley felt a flash of guilt but stood her ground. "We were just trying to help the investigation," she replied, though she knew it would do little to calm Lester's rage.

"Help?" Lester scoffed. "You've done nothing but make things worse! I'll be filing a wrongful arrest suit against you, Sergio, and the entire police department."

Sergio remained unflappable. "You're welcome to call your lawyer, Lester. But we have to follow the law, and the evidence as it stands points to Alan. He needs to come with us."

Alan stood slowly, his face pale as Sergio moved to cuff him. The young man shot his father a panicked glance, but Lester's stern expression offered no comfort. Alan said nothing as Sergio led him out of the house, his silence more damning than any confession.

Hayley sensed some movement at the top of the stairs as they all walked out. Bo stood on the top step, his face etched with confusion, as he watched Chief Sergio escort his brother Alan, now in handcuffs, out of the house.

As Sergio secured Alan in the back seat, Hayley could not shake the feeling that this was far from over. There were still questions to be answered, still pieces of the puzzle that did not quite fit. But for now, they had done their part, and the law would take its course.

With a final glance at the Murdock home and its dilapidated barn a stone's throw distance, Hayley and Bruce climbed into their car and followed Sergio back to the station.

Chapter 13

Hayley stood in the brightly lit hallway of the Bar Harbor Police Station, the dull hum of fluorescent lights above her doing little to ease her nerves. Bruce was by her side, his arms crossed as he observed the scene unfolding in front of them. Through the small window of the interrogation room door, they could see Alan Murdock sitting stiffly in a metal chair, his hands clasped tightly together on the table in front of him. His face was pale, and his eyes were fixed on the empty chair across from him.

Chief Sergio paced back and forth in the interrogation room, his usual calm demeanor replaced by an intensity that was palpable even from where Hayley stood. He had been questioning Alan for nearly an hour now, and while Alan had responded to each question, his answers had been careful and measured, revealing little more than the basic facts of his whereabouts during the turkey shoot.

As Sergio stopped pacing and leaned in close to Alan, Hayley could see the tension in the young man's shoulders. She knew that Sergio was getting close to breaking him, but Alan's resolve was still strong. Just as Sergio was about to ask another question, his phone buzzed in his pocket. He pulled it out, frowned, and excused himself from the room.

As he blew past Hayley and Bruce without a word, Hayley took a deep breath, glancing at Bruce.

"I think Lester Murdock's high-priced lawyer probably just arrived," Hayley guessed.

"Danny Maddox, I bet. Down from Bangor," Bruce surmised. "He's an old fishing buddy from when we were kids. Haven't seen him in years. I bet he'd be glad to see me and want to catch up for a few minutes out in reception . . ."

His voice trailed off, but Hayley knew exactly what he was saying. A smile crept across her lips.

This was her chance.

Bruce nodded at her. "Go. I'll stall as long as I can," he whispered, already moving toward the entrance as the rubber soles of his hiking boots squeaked, echoing down the hallway.

Hayley quickly slipped into the interrogation room, closing the door softly behind her.

Alan looked up in surprise, his tense expression softening slightly when he recognized her.

"Hayley?" he asked, his voice tinged with confusion. "What are you doing here?"

"I thought I'd check in on you, Alan," Hayley said, pulling out the chair across from him and sitting down. She smiled warmly, hoping to put him at ease. "You look like you could use a friendly face right about now."

Alan's shoulders relaxed a fraction, and he leaned back in his chair, though his hands remained tightly clasped. "Yeah, I guess so. It's been a rough day."

Hayley nodded sympathetically. "I can imagine. It's never easy being in a situation like this. But I thought maybe talking to someone who isn't trying to trip you up might help."

Alan gave her a small, grateful smile. "Thanks, Hayley. I appreciate that."

They sat in comfortable silence for a moment, and then Hayley casually asked, "So, how's college treating you? Bowdoin, right? Last I heard, you were doing well."

Alan's expression brightened slightly at the mention of college. "Yeah, it's going okay. I'm majoring in Environmental Studies, which I love, but Dad doesn't really approve. He's been pushing me to get into Economics or Computer Science, like him."

"You have to follow your passion," Hayley said softly.

Alan gave her a wan smile that seemed to say, *"Easier said than done."*

"I remember you always had a knack for that kind of thing when you were younger, leading an eighth grade protest on government inaction on climate change at the town pier, as I recall."

"Oh, yeah, Dad wasn't happy that day, especially

since his fraternity brother who owned the plant we were targeting for their excessive carbon emissions was visiting us that weekend."

Hayley chuckled. "It's natural for fathers and sons to butt heads, I suppose."

"I don't know," he shrugged. "We seem to be doing it all the time. I can't catch a break." He glanced over at Hayley. "The only thing we seem to agree on lately is we both love the shrimp scampi at your restaurant."

"You're always welcome at Hayley's Kitchen whenever you're home from college, but I thought our lobster rolls were your favorite dish."

Alan chuckled, some of the tension leaving his face. "They were. Until I tried the scampi. I've missed eating there while I've been away at school."

"Well, next time you're back, I'll make sure to have an order of the scampi waiting for you, on the house," Hayley said with a wink. "You know, Alan, you've always been a good kid. I'm sure your dad's proud of you."

Alan's smile faltered slightly, and he looked down at his hands. "I don't know about that. Dad . . . he's tough to please. I feel like nothing I do is ever good enough."

Hayley reached out and placed a comforting hand on his. "I'm sure he doesn't mean to be so hard on you. He's just got a lot on his plate with the whole property deal, right?"

Alan nodded slowly. "Yeah. That's been really stressing him out. He's been so focused on selling the old property so we can get this new estate in Northeast Harbor. It's like nothing else matters."

Hayley gently squeezed his hand. "And then Tom

Farley goes and refuses to sell, holding up the entire deal. That must have been frustrating for both of you."

Alan's eyes flickered with something—regret, maybe, or fear. "Yeah, it was. Dad was furious. I've never seen him that mad before. He was worried we were going to lose everything. We didn't have enough cash for the down payment on the new place. We needed the sale of the old property to make it work."

Hayley's heart quickened. She could feel she was getting close. "So, you decided to help him out, right? Take matters into your own hands to protect your family's future?"

Alan looked away, his jaw clenching. "I . . . I just wanted to help. I thought if I could . . . I was just hoping we could finally close the deal and everything would be okay."

Hayley nodded, keeping her voice soft and nonjudgmental. "So you stowed a gun in the back of the family SUV, parked it near the food tent, waited for the right moment, and used the truck as cover to shoot Tom at the turkey shoot. Then, when no one was looking, you broke the rifle down and dropped it in with the food scraps that were hauled away to the fire chief's farm, planning to go back later and retrieve it."

Alan did not say anything, but the look in his eyes told Hayley that she was dead on with her theory.

He had not wanted to hurt anyone, but the pressure from his father, the fear of losing everything, had driven him to make a terrible, tragic mistake.

Before she could say anything more, the door to the interrogation room burst open, and Lester Murdock's lawyer Danny Maddox stormed in, his face a mask of fury. "What the hell is going on here?" he demanded, his eyes narrowing at Hayley. "You have no business being in here!"

Hayley stood up, giving Alan's hand one last reassuring squeeze. "I was just having a chat with Alan. But I'll leave you to your work now."

Maddox scowled at her as she breezed past him, but Hayley did not care. She had gotten what she needed. As she stepped out into the hallway, Bruce was waiting for her, his expression a mix of curiosity and concern.

"Well?" he asked, falling into step beside her as they headed for the exit.

Hayley let out a slow breath, the weight of what she had just uncovered settling on her shoulders. "Alan didn't confess outright, but I'm pretty sure he did it. He was trying to help his father, but it all went horribly wrong."

Bruce nodded thoughtfully. "And now it's up to Sergio to figure out the rest."

Hayley glanced back at the station as they stepped out into the cool evening air. "I just hope Alan can find a way to make things right. He's not a bad kid, Bruce. He just got caught up in something bigger than himself."

Bruce slipped an arm around her shoulders as they walked toward the car. "I know, Hayley. But sometimes, even good people make bad choices. We just have to trust that justice will be served, one way or another."

"Sounds like the last paragraph of one of your columns. Are you trying it out for a spin before you officially submit your story?"

"Maybe. We'll see how it plays out. I don't want to jump the gun until we have all the facts."

As they drove home, the glow of the streetlights flickering by, Hayley's mind raced with everything that had just happened.

The facts as she knew them.

She had gotten Alan to open up.

Not completely.

There was no outright confession.

But that would most likely come in time.

And then the mystery of who shot Tom Farley would finally be solved. Hayley, however, could not shake the feeling that the case was far from over. That things very quickly could go from bad to worse.

Much worse.

Chapter 14

Hayley Powell had never seen her restaurant, Hayley's Kitchen, this packed, not even during peak tourist season. Every table was occupied, and a line of hopeful diners stretched out the door and down Rodick Street. The air inside was filled with the clatter of silverware, the murmur of conversations, and the occasional burst of laughter, all underscored by the constant buzz of the kitchen's chaos.

"Table for two?" the temporary hostess, Caroline, squeaked from behind the podium. She was a college student who had started just two days ago to fill in while on her Thanksgiving break, and with Betty on vacation visiting family in Bucksport, the new girl was overwhelmed.

"Three actually," said a woman who looked like she was on the verge of exploding, two kids in tow who were tugging at her skirt.

Caroline's eyes darted frantically across the seating chart. "Uh, it's going to be about twenty minutes."

"Twenty minutes? We have a reservation!" the woman snapped.

Hayley swooped in, all smiles. "I'm so sorry about the wait. We're a bit busier than usual tonight. Caroline here will get you seated as quickly as possible." She shot Caroline an encouraging look before turning back to the woman. "You can wait at the bar. Can I bring you some appetizers while you wait? On the house, of course."

The woman's expression softened slightly. "That would be nice."

"Perfect. I'll have a basket of our famous lobster sliders out to you in just a minute." Hayley flashed her most reassuring smile and made a mental note to ask the kitchen to rush those sliders.

As she glided through the dining room, Hayley noticed her husband, Bruce, sitting at a corner table near the fireplace with Alley Roberts, the local Assistant District Attorney. Alley was petite in size but a force of nature, a spitfire, and a real brawler in the courtroom.

Bruce was jotting down notes, a serious expression on his face. Hayley's curiosity piqued—she knew they were discussing the Alan Murdock case, the latest drama to rock Bar Harbor. Alan Murdock was facing charges for the attempted murder of Tom Farley at the turkey shoot, and the entire town was buzzing about it.

But there was no time to linger. The sous-chef, Greg, poked his head out from the kitchen, eyes wide with panic. "Hayley! We're drowning back here! The fryer's acting up, and we're out of clams for the chowder!"

Of course Kelton, her chef, had called in sick.

Tonight of all nights.

Leaving his second in command, Greg, who already wrestled with anxiety issues, in charge.

And they were overbooked.

She could see Greg drowning.

"Greg, take a deep breath," Hayley instructed calmly, stepping into the kitchen to assess the situation. "I'll handle the fryer. You focus on getting those lobster rolls out. And tell Sam to run over to the Shop 'n Save for more clams. They'll hold some for us."

Greg nodded, looking relieved to have a plan. The kitchen was a whirlwind of activity—pots clanged, steam billowed, and the sharp scent of searing seafood filled the air. Despite the chaos, Hayley felt a sense of pride. This was her domain, her creation, and no matter how many fires she had to put out—sometimes literally—she would not trade it for anything.

As she fixed the fryer, her thoughts drifted back to the corner table where Bruce and Alley were still deep in conversation. Once she was done, she returned to the dining room to check on her customers, passing by Bruce and Alley's table several times hoping to eavesdrop. She could only catch snippets as she darted in and out, but what she heard made her heart race.

"The evidence against Alan is pretty solid," Alley was saying, her voice low but firm. "Danny Maddox wants to cop a plea, but Lester Murdock won't have it. He thinks he can strong-arm me into dropping the charges altogether."

"Is that even possible?" Bruce asked, his brow furrowed.

"Not on my watch," Alley replied sharply. "Alan needs to pay for his crime. He put Tom Farley in the hospital—he doesn't just get to walk away scot-free. But . . . given his obvious remorse, I'm willing to recommend a lighter sentence."

Hayley pretended to be adjusting a sconce on the wall as she leaned in closer to hear more.

"Lester's not used to being told no," Alley continued. "But I'm not budging. Alan's going to do time—how much is up to the judge, but there's no way he's avoiding jail altogether."

Hayley's mind raced. Lester Murdock was known around town as a bully who always got his way, but this time, he seemed to have met his match in Alley Roberts. The thought of Alan, who was just a kid really, going to prison was troubling, but Hayley could not forget the image of Tom Farley lying in that hospital bed, pale and bandaged.

"Hayley! Table nine needs refills!"

Hayley spun around.

It was Debbie, one of her overwhelmed waitresses, balancing six entrees in her arms, her voice snapping her back to reality.

"On it!" Hayley called, grabbing a pitcher of water as she made her way through the maze of tables. As she passed the corner table near the fireplace again, she caught sight of her brother Randy and his husband Chief Sergio, waiting at the hostess stand.

"Finally," Sergio muttered when Hayley greeted them. "I'm in desperate need of a cocktail after the day I've had."

Hayley chuckled, motioning for Caroline to take a break. "Come on, I'll seat you myself."

She led them to a recently vacated table that had just been bussed and set. "What can I get you, Sergio?"

"Something strong and Brazilian," Sergio replied with a sigh. "Maybe a Caipirinha."

"I'll get that right out to you," Hayley said, pausing as she noticed the lines of stress on Sergio's face. "Rough day?"

"You could say that," Sergio replied, his voice low. "Lester Murdock showed up at the Thirsty Whale while I was grabbing lunch. He tried to bribe me—actually tried to slip me an envelope—wanted me to put pressure on the DA to drop the charges against Alan."

Hayley's eyes widened. "You're kidding."

"I wish I was. I laughed in his face, told him if he tries bribing a law enforcement officer again, he'll be joining his son in a jail cell."

Randy shook his head, exasperated. "The man's unbelievable. He really thinks he can buy his way out of anything."

"Well, he's not going to get his way this time," Hayley said firmly, feeling a surge of admiration for her brother-in-law. "Alley Roberts isn't one to be intimidated, and neither are you."

"Let's hope you're right," Sergio said, managing a tired smile. "Now, about that cocktail . . ."

"I'm on it," Hayley said, patting his shoulder before scooting back to the bar. As she passed by Bruce and Alley's table once more, she heard the prosecutor say something that stopped her in her tracks.

"If Lester keeps pushing, he might just make things worse for Alan. There's talk that the DA might even tack on more charges if he doesn't back off."

Hayley frowned.

More charges?

That would be a disaster for Alan, who was already way in over his head. She needed to get back to tending to her customers, but her mind was spinning with everything she had just overheard.

Behind the bar, Hayley quickly mixed Sergio's Caipirinha, her hands moving automatically as her thoughts raced. Lester Murdock was playing a dangerous game, and it was clear that neither Alley nor Sergio had any attention of letting him win.

But what if he found another way?

Someone like Lester would not just give up.

He was bound to try something else, something underhanded.

Hayley made a mental note to keep an eye on Lester—and to warn her brother and Sergio to do the same. For now, though, she had a restaurant to run.

Taking a deep breath, she slipped back into the controlled chaos of the kitchen, ready to tackle whatever crisis came next.

As the night wore on, the restaurant gradually began to empty out. The last of the tables were served, and the noise level eventually dropped to a dull hum. Hayley finally had a moment to breathe, leaning against the bar and surveying the room with satisfaction. Despite everything, they had made it through another night relatively unscathed.

Bruce joined her at the bar, his notebook tucked under his arm. "You okay?" he asked, wrapping an arm around her shoulders.

"I think so," she replied with a tired smile. "Just another day at the office."

Bruce laughed softly, kissing her temple. "You handled it all like a pro. Even eavesdropping on our conversation."

Hayley grinned sheepishly. "Couldn't help it. Sounds like the Murdocks are in deeper than I thought."

"Yeah," Bruce agreed, his expression serious. "And I have a feeling it's going to get worse before it gets better."

But that was a problem for another day. For now, she was going to enjoy the relative peace of the empty restaurant, her husband by her side, and a well-deserved glass of wine.

Chapter 15

Hayley and Bruce stepped through the automatic sliding glass doors of Bar Harbor Hospital, the sharp scent of antiseptic hitting their nostrils immediately. Hayley had been here plenty of times, usually for minor emergencies involving her kids, and in her role as the local amateur sleuth, but this visit had a different feel. They were here to deliver some rather significant news to the cantankerous turkey farmer Tom Farley who had recently been on the wrong end of a gunshot at the Thanksgiving turkey shoot. Now that Alan Murdock, Tom's neighbor, had been arrested, Hayley was eager to see Tom's reaction.

"Do you think he'll be surprised?" Hayley asked as they stepped into the elevator.

"Surprised that someone wanted to shoot him? No," Bruce replied, pressing the button for the second floor. "But maybe surprised that it was Alan Murdock who

actually pulled the trigger. I would bet Tom underesti-
mated the kid."

The elevator doors slid open with a soft ding, and
Hayley immediately noticed something strange. The
distant sound of music—cheerful, upbeat—was drifting
down the hallway. As they walked towards Tom's room,
the music grew louder, and by the time they reached
the door, they could make out the lyrics clearly.

"Kool and the Gang?" Hayley muttered in disbelief.
"Is that *Celebration*?"

Bruce raised an eyebrow and pushed the door open.
They were greeted by the sight of a full-blown party in
Tom Farley's hospital room. Nurses, orderlies, and
even a couple of doctors were gathered around, sipping
champagne and swaying to the music. The bed was
empty, the sheets neatly folded, and there was no sign
of Tom anywhere.

"What's happening here?" Hayley asked, blinking in
astonishment.

One of the staff, Nurse Tilly, turned around and waved,
holding up a champagne flute. "Hayley! Bruce! Come
join the party!" she called out, her voice a little too
cheerful. She took a sip of champagne, her cheeks flushed
from the excitement. She plucked a half empty bottle
of champagne from the nightstand and started refilling
her glass. "Don't worry, I got off duty a half hour ago
and my sweetie Donnie is picking me up, so I don't
have to drive home!"

Hayley exchanged a baffled look with Bruce before
stepping into the room. "Uh, where's Tom?" she asked.

Tilly let out a light, tipsy laugh. "Oh, he's gone, thank
goodness! Discharged this morning."

"Discharged?" Bruce echoed, still trying to process the scene in front of him. "But he was shot just a few days ago."

Tilly nodded enthusiastically. "Yup! And he's been the biggest pain in the neck ever since. Honestly, we've never been happier to see a patient leave so we're celebrating!"

Hayley's eyes widened. "*Celebrating*?"

"Champagne and everything! From Dr. Cormack's personal stash," Tilly said, swirling the bubbly in her glass. "Tom Farley was the absolute worst. The only other patient who even came close was your friend, Mona Barnes, when she had that foot surgery last year. Remember how she called the nurses station every five minutes?"

Hayley winced, recalling Mona's endless complaining about the hospital food, the stiff sheets, and the temperature of her room. "I think she'd be mortified if she knew you were comparing her to Tom Farley."

Tilly shrugged, unbothered. "We needed a reason to pop some bubbly. It's been so stressful around here. And Tom finally gave us one by finally leaving!"

Bruce chuckled under his breath. "I can't say I blame you. Tom's not exactly Mr. Charming."

"No kidding!" Tilly agreed, raising her glass in a mock toast. "So, what brings you two here?"

"We were actually here to let Tom know that someone's been arrested for the shooting," Hayley explained.

Tilly's eyes widened with surprise. "Really? Who?"

"Alan Murdock," Bruce replied. "Lester Murdock's son."

Tilly let out a low whistle. "Well, I guess Tom won't be too happy about that. But like I said, he's gone. Discharged bright and early this morning. And good riddance, if you ask me."

Hayley and Bruce exchanged glances. The idea of Tom being back home so soon was unsettling, especially with his temper and his habit of holding grudges. "Well, thanks for the update, Tilly," Hayley said, forcing a smile. "But I think we'll pass on the champagne."

"Suit yourselves!" Tilly said with a grin, turning back to the party as the song changed to Gloria Gaynor's *I Will Survive*.

Tilly grabbed another nurse, and they cut loose, singing at the top of their lungs, rewriting the lyrics "*First we were afraid, we were petrified, having to bring a bedpan to Tom's bedside . . . But yes, we survived! Oh, we survived!*"

Hayley and Bruce left the hospital room, the sounds of the celebration fading behind them as they walked back to the car.

"You know, I almost feel bad for Tom," Hayley said as they stepped out into the parking lot. "He must have been really miserable and in pain to be that difficult, especially if the hospital staff is throwing a party just because he's gone."

"I wouldn't waste too much sympathy on him," Bruce said, unlocking the car. "Tom's tough. I'm more worried about what he's going to do now that he's probably heard who shot him."

The drive to Tom's farm was quiet, the weight of the situation settling over them. When they arrived, something immediately seemed off. The usual row of turkeys were in complete disarray, flapping their wings and squawking loudly. Some were outside their pens, wandering near the house, while others were pacing nervously inside their enclosures.

"What on earth . . . Hayley murmured, stepping out of the car.

The farm was in chaos. Feathers were strewn across the yard, and the air was thick with the frenzied clucks and gobbles of the distressed birds.

Bruce joined Hayley, frowning as he took in the scene. "Something's wrong," he said, stating the obvious.

"Where's Tom?" Hayley wondered aloud, her eyes scanning the property. She had expected to see him up and about, maybe working on his farm despite his recent injury.

But there was no sign of him anywhere.

"Let's check inside," Bruce suggested, heading towards the house.

They walked up the front steps, noticing that the door was slightly ajar. Bruce pushed it open, and they stepped into the living room. The place was a mess. Papers were scattered across the coffee table, a half-empty glass of whiskey sat on the mantle, and muddy footprints, most likely Tom's, led from the front door deeper into the house.

"Tom?" Hayley called out, but there was no response. The only sound was the muffled clucking of turkeys outside. And a couple inside the house exploring the kitchen.

They moved through the house, checking each room, but found nothing. Everything was in disarray, as if someone had left in a hurry. Finally, they reached the back door, which was also slightly open. As they stepped outside, they were greeted by an even more disturbing sight.

Near the barn, where Tom kept his equipment, the woodchipper was running, its engine rumbling loudly. Bruce and Hayley exchanged uneasy glances.

"Why would he be running that thing now?" Bruce muttered, more to himself than to Hayley.

They approached the machine cautiously. The ground was muddy from recent rains, and as they got closer, Hayley noticed something that made her stomach drop— a muddy footprint near the woodchipper, larger than any she had seen Tom make inside the house.

Bruce knelt down to examine it. "This doesn't look like Tom's shoe size," he said, his voice tense. "And why would he be out here in the mud?"

Hayley's mind was racing, her heart pounding in her chest. "Bruce, we need to turn that thing off," she whispered.

Bruce reached out and shut off the woodchipper. As the machine sputtered to a stop, they both leaned in, dread pooling in their stomachs. There, amid the splintered wood chips, was something that made Hayley gasp in horror—a piece of fabric, blood-soaked, tangled with what could only be . . .

Human remains.

Hayley stumbled back, covering her mouth with her hand. "Oh my God, Bruce . . ."

Bruce looked as pale as she felt, his eyes wide as he took in the grisly sight. "We need to call the police," he said, his voice steady but tight with urgency.

Hayley nodded, her mind a whirlwind of thoughts.

"And fast," she added, glancing around as if expecting someone to suddenly jump out of the shadows.

Bruce pulled out his phone and quickly dialed 911, giving the dispatcher a brief rundown of what they had found. As he spoke, Hayley's eyes wandered back to the footprint in the mud. It was fresh, but it was not the only one. There were several others, leading away from the woodchipper towards the back of the property.

"Bruce," Hayley whispered, tugging on his sleeve. "There's more."

He followed her gaze, his eyes narrowing as he tracked the line of footprints. "Stay close," he instructed, his voice taking on a protective tone.

They followed the muddy trail, their shoes squelching with each step. The footprints led them through the yard, past the frantic turkeys, and towards the tree line at the edge of the property. The trees were dense here, the underbrush thick and tangled.

"Whoever did this couldn't have gotten far," Hayley said, her voice low. "And if they're still around . . ."

Bruce placed a reassuring hand on her shoulder. "We'll let the police handle it. Let's get back to the house."

As they turned to head back, a rustling sound came from the bushes nearby. Both of them froze, their breath caught in their throats. The sound grew louder, something—or someone—was moving fast towards them.

Before they could react, a figure burst through the underbrush—a deer, startled by their presence, bolted past them and disappeared into the woods.

Hayley exhaled a shaky breath, her pulse racing.

"Let's go," Bruce urged, taking her hand and leading her back towards the house.

By the time they reached the woodchipper again, the sound of sirens was approaching, the flashing lights of police cars visible down the long driveway. Hayley clung to Bruce's arm, her mind reeling from the discovery.

Tom Farley might have survived the shooting, but it seemed that his luck had finally run out.

ISLAND FOOD & SPIRITS
BY
HAYLEY POWELL

I didn't realize how many Thanksgiving recipes I've come to love over the years. And, folks, I stumbled across another winner recently—sweet potato muffins! They're the perfect way to use up that leftover sweet potato casserole from your holiday spread, and trust me, they're a real crowd-pleaser. But before we dive into that deliciousness, let me share a little story about the Thanksgiving that almost wasn't . . .

Last year, Bruce and I accepted an invite to his cousin Bill and his wife Sue's place in Boston. Now, don't get me wrong, I love Bill and Sue, but Thanksgiving at home with my turkey, stuffing, and mashed potatoes is sacred. So, there was a bit of hesitation. But we packed our stretchy pants, because when we visit, we eat like kings.

Imagine my surprise when we pulled up to their house and saw Bill and Sue looking . . . trim. Like, they-dropped-the-entire-dessert-table trim. As soon as we sat down for lunch, Sue placed a perfectly measured balsamic-dressed salad in front of us. Bruce was scraping the bottom of his bowl like a man on a deserted island! And as Sue cheerfully announced dinner would be a cheese-less veggie pizza, Bruce's horrified look said it all.

For three days, we endured salads. We walked. We did yoga. And I kept telling Bruce, "It's only four days 'til Thanksgiving!" But when Sue announced her grand Thanksgiving meal—mixed lettuce, smoked deli turkey, and mustard vinaigrette—I knew I had to take action. I made a very dramatic call to my brother Randy. You see, Leroy (our dog) was suddenly "sick", and we had to rush home.

Twenty minutes later, Bruce and I were driving back to Bar Harbor, devouring burgers and fries like it was our last meal. Not my proudest moment, but hey, sometimes a girl's gotta do what a girl's gotta do.

Now, to help you avoid such Thanksgiving drama, I'm sharing my Leftover Sweet Potato Muffin recipe. They're sweet, comforting, and a great way to put those leftovers to good use! But first, a perfect fall cocktail.

I have been on a fall margarita kick and this delectable cocktail recipe has been heartily approved by my brother-in-law, Bar Harbor's finest, Police Chief Sergio Alvarez!

SERGIO'S SPICY CUCUMBER MARGARITA

INGREDIENTS:
2 ounces white tequila
1 ounce lime juice
3 slices cucumber
2 slices Serrano pepper

Muddle your cucumbers, peppers and lime juice in a cocktail shaker.

Add the tequila and shake to combine.

Strain into a chilled martini glass and enjoy.

Leftover Sweet Potato Muffins

Ingredients:
2 cups flour
2 tsp cinnamon
1 tbsp baking powder
1 egg
1 tsp salt
1 cup sugar ($\frac{1}{2}$ cup more if you like them sweeter)
$\frac{1}{2}$ cup vegetable oil
$\frac{1}{2}$ cup applesauce (skip if your sweet potatoes had apple pie filling)
2 cups leftover mashed sweet potatoes

Preheat your oven to 375°F.

Mix flour, cinnamon, baking powder, and salt in a bowl.

In another bowl, combine the egg, sugar, oil, applesauce (if using), and sweet potatoes.

Stir the wet ingredients into the dry until just combined.

Divide the batter into a lined or greased 12-cup muffin tin.

Bake for 25 minutes or until a toothpick comes out clean. Cool for 10 minutes.

Enjoy these muffins and may your Thanksgiving leftovers always bring joy (and fewer salads)!

Chapter 16

Thanksgiving at Randy and Sergio's home was always an event to look forward to. Their beautifully restored Victorian house, perched on the shore path of Bar Harbor, offered a breathtaking view of the Atlantic Ocean, where waves gently lapped against the rocky coastline. The dining room was a vision of holiday cheer, with a long table draped in a rich, burgundy cloth and set for eight, far more than the usual four.

Hayley walked in, balancing her homemade pumpkin pie, and immediately noticed the extra place settings. Her brother Randy was bustling around the kitchen, his excitement palpable as he greeted her.

"Pumpkin pie, as promised!" Hayley announced, placing the dessert on the counter. Bruce followed behind, carefully carrying a tray of his signature Thanksgiving cocktails—cranberry-orange whiskey sours garnished with a sprig of rosemary.

Randy flashed a mischievous grin as he caught Hayley's curious glance at the table. "Surprise guests tonight, sis," he said with a wink, clearly enjoying keeping the secret.

Before Hayley could press for more details, the door swung open, and in walked Mona with Sergeant Earl by her side. Earl, short and squat, and dressed sharply as always, looked slightly uncomfortable. He worked for Police Chief Sergio, which made for an awkward Thanksgiving dinner with his boss.

"Chief," Earl said respectfully, nodding at Sergio.

Sergio sighed, rolling his eyes good-naturedly. "Earl, we're off duty. Call me Sergio, please."

Earl nodded, though it was clear he was still mentally at work. Mona, catching the slight tension, smirked and said, "Give it up, Chief. Earl's never going to drop the formalities. He's too by-the-book."

Earl chided playfully. "That's not what you said last night when we—"

"Not here, Earl!" Mona snapped.

The group chuckled, but Mona quickly fixed them all with a sharp look. "And before anyone gets any ideas, my private life stays private. I'm not here to be the subject of any dinner party gossip, got it?"

Randy raised his hands in mock surrender. "No gossip, I swear."

"Good," Mona huffed. "Because I'm sick of hearing those chattering hens in town fixated on the obvious age difference between us."

At least two decades.

But who was counting?

"It's none of their business," Hayley said.

"Damn right it's not! I've got enough on my plate with my grandkids aging me by the minute. Why would I want to go to Disney World with a bunch of marauding, screaming rug rats when I can be here, trying to relax?"

Mona's family—kids, grandkids, the whole bunch—had jetted off to Disney World for Thanksgiving, leaving her to fend for herself. But Mona had made it very clear she had no intention of joining them in the land of Mickey Mouse.

"Too happy," Mona had said with a scowl when she first told Hayley about the trip. "All that artificial cheerfulness annoys the hell out of me! I got no use for it!"

"The last time Mona took her kids to Disney World she ended up punching Goofy in the nose," Hayley noted.

"He was gettin' a little too cozy, if you know what I mean!" Mona bellowed.

"He just put his arm around you when your ex Dennis tried to take a family photo in front of Cinderella's castle!" Hayley exclaimed.

"Yeah, well now he knows to ask next time!"

Everyone chuckled again, and the mood lightened as they gathered in the living room for cocktails. The room was warm with laughter, and the aroma of roasting turkey mingled with the scent of Bruce's cocktails. The conversation naturally drifted to the talk of the town: the grisly discovery that Hayley and Bruce had made at Tom Farley's turkey farm.

"I still can't believe it's real," Randy said, shaking his head as he passed around appetizers. "Tom Farley, ground up in his own woodchipper. How does something like that even happen?"

Sergio, sipping his drink, maintained a carefully neutral expression. "It's an ongoing investigation, Randy. I can't speculate on the details."

"The Chief's right," Earl agreed.

Sergio threw him a look. "Earl, what did I say about calling me—?"

"I know, I know, but I can't, Chief. I just can't."

"Fine. Call me whatever makes you feel comfortable."

"Thanks, Chief."

Earl sat back, relieved.

"Oh, come on, Sergio," Bruce prodded. "We all know it wasn't an accident. You don't just fall into a woodchipper."

Mona jumped in, her voice tinged with exasperation. "Exactly! And now I'm sitting here with the guy heading the investigation, and I can't even get the details on the town's biggest scandal?"

Sergio held up his hands, a small smile playing at his lips. "I'm not giving you anything, Mona. It's not just town gossip; it's an active case."

"Hey, weren't you the one who said no gossiping at Thanksgiving dinner?" Bruce asked with a wry smile.

"No gossiping about *me*! When it comes to who offed that old grouch Tom Farley, all bets are off!"

Sergio mimed zipping his lips.

Everyone groaned in playful frustration, but it was clear Sergio was not going to budge. Still, the speculation continued, with everyone offering their own theories.

"It had to be one of his neighbors," Hayley said, her mind racing through the possibilities. "And I'd bet good money it was Lester Murdock. He's been gunning for Tom ever since Tom first refused to sell his land."

"What about his son Alan? He's already been charged with attempted murder?" Earl asked.

"I think Daddy Lester finished the job his boy Alan couldn't see through all the way," Hayley concluded.

Bruce took a thoughtful sip of his cocktail. "Maybe. But sometimes the most unlikely suspects turn out to be the true culprits. Like that sweet young couple, the Sweets. Who would ever suspect them?"

Randy immediately jumped to Daniel's defense. "Hey, don't go pointing fingers at Daniel. He's a good kid. Honest, decent. There's no way he's involved in something like this."

Just as Bruce opened his mouth to respond, the doorbell rang. Randy exchanged a quick glance with Sergio before heading to the door, leaving the others to ponder Bruce's suggestion.

"Could you imagine?" Mona scoffed, rolling her eyes. "Daniel and Hannah Sweet? The couple who just moved into that tiny double-wide trailer? She's about to have a baby, for crying out loud!"

Randy reappeared in the doorway, his face composed but his eyes twinkling with a mixture of excitement and unease. Behind him, standing awkwardly in the entrance, were Daniel and Hannah Sweet.

They looked just as surprised as everyone else to be there.

"Sorry we're late," Daniel said, his voice soft and slightly apologetic. "We got caught up—"

But he trailed off as he caught the look on everyone's faces. The room was so quiet you could hear the waves crashing outside.

Bruce cleared his throat, the silence stretching unbearably. "We were just discussing, uh, some possibilities in the investigation of Tom Farley's death."

Hannah's hand went protectively to her swollen belly as she glanced at Daniel. "Are . . . are we suspects?"

Hayley felt the air in the room grow thick with tension, and for the first time all evening, she did not know what to say.

Randy, ever the diplomat, stepped forward, his voice light and welcoming. "Well, come in! Grab a drink! We've got a lovely dinner waiting for us. Let's not let talk of woodchippers and dead bodies ruin our Thanksgiving, shall we?"

Mona nodded, popping a cranberry brie bite, one of Randy's appetizers, into her mouth. "He's right. Just the thought of ground up human remains almost makes me lose my appetite." She chewed and swallowed. "Oh, these are really good."

Bruce, mouth open, quickly closed it and put his brie bite back down on his small plate.

Hayley noticed Daniel and Hannah were both flushed with embarrassment from having overheard snippets of the speculation about them. "Let's move to the dining room, shall we?"

As they all picked up their drinks and moved towards the beautifully set dining room table, the awkwardness lingered like a shadow, darkening what was supposed to be a festive evening.

Chapter 17

The Thanksgiving dinner at Randy and Sergio's home had started as a warm, chaotic gathering, but it had quickly turned into a battlefield of accusations and defenses. The aroma of turkey, stuffing, and sweet potatoes filled the air, but the tension was thick enough to cut with a knife.

Hayley sat next to Bruce as they watched Randy vociferously defend his new bar manager, Daniel Sweet, and his wife, Hannah.

"There's no way," Randy insisted, waving his fork in the air for emphasis. "No way this adorable young couple could hurt anyone! I mean, look at them!" He gestured toward Daniel and Hannah, who were sitting across the table, their faces pale and their eyes wide as they absorbed the unsettling conversation.

Daniel, his hands trembling slightly, shakily set

down his half empty wine glass. "We wouldn't . . . We didn't . . ." he stammered, his voice barely above a whisper. Hannah reached out to squeeze his hand, her expression a mixture of fear and bewilderment.

"We're just . . . shocked," Hannah added, her voice small and tight. "We didn't realize people thought we were . . . capable of something like this."

Randy's eyes softened as he looked at them. "Of course you're shocked. You're good kids, that's why I hired you, Daniel. Everyone here knows it. Believe me, once people get to know you, they'll realize you're not Bar Harbor's Bonnie and Clyde."

Daniel and Hannah exchanged a confused look and then both asked in unison, "Who?"

"I forget how young you really are," Randy moaned. "Never mind. I'll show you the movie one day."

Bruce leaned back in his chair, crossing his arms. "If not them, then who?" he asked, his tone skeptical. He turned to Hayley, his brows raised in question. "What do you think?"

Hayley shook her head slowly. "It's hard to say. I mean, I really don't think it could be Lori Gunning. She's got that agoraphobia—she's terrified to leave her house. And she's more likely to shut herself away from the world than do something like this."

Mona, who had been quietly sipping her wine, leaned forward. "But what if that's all an act?" she suggested, her voice low and conspiratorial. "It would be the perfect cover. No one would suspect her if she's too 'afraid' to leave the house. Maybe that's exactly what she wants us to think."

Hayley considered this for a moment, but then shook

her head again. "I don't know, Mona. Lori seemed pretty genuine to me. And besides, if she were going to snap, wouldn't she have done something to Tom years ago? He's been tormenting her for ages."

"Maybe," Mona conceded, "but people have their breaking points."

Bruce, who had been listening with a furrowed brow, scoffed. "What about Reid Norton? I wouldn't put it past him."

Mona frowned. "Reid? But I've known him for years. He's a friend of my parents. Sure, he's a bit rough around the edges, but he's a decent man."

Bruce snorted. "Decent? I've had a few run-ins with him, and that's not the word I would use to describe him. He's got a temper, and he's not exactly subtle about his dislike for Tom."

"He was pretty angry over Tom suing him for assault and he did tell me he's a sharpshooter, and he's certainly big enough and strong enough to push Tom into that woodchipper," Hayley added.

"Maybe so," Mona admitted, "but it still seems farfetched. What about the Murdocks? Hayley has put her money on Lester, but it could have been any one from that freak show of a family!"

The discussion dissolved into a heated debate, with everyone at the table throwing out names and theories, their voices rising as they tried to make their points heard over the clatter of dishes and the hum of the oven.

Daniel and Hannah sat in stunned silence, glancing at each other as the accusations flew around the table. They had come to Randy and Sergio's home expecting a festive Thanksgiving dinner, not a full-blown murder mystery discussion with themselves as potential suspects.

Randy, noticing their discomfort, raised his voice to be heard over the din. "Enough, everyone! I'm telling you, Daniel and Hannah are not involved in this mess. They're just trying to get by, like the rest of us."

Sergio nodded in agreement, placing a comforting hand on Randy's shoulder. "Let's not jump to conclusions. We need to keep an open mind. But as I've already said, I cannot speculate on an ongoing police investigation so can we please counter this whole discussion?"

"Counter what?" Mona asked.

"The discussion. Counter the discussion. It's a saying," Sergio argued.

"No, it's not," Mona laughed.

Hayley jumped in. "He means table. Let's table the discussion?"

"Counter, table, what difference does it make?" Sergio huffed.

They managed to focus on more mundane topics from that point forward, especially the succulent turkey and fluffy cornbread stuffing, but Bruce, unable to let the subject drop, turned back to Hayley. "So if it wasn't Lori, and you don't think it was Reid, who does that leave? We've already ruled out the Sweets. We're running out of suspects."

Hayley sighed, pushing a piece of turkey around her plate with her fork. "Since Alan Murdock has already been charged with attempted murder, logically the trail should lead straight to the Murdocks. I want to believe it was Lester, but my judgement could be clouded because I just don't like the guy. Honestly, I'm starting to wonder if it was any of the neighbors."

Mona raised an eyebrow. "What do you mean? They all had a motive to kill him, even Ken and Barbie here, no offense."

Daniel gave a weak smile. "It's okay. We're starting to get used to it."

Hayley set down her fork and leaned forward, her expression thoughtful. "Think about it. We're all focused on Tom's neighbors because they had the most to gain if he was out of the picture. But what if we're looking at this the wrong way? What if the real culprit isn't any of them?"

Daniel, who had been quietly absorbing the conversation, spoke up. "You mean someone from the development company?"

Hayley nodded slowly. "Exactly. They had millions at stake if this resort deal went through. Tom was the lone holdout, the only thing standing in their way. Maybe someone there decided they couldn't wait any longer."

Hannah, who had been sitting quietly beside Daniel, finally found her voice. "But how would they have done it? They're not from around here. How would they even know when and where to strike?"

"That's a good question," Bruce mused, rubbing his chin. "But they'd need someone on the inside. Someone who knows the area, knows Tom's routines, and could pull it off without drawing attention."

Randy's eyes narrowed. "Someone who could blend in. Maybe even someone we know."

The table fell silent as the weight of his words sank

in. Hayley could see the gears turning in everyone's minds, the suspicion spreading like wildfire.

"So, who fits that description?" Mona asked, breaking the silence.

Hayley thought for a moment before answering. "Well, who would have had the most contact at the development company? Who would have known their plans, their timeline?"

Daniel snapped his fingers. "The realtor! Liddy, wasn't it? She's been pushing hard to get everyone to sell. She's been in constant contact with all the property owners and the development company, and she would have known exactly what Tom was up to."

Hayley frowned. "*Liddy*? That's insane. She's my best friend in the whole world!" She noticed Mona scowling from across the table. "*One* of my best friends! She is not capable of murder, she couldn't kill anyone."

"Except with her cooking," Mona joked.

Bruce shrugged. "I don't know. But if the development company was desperate enough, and she stood to make a huge commission from the deal, maybe she saw an opportunity."

Hayley gasped. "Bruce, are you actually being serious right now?"

"We're just talking, throwing out theories. We have to consider everyone. Do I think Liddy is somehow involved? Probably not."

"*Definitely* not!" Hayley cried. "And she's barely five foot four. How on earth could she hurl Tom into a woodchipper? Now, please, let's move on to someone else!"

The room fell silent again, everyone deep in thought. Finally, Bruce broke the silence with a nod. "Daniel's right. We've been so focused on the neighbors, we might have missed the bigger picture. Who's in charge of the deal at the development company?"

"I don't know, but I'm sure we can find out," Hayley said, feeling a renewed sense of determination. "Let's start digging into the development company. If there's something there, we'll find it."

Randy, his voice steady, added, "And in the meantime, let's not turn on each other. We've all been through enough without tearing each other apart."

Everyone nodded in agreement, the tension in the room finally beginning to ease. Hayley felt a flicker of hope. They were getting closer to the truth, and while they still had a long way to go, at least they were back on track.

As the dinner resumed, the conversation turned to lighter topics—Mona's rambunctious grandkids, Randy's instructions on spatchcocking a turkey, and Bruce's amusing anecdotes from the world of crime reporting. But the mystery of Tom Farley's death still hung over them, like a dark cloud on an otherwise bright day.

Hayley caught Bruce's eye across the table and smiled faintly. They had a new lead, and with any luck, it would bring them closer to solving the case. But for now, they would focus on what they did best: eating good food, sharing stories, and enjoying the warmth of friends and family.

And tomorrow, they would start digging deeper into the shadows where the truth was hiding, determined to find out who had really pushed Tom Farley into that woodchipper.

Chapter 18

Hayley stepped out of her car and took a deep breath. The sleek glass façade of Acadia Resorts Incorporated loomed above her, a stark contrast to the quaint, weathered buildings of Bar Harbor. The property development company had only recently opened its local office on West Street across from the town pier. She was not sure what she expected when she decided to confront the CEO of the company behind the controversial hotel and resort project, but as she stood at the entrance, her nerves began to creep in.

Steeling herself, she pushed through the heavy glass doors and approached the reception desk. The young woman behind it barely looked up as Hayley introduced herself and asked to see the CEO.

"Do you have an appointment?" the secretary asked, her tone as flat as her expression.

"No, I don't," Hayley replied, offering her best disarming smile. "But I believe it's important."

The secretary did not bother hiding her skepticism. "I'm sorry, but the CEO has a very busy schedule. If you'd like to make an appointment, I can see what's available next month."

Hayley opened her mouth to protest, but before she could say anything, the door to the CEO's office swung open. A tall, elegant woman with dark auburn hair swept back in a sleek bun emerged, her heels clicking on the polished floor. "I'm heading out for a bite to eat," she told the secretary. "I haven't had a thing all morning, and I'm starving."

She was halfway through the doorway when she suddenly froze, her eyes landing on Hayley.

"Hayley Powell?" The woman's voice was rich with surprise, yet carried an unmistakable tone of familiarity. A smile spread across her lips, and Hayley suddenly felt her stomach drop.

"Tabitha Collins?" Hayley stammered, caught completely off guard. The last person she expected to see running this company was Bruce's ex-girlfriend, the former CEO of Boston Common Seafood. The same Tabitha who had once tried to convince her to franchise Hayley's Kitchen, and who had, once upon a time, shared a life with her husband.

Tabitha's smile widened, and she strode over to Hayley, completely ignoring the bewildered secretary. "It's been ages! How are you?" she asked, her tone warm, almost as if they were old friends.

Hayley forced herself to smile back, though her mind was racing.

What were the odds?

And what, exactly, was Tabitha doing here?

"I'm . . . fine," Hayley managed to reply. "I didn't expect to see you here."

Tabitha chuckled, a sound that was too smooth to be anything but practiced. "It's a small world, isn't it? Come on, let's catch up. How about we grab some lunch? There's a great spot across the street near the pier."

Hayley hesitated, but what choice did she have? If she wanted answers, she would have to play along. "Sure, that sounds good," she agreed, even though the thought of spending an hour in Tabitha's company made her uneasy.

The two women walked together, the conversation flowing as easily as the breeze off the water, but beneath the surface, Hayley felt the tension. She could not forget that this was the same woman who had a history with Bruce. Despite her polite façade, Tabitha was a shrewd businesswoman, and Hayley knew she would have to be careful. Because she was painfully aware that Tabitha had once gone behind her back to try to reclaim Bruce.

But luckily she had failed in her mission.

Bruce had made no bones about his feelings. He told Tabitha he had no intention of ever leaving Hayley. And she appeared to get the message. So what was she doing back in town?

At the pier, they found a small seafood shack with outdoor picnic tables. The smell of fried clams wafted through the air, mingling with the scent of saltwater.

Tabitha ordered for both of them, as if it were the most natural thing in the world, and they took a seat at a table overlooking the harbor.

Hayley watched as Tabitha dipped a fried clam into a paper cup of tartar sauce and popped it into her mouth, chewing thoughtfully before turning to her with that same polished smile. "So, what brought you to my office, Hayley? I assume this wasn't just a social call."

Hayley met her gaze, trying to read the woman who sat across from her. "I've been looking into the shooting at the Thanksgiving turkey shoot. Tom Farley."

Tabitha raised an eyebrow, though she did not seem particularly surprised. "Ah, yes. Tom. I heard about what happened. Terrible business. I was relieved to hear he survived."

"Yes, but I'm sure you've heard by now that he wasn't so lucky when he got home from the hospital and supposedly fell headfirst into his woodchipper."

Tabitha gasped, in shock. "What? No, I didn't! How awful!"

Hayley studied her face. "You really didn't know?"

"No! I haven't been paying too much attention to the news lately. I've been so busy at work."

Hayley nodded, leaning in slightly. "Tom was the only holdout in the sale of the properties near the hotel site. That project was your priority, wasn't it?"

Tabitha sighed, setting down her fork. "It was. When Acadia Resorts lured me away from Boston Common to be company CEO, the hotel project was already in motion, but it was clear that Tom was going to be a problem. All the owners of the neighboring properties were eager to sell. They saw the money, the opportunity, and they were on board from the start. But Tom? He was stubborn." She shook her head, a hint of frustration creeping into her voice. "I made him offer after offer, money that would have changed his life, but he refused. It wasn't about the money for him. He was holding on to something—some principle, I suppose."

Hayley nodded, her suspicion growing. "And the neighbors? How did they feel about his refusal?"

Tabitha's smile faded slightly, replaced by a more serious expression. "They were desperate, Hayley. They were counting on that sale to go through. Some of them were in financial trouble, and others just wanted to be rid of the place. Every time Tom refused, it made things harder for everyone. There were times when I considered walking away from the whole project, but I'm tenacious. I don't give up easily."

She paused, her blue eyes narrowing slightly. "But I would never resort to violence, if that's what you're implying. I wanted Tom on board, yes, but *killing* him? That's not my style. I can't even watch those *Dateline* shows. They cause me too much anxiety."

Hayley studied her, trying to gauge the sincerity in her words. Tabitha was a master of her craft, a woman who knew how to manipulate a conversation to her advantage.

But was she telling the truth?

Tabitha laughed lightly, breaking the tension. "Besides, even if I did want him out of the way, I wouldn't do something as dramatic as that. There are other ways to get what you want."

Hayley forced a smile, though her mind was still

turning over everything Tabitha had said. "You're right, of course. I didn't mean to suggest anything like that."

Tabitha waved her hand dismissively. "Don't worry about it. I understand why you're asking. But believe me, Hayley, I wanted Tom to agree to the sale, not to disappear."

Hayley nodded, though she remained unconvinced. Tabitha was too polished, too smooth, and there was something about her that Hayley did not trust. Maybe it was her history with Bruce, or maybe it was just the fact that Tabitha had always seemed to have an agenda.

Tabitha ate her last clam. "So how's Bruce doing?"

"He's fine," Hayley muttered.

There was a lingering tension still in the air.

Did Bruce know she was back in town?

As they finished their lunch and parted ways, Hayley could not shake the feeling that Tabitha was hiding something. The woman had been too eager to play the role of the reasonable businesswoman, too quick to dismiss the possibility that she could have been involved in something more sinister.

And yet, Hayley knew she needed more than just a gut feeling. She needed proof. As she walked back to her car, her mind was already working through the possibilities. She would have to dig deeper, ask more questions, and see if there was anyone else who could shed light on Tabitha's true role in all of this.

Liddy popped into her head. She was the realtor who had been working with the Murdocks and trying to hustle her way into representing the other properties in the big sale.

But why had Liddy not mentioned Tabitha?

She knew the history—knew all about Bruce and Tabitha's past. Surely, Liddy would have alerted her to the fact that Bruce's ex was back in town.

Had she intentionally kept this from her?

And if so, why?

One thing was certain. Hayley was more determined than ever to uncover the truth. Even if it meant confronting the ghosts of the past—Bruce's past, and her own.

Chapter 19

As Bruce and Hayley drove along the winding roads to Southwest Harbor, for a moment, Hayley allowed herself to relax, rolling down the window and breathing in the crisp air. Despite everything that had happened, she loved mornings like these—quiet, serene, and full of promise.

As they pulled into the small parking lot of the Common Good Kitchen Cafe, the sound of strumming ukuleles and the scent of freshly baked popovers welcomed them. This local food pantry was more than just a place to grab a bite; it was a beacon of community spirit. The homemade hams and maple butter, warm oatmeal, and rich coffee were not just a treat—they were a lifeline to those in need during the harsh Maine winters. Bruce and Hayley made it a point to visit often, knowing their donations went to a good cause.

Bruce turned off the engine and looked over at Hayley, his expression serious. "I swear, Hayley, I had no clue that Tabitha was in town. And if I had known she was the new CEO of Acadia Resorts, I would've told you immediately."

"I know, Bruce, this is the third time you've brought it up."

"I just want to be clear. I haven't spoken to her since the last time she showed up in town a couple years ago."

Hayley studied his face, searching for any hint of deception, but all she saw was sincerity mixed with a hint of discomfort. "It's just . . . surprising, that's all," she said, trying to keep her voice light. "Of all the places she could end up, she's here, right in the middle of this whole mess."

Bruce sighed and ran a hand through his hair. "I know. But you have to believe me—whatever happened between us is ancient history. I'm with you now, Hayley, and that's all that matters."

She smiled, taking his hand and squeezing it. "I know. But you can't blame a girl for being a little wary."

He smiled back, and for a moment, the tension between them eased. "Let's go get some popovers before they're all gone," Bruce said, his tone lightening as he flung open his door.

Inside the café, the warmth of the wood-paneled walls and the sound of laughter greeted them. They quickly spotted their favorite table by the window, but before they could sit down, a familiar voice called out to them.

"Hayley! Bruce!"

Turning, they saw Liddy hurrying over, a wide smile

on her face. She was dressed in a smart blazer and jeans, clearly coming from a house showing, but the telltale sign of craving hung on her features—a desperate need for a popover.

"Liddy! Just the person we needed to see," Hayley said, embracing her friend. "You're here for the popovers, I assume?"

"You know me too well," Liddy laughed. "I've been dreaming about them all morning. The house I just showed was beautiful, but all I could think about was that golden, buttery perfection. I'm surprised I didn't get a speeding ticket on my way over here from Somesville."

As they approached the counter, Hayley leaned in closer to Liddy, lowering her voice. "Did you know about Tabitha?"

Liddy frowned, puzzled. "Tabitha? Who's Tabitha?"

"Tabitha Collins. Bruce's ex-girlfriend and the new CEO of Acadia Resorts," Hayley explained, watching Liddy's reaction closely.

Liddy's eyes widened in genuine surprise. "Are you serious? I had no idea! I've been dealing directly with a project manager this whole time. Tabitha must've been pulling the strings behind the scenes. But I swear, Hayley, I didn't know."

Hayley nodded slowly, considering her friend's words. Liddy had never been one to withhold information—especially not something as juicy as this. "That's strange. It's almost like she's hiding."

"Or keeping a low profile," Bruce added as he paid for their popovers. "It wouldn't be the first time a CEO lets others do the dirty work."

They carried their trays to a table in the corner, where they could enjoy the music. The Common Good Ukulele Band was in full swing, their cheerful melodies filling the air. Hayley was about to take a bite of her popover when she noticed something—or rather, someone—familiar on the small stage.

"Is that . . . Daniel?" Hayley whispered, nudging Bruce.

It was indeed Daniel, strumming away on a ukulele, looking more at ease than Hayley had ever seen him. His fingers danced across the strings as he belted out a country tune, his voice rich and soulful. The room fell silent as everyone turned to listen, captivated by his unexpected talent.

Up front at a table, Hannah sat with her hands clasped under her chin, her eyes glued to Daniel with a look of pride that Hayley could not help but notice. It was a sweet scene, and for a moment, all the suspicions that had swirled around the young couple seemed ridiculous.

Bruce leaned over, speaking quietly to Hayley. "There's no way a couple like that could be involved in anything sinister. Look at them—Daniel's playing ukulele in a band for a food pantry, for crying out loud."

Hayley wanted to agree, to dismiss the nagging doubts that still lingered. But then, out of the corner of her eye, she saw something that made her pause—a young man, around Hannah's age, approaching her from across the room. His posture was hesitant, almost shy, but there was a recognition in his eyes, as if he knew Hannah from somewhere.

Hannah's smile faltered the moment she saw him. The color drained from her face, and she stiffened in her chair. The young man said something to her, but Hayley could not hear over the music. Whatever it was, it spooked Hannah enough that she shot up from her seat, tears welling in her eyes. Without another word, she bolted from the café, leaving the young man standing there, confused and concerned.

Hayley immediately got up, her instincts kicking in. "I'll be right back," she murmured to Bruce, already moving toward the door.

Outside, the fresh air did little to soothe the knot in the pit of her stomach. She spotted Hannah a few steps ahead, leaning against the wall of the building, her shoulders shaking as she sobbed quietly.

"Hannah?" Hayley called softly as she approached. "Are you okay?"

Hannah quickly wiped her eyes, trying to compose herself. "I'm fine. I just . . . I needed some air."

Hayley was not buying it. "Who was that guy? He seemed to know you."

Hannah shook her head vigorously. "No, it's nothing. Just a misunderstanding. Really, I'm fine."

But Hayley could see the fear in her eyes, the way her hands trembled as she tried to brush off whatever had just happened. "Hannah, if something's wrong, you can tell me. I want to help."

For a moment, it looked like Hannah might open up. Her lips parted, and she glanced back toward the café as if considering whether to confide in Hayley. But then, she shook her head again, this time more decisively. "It's nothing, Hayley. Really. I just . . . I need to get back inside. Daniel's probably wondering where I went."

Hayley wanted to push her some more, to demand answers, but she could see that Hannah was not ready to confide in her. Not yet, anyway. So she nodded, giving the young woman a reassuring smile. "Okay. But if you ever want to talk, you know where to find me."

Hannah gave her a small, grateful smile in return before brushing past her and scurrying back into the café.

Hayley lingered outside for a moment, watching her go. There was something more to this story, something Hannah was not telling her. And whatever it was, Hayley had a feeling it was tied to the murder.

One thing was clear. They could not afford to cross anyone off the suspect list just yet. Not even the sweet young couple who seemed to have nothing to hide.

Chapter 20

Hayley and Bruce walked into their kitchen, both eager to unwind after a long day. The promise of a quiet evening at home, complete with a glass of wine, was a welcome relief from the day's events.

Hayley opened a bottle of Pinot Noir while Bruce grabbed two glasses from the cupboard. She poured, and they clinked their glasses together in a silent toast to some much-needed relaxation.

As they hung up their coats and settled in, the familiar crackle of the police scanner on top of the refrigerator broke the silence. It was a sound that had become a constant presence in their lives—one that Hayley had first brought into their home out of pure curiosity as an amateur sleuth. She had always been fascinated by the goings-on in Bar Harbor, and the scanner had given her a front-row seat to all the town's dramas. But when she married Bruce, a crime reporter with a nose for news, he had insisted on upgrading it to a state-of-the-art model, claiming it was essential for both of their "occupations."

Now, as Hayley took a sip of her wine, the urgent tone of the dispatcher's voice cut through the kitchen, pulling her attention away from the glass in her hand.

"All units, report of shots fired at 83 Windward Lane, Reid Norton's property. Repeat, shots fired."

Hayley and Bruce exchanged a worried look. The peaceful evening they had hoped for vanished in an instant.

"Never a dull moment when it comes to Reid Norton," Bruce sighed, already heading for the door.

Hayley quickly set her glass down and followed him, her heart racing. Reid Norton was not exactly known for his calm demeanor, especially when it came to his late neighbor, Tom Farley. The two men had been at odds for years, but with Tom recently meeting a gruesome end, Hayley could not help but wonder what else could have possibly set Reid off now? Unless it was someone else taking potshots at Reid.

They bolted out of the house to Bruce's truck. A few minutes later, they were driving down the narrow road that led to Reid's property. As they approached, the flashing blue lights of a police cruiser came into view, casting the yard in eerie, strobing shadows.

Reid's yard was in complete disarray. Turkeys—Tom's turkeys—were scattering in all directions, their feathers ruffled and their eyes wide with fear. In the middle of it all stood Reid Norton, a shotgun clutched tightly in his hands, his face a mix of rage and desperation.

"Put the gun down, Reid," Police Chief Sergio called out, his voice firm but edged with concern. Lieutenant Donnie was beside him, slowly circling to cut off any potential escape route.

Reid shook his head, his grip tightening on the shotgun. "I'm not putting this down until someone does something about these damn birds! They've been wandering over here for days—nobody's taking care of them! If no one else will get rid of them, I will!"

He cocked his shotgun.

Sergio reached for his gun holster, his hand steady, ready to withdraw at a moment's notice.

Reid watched as one panicked turkey fluttered by him. He kicked some dirt at it with his boot but did not shoot at it.

Hayley and Bruce exchanged a worried glance as they parked at the edge of the property. This was a situation that could escalate quickly. While Bruce hung back, Hayley cautiously approached, trying to assess just how close Reid was to the edge.

"Reid, please," Sergio tried again, his voice calming but urgent. "This isn't the way to handle it. Let's talk about this."

Reid was not listening. His eyes darted wildly between the turkeys and the officers. "Every time I aim at one of these birds, I see Tom's face," he muttered to himself, his voice breaking. "It's like he's still here, taunting me, even after he's gone."

Sergio exchanged a worried glance with Donnie, who was inching closer to Reid. "Reid, I'm asking you one more time to put the gun down. We can help you, but not like this."

Hayley's mind raced as she watched the situation teeter on the brink of disaster. Then, an idea struck her. She quickly pulled out her phone and dialed Mona's number, praying she would pick up.

"Mona? It's Hayley. We're over at Reid's place. He's got a gun, and he's threatening to shoot Tom's turkeys. Can you get over here quick? I think you might be the only one who can calm him down at this point."

Mona didn't hesitate. "I'm on my way."

Within minutes, Mona's truck pulled up behind Bruce's, and she jumped out with a determined expression. Sergio and Lieutenant Donnie were still holding Reid at bay but losing patience.

Without wasting any time, Mona marched straight toward Reid, her confidence cutting through the tension in the air.

"Reid Norton!" she called out, her voice firm and commanding. "What the hell do you think you're doing? Are you out of your mind? Put that gun down this instant, or you're going to regret it."

Reid's head snapped around, his grip on the shotgun faltering as he registered Mona's presence. "Mona . . . I . . ."

"I don't want to hear any of your excuses," Mona cut him off, closing the distance between them. "This isn't who you are, Reid. You know better than this. These turkeys didn't do anything to you, and this isn't how you deal with what you're feeling."

Hayley watched Mona, impressed.

Reid's shoulders slumped, the fight draining out of him. His hands trembled as he slowly lowered the shotgun. "But they're everywhere, Mona . . . And Tom . . ."

I just can't stop thinking about him. These damn turkeys are a constant reminder of what that man put me through."

Mona stepped closer, gently taking the shotgun from his hands. "I know, Reid. I know it's been hard. But this isn't the way to cope with it."

Reid let out a shaky breath, his eyes welling up with tears. He looked utterly defeated, a stark contrast to the gruff, tough exterior he usually projected.

Mona handed the shotgun over to Sergio, who quickly unloaded it and set it aside. "Thank you, Mona," he said quietly, his relief evident.

Mona nodded but kept her attention on Reid. "Come on, Reid. Let's go inside and get you settled. I'll bring you some fresh lobsters later, free of charge."

Hayley watched as Mona quietly led Reid into his house.

Sergio and Donnie exchanged relieved glances, grateful that the situation had not escalated further. As they began to wrap up the scene, Mona reemerged from the house, looking tired but resolute.

She approached Hayley and Sergio, wiping her hands on her jeans. "He's calmed down now. I'll stay with him for a bit, make sure he doesn't do anything else stupid."

Hayley nodded, still trying to piece everything together. "Mona, I have to ask . . . what's going on with Reid? Why was he so on edge?"

Mona sighed, her expression softening as she looked back at the house. "Reid's a good man, Hayley. He's got a tough exterior, but he's been through a lot. I know he's quick-tempered, pig-headed . . ."

"With a lot of toxic masculinity," Hayley added.

"I don't know anything about any of those modern phrases, he can be a real bastard, okay? I'll admit that. But I will always be loyal to that man."

"Why?" Lieutenant Donnie asked.

Mona gave Donnie the once over, about to tell him to mind his own damn business, but then she shrugged, deciding to come clean. "Years ago, when my lobster business was struggling, Reid was the one who floated me a loan to keep it afloat. He never asked for anything in return, just told me to pay it back when I could. And I did, with interest, once things picked up again. But that's just who Reid is—he helps people, even if he doesn't show it."

Sergio crossed his arms, still processing what Mona was saying. "That's surprising."

"I know, that's not how he comes across at all, but my family has known him for years. We know the real Reid Norton. He's got a good heart. That's why I can't believe he had anything to do with Tom's death, despite their history. Reid's not a killer, no matter how bad things got between him and Tom."

Hayley considered Mona's words, still skeptical but willing to keep an open mind. "I hope you're right, Mona. But we can't rule anything out just yet. Reid's behavior tonight . . . it's troubling, to say the least."

Mona looked back toward the house, her expression sad but determined. "I know. I'll stay with him tonight, make sure he's okay. But please, Hayley . . . don't judge him too harshly. He's going through something, and I don't think he even knows how to handle it."

Hayley nodded, appreciating Mona's loyalty but still feeling unsettled.

As they drove home, the events of the night played over and over in Hayley's mind. Reid might not have been the one to push Tom into that woodchipper, but his actions and words suggested he was haunted by something. And until Hayley figured out what that was, she knew she would not be able to rest.

Chapter 21

When Hayley Powell pulled up to the Hancock County Courthouse to drop Bruce off who was covering a trial for the Island Times, Bruce, sitting in the passenger seat, was already scanning the front entrance, his journalist instincts kicking into high gear. He had a knack for spotting potential stories, and today was no exception.

"Looks like something's brewing," he muttered, nodding toward the small crowd of reporters gathered near the entrance.

Hayley followed his gaze and saw Lester Murdock, the patriarch of the troubled Murdock family, holding court with the press. Even from a distance, Hayley could sense the oily charm that Lester exuded, a man who knew how to manipulate any situation to his advantage. She parked the car, and they both got out, curious to see what the man had to say.

As they approached, Lester's voice rang out, thick with a manufactured sorrow. "It's a tragedy, an absolute tragedy. Tom was a good man, a neighbor, someone we all respected deeply."

The reporters scribbled furiously in their notebooks, capturing every word of the rehearsed eulogy.

Hayley felt her stomach churn. She knew the truth about the relationship between Tom Farley and Lester Murdock. It had been anything but respectful. Far from the grieving friend he was pretending to be, Lester had seen Tom as an obstacle, nothing more.

One of the reporters, a young woman with sharp eyes, pressed him further. "But Mr. Murdock, wasn't there some animosity between your family and Mr. Farley? I mean let's face it, your son Alan, for instance, shot Mr. Farley during the Thanksgiving turkey shoot."

Lester's expression did not falter, but his eyes hardened for a split second. "A small dispute blown way out of proportion," he said smoothly. "My misguided son acted rashly, but Tom was making a full recovery. Before someone, some vile, violent killer, pushed him into that woodchipper. It was a grim and unimaginable death, and now we must all mourn his loss and focus on finding the real perpetrator."

Hayley clenched her teeth. The way Lester spoke about Tom, as if his death was just an unfortunate hiccup in an otherwise peaceful neighborly relationship, made her blood boil. She exchanged a look with Bruce, who was just as unimpressed.

As the reporters began to disperse, Hayley and Bruce followed Lester into the courthouse. The change in his demeanor was immediate. The false empathy vanished, replaced by a demanding, almost dictatorial presence. Lester marched through the courthouse halls like a man who owned the place, his footsteps echoing against the marble floors.

They trailed behind him, staying close enough to observe without drawing attention to themselves. When Lester reached the office of Hancock County Assistant District Attorney Alley Roberts, he did not bother to knock. He pushed the door open, barging in as if he had every right to do so.

"Roberts," Lester barked, his tone dripping with authority. "We need to talk about these charges against my son. This whole thing has gone on long enough."

Alley Roberts looked up from her desk, unfazed by Lester's intrusion. "Mr. Murdock, I thought I made it clear that the charges against your son stand. Alan shot a man, and that's not something I'm willing or able to overlook."

Lester's face darkened. "You have no idea who you're dealing with. The Murdock family has been a pillar of this community for generations. I won't let you ruin my son's life over a simple misunderstanding."

Alley did not flinch. "Alan's actions have consequences, Mr. Murdock. That's not a simple misunderstanding; that's the law."

Hayley admired Alley's composure. She could see Lester was used to getting his way, and it was infuriating him that Alley was not budging.

"You'll regret this," Lester hissed, his voice low and menacing. "I have the power to ruin your career, Roberts. Don't think for a second that I won't use it."

Alley met his gaze, unyielding. "Do what you need to do, Mr. Murdock. But I'm not dropping the charges."

Hayley felt a surge of respect for Alley. The assistant DA was not going to be intimidated by a man like Lester Murdock. But beneath her admiration, Hayley's suspicion was growing. Lester's desperation to sweep the entire Tom Farley situation under the rug was glaringly obvious. The man who had just feigned sorrow in front of the press was now trying to make the whole tragic situation just disappear.

And that raised a red flag in Hayley's mind.

Lester turned on his heel and stormed out of the office, his face a mask of barely contained fury. Hayley and Bruce quickly moved aside, watching him as he stalked down the hallway.

"I don't trust him," Hayley whispered to Bruce once Lester was out of earshot. "Not one bit."

Bruce nodded. "Neither do I. He's too eager to close the book on Tom Farley. And that act outside with the reporters? That was just that—an act."

Hayley's thoughts churned as she exited the courthouse. Lester Murdock's performance in front of the press and his true nature behind closed doors only confirmed her suspicions. This was not just about clearing Alan's name; this was about covering up something much bigger.

As they walked back to the car, Hayley could not shake the feeling that Lester was hiding more than just his son's reckless behavior. The question was, how far would he go to protect his family's name—and was that desperation enough to drive him to murder?

She had a feeling she was going to find out sooner rather than later.

Chapter 22

The soft chime of the bell over the Island Times office door sounded as Hayley Powell stepped in, balancing a box of treats in one hand and a steaming cup of coffee in the other. The office still had that familiar scent of old newsprint and ink, though the staff had thinned out over the years. But one constant remained: Sal Moretti, her former editor and longtime expert in state law stories, sat at his cluttered desk in his office at the end of the back bullpen, chewing on the end of a pen.

Sal looked up as Hayley approached, his eyes immediately narrowing at the sight of the bakery box. "What are you doing here, Hayley? Your column's not due until tomorrow, which you always just email to me these days," he grunted, trying to sound annoyed, but failing miserably. "I know that look. And that box. You're after something."

Hayley flashed him a bright smile. "*Me*? After something? Come on, Sal, I'm just here to catch up. And, well, I did happen to stop by A Slice of Eden, your favorite bakery, on the way over. I figured I'd bring some goodies for my favorite editor."

Sal's eyes shifted to the box again, and despite himself, a glimmer of interest sparked in them. "Don't tempt me. I'm on a diet," he said, almost as if reminding himself.

No doubt his wife Roseanna was worried about his health again.

"So don't try to tempt me. I know all your tricks."

Hayley plopped herself down in the chair across from him, crossing her legs and setting the coffee on his desk with a decisive thud. "I completely understand. I'm constantly on a diet too, as you know from years of us working together. But honestly, what kind of diet lets you skip these?" She opened the box with a flourish, revealing a variety of decadent pastries—cream-filled éclairs, chocolate croissants, and sugar-dusted donuts.

Sal grumbled something under his breath and looked away, but Hayley caught his lips twitching in what could have been a suppressed smile.

"So," Hayley said, leaning back casually, "I've been doing some thinking about Tom Farley's property."

Sal shot her a wary glance. "Farley? That crank who got himself thrown into his own woodchipper?"

Hayley nodded and picked up an éclair, making sure to take a dramatic bite, letting the cream ooze out a little. "Oh, wow, that's so good!" Hayley moaned wiping a bit of cream off the side of her mouth with a napkin.

"Who does his property belong to now that he's gone? What happens to it? Any idea?"

Sal sighed heavily, keeping his gaze firmly away from the pastries. "Why do you care about that? You give up on your restaurant to run your own real estate business now?"

"Just curious," Hayley said through another bite. "You know, Bar Harbor is a small town. People are talking."

Sal leaned back in his chair and crossed his arms over his broad chest. "Uh-huh. Sure. And you just happened to wander in here with a box of baked goods."

Hayley smirked. "I didn't pick these up for you. These are for Bruce. If they end up making it home."

Sal glared at her suspiciously. "I'm not falling for it."

"Suit yourself." Hayley picked up a chocolate croissant next and took an exaggeratedly slow bite. The flaky pastry crumbled under her teeth, and she let out a little moan of satisfaction that caused Sal's eyes to flick toward the box involuntarily. "Heaven. Absolute heaven."

Sal lasted a full thirty more seconds before his willpower crumbled faster than the pastry. "All right, fine. But you owe me one." He reached for an éclair, and Hayley stifled a victorious grin.

"For each piece of information you give me, I'll let you try something new," Hayley bargained, leaning forward.

"Deal," Sal said with a grunt, greedily stuffing half of the éclair into his mouth. He chewed thoughtfully for a moment before wiping his mouth with the back of his hand. "Farley's property, huh? Let me think . . . Old man, never married, no kids. His parents are long gone. I'd bet the state takes it."

"State?" Hayley asked, eyebrows raised as she handed over a chocolate croissant in exchange for more information.

"Yeah," Sal said between bites. "If someone dies without a will or next of kin, Maine law says the state takes over. They'll sell it off to make money, especially if it's valuable property—which in Tom's case, it definitely is. Developers have been drooling over that land for years."

Hayley nodded, absorbing the information. "And what about his family? Was there anyone else? Cousins, siblings?"

Sal shook his head, his hand already hovering over a sugar-dusted donut. "Nope. He had one brother, but he died years ago. No relatives that I can find."

"So . . . the state would be more than happy to sell the land to Acadia Resorts, then?" Hayley asked, watching Sal as he took a bite of the donut, powdered sugar dusting his shirt.

"Of course. Big developers like Acadia? They've got deep pockets. The state will get top dollar for that land, and Tabitha Collins—well, she's not going to let this deal slip away after all the effort she's made to keep it from collapsing in on her."

At the mention of Tabitha, Hayley felt her stomach knot. Tabitha had far too much riding on this project. If Tom's property was up for grabs, there was nothing standing in the way of her and the resort. But could she have gone as far as pushing Tom into a woodchipper to ensure the sale?

Sal leaned back in his chair, licking his fingers. "So, what's this really about, Hayley? You think someone killed Tom to get their hands on his land?"

Hayley shrugged, feigning nonchalance. "I'm just trying to put all the pieces together. Tom wasn't exactly well-liked, and now his land is worth a fortune. It's not a stretch to think someone might have wanted him out of the way."

"You mean besides the Murdock kid they arrested for taking a potshot at him during the turkey shoot?"

Hayley nodded. "But Alan has an alibi for the wood-chipper incident. He was in jail. No, it was someone else."

"Sounds like you've got a suspect in mind," Sal said, eyeing the last pastry in the box—a buttery almond croissant.

Hayley did not respond immediately, her mind whirring. Tabitha had motive, opportunity, and the ruthlessness required to pull off such a brutal act. And as much as she did not want to admit it, her husband's past relationship with Tabitha complicated things.

"Let's just say I'm not ruling anyone out," Hayley said carefully.

Sal chuckled. "Well, good luck with that. Just remember, land disputes and money make people do crazy things."

As she handed Sal the last croissant, Hayley could not help but agree. She rose from the chair and gathered her things. "Thanks for the help, Sal. I'll be in touch."

"Don't wait so long next time," Sal called after her,

his voice muffled by the croissant. "And bring more of those éclairs."

As Hayley left the office, she was convinced that Tabitha Collins was at the center of it all, she never trusted her from the moment they first met, and if Hayley was not careful, she might find herself in over her head.

And Tabitha did not appear to be the type to leave loose ends lying around.

ISLAND FOOD & SPIRITS
By
Hayley Powell

Back in the day, when I was married to my first husband, Danny, money was as tight as a lid on a jar of pickles. We were newlyweds, which meant I was working two part-time jobs to help pay bills, and Danny, bless him, spent more time cooking up get-rich-quick schemes than actual meals. Not that I'm bitter . . . anymore.

It was the week before Thanksgiving, a holiday we both loved—mostly because we couldn't wait for turkey leftovers to make our favorite: turkey quesadillas. With family coming over, Danny and I were hustling to save up for our first big Thanksgiving dinner. Danny was working night shifts at the Big Apple convenience store, a job he hated almost as much as his get-rich ideas. So, when his softball buddy Hank strolled in one night, waving a fat wad of cash and bragging about bartending at a new club called Happenings up in Bangor, Danny was all ears.

Before I could blink, Danny quit his job and declared himself Bangor's next top bartender. I thought he'd lost his mind. But somehow, he convinced me to let him give it a trial run. And after a few weeks of decent paychecks, I had to admit—I was impressed.

Until one Saturday night, when my best friends Mona and Liddy came over, and they looked like two guilty cats. Liddy spilled the beans: word on the street was that Happenings was more wild than welcoming, with noise complaints piling up. I didn't believe her for a second. Danny hadn't mentioned a peep.

But curiosity got the best of me, and before I knew it, we were in the car, heading to the club in Bangor.

Let me tell you, the moment we pulled into that packed parking lot, I knew something was up. The music was so loud I thought my eardrums would burst, and inside was a scene straight out of *Coyote Ugly*. Shirtless bartenders—including Danny—were dancing on the bar, pouring shots for the screaming crowd. Women stuffing dollar bills down his pants!

It was like a Lifetime TV movie I saw once called *I Married a Male Stripper*!

Okay, I may have seen it twice.

Mona grabbed a beer, Liddy laughed herself silly, and I . . . well, I yanked on Danny's pant leg, yelling for him to get down before the burly bouncer dragged me away. Danny swooped down, planted a kiss on me, and I forgave him—mostly because he looked so darn cute. We made a deal: he'd finish the holiday season, and if the place shut down (which it did), he'd go back to a "normal" job.

But hey, we had a little extra cash, a few good stories, and a freezer full of leftover turkey for our favorite quesadillas.

Still, a little kick before you get started is always helpful for the chef so here is another mouthwatering margarita recipe idea.

MONA'S MARGARITA ON THE ROCKS

INGREDIENTS:
2 ounces tequila
1 ounce orange liqueur
2 ounces margarita mix
Lime wedge
Margarita salt for rimming glass

Pour some margarita salt on a small plate. Run your lime wedge around rim of glass and then dip glass into the salt and set aside.

In a shaker half filled with ice add your tequila, orange liqueur and margarita mix.

Shake well and add to an ice-filled rocks glass garnish with lime wedge and enjoy!

Leftover Turkey Quesadillas

Ingredients:
1 tablespoon oil
Butter
½ red onion, chopped
½ bell pepper, chopped
2 cups leftover turkey, chopped
1 can black beans, drained and rinsed
½ cup sweet corn, drained and rinsed
⅓ cup cilantro (optional)
⅓ cup green onions, chopped
2 cups shredded Mexican cheese blend (more if you
    like it cheesy!)
Sour cream (optional)
Salsa (optional)
Flour tortillas

Heat oil in a large skillet on medium heat. Add onions
and peppers, sauté until soft.

Add turkey, sauté for 1-2 minutes, then toss in beans,
corn, green onions, and cilantro. Mix well and set aside.

Wipe out the skillet, then heat a bit of butter. Place a
tortilla in the pan, add cheese on one half, then spoon
on the turkey mixture. Top with more cheese, fold the
tortilla, and brown each side.

Serve with sour cream and salsa. Enjoy!

There's no better way to savor the season—and your
leftovers!

Chapter 23

Hayley hustled through the doors of her restaurant, Hayley's Kitchen, just as the dinner rush hit its peak. Betty, her dependable manager, back from her Thanksgiving vacation, stood behind the counter, frazzled and red-faced, trying to juggle orders and direct the waitstaff all at once.

"Hayley! Thank God you're here!" Betty exclaimed, looking like she was ready to either scream or cry. "We're swamped, the fryer's on the fritz again, and two tables just sent back their appetizers because they said the shrimp was cold."

This was even worse than when Betty was gone.

And Betty's meltdown was just as bad as Caroline's, her temporary replacement during Thanksgiving week.

"It's okay, Betty. I've got this," Hayley said, laying a calming hand on her shoulder. "You go grab a glass of wine and take a break. I'll handle it."

Betty hesitated, torn between staying to keep the chaos in check and the undeniable pull of a much-needed glass of Chardonnay. "Are you sure?"

"Positive. You've earned it," Hayley reassured her with a wink, then swiveled to take charge of the bustling kitchen.

She slipped seamlessly into work mode, moving through the kitchen with practiced ease, inspecting the seafood specials that were flying out the door, double-checking plating, and calling out instructions to the line cooks. She could feel the tension melt away as she settled into the comforting rhythm of her restaurant. For now, she had control over something, even if the investigation into Tom Farley's death was slipping further into murky waters.

As she made her way to the dining area to check on the tables, Hayley overheard snippets of conversation, her ears perking up as the familiar name of Tom Farley surfaced among the diners.

"I heard that guy was a real piece of work," one man at a corner table muttered to his companions. "No wonder someone finally snapped."

"Can't say I'm surprised," a woman responded, sipping her wine. "Everyone around here hated him."

Hayley could not help but feel a pang of discomfort at the way they were talking about Tom. He had been difficult, prickly even, but no one deserved to die the way he had. She found herself walking over before she could think better of it.

"Excuse me," she said, flashing a smile that felt just a little too tight. "I couldn't help overhearing. I know Tom Farley wasn't always the easiest person to deal with, but let's not forget, someone may have murdered him, the police are still trying to make a determination. It's a tragedy, regardless of how you felt about him."

The diners blinked, caught off guard by her interruption. The man cleared his throat awkwardly. "Oh, uh, of course. We didn't mean anything by it."

"Good. Just remember, everyone has their reasons for the way they act," she said, before turning on her heel and continuing her rounds.

Hayley knew she was not following her own rule.

The customer was always right.

But she just could not help herself.

She felt oddly protective of ornery old Tom.

Especially given the horrific circumstances of his death.

As she made her way to the far side of the dining room, a familiar face caught her eye. Tabitha Collins was sitting alone at a table, looking far too relaxed for someone who had been butting heads with Tom Farley in the weeks leading up to his murder.

Hayley's pulse quickened.

Tabitha was a prime suspect in her mind, though nothing she had done so far could be tied to the crime. At least, not yet. But her conversation with Sal in his office earlier had been too enticing to ignore.

With a quick, strategic smile, Hayley approached her. "Tabitha, nice to see you. How's dinner?"

"Delicious, as always," Tabitha replied, looking up from her nearly empty plate. "You always did know how to make a great meal, Hayley. This shrimp scampi is divine."

"Glad to hear it. It seems to be a favorite." Hayley

motioned to the waitress. "Can I get you a glass of wine? On the house."

Tabitha's eyebrows lifted in surprise, but she did not refuse. "How generous of you. Yes, I'll take a glass of the Pinot Grigio."

Hayley nodded and gestured to Debbie the waitress, before taking the opportunity to sit down opposite Tabitha. She leaned in, adopting a casual tone, though her mind was anything but. "I was just thinking about Tom Farley. Such a tragedy, isn't it?"

"Tragedy?" Tabitha repeated, swirling her wine glass as it was placed in front of her. "I suppose it is. But from what I've heard, plenty of people won't be shedding any tears."

Hayley studied her carefully. "True, but it's still shocking. You know, I've been wondering how much you knew about Tom's family situation. Did you ever meet any of them? A sibling, maybe?"

Tabitha shook her head dismissively. "Not at all. I assume the property will go to an heir, but I haven't bothered looking into it. Whoever inherits will likely sell—everyone has their price, after all. And if there's no family, then I imagine it'll go to the state. And I'll be first in line to buy."

Tabitha was obviously also aware of state laws regarding the property of a deceased landowner.

"Of course." Hayley gave a small, knowing smile. "And you're prepared to make it worth their while?"

"Absolutely." Tabitha's smile was sharp and confident. "I'm not worried. Whoever comes into control of that land will sell. It's inevitable."

Hayley leaned back, her suspicion deepening. Tabitha was too calm, too sure of herself. There was something off here, and it was not just her casual dismissal of the tragedy. She had to know about Tom's family—or lack thereof. That made the land even more valuable to someone like her. And with Tom dead, there was no one standing in her way. Hayley's entire theory was tracking. But she still needed proof.

Tabitha eyed Hayley warily. "You're not still considering me as a suspect, are you? I thought we put this to bed the other day when we had lunch. I didn't kill Tom."

Just as Hayley was about to press further, Bruce strolled in through the front door, looking around until he spotted Hayley. He waved, making his way over.

"Hey, honey," he said, hugging her with a grin. "There's nothing in the fridge, so I figured I'd come here for dinner. Free food, right?"

Tabitha chuckled, raising her glass. "Join me, Bruce. I'd love the company."

Bruce hesitated, glancing at Hayley, who gave him a sweet but strained smile. "Go ahead," she said, even though the thought of her husband dining with his ex made her stomach tighten. "Enjoy yourself."

Bruce, oblivious to the tension, shrugged and took a seat, eyeing the menu.

The three of them made polite conversation, but Hayley kept her focus on Tabitha, her mind racing with all the possible scenarios involving Tom Farley's woodchipper. After a while, Tabitha finished her wine, stood, and offered a friendly goodbye to them both.

"Always a pleasure, Hayley. Bruce, good to see you

again." Her gaze lingered a bit too long on Bruce for Hayley's comfort, but she refrained from commenting.

As soon as Tabitha left, Hayley slid into her seat, eyes narrowed and faced Bruce. "I'm almost certain Tabitha killed Tom."

Bruce let out a bark of laughter, nearly choking on his water. "Tabitha? No way, Hayley. You're just jealous."

"I am not!" Hayley protested, though she knew her defensiveness did not help her case. "It makes sense. She needed his land, and now she'll get it. With Tom gone, there's no one left to stand in her way."

Bruce wiped his mouth, still chuckling. "Look, I know Tabitha. I lived with her once in Boston, remember?"

"How can I forget?" Hayley spat out.

"Look, she's ruthless in business, sure, but she's not a killer. You're letting your imagination run wild."

Hayley scowled. "Maybe, but I've got a gut feeling, and I'm not going to ignore it."

Bruce shook his head, amusement still dancing in his eyes. "You say that like I'm learning something new, Hayley. You're like a dog with a bone, you can't ever let it go. That's the woman I fell in love with and married. Just be careful, okay? Don't go around accusing people without evidence."

"I know what I'm doing," Hayley muttered, more to herself than to Bruce. But even as she said it, she knew that if Tabitha Collins had anything to do with Tom Farley's murder, she would have to tread carefully. People like Tabitha did not just play the game—they owned the board.

Chapter 24

Hayley was in the middle of scanning the shelves for breadcrumbs in the Shop 'n Save grocery store when she nearly bumped into Assistant District Attorney Alley Roberts, who looked frazzled and distracted as she fumbled with her shopping list.

"Alley! How are you?" Hayley asked with a friendly smile, her hand poised on the shopping cart.

Alley blinked, as though startled out of deep thought. "Hayley! Oh, thank God. I was just thinking about you."

"About *me*? Well, that's flattering. What's going on?"

Alley let out a deep sigh, tucking a strand of hair behind her ear. "My parents are coming over for dinner tonight, and I have no idea what to cook. I was hoping to find something quick and foolproof, but I'm not exactly . . . *you*."

Hayley chuckled. "I'm sure you're better than you

think, but I've got just the thing. How about a classic New England dish—baked haddock with butter and Ritz cracker crumbs? Simple, delicious, and you'll impress the heck out of them. Plus, it's pretty hard to mess up."

Alley's eyes lit up, but her face still held traces of frustration. "That sounds perfect, but I don't know where to start. Can you help me find everything?"

"Of course! Follow me," Hayley said, wheeling her cart beside Alley's as they navigated the aisles together.

As they grabbed haddock fillets from the seafood counter, crackers from the snack aisle, and a few sticks of butter from the dairy section, Hayley could not help but notice that Alley was unusually tense. She complained about the price of butter and even muttered something about the injustice of potato prices. But it was not just the cost of groceries that had her wound up—there was something deeper eating at her.

Hayley tossed the crackers into her cart and glanced over at her friend. "Okay, spill. What's really bothering you?"

"I really shouldn't talk about it."

Of course this just made Hayley more curious.

She could see that Alley was debating with herself whether or not she should talk freely with her, so Hayley waited patiently, hoping she might decide to just go for it.

Alley hesitated, biting her lip, but after a long pause, she finally sighed. "It's work. My boss just forced me to dismiss the charges against Alan Murdock."

"Wait—what?" Hayley stopped short, her cart roll-

ing to a halt. "You mean the charges for taking a shot at
Tom Farley during the turkey shoot? He all but confessed!"

"And then retracted once the lawyers got involved.
They're claiming it was coerced and that you never
should have been allowed near him."

They were probably right about that.

"It's so typical of this boys' club we've still got in
this town." Alley's voice was tight with anger, and she
clenched her shopping list in her hand. "I had a solid
case against him, but now it's gone. All because my
boss is buddies with Lester Murdock. They golf together every other weekend, and I'm sure Lester pulled
some strings. And guess what? Justice isn't so blind
when you've got deep pockets and influential friends."

Hayley felt a surge of indignation on Alley's behalf.
"That's outrageous! You had enough evidence to nail
Alan, didn't you?"

"I did!" Alley grabbed a carton of cream for her haddock recipe, her hands trembling with frustration. "I
was so close. But when I pushed back, my boss had the
nerve to suggest that I was pursuing a personal ven-
detta against the Murdocks. Can you believe that? Like
I'm some rogue prosecutor with an agenda."

"That's absurd. Everyone knows the Murdocks have
gotten away with all sorts of things over the years."
Hayley frowned. "But dismissing the charges? That
feels . . . shady."

"It is shady. Since the Murdocks are now pushing
the story that the shooting was just an accident, and

that Alan had a sturdy alibi for the day Tom was killed, so why not just let it go? Can you believe that?"

"So what's your next move?"

"The boss says I should be paying attention to more important cases like actual murders so, okay, then I will. I'm going to focus on tying Lester to Tom Farley's murder," Alley whispered, lowering her voice as a few other shoppers passed by. "I'm convinced Lester was the one who shoved Tom into that woodchipper."

Hayley's heart skipped a beat. She had suspected Lester Murdock might be the killer too, but hearing Alley say it out loud made it all the more real. "You honestly think Lester did it?"

Alley nodded, her face set in determination. "It makes sense. He had the most to gain—Tom was holding up that massive real estate deal with Acadia Resorts. Once Tom was out of the way, the Murdocks were free to sell, and Tabitha Collins was ready to buy. And Lester? We both know he's ruthless enough to make it all happen."

Hayley grabbed a jar of lemon juice, her mind spinning. "But do you have any evidence?"

"I'm working on it," Alley said, her voice low but intense. "We found those muddy footprints at the scene, remember? I'm trying to get it matched to Lester. But every time I request an interview with him, his lawyers stonewall me. It's like they know I'm circling him, and they're doing everything they can to keep me at bay."

Hayley glanced down at the breadcrumbs in her cart, suddenly feeling the weight of the conversation. "So you think Lester Murdock killed Tom, and now he's just going to walk free because he's got the right connections?"

"Not if I can help it," Alley muttered darkly. "Trust me. I won't let him get away with it. But I need more time—and I need that footprint to be the smoking gun. My boss can't ignore that kind of evidence."

"That's tough," Hayley said, her voice thoughtful. "I've been looking at Tabitha Collins, too. She's got plenty to gain from Tom's death, and she's not afraid to throw money around to get what she wants."

Alley gave her a sideways glance. "Tabitha's definitely in the mix, but I think Lester's the one who got his hands dirty. He's the kind of guy who likes to do his own dirty work when the stakes are high enough."

They turned into the checkout line, their carts filled with ingredients. Alley gave Hayley a grateful smile. "Thanks for helping me with dinner. I'd be lost without you."

"Anytime. Just let me know how it turns out," Hayley said, but her thoughts were still with Lester Murdock.

As she watched Alley pay for her groceries, Hayley wondered if it was possible that both Tabitha and Lester were involved.

A partnership of convenience, perhaps?

Or maybe they each had their own reasons for wanting Tom Farley out of the picture, and one of them had simply acted first.

Hayley left the store with a mental list longer than her grocery one. She needed to dig deeper into Lester Murdock's history—and fast. If Alley was onto something, then Hayley was more determined than ever to help her bring justice to Tom Farley's killer. Even if it meant going toe-to-toe with a man as powerful as Lester Murdock. She would not allow herself to be intimidated by him.

Or anyone else for that matter.

Even if it eventually put her own life in danger.

Chapter 25

Hayley sat at her kitchen table, her laptop glowing softly in the dim afternoon light. She stared at the screen as the search results finished loading. She had not been able to shake the strange encounter between Hannah Sweet and that man at the Common Good food pantry. The way he had confronted her, how pale and rattled she had become. There was something off about it, and Hayley's instincts told her she needed to dig deeper.

A quick Google search of Hannah's maiden name—Corbin—led her straight to the answers. *Hannah Corbin of Pittsfield, Maine*, the headline read, *Teen Convicted in Tragic Hit-and-Run*. Hayley scrolled through the details, her heart sinking with each sentence. As a teenager, Hannah had gone joyriding with friends and struck an elderly woman in a crosswalk. Worse, she had fled the scene. When she was caught, the courts treated it as a hit-and-run. Hannah had been convicted and served time in prison.

Hayley leaned back in her chair, her mind racing. This was a painful secret—one that Hannah had likely carried for years, and one she had surely tried to bury.

But had she told Daniel?

Hayley doubted it.

The young couple had always seemed so in love, and Hayley could not help but wonder how Daniel would react to learning such a dark truth.

Had Tom Farley somehow found out her secret?

That would be motive enough for Hannah to try and keep him from talking.

But the thought of a woman eight months pregnant lifting a grown man and dropping him into a wood-chipper seemed a remote possibility at best.

An hour later, Hayley found herself pulling up the long, dirt driveway to the Sweets' double-wide trailer. Hayley could see Hannah through the window, moving slowly around the kitchen, her hand resting protectively on her lower belly. The sight made Hayley's heart ache. She was not just dealing with the weight of her past—she had a future to think about now, too.

Gathering her courage, Hayley walked up to the door and knocked softly. After a moment, Hannah appeared, her expression shifting from surprise to worry.

"Hayley? What are you doing here?"

"Can I come in?" Hayley asked gently. "I think we need to talk."

Hannah hesitated but nodded, stepping aside to let Hayley into the small but cozy living room. Hannah instinctively knew this was not a social call.

They sat down, and Hayley took a deep breath. "I know about your past. What happened in Pittsfield. The accident."

Hannah's face went white as a sheet, her eyes widening in fear. "How—how did you—"

"I did some digging," Hayley admitted, her voice soft but firm. "That man at the pantry . . . he recognized you, didn't he? From the trial?"

Hannah's hands trembled as she clasped them in her lap, her gaze dropping to the floor. "Yes," she whispered. "He did. I thought I could escape it when I moved to New Hampshire my senior year and met Daniel, but . . . it's always there. Lurking, waiting to ruin everything."

Tears welled up in her eyes as she looked up at Hayley, her voice cracking. "I didn't mean to hurt that woman. I was a stupid, reckless kid. But I panicked, and I ran, and now I have to live with that every day. I've tried to move on, but . . . how can I, when I've never even told Daniel? And now . . . with the baby . . ."

She placed a trembling hand on her stomach, her voice breaking.

Hayley felt her heart clench. "Hannah, I know this is terrifying, but you can't keep this from him. He loves you, and you're about to start a family together. You need to be honest with him."

Hannah wiped her eyes, shaking her head. "You don't understand. I've seen people walk away when they find out the truth. I've seen the disgust in their eyes. What if Daniel leaves me too? What if he doesn't want this baby anymore?"

Hayley reached over, gently placing a hand on Hannah's arm. "I've seen the way Daniel looks at you. He adores you, and I don't think anything—certainly not something you did as a teenager—is going to change that. But you have to give him the chance to prove that to you. You can't build a life on secrets."

Hannah sniffled, her fingers tightening around the hem of her shirt. "I don't know if I'm strong enough."

"You are," Hayley said firmly. "And I'll be here with you, if you want."

Hannah nodded, her face filled with a mixture of fear and determination. Before she could say more, the front door creaked open. Daniel stepped inside, his boots caked in mud, his face lined with fatigue. He froze when he saw the two of them sitting on the couch, his brow furrowing in confusion.

"What's going on?" he asked, setting his things down and walking over to them.

Hannah sucked in a shaky breath, glancing at Hayley for support. "Daniel . . . there's something I need to tell you. It's about my past—something I should have told you a long time ago."

Daniel's expression darkened with concern, and he knelt in front of her, taking her hands in his. "What is it, Hannah? You're scaring me."

Hannah's voice cracked as she began to speak, recounting the story of her teenage years, the joyride that ended in tragedy, the trial, the prison sentence. She left nothing out, her words spilling out in a rush as if she could finally unburden herself. When she finished, she sat back, her entire body shaking, waiting for Daniel's response.

Daniel was silent for a long moment, his face unreadable. Hayley held her breath, watching the emotions play across his face—shock, sadness, but no anger. Finally, he reached up and cupped Hannah's face in his hands, his voice low and steady.

"Hannah, you made a mistake. A terrible one. But that doesn't change how much I love you, or how much I want to be with you. You and this baby—you're my family now. And nothing from your past is going to change that."

Hannah's breath hitched as tears filled her eyes again, but this time they were tears of relief. "You—you still want to be with me? Even after everything?"

"Of course I do," Daniel said, pulling her into his arms. "We'll get through this together. I'm not going anywhere."

Hannah sobbed into his shoulder, clinging to him as if afraid he might slip away. But Daniel held her tightly, his grip unwavering.

Hayley watched, her heart full as the young couple shared this tender moment of truth and forgiveness. She knew how difficult it had been for Hannah to come clean, and she was glad to see that Daniel's love was as steadfast as she had hoped.

When Daniel finally looked over at Hayley, his eyes were filled with gratitude. "Thank you, Hayley," he said softly. "For helping her—and for being here."

Hayley smiled, her heart warm. "You don't need to thank me. I'm just glad Hannah doesn't have to carry this alone anymore. But I have to ask . . ." She hesitated, not wanting to do this.

They both looked at her expectantly.

"Did Tom Farley somehow discover what happened to you when you were young, Hannah? Did he know?"

Hannah gasped. "What? No, of course not. Why? Do you think I could have—?"

"No, I just had to ask. I'm sorry."

They both nodded, understanding.

"I'll leave you two alone now."

As she made her way out of the trailer, Hayley's thoughts drifted back to the tangled mystery of Tom Farley's death. She was certain now that Daniel and Hannah were innocent. But someone was still responsible for what had happened to Tom.

Lester Murdock.

His wife and sons.

Reid Norton.

Lori the agoraphobic.

And especially Tabitha Collins.

All still likely suspects with or without alibis.

Because it was possible the killer may not have acted alone.

In fact, this could involve a whole conspiracy.

Chapter 26

Late that night, Hayley lay wide awake in bed, her phone glowing in the darkness while Bruce snored lightly beside her. The hum of the furnace filled the room, but Hayley barely noticed as her thumb scrolled through the endless stream of social media posts. Her eyes darted from one profile to the next, each click inching her closer to her goal: digging up dirt on Tabitha Collins. Hayley was convinced that Tabitha, with her polished smile and sharp business acumen, was somehow behind the gruesome murder of Tom Farley.

It was the kind of sleepless obsession she used to reserve for tweaking recipes or hunting down rare ingredients, but now, she was chasing something far more sinister—a clear motive.

Tabitha had been aggressively courting all the local property owners around Tom's farm for Acadia Resorts, determined to build her fancy new resort in Bar Harbor. Tom, stubborn and ornery, had been the lone hold-out. That alone would have been enough to make him a nuisance, but the fact that he had been found ground up in his own woodchipper seemed like overkill, even for a woman like Tabitha. Hayley narrowed her eyes, clicking on another post about Tabitha's time as CEO of Boston Common Seafood, the company she had run before moving over to Acadia Resorts.

The flood of negative comments was impressive. People really did not have nice things to say about her. Allegations of bullying, intimidation, and an overall toxic work environment littered her history.

"Fishy," Hayley muttered under her breath, smirking at the irony. There were even rumors of threats to employees who had dared to oppose her ideas.

But one post in particular caught her attention. Bethany—a former employee of Boston Common Seafood—had left an exceptionally scathing comment about Tabitha. *She ruined my life. I'll never forget what she did to me and my team. Tabitha Collins is a monster who hides behind her pretty face and corporate power. She should be in jail for half the things she's done.*

Hayley sat up straight in bed. This was what she needed—a first-hand account of Tabitha's behavior, someone who had seen behind the façade. Without thinking twice, Hayley sent a direct message to Bethany.

Hi Bethany—this is Hayley Powell from Bar Harbor. I read your post about Tabitha Collins, and I was wondering if you'd be willing to talk about your experience. I have a few questions I'd love to ask you. Let me know!

To her surprise, Bethany responded almost immediately.

Of course. I have A LOT to say about that woman. I'm in Bangor—only about an hour away. I can drive down tomorrow if that works for you?

Hayley grinned, typing back quickly. *That works perfectly. How about we meet at Drinks Like a Fish? I'll treat you to lunch and we can talk over fried clams and beer.*

Bethany agreed, and as Hayley was about to set her phone down, Bruce stirred beside her, blinking groggily.

"What're you up to?" he mumbled, his voice thick with sleep.

Hayley's heart jumped, but she managed to keep her voice casual. "Just . . . checking out some things for a column I'm working on," she said, glancing at her phone before tucking it under her pillow. She did not care to mention that she was digging up dirt on his ex-girlfriend.

No need to open that can of worms at one in the morning.

Bruce muttered something unintelligible and rolled over, his soft snores resuming within seconds. Hayley exhaled, sinking back into her pillow.

Tomorrow was going to be interesting.

The next day, Hayley arrived at Drinks Like a Fish, scanning the room for Bethany. The bar was filled with the comforting scent of fried seafood and the low hum of conversation. Randy was at his usual post behind the bar, chatting with some locals, but when he caught sight of Hayley, he gave her a nod. She waved back, but her eyes were focused on the young woman sitting alone at a table near the window.

Bethany looked even more intense in person than in her profile picture. She wore a leather jacket and had her arms crossed, but as soon as she saw Hayley, she uncrossed them and gave a small wave. Her expression softened slightly, but it was clear that she was not here to exchange pleasantries.

Hayley sat down across from her, offering a polite smile. "Bethany, thanks for meeting with me."

Bethany nodded and leaned back in her seat. "No problem. I'm guessing you want the dirt on Tabitha?"

Hayley chuckled. "Something like that. I've heard some things, but I'd rather hear it from someone who actually worked with her."

Before Bethany could respond, Randy appeared at the table with a tray of fried clams and two beers. "On the house," he said with a grin, setting them down. "Figured you ladies could use a little fuel."

"Thanks, Randy," Hayley said, grateful for the distraction. She turned back to Bethany, who was already reaching for a clam. "He's my brother so I tend to get the royal treatment around here."

"Nice," Bethany said, chewing thoughtfully.

Hayley waited patiently until Bethany swallowed her first clam before gently prodding, "So . . . Tabitha?"

As Bethany reached for another clam, she suddenly stopped. "I just remembered how much Tabitha loves clams." She withdrew her hand from the plate. "I've lost my appetite."

Hayley remembered her lunch with Tabitha when she devoured the clams, but unfortunately nothing ever spoiled Hayley's appetite. She could finish the rest of the plate of clams no problem. After popping one in her mouth, she said, "You were about to tell me about your experience working for Tabitha?"

Bethany rolled her eyes. "Where do I even start? Tabitha Collins is one of those people who never has to face consequences for anything. She's manipulative, ruthless, and downright toxic. Back at Boston Common Seafood, she ran the company like it was her personal fiefdom. If you crossed her, you were done. She'd make your life miserable until you couldn't take it anymore and quit."

Hayley leaned in, intrigued. "That bad, huh?"

Bethany scoffed. "Worse. She was known for making threats to people who stood in her way. Intimidation was her go-to tactic. I personally filed three complaints with HR about her, and I wasn't the only one. At least half a dozen people did the same, but nothing ever came of it. She had the board in her pocket."

Hayley sipped her beer, trying to keep her excitement in check. "So what happened? How did she end up leaving?"

Bethany smirked, as if savoring a long-awaited punchline. "Eventually, the complaints piled up. She became a liability, so the board had no choice but to push her out. Of course, she didn't leave empty-handed. They gave her a nice fat severance package, and she landed at Acadia Resorts like nothing happened. She's been failing upward ever since. It's a running joke between my husband and our friends—no matter how many people she screws over, she just keeps getting promoted."

Hayley nodded, processing the information. She was not surprised by what she was hearing. Tabitha was exactly the type of person she suspected her to be. "Do you think she's capable of something . . . more extreme? Like, pushing someone out of the way—permanently?"

Bethany paused, studying Hayley's face. "You're talking about that turkey farmer, right? The one who ended up in his own woodchipper? God, what a grisly way to go."

Hayley nodded, her heart racing. "Tom Farley. He was the only property owner holding out against Acadia Resorts."

Bethany took a long sip of her beer before answering. "I wouldn't put anything past her. If Tom was standing in the way of what she wanted, I could see her taking drastic measures. She always had this 'ends justify the means' attitude. It was like a game to her, and she always had to win."

Hayley felt a shiver run down her spine. She could almost hear Tabitha's smooth, confident voice in her head, issuing threats with that same icy smile she remembered from their brief encounters.

Bethany glanced around the bar before lowering her voice. "I wasn't sure if I should bring this up, but . . . I have a friend. She's a Tri Delta sorority sister from back when I went to the University of Maine at Orono. She worked at Acadia Resorts for a bit, doing some temporary project management. She knew how much I hated Tabitha, so when she came across some internal emails—ones that specifically mentioned Tom Farley— she thought I'd be interested."

Hayley's breath caught. "Emails? What did they say?"

Bethany pulled out her phone and started scrolling through her messages. "It's not pretty. Tabitha was threatening Tom, practically admitting she'd do whatever it took to get him out of the way. Here, I'll forward them to you."

Hayley quickly rattled off her email address.

Bethany typed a few quick words, and within seconds, Hayley's phone buzzed with a new email alert. Hayley opened it immediately, her heart pounding as she read the subject lines.

RE: Farley Problem

The first email, dated a few weeks before Tom's death, was chilling:

Tom, I've been patient long enough. This deal is going through, with or without your cooperation. I'll do whatever it takes to get you out of the way.

Very on the nose.

Even for someone as direct as Tabitha.

Hayley scrolled to the next email, her pulse quickening as she read more. In each one, Tabitha's tone became more aggressive. She threatened to pull legal strings, to discredit him publicly, to tie him up in so many lawsuits he would have no choice but to sell. But it was the last email, sent just a few days before Tom's body was found in the woodchipper, that made Hayley's blood run cold:

You've left me no choice. This ends now.

Hayley put her phone down, her hand shaking slightly. She took a deep breath, steadying herself before meeting Bethany's eyes.

Bethany leaned back, crossing her arms again. "Told you she's ruthless. And now you've got proof."

Hayley nodded, her mind spinning with the possibilities. This was exactly what she needed—concrete evidence that Tabitha had targeted Tom. Maybe it was not a direct admission of murder, but it sure as hell painted her in a suspicious light.

"Bethany," Hayley said slowly, "this changes everything."

Bethany gave a small, grim smile. "Yeah, it does. You really think she could have done it? Killed this Tom guy?"

"I don't know," Hayley admitted. "But these emails give us motive. She clearly hated Tom for standing in the way of her project. If she didn't do it herself, I wouldn't be surprised if she found someone to do it for her."

Bethany took a final sip of her beer, her eyes thoughtful. "Tabitha's the kind of person who always gets what she wants. Like I said, she'd do anything to win, no matter the cost. And sadly she's probably going to get away with it again."

"Not on my watch," Hayley promised, downing more of her beer. "Thanks for sharing this with me, Bethany."

Bethany watched Hayley pop the last clam in her mouth and wash it down with a gulp of her beer.

Bethany guzzled the rest of her beer and slammed the mug down on the table. "Whatever I can do to make that woman pay for all the bad things she's done." Then she stood up. "It was nice meeting you, Hayley. I have to get back to Bangor. My husband and I are celebrating our third wedding anniversary at Timber tonight."

"Happy anniversary!" Hayley chirped.

As Bethany left the bar, Hayley stared at her phone, the emails still open on the screen. She now had undeniable proof of how much Tabitha wanted Tom gone. But if Tabitha had gone so far as to murder him, Hayley knew she would need to tread carefully. People like Tabitha did not go down without a fight, and this was one battle Hayley had no intention of losing.

Chapter 27

Hayley rushed into Bruce's office at the *Island Times*, her laptop tucked under one arm and a look of determined excitement on her face. She barely had time to close the door behind her before she was at his desk, flipping open her computer and angling it so Bruce could see the screen.

"Look at this," she said breathlessly, pulling up a string of emails she had been poring through for the past two hours. "It's bad, Bruce. Really bad. I'm not done yet, but this one in particular—" she pointed to a highlighted message, "—this one is . . . well, you'll see."

Bruce leaned in, squinting at the screen, his brows knitting together as he read through the email chain. "Hayley . . . you really think Tabitha's involved in this? I mean, yeah, this doesn't look good, but—"

"'Doesn't look good'? Bruce, that's the understatement of the century," Hayley cut in, her voice sharp. "You're missing the point. She was threatening him. She said if he didn't cooperate, she'd—"

"'Chop him up into little pieces,'" Bruce finished reading aloud, his voice skeptical. "Hayley, that's just a figure of speech. People say things like that when they're frustrated. It doesn't mean she actually—"

"He was found in a woodchipper, Bruce!" Hayley exclaimed, throwing her hands up in frustration. "How can you defend her after seeing this?"

Bruce sighed, leaning back in his chair. "I'm not defending her, I'm just saying we don't know for sure. Tabitha's ruthless in business, yes, but that doesn't make her a murderer."

Hayley's eyes narrowed. "Why are you so sure she's innocent? Do you know something I don't?"

Bruce hesitated, a brief flicker of discomfort crossing his face. "Hayley, come on—"

"Oh my God," Hayley said, her voice low and accusing as the realization hit her. "You do still have feelings for her."

Bruce's eyes widened. "What? No! That's not it at all."

"Then why are you constantly defending her?" Hayley demanded, crossing her arms. "Every time Tabitha's name comes up, you're so quick to say she couldn't have done it. Why, Bruce? The only explanation is because you still have a thing for her!"

"I do not have a thing for Tabitha," Bruce shot back, his voice rising in frustration. "I'm just saying we need to be careful here. You're accusing her of murder based on a couple of emails."

Before Hayley could respond, her phone buzzed with a notification. She glanced down at the screen and her eyes widened.

"Look at this," she said, turning the phone to show Bruce. It was a social media post from Liddy, time-stamped just a few minutes earlier. She was at a house, celebrating with none other than Tabitha Collins.

"'Celebrating Tabitha's offer on this gorgeous property,'" Hayley read aloud, her voice dripping with disbelief. "She's celebrating while Tom's body is barely cold in the morgue."

Bruce leaned in, scanning the post. "Wait a minute, I know that house . . . isn't that where we went to that Christmas party last year? The one with the big wrap-around porch and the fireplace in the kitchen?"

"Exactly," Hayley said, already grabbing her bag. "The Jensens. Lovely couple. I remember them talking about selling and retiring to Florida sometime this year. Looks like Tabitha's the buyer. Come on, we need to get over there."

Bruce sighed but grabbed his jacket. "You're not going to let this go, are you?"

Hayley shot him a determined look. "Not a chance."

They pulled up to the house a short while later, the sound of laughter and the faint clinking of champagne glasses drifting out from the front porch. As they approached, they could hear Tabitha's voice, loud and slightly slurred.

"And I'm telling you, Liddy, I'm going to gut this place," Tabitha was saying excitedly. "Rip out the old wood paneling, get rid of that ridiculous vintage stove—who needs charm when you can have sleek and modern?"

Hayley's stomach turned at the thought. The house had been so warm and welcoming during that Christmas party, full of history and character. Now Tabitha was planning to turn it into a soulless showroom.

Tabitha spotted them approaching and waved, still holding her champagne glass. "Well, well, look who it is! Bruce and Hayley, come join the party!"

Liddy was practically bouncing she was so happy, no doubt at the hefty commission she was going to make from what was probably an inflated sale price.

Hayley did not waste time on pleasantries. "We need to talk," she said, her tone sharp as she held up her laptop. "About these emails."

The smile froze on Tabitha's face as she took in Hayley's serious expression. "Emails?"

"Yeah, the ones where you threatened Tom," Hayley said, flipping the screen to show her. "The ones where you said you'd chop him into little pieces if he didn't cooperate."

Tabitha's face drained of color, and for a moment, she looked genuinely shaken. But then she straightened, taking a deep breath. "That's just a figure of speech, Hayley. You should know that."

Hayley glanced at Bruce who looked exceedingly nervous.

Odd they had both said the same thing.

Had they discussed this beforehand?

Hayley shook that unpleasant thought right out of her head.

"Sure," Hayley said coldly. "Except Tom was actually chopped up—into very small pieces."

Tabitha blinked, her eyes flicking to Bruce as if for support. "Bruce, you don't seriously think—?"

Bruce crossed his arms. "It doesn't look good, Tabitha."

"But you—?" Her composure wavered. She appeared confused at Bruce's behavior at first, but then relaxed, realizing what was going on.

Tabitha quickly recovered, setting her champagne glass down on the porch railing. "Look, those emails prove nothing. They were just heated business exchanges. If you think they're enough to accuse me of murder, you're out of your mind."

Hayley's gaze was unrelenting. "You can call it a figure of speech all you want, but Tom was found dead in the most horrific way possible, and you were the one pressuring him."

Tabitha opened her mouth to protest, but then stopped herself. Her eyes darted back to Bruce, and for the first time, there was real fear in her voice. "I have an alibi."

Hayley folded her arms. "Oh yeah? Let's hear it."

Tabitha hesitated, and Bruce visibly tensed beside her. "I'm sorry, Bruce, but I'm not going down for a crime I did not commit." She turned to Hayley. "I had lunch with Bruce that day. Right before you called him and told him to meet you at the hospital to see Tom."

"He had been discharged that morning, so we went over to his farm to check on him . . ." Hayley's voice trailed off.

"Where you found him in itty bitty pieces. See, I

couldn't have done it. I was with Bruce during the time he was killed."

The world tilted beneath Hayley's feet. She turned to Bruce, searching his face for some sign that this was all one big mistake. "Is that . . . is that true?"

Bruce let out a long sigh, rubbing the back of his neck. "Yeah. She's telling the truth. We had lunch. She tried to—"

"*What*?" Hayley's voice was a mix of disbelief and anger.

Bruce's jaw tightened as he shot Tabitha a look. "She tried to rekindle things. Again. But I told her, just like I've told her before—I'm not interested. I love you, Hayley."

Tabitha gave a bitter smile. "He's telling you the truth, Hayley. I lost. Again. Bruce isn't coming back to me, no matter how many times I try."

"I wanted to tell you, I was just scared about how you might react," Bruce murmured.

"Like how I'm acting right now, shocked and enraged?"

Bruce stared at his shoes. "Yeah, pretty much."

Hayley's heart pounded in her chest as she turned back to Tabitha. "Stay away from my husband. And maybe work on finding someone who isn't already taken."

Tabitha shrugged; her earlier bravado gone. "There are plenty of men in Bar Harbor. I'll be sure to take your advice."

"There aren't that many unattached men in this town, believe me!" Liddy piped in before her eyes fell on Hayley's flushed and angry face. "But Hayley, my best friend, is right, you should probably focus on the few single ones who can stay sober past five o'clock or don't smell like a fishing trawler."

On the way back to the car, Hayley noticed Bruce silently bracing himself for the inevitable explosion that was about to come, but to his surprise, Hayley stopped walking and turned to him with a soft smile. Before he could say anything, she kissed him softly on the lips.

He pulled back, blinking in confusion. "You're not mad?"

Hayley shook her head, her hand resting on his chest. "I know you love me, Bruce. And I know you'll never leave me for someone like Tabitha."

Bruce let out a relieved breath, pulling her into a hug. "You have nothing to worry about. Not now, not ever."

"Good," Hayley murmured, her gaze softening. "Because we still have a killer to catch."

Chapter 28

Hayley slipped into Kathy's Salon, the bells on the door tinkling cheerfully, in sharp contrast to her mood. She was grateful for this break, even if it was just a quick shampoo and blow-dry. Kathy's salon always had the aroma of hairspray and gossip—a mixture both comforting and distracting.

"Hayley, sweetie darling! Get in here!" Kathy trilled from across the room, her rollers bouncing as she popped up from behind the reception desk.

"Hey, Kathy." Hayley gave a weak smile, pulling her coat off. She did not feel up for the usual gossip-fest, but she needed a breather, especially after finding human remains in a woodchipper and finding out Tabitha Collins had once again made a play for Bruce.

It was all a bit too much.

"Grab a seat! I'll get to you in just a sec. Got a lot to

tell you!" Kathy winked, already bubbling over with excitement.

Hayley's reputation as the town's amateur sleuth preceded her. As for Kathy, Hayley sometimes wondered if she had gotten her cosmetology degree as an excuse to pump all the locals for the latest juicy gossip when they were under her hair dryer.

Hayley sat in the familiar leather chair and closed her eyes for a moment as Kathy fussed behind her. "You're not going to believe this, but I think I know who killed Tom Farley."

Hayley stiffened but kept her face neutral. "Oh? And who might that be?" She opened her eyes and met Kathy's through the mirror.

"Reid Norton," Kathy declared, as if the truth had been sitting right there all along. "I never liked him. Not since he backed into my car in the Shop 'n Save parking lot five years ago. And you know what he did? He yelled at me! Like it was *my* fault!" Kathy fluffed Hayley's hair aggressively, as if Reid were hidden somewhere in the strands.

Hayley managed a soft laugh. "I'm sure that wasn't pleasant, but that doesn't make him a murderer, Kathy."

Kathy stopped mid-fluff and narrowed her eyes at Hayley's reflection. "You're too nice. He's got a legendary temper, and poor Tom lived right next door. You do the math."

"I'm not saying you're wrong . . ." Hayley trailed off diplomatically. Kathy was not one to be swayed by pesky facts when she got a wild idea in her head. And right now, her theory was Reid Norton did it, based on a fender bender from five years ago. But Hayley knew better than to stoke the flames of small-town gossip.

Best to just let it run its course.

Before Kathy could continue, the door of the salon flew open, and Liddy breezed in, all fluttering scarves and bright apologies.

"Hayley!" she exclaimed, rushing over. "I am so, so sorry about Tabitha! I swear, if I had known she was trying to steal Bruce right out from under you, I never, ever would have taken her on as a client! Not in a million years!" Liddy's voice was dramatic, layered with righteous indignation.

And loud enough for all the customers in the shop, as well as Kathy and her staff, to stop chatting and be all ears.

Hayley stifled a smile. Liddy was as loyal as a golden retriever when it suited her, though she would sell out her own mother for a good commission. "It's fine, Liddy," Hayley said with a shake of her head. "Water under the bridge."

"No, no, it's not fine! I'm one hundred percent on your side. BFFs forever, right?" Liddy slid into the chair next to Hayley, wrapping her arm around her in a gesture of solidarity.

Hayley smiled indulgently. "Of course. BFFs."

Liddy straightened up, satisfied. "I'm just glad that's settled."

Hayley turned and gave Liddy a smirk. "So are you dropping her as a client? Maybe reassign the closing of the sale to another agent in the office?"

Liddy's eyes widened in panic as the blood drained

from her face. "Um, well, I just assumed since the offer was already accepted before I found out what Tabitha had tried to do, then it's okay for me to accept the commission, right? What I meant was, from this point forward, I am loyal to you one hundred percent."

Hayley chuckled.

"It's a one-point-five-million-dollar sale, Hayley, think of the cashmere sweaters I can buy at Bergdorf Goodman the next time I'm in New York!"

Hayley placed a reassuring hand on Liddy's arm. "It's fine, Liddy, really. You deserve every penny you make on that sale."

Liddy breathed a huge sigh of relief.

As Kathy resumed working on Hayley's hair, the door jingled again, and in walked Caitlin Rivers, the new Mrs. Sonny Rivers, all grace and sharp angles. Her perfectly tailored coat and sleek hair made her seem out of place in the cozy, chaotic salon.

Sonny Rivers was a local attorney to whom Liddy had once been engaged.

Actually they were more than just engaged.

Liddy was in her wedding dress at the altar with a church packed with family and friends.

And Sonny had been a no show.

It turned out to be a blessing in disguise given his checkered past that came to light later.

"Hey there, Caitlin! We're running just a little behind. The shampoo girl is out sick," Kathy called out cheerfully, though there was a slight edge to her voice.

Caitlin was a newcomer, and in Bar Harbor, newcomers had to earn their place.

Caitlin did not bother hiding her annoyance. "I have an appointment at eleven. I'll wait a little while, but I have things to do," she said, sitting down and tapping her fingernails impatiently on the arm of the chair.

Hayley glanced at Liddy, who raised an eyebrow. Caitlin always seemed so polished, like she did not have time for anyone or anything, not even the typical small-town pleasantries.

"Well, while we're waiting . . ." Liddy said loudly, her eyes sparkling as she eyed Caitlin. "Good morning, Caitlin!"

Caitlin raised her eyes, surprised to see Liddy, her husband's ex-fiancée, with a bright smile on her face.

"Uh, hello," she muttered, quickly returning to rifle through the magazine she had picked up off the side table.

"How's life with Sonny?" Liddy chirped.

Caitlin's expression tightened. "It's fine," she said coolly. She did not elaborate.

"Good to hear," Liddy replied. "It's a relief actually given, well, you know the whole sordid story. You're brave, you know, marrying a man with his, how shall I say, colorful past."

Hayley sighed inwardly. It was just like Liddy to dig into old drama. Sonny Rivers had been the talk of the town after it came out that he was a polygamist, juggling multiple families. And while he somehow managed to hold onto his law license after serving a little time, Liddy was not about to let anyone in town forget it.

Caitlin, though, did not seem fazed. "Everyone deserves a second chance," she said firmly, though her eyes flitted briefly to Liddy. "Besides, Sonny's doing fine now. He's back to practicing law and has been very busy. Actually, he's handling Tom Farley's estate."

Hayley and Liddy exchanged a surprised glance.

That was news.

"Tom had a will?" Hayley asked, surprised. She had not considered that Tom would bother with formal arrangements like that.

Caitlin nodded. "Yes. Sonny told me that he's scheduled the reading of the will for tomorrow. He's been out of town, but he got home last night. He wanted to wait until he was back before proceeding with all the legal mumbo jumbo."

Hayley's mind whirled.

A will could change everything.

If Tom left his property to someone, that person could still block the sale to Acadia Resorts.

And suddenly, the stakes felt higher than ever.

Liddy's face lit up. "Really? Tomorrow?" She leaned in, her tone shifting from predatory to friendly in an instant. "You and I should catch up soon, Caitlin. Maybe lunch?"

Caitlin raised an eyebrow but nodded slowly. "Sure, I suppose."

Hayley watched Liddy with a bemused smile. Trust Liddy to switch alliances the moment an opportunity presented itself. But that was Liddy—always adapting to the winds of fortune.

Kathy finally stepped back from Hayley's hair and announced, "All done! You're looking fabulous, as always."

Hayley stood, feeling refreshed, but her mind was racing. Tomorrow's will reading could provide answers—answers that someone might not want to get out. As she and Liddy said their goodbyes to Caitlin, Hayley could not shake the feeling that things were about to get a whole lot more complicated.

And in Bar Harbor, it seemed complications were never far from danger.

Chapter 29

Thanksgiving Leftovers Night at Hayley's Kitchen had always been a local favorite. A cozy warmth spread through the small restaurant, the smell of sage stuffing, cranberry compote, and roast turkey filling the air. The tables were packed with regulars and visitors alike, many hoping to relive the flavors of the holiday without the hassle of all that cooking and preparation. The restaurant hummed with conversation, the clinking of glasses, and the scrape of utensils on plates. It was a busy night, but not a madhouse, which was usually the case.

At a table near the window, the Murdocks sat, their expensive clothes a stark contrast to the casual, homey atmosphere. Lester Murdock wore a deep scowl as he tore into his turkey sandwich, his wife Melody casting nervous glances around the room. Their sons, Alan and Bo, sat stiffly beside them, barely touching their food.

Across from them, Reid Norton, who seemed to be perpetually irritated with the world, grimaced into his drink, making little effort to engage with the others around him.

Nearby, Daniel and Hannah Sweet exchanged polite smiles, though there was a subtle tension beneath the surface. The room buzzed with the quiet acknowledgment of shared suspicion, though no one dared to voice it.

The only neighbor missing was agoraphobic Lori Gunning, for obvious reasons.

Hayley made her rounds, checking in on her guests with practiced ease, though her mind was far from the comforting routine of the night. As she approached the Murdocks' table, she could feel the weight of the tension surrounding Tom Farley's murder. His neighbors, the very people now seated just a few feet from each other, all harbored motives—secrets, grudges, and desires that swirled around like the late fall wind.

"Everything tasting good tonight?" she asked, her tone chipper as she approached the Murdocks.

Lester barely glanced up, his voice gruff. "It's fine."

Melody, ever the peacemaker, forced a smile. "Delicious, Hayley, as always. You do a wonderful job here." Then she downed the rest of her Rose Kennedy, her hand shaking slightly.

Alan and Bo mumbled in agreement, though they seemed distracted, their eyes darting toward Reid and the Sweets, as if trying to gauge what the others were thinking.

"Glad to hear it," Hayley replied, her own smile genuine but masking the nervous flutter in her stomach. Alan was the only Murdock who did not order from the special Thanksgiving leftovers menu. "Enjoying the scampi, Alan? I know it's your favorite."

He did not meet her gaze and just shrugged. "It's good."

Hayley could only imagine what wheels Lester must have greased to get such a favorable outcome after what Alan did at the turkey shoot. All charges dropped. A gross miscarriage of justice. And there was nothing ADA Alley Roberts could do about it.

The conversation she had overheard at the salon earlier still played on her mind. Tom's will, the one no one seemed to know about except Sonny Rivers and his wife, Caitlin. It was only a matter of time before the secret slipped out, and she feared that tonight might be the night.

She moved on to the Sweets' table next, her hand resting lightly on the back of Hannah's chair. "How's everything, Hannah? Daniel? Anything you need? There's plenty of stuffing still left in the kitchen."

Hannah looked up with a warm smile, though her eyes betrayed a weariness that Hayley knew came with the pregnancy.

"No, but thank you, Hayley. I'm stuffed," Daniel moaned.

"Not me," Hannah piped in. "I could scarf down your cranberry sauce all night."

"I'll make sure to pack you up some to take home," Hayley offered with a wink. "You've got to keep those midnight cravings satisfied."

Daniel chuckled, his attention shifting between his wife and the other diners. He was more observant than people gave him credit for, and Hayley could tell he was picking up on the same tensions she was. Everyone in the room was on edge, though none of them knew just how precarious the situation was about to become.

Excusing herself from the table, Hayley headed over to the hostess station, where Betty stood, greeting guests with her usual warmth. Betty had been with Hayley from the beginning and was as reliable as they came. Her wide smile faltered slightly as Hayley approached, a telltale sign that something was on her mind.

"Not as busy as usual," Hayley commented, leaning against the counter.

Betty nodded. "Yes, we've had a few last-minute cancellations actually."

"Anyone I should know about?" Hayley asked, glancing at the reservation list.

Betty hesitated, then said quietly, "Sonny and Caitlin Rivers called to cancel. Caitlin said Sonny's wiped out, and he has to be in the office extra early tomorrow for the reading of Tom Farley's will."

Hayley's heart skipped a beat. She leaned in, her voice a sharp whisper. "Betty! Keep your voice down." Her eyes flicked toward the tables, where Tom's neighbors sat, oblivious for the moment.

Betty's eyes widened, and she quickly zipped her lips with a mock gesture. "I'm sorry, I didn't think it was such a big secret—" she started, but Hayley waved her off.

"No, no, it's fine. Just . . . the last thing we need is for them"—she nodded discreetly in the direction of the Murdocks, the Sweets, and Reid Norton—"to hear about that here."

"I won't say another word," Betty promised, crossing her heart dramatically. "But you should know, our last reservation of the night is Liddy Crawford. She requested the corner table by the fireplace."

Hayley blinked in surprise. Liddy—the only other person aside from Sonny Rivers who knew about Tom's will—was dining here tonight?

"Liddy's coming here?" Hayley asked, trying to keep her voice steady.

Betty nodded. "Yeah, she should be here any minute. A couple's still at her table, but the check's down. They'll be out of here soon."

Hayley's mind raced. Liddy was a wild card. If anyone was going to inadvertently spill the beans about Tom's will, it would be her. The last thing Hayley wanted was for all of Tom's neighbors to find out, right here in the middle of her restaurant, that their plans to sell their properties to Acadia Resorts for a fortune were about to possibly be blown to smithereens.

"Let me know the second she gets here," Hayley said. "I need to make sure she doesn't say anything."

Betty gave a quick nod. "Got it. Actually . . ." She glanced over Hayley's shoulder. "She's already here."

Hayley turned to look, scanning the restaurant. "Where?"

"She must have slipped in while you were talking to me just now," Betty explained. "She's over there."

Hayley's eyes widened in alarm as she spotted Liddy already halfway across the dining room, marching with purpose toward the Murdock table.

"No, no, no," Hayley muttered under her breath, making a beeline toward Liddy, but it was too late.

Liddy stopped at the edge of the Murdocks' table, her voice cheerful and oblivious to the looming disaster. "Lester! I wanted to let you know, I've scheduled the inspection of your new property for tomorrow afternoon."

Lester looked up, a thin smile on his lips. "Can't do afternoon. How about the morning?"

Before Hayley could intervene, Liddy tilted her head and said, "I thought you'd be at the reading of Tom Farley's will in the morning."

Lester froze, his fork halfway to his mouth. His eyes bulged, and he nearly choked on his turkey. "What will?"

The room seemed to hush in an instant, the other tables suddenly quiet as people strained to hear the conversation.

Liddy blinked in confusion, clearly unaware of the bombshell she had just dropped.

"Oh, didn't you know?" she said, her tone light. "Sonny Rivers is reading Tom Farley's will tomorrow morning. Apparently, Sonny is the executor."

Lester's face turned red, his voice rising in disbelief. "A will? Tom wasn't supposed to have any family! How can there be a will?"

Reid Norton leaned back in his chair, a dark grimace creeping across his face. "Well, well. This changes things, doesn't it?"

Even the normally mild-mannered Sweets exchanged worried glances. Daniel looked down at his plate, frowning, while Hannah's hand instinctively went to her belly as if to shield the baby from the chaos erupting around them.

"Ruins *everything*, is more like it!" Lester bellowed, slamming his fist on the table. "This whole sale—everything—it's all going to hell if Tom had a will!"

The outburst drew the attention of nearly every diner in the restaurant. Hayley, now standing helplessly at the edge of the fray, closed her eyes for a brief moment, cursing her bad luck.

Liddy looked perplexed, blinking innocently. "Was it something I said?"

I was young and married to my ex-husband Danny when it became clear my mother had . . . let's say, "thoughts" about him. She wasn't a fan, and she didn't hide it. I mean, she practically blamed him for ruining my "career"—which, by the way, I hadn't even figured out at the time!

Danny, bless his heart, tried everything to win her over, from ambitious job plans to promises of bright new horizons. Her response? "I'll believe it when I see it." Needless to say, her holiday parties became minefields of tense small talk and side-eye.

One Labor Day, after a particularly scathing remark about Danny's grilling skills (she likened his burgers to hockey pucks), I finally snapped. I stormed out with him, declaring a ban on family gatherings until she apologized. It took a month and four days, but she finally picked up the phone to apologize. Well, sort of—she only half-apologized and managed to avoid saying sorry to Danny. So, I decided to up the ante and offered to host Thanksgiving. I thought it'd make her beg to take it back. Imagine my shock when she agreed. I was hosting Thanksgiving—with zero experience.

Fast forward to Thanksgiving morning: somehow, with help from Liddy and Mona, I pulled together sides, set the table, and even managed to get the turkey in the oven. I just needed Danny to set the timer while I welcomed the guests. Everything was going swimmingly; even my mom wasn't being her usual sarcastic self.

Until . . . I realized the timer was off by an hour, and the oven door wouldn't open. Danny had accidentally hit the self-cleaning mode.

I was ready to strangle him. By the time the oven unlocked, the turkey was literal dust. But instead of piling on Danny, my mom surprised us all by defending him. And then she brought in a fully cooked backup turkey from her car, just in case. Turns out, she was always prepared for me to fail.

That Thanksgiving, amidst laughter over our "incinerated turkey," something softened between Danny and my mother. She even brought mashed potatoes and green beans as backup—who could stay mad? It was a messy Thanksgiving miracle.

Randy's Strawberry Margarita

For those summer days when you're laughing about past holiday mishaps.

Ingredients:
16 ounces frozen strawberries
1 cup tequila
$\frac{1}{2}$ cup fresh-squeezed lime juice
$\frac{1}{2}$ cup orange liqueur
$\frac{1}{3}$ cup honey (adjust to taste)
Margarita salt and lime wedges for garnish

Run a lime wedge around the rim of your glasses and dip in salt. Blend strawberries, tequila, lime juice, orange liqueur, and honey. Adjust to taste, pour, and garnish with lime. Enjoy!

HAYLEY'S POST-THANKSGIVING POTATO CAKES

Perfect for using up those leftover mashed potatoes after the holiday.

INGREDIENTS:
2 large eggs
2 cups cold mashed potatoes
½ cup flour (add more if needed)
1 tsp each onion powder, garlic powder
1 tsp Cajun seasoning (optional, for a kick)
½ tsp kosher salt
½ cup shredded cheddar
1 tbsp minced onion
2 tbsp canola oil or cooking spray for frying
Sour cream for dipping

Mix eggs with potatoes, add flour, seasonings, cheese, and minced onion. Form patties and fry in oil until golden on both sides. Serve with sour cream and savor the taste of Thanksgiving all over again.

Here's to family, Thanksgiving, and always having a backup!

Chapter 30

Hayley Powell knew that delivering a Thanksgiving Leftovers takeout special to Sonny and Caitlin Rivers' house was not entirely about spreading goodwill. Sure, the food from her restaurant, Hayley's Kitchen, was mouthwatering as usual, but the timing of Sonny's cancellation had piqued her curiosity. And after Caitlin had dropped the bombshell at the hair salon about Tom Farley having a will—and Sonny being the executor—Hayley's amateur sleuthing instincts went into overdrive.

"I think it's sweet that you're dropping off food," Liddy commented dryly as Hayley packed up the boxes of turkey, mashed potatoes, and stuffing into a bag. "But let's not kid ourselves. You're going there to find out what's in that will."

Hayley made a vague protest, although her heart was

not in it. "It's completely unethical for me to ask him about it," she said, but her words lacked conviction. She turned to Liddy, who raised a perfectly arched eyebrow. "Okay, fine! Yes, I want to know what's in the will. You caught me."

Liddy smiled triumphantly. "I knew it. And by the way, I'm coming with you."

"No, you're not," Hayley shot back. "I can't have you causing a scene."

Liddy narrowed her eyes, clearly offended. "A scene? *Moi*? When have I ever caused a scene?"

Hayley's mouth dropped open.

Liddy ignored her. "I honestly think that's the most insulting thing you've ever said to me. I just want to wish him well on his new marriage, that's all."

Hayley crossed her arms. "You're telling me you want to 'wish him well'—the man who stood you up at the altar?"

Liddy tilted her head, smiling sweetly. "Honey, I've moved on. Haven't you heard? I'm a mature forgiving woman now. Water off a duck's back. No hard feelings."

Hayley sighed. Arguing with Liddy was like trying to hold back the tide. "Fine. Just don't say anything to make the situation more uncomfortable than it already is."

Liddy laughed. "Oh, honey, where's the fun in that?"

The drive to Sonny and Caitlin's house passed by in a blur of winter twilight and swirling thoughts about Tom Farley's will. The more Hayley thought about it, the more she realized how strange it all seemed. None of Tom's neighbors had mentioned any family. For that matter, Tom had never mentioned anyone else in his life but his marauding turkeys. Yet, here was a will, executed by Sonny, about to be unsealed in the morning. She was not just curious—she had to know what was going on.

Hayley and Liddy walked up the front steps of the Rivers' charming Cape Cod-style home, which was softly lit from the inside. Hayley could smell wood smoke from the chimney and heard the faint murmur of a television coming from inside. Caitlin was surprised to see them when she opened the door. Her eyes flicked from Hayley to Liddy and back again, trying to mask her confusion.

"Hayley," Caitlin said, her voice carefully polite. "What a surprise. We weren't expecting visitors."

Hayley smiled, holding up the bag of food. "I brought over some Thanksgiving leftovers from the restaurant. Since you couldn't make it tonight, I thought you might enjoy some anyway."

Caitlin blinked in surprise. "That's . . . very thoughtful of you."

Hayley handed the bag to Caitlin, who accepted it with a cautious smile. "Come in," she said, stepping aside. "I'm sure Sonny will want to thank you personally."

As they stepped into the cozy foyer, Caitlin's gaze lingered on Liddy, her expression wary but neutral. "Liddy," she said smoothly, though there was an undeniable edge to her voice. "I'm surprised you're here."

Liddy gave a cool, almost demure smile. "I was dining at the restaurant tonight. When Hayley told me you had to cancel, I said to her, they're such a lovely couple, I hate to think of them eating baloney sandwiches, why not bring them a Thanksgiving feast? It was my idea, wasn't it, Hayley?"

Hayley stifled a groan. "Right. Your idea."

Caitlin clearly was not fooled, but she led them into the living room, where Sonny was working on his laptop. He glanced up, and his eyes widened in shock when he saw Liddy standing in his home.

"Liddy?" Sonny nearly spilled his coffee down the front of his shirt. He set the mug down with a clatter, his face caught somewhere between panic and bewilderment.

Liddy, ever graceful, smiled warmly. "Sonny, you look . . . wonderful. I just wanted to wish you the best, now that you've found such a lovely woman to share your life with."

Hayley watched as Sonny visibly relaxed at Liddy's words, a faint smile tugging at his lips. "Thanks, Liddy," he said, sounding almost sheepish. "I appreciate that."

Liddy continued, her tone light. "It's nice to see you happy. Really."

Before Hayley could intervene, Sonny chuckled. "Thank you for bringing us dinner, Hayley. It's such a kind gesture. Truly neighborly. Maybe I'll return the favor someday."

Hayley perked up, seizing the opportunity. "Actually, Sonny, if you don't mind, I'd like to take you up on that offer now."

Sonny blinked, clearly thrown off. "Uh . . . now?"

Caitlin, still standing in the doorway, looked between Hayley and Sonny, her brows furrowing. "Why don't I go set up the food in the kitchen?" she suggested, though it was obvious she did not want to leave Liddy alone with her husband.

"I'll help you," Hayley offered, but Caitlin shook her head. "No, you stay. I can handle it."

"Are you sure?" Hayley asked.

"Yes. I'm sure. Stay."

With one last glance at Liddy, Caitlin left the room.

As soon as Caitlin was out of earshot, Hayley turned to Sonny. "So, about Tom Farley's will . . ."

Sonny stiffened, his professional veneer snapping back into place. "Hayley, you know I can't discuss the details of the will with you. Client confidentiality and all."

Liddy stepped in, her tone silky. "Oh, come on, Sonny. We're just friends catching up. Surely there's no harm in sharing a little detail here and there?"

Sonny hesitated, but Liddy leaned in slightly, her eyes twinkling. "Remember that time when I got you to spill that secret about Councilman Rodman's affair with his defense council during his bribery trial? You were trying to be so tight-lipped, but I dragged it out of you. It took a lot of tickling you, but I finally got you to talk!"

Sonny chuckled at the memory, his shoulders relaxing as he remembered. "I can't believe you're bringing that up."

Liddy gave a soft laugh. "You were impossible back then. But somehow, I always managed to get what I needed from you."

Sonny shook his head, a grin forming as he looked at her. "You haven't changed a bit."

Hayley watched the exchange, her curiosity growing. It was clear that there was still something between them, a familiarity that had not faded despite everything.

"Come on, Sonny," Liddy coaxed. "Just a little hint. For old times' sake." Liddy then leaned in, her voice soft and coaxing. "We're all friends here, aren't we? A teeny tiny little hint wouldn't hurt."

Hayley watched in amazement as Sonny visibly softened under Liddy's charm, his resolve cracking. "Well, I suppose there's one thing I can tell you," he said, lowering his voice. "Tom has a niece. He only found out about her recently."

Hayley blinked in surprise. "A niece? Tom never mentioned any family."

Sonny nodded. "That's because he didn't know about her for most of the girl's life. His brother fathered a daughter with another woman while he was still married. The woman's sister raised her, and the girl never knew who her real father was until the truth came out on the sister's deathbed."

Liddy's eyes widened. "So, this niece—what's her name?"

"Emily," Sonny said. "She's in her twenties now. She came to visit Tom after finding out who her birth father was, but it was only a brief meeting. After that, for reasons I'm not entirely sure of, Tom decided to include her in his will."

Hayley's mind raced.

A secret niece?

And she had only met Tom once?

"So this Emily is going to inherit everything?" she asked, trying to keep her voice neutral.

Sonny shook his head, leaning in conspiratorially. "Not everything," he whispered. "There's someone else named in the will."

Hayley and Liddy exchanged glances.

Another mystery.

Hayley's stomach fluttered with anticipation.

"Who?" Liddy breathed, her curiosity fully piqued.

Sonny smiled faintly, clearly relishing the suspense. "I can't tell you that," he said, leaning back in his chair with a grin. "I need to draw the line somewhere!"

Liddy was not deterred. She smiled, accepting the challenge. This was not new territory for her. Liddy tilted her head, her smile turning flirtatious. "Sonny, those biceps! Have you been working out?"

Sonny's grin faltered, just for a second, as if she had struck a nerve. Liddy leaned in a bit closer, brushing a hand lightly over his arm. "You always had such a strong build. I bet you're lifting weights again, aren't you?"

Sonny chuckled, clearly flustered. "Well, you know, I've been hitting the gym every now and then . . ."

"Of course you have," Liddy purred. "You always were the strong, not-so-silent type."

Hayley watched, holding her breath as Sonny's resolve visibly wavered.

Liddy had him right where she wanted him, and they both knew it.

They had a name in less than a minute.

Chapter 31

Hayley woke early the next morning, a little groggy but determined. Now that the reading of Tom Farley's will was on the horizon, there were more questions than answers. One thing was clear: every one of his neighbors had a reason to want him gone. But it was the revelation from Sonny Rivers, Tom's lawyer, that made Hayley sit up in bed and reach for her phone.

Lori Gunning, Tom's agoraphobic neighbor, had been named in his will. They hated each other—everyone knew that. But still, there she was, one of only two beneficiaries. Hayley needed to tell her before the reading. Convincing Lori to step outside her fortress-like house was another matter entirely.

After finishing her coffee, Hayley made the short drive to Lori's place, her mind racing with the possibilities. Tom Farley was a master of torment, from blasting music late at night to letting his turkeys run amok in Lori's yard. Why would he leave her anything? The man never did anything without a reason, and this had revenge written all over it.

When she arrived at Lori's house, she noticed the blinds were still drawn, the way they always were. The property looked forlorn and unwelcoming. Hayley took a deep breath and knocked.

After what felt like an eternity, the door creaked open a few inches. Lori's pale face appeared in the crack, her eyes wide with suspicion.

"Hayley? What are you doing here?" Lori's voice was a shaky whisper, as though even talking too loudly might invite disaster.

"We need to talk," Hayley said, her tone gentle but firm. "About Tom."

Lori's face darkened. "I don't want to talk about him. I don't care what happened to him."

"You might care about this." Hayley glanced over her shoulder, as if checking for eavesdroppers. "Tom left you something in his will."

Lori blinked, stepping back into the shadows of her hallway. "What?"

"Sonny Rivers told me last night. You need to go to the reading later this morning. You're one of the bene-ficiaries."

Lori opened the door a little wider but did not step out. She looked baffled, more so than Hayley expected. "That doesn't make any sense. He hated me. We hated each other."

"I know, but for some reason, he's left you some-thing. And you need to be there to find out what it is."

Lori's eyes flicked toward the living room, where

the faint glow of a television showed she had been sitting alone in the dark watching a morning news program. "I don't like to leave the house, Hayley. You know that."

"I understand," Hayley said, stepping closer. "But this is important. You might not get another chance to know what Tom had in store for you. Aren't you the least bit curious to find out?"

Lori hesitated, chewing her lip. "Why would he leave me anything?"

"I have no idea, but whatever it is, don't you think it's better to know than to be left wondering forever?"

"Can't someone just call me when it's over and tell me what I got?"

"Yes, but if he left you his property, you need to make plans. We could be talking about a lot of money. It's better to get ahead of these things."

Lori nodded slightly but was still not convinced enough to muster the courage to leave her house.

Hayley softened her voice. "I'll be there with you. Every step of the way. You won't have to go through this alone."

Lori stood still for a long moment, and Hayley could practically see the gears turning in her mind. Finally, Lori let out a breath and nodded. "Okay. But only because I want to know what that miserable man left me. And on the condition you stay with me the whole time."

"I promise. I will never leave your side."

* * *

The law office of Sonny Rivers was a far cry from what anyone would expect of a small-town attorney. His office had an air of sophistication, with leather chairs, polished oak bookshelves, and a sprawling mahogany desk. Hayley and Lori arrived just before the reading was set to begin. Hayley had barely managed to get Lori into the car without her backing out at the last second.

But they had finally made it.

As they walked inside, Lori clutched her bag to her chest like a shield, her knuckles white. "I'm not staying long," she whispered.

"You'll be fine," Hayley assured her. "It'll be over before you know it."

In the waiting room, they found a few others already gathered. Emily McCloud, the niece Tom apparently never knew he had until the last year of his life, sat next to her boyfriend, John David Lynch—or JD, as he called himself far too often for Hayley's taste. JD was tall, with slicked-back hair and a grin that never seemed to reach his eyes. The moment Hayley walked in with Lori, JD's eyes lit up like a greedy child at Christmas.

"Well, well! The gang's all here!" JD said with an obnoxious chuckle. "Can't wait to see what good ol' Uncle Tom has left for us, eh, Em?"

Emily gave a tight smile, her eyes flicking to Lori with what Hayley guessed was a mix of curiosity and nervousness. Emily seemed nice enough, but her choice in boyfriends was questionable at best.

"Should be interesting," Hayley said, sizing up JD. There was something about him that set off alarm bells in her head. Maybe it was the too-slick way he talked, or the way his eyes kept darting around like he was trying to find an angle. He struck her as untrustworthy.

Greedy, even.

Sonny emerged from this office into the reception area, welcoming everyone, offering coffee, before they were to begin.

Before he could say anything more, the front entrance door to Sonny Rivers' office building opened, and in stepped none other than Lester Murdock. He had not been invited, that much was clear, and Sonny looked none too pleased as he physically moved to block Lester from entering any further.

"What are you doing here, Lester?" Sonny asked, crossing his arms.

"Just curious about what's going on, Sonny." Lester's smarmy smile turned predatory. "Can't a concerned neighbor drop in as a spectator?"

"No," Sonny replied bluntly. "This is a private matter."

Lester threw a snarling look at Hayley. "Then what's *she* doing here?"

"She's with me," Lori said firmly, clutching her bag so tightly her knuckles were white.

Hayley put a comforting arm around Lori. "Lori's been named in the will, so I'm here for moral support."

Lester went pale. "What? You're in the—? But why? I don't understand. Why would Farley—?"

"I'm just as in the dark as you, Lester," Lori said. "I haven't a clue."

Sonny inserted himself between Murdock and the others. "I'm sorry, Lester, but it's time to go."

Lester's eyes blazed. "You have no idea what you're dealing with. But you will. This isn't over." He glared at Emily, then Lori, before stalking back out.

Sonny sighed, visibly relieved. "All right, now that we've gotten rid of that, let's proceed." He ushered everyone inside, and Hayley took a seat next to Lori, who looked like she was about to bolt at the slightest provocation.

The reading began in the usual, formal way. Sonny listed off Tom's possessions, from his land to his farm equipment, all of it bequeathed to Emily.

JD's eyes gleamed with barely concealed excitement, and he actually nudged Emily, who kept her expression neutral.

Then Sonny paused and cleared his throat. "There is one additional clause in the will."

Lori sat up, gripping the armrests of her chair.

"Tom Farley bequeaths custody of all his live turkeys to Lori Gunning."

There was a stunned silence in the room. Hayley could see Lori's face turning red as the words sank in.

"Turkeys?" Lori sputtered. "He left me the damn turkeys?"

Sonny nodded, his tone sympathetic but firm. "Yes, all of his turkeys. The entirety of his flock."

Lori's hands clenched into fists, and her voice shook with disbelief. "He did this to get back at me. He knew I hated those awful birds! He let them into my house, my yard, just to torment me. This is his way of getting revenge, even from beyond the grave! What kind of Alfred Hitchcock nightmare is this? Hayley, what am I going to do with a bunch of filthy, disgusting turkeys?"

"You could throw one hell of a Thanksgiving dinner for the whole town," JD suggested, amused.

Lori threw him a death stare.

Hayley placed a hand on Lori's arm to calm her. "We'll figure this out," she promised. "We can find homes for the turkeys. You won't have to deal with them alone."

But Lori's face was set in a deep frown, her eyes full of bitterness. "That man couldn't leave me in peace, even after he's dead."

As the group dispersed, Hayley could not shake the feeling that there was more to this than a petty final act of revenge. Tom Farley had played a cruel game with everyone around him—neighbors, family, even enemies. And now, in death, his twisted legacy continued.

But one thing was for sure. Now that a young woman no one had ever heard of before today was the new owner of Tom Farley's property, this turkey farm was about to become even more of a battleground than it already had been.

Chapter 32

As the reading of Tom Farley's will concluded, the room thinned out, Emily and JD lingered behind, discussing details with Sonny, while the rest of the group had already started to leave. Hayley glanced at Lori Gunning, who sat stiff and silent beside her, her face drained of color. Tom's will had delivered a cruel blow—Emily had inherited his land, but Lori, Tom's ex-girlfriend and long-suffering neighbor, was now the reluctant owner of his mean-spirited turkeys.

Lori seemed too stunned to speak. Hayley gently placed a hand on her arm. "Come on, Lori," she said softly. "Let's get you out of here."

Lori did not respond but allowed Hayley to pull her to her feet. The two of them walked slowly out of Sonny's office, the weight of the will pressing down on Lori's small frame. Hayley had known this would be hard on her, but Lori's shock seemed deeper than she had anticipated. The poor woman had been through enough, especially with her battle against agoraphobia. This cruel twist from Tom had clearly rattled her.

As they neared the office building's exit doors, the sound of voices and camera flashes suddenly assaulted them. Hayley paused, her instincts flaring. She had not expected this—a pack of reporters from the surrounding areas waited outside, their lenses trained on the door. The second they spotted her and Lori, the shouting began.

"Ms. Gunning, how do you feel about inheriting Tom's turkeys?"

Hayley reared back, stunned. "Wait, how did you already hear about—?"

Who had told them?

Hayley suspected Liddy was not the only one who could charm the words right out of Sonny Rivers' mouth.

And her suspicious brain immediately went to Tabitha Collins.

The reporters kept shouting questions at Lori.

"Are you going to sell them off?"

"What did the will say about the property?"

"Is Acadia Resorts getting the land or not?"

Lori froze beside her, her breath coming in shallow, rapid bursts. Hayley tightened her grip on Lori's arm, trying to push through the crowd of reporters, but the questions kept coming, a rapid-fire barrage.

"A statement from Tabitha Collins, CEO of Acadia Resorts, says they're banking on the sale. What's your take, Ms. Gunning?"

The name Tabitha Collins made Hayley's stomach

twist. Her suspicions were suddenly confirmed in her mind.

But who was at the reading feeding her information?

She did see Emily's boyfriend JD texting at one point.

Did the two of them secretly know each other?

Or was that just a coincidence?

One thing was perfectly clear.

This was not just a local story—it was big news statewide. And apparently, the future of the entire resort project depended on what was in that will.

Lori was trembling violently now, her eyes wide with panic. Her breathing had turned shallow, ragged. Hayley recognized the signs of a full-blown panic attack, and her protective instincts kicked into high gear.

"Move!" Hayley barked at the reporters, pushing forward with determination. "Get out of the way!"

The crowd parted slightly, enough for Hayley to pull Lori toward her car parked nearby. Lori stumbled alongside her, gasping for breath, her face pale and her hands shaking uncontrollably.

"I can't . . . I can't breathe," Lori whimpered, clutching at her chest as Hayley helped her into the passenger seat.

"Shh, it's okay," Hayley soothed, quickly shutting the door and locking it behind her. "Just breathe, Lori. You're safe now."

Lori's panic continued, but she was at least sheltered from the mob outside. Hayley stood by the car for a moment, catching her own breath, her mind racing with everything that had just unfolded.

Tom's turkeys?

That's all Lori got?

It did not seem like the sort of cruel joke he would pull—unless there was something more behind it.

But she had no time to dwell on it, because at that moment, Emily and JD emerged from Sonny's office. The reporters, sensing fresh meat, swiveled their attention to the couple. Hayley stayed by Lori's side, watching the scene unfold with an uneasy feeling in her gut.

Emily looked confident, almost defiant, her chin held high as she faced the barrage of questions. JD stood beside her, his arm protectively draped over her shoulder, his expression smug, like a man who had already won a game no one else knew they were playing.

Emily raised her voice over the din of the reporters. "I won't be selling Tom's property to Acadia Resorts," she announced, her voice firm and steady. "Instead, I plan to turn it into a bird sanctuary to honor my uncle's memory."

The crowd buzzed with surprise.

A bird sanctuary?

Hayley's brow furrowed in confusion. She had never known Tom to care about birds—except, of course, for his turkeys. The idea of him wanting to preserve land for wildlife felt completely out of character.

But before she could make sense of it, Lester Murdock stormed into the scene, his face red with fury. He was counting on that sale, just like the others. It seemed Emily was stepping into her uncle's shoes, much to Lester's rage.

"Just like your damned uncle, aren't you?" Lester

growled, pointing a trembling finger at Emily. "Holding out, trying to squeeze more money out of the deal!"

Emily did not flinch. She stared Lester down with a calm that seemed unnerving under the circumstances. "I'm not holding out, Mr. Murdock. I've made my decision. I'm not selling. It's personal. I don't expect you to understand."

Lester's lips curled into a snarl. "Don't play dumb with me, little girl. We all know what this is—some ploy to drive up the price! There's only so much Tabitha Collins is willing to pay, and you're testing her limits. You're about to blow the whole damn deal. For all of us!"

Emily stood firm, but JD's expression shifted. That same self-satisfied smile crept across his face, and Hayley knew instantly that he was the one pulling the strings. JD had probably always been a manipulator, and now it seemed like he was using Emily to push Acadia Resorts into a corner.

"I'm not selling," Emily repeated, her voice stronger this time. "The land stays with me. End of discussion."

Lester's fists clenched at his sides, his face a mix of fury and desperation. He took a step closer to Emily. "You don't know who you're dealing with," he hissed. "If this deal falls through, you and that gold-digging boyfriend of yours are going to wish you'd never come to Bar Harbor. I'll make sure of it."

JD's arm tightened around Emily, but his smug grin remained intact.

Hayley's unease deepened.

There was more going on here.

JD was enjoying this too much, like a man who was playing the long game, setting the pieces in place to benefit himself, no matter what it cost everyone else.

Lester's parting threat hung in the air as he stormed off, leaving Emily and JD surrounded by reporters who were now bombarding them with questions about the bird sanctuary, Acadia Resorts, and what would happen next.

But Hayley barely heard any of it.

Her mind was already racing.

Tom's death, the will, the property dispute—it was all connected. And now, with Emily's unexpected stand against Acadia, the stakes had risen even higher. There was something Emily and JD were not saying, and Hayley had a sinking feeling that JD's involvement went much deeper than just being a supportive boyfriend.

She glanced back at Lori, still trembling in the car.

This was not just about a will anymore.

It was about power, greed, and control—and the real fight had only just begun.

Hayley knew she would have to dig deeper if she was going to unravel the truth behind Tom's death. And this time, it was not just about finding a killer. It was about stopping a much larger conspiracy before it consumed the whole town.

Chapter 33

Hayley sat behind the wheel of her car, tapping her fingers on the steering wheel as she waited for Bruce to finish up inside the *Island Times* office. She glanced at the clock on the dashboard—Bruce had promised he would be ready by now, but her crime reporter husband often got caught up in the flurry of deadlines and stories and would lose track of time.

The door to the *Island Times* swung open just as Hayley was about to honk. Bruce emerged, but behind him was the rumpled figure of Sal, the paper's editor in chief. Sal waved a sheaf of papers in the air, looking more animated than usual.

"You won't believe this," Bruce said as he climbed into the passenger seat. "Sal just got back from an interview with Tabitha Collins."

The name made Hayley sit up straight.

"What's the scoop?" Hayley asked, her curiosity piqued.

Bruce buckled his seatbelt. "It's bad. Or good, depending on which side you're on. Apparently, Emily— the niece who just inherited Tom's turkey farm— demanded some astronomical price for the land. Tabitha balked, called her bluff, and walked away. Acadia Resorts has officially pulled out."

"*What*?" Hayley's eyes widened. "What happened to the bird sanctuary she was so determined to erect in honor of Tom?"

Bruce shrugged his shoulders. "Beats me."

"So, no luxury hotel? No development?"

"Yup, it's over. No resort, no huge payday for the neighbors. And all those offers Acadia made on the other properties have been rescinded."

Hayley whistled low. "Lester Murdock is going to lose it. He was already furious about Emily holding out, and now that the deal's off . . ."

Bruce leaned back in his seat, shaking his head. "Yeah, we were just talking about how bad this could get. Lester was counting on selling his land so he could buy that massive new house in Northeast Harbor he's been bragging about."

"And not just him," Hayley muttered. "I can only imagine how hothead Reid Norton is going to react."

Hayley's mind was already racing, thinking of all the other people in town who would be affected by the news. Tom Farley had always been the lone holdout, but now it seemed his niece had taken over the mantle, and her interference had just cost the entire neighborhood a fortune. Tensions had already been high, and with the deal dead, things were likely to get even worse.

"Sal's writing it up now," Bruce said. "He wants to post it online before tomorrow's print edition. It's going to hit the town like a bomb."

Hayley nodded, still absorbing the news. "I wouldn't want to be Emily right now. Or JD," she added, thinking of Emily's smug boyfriend, who she suspected had been the one pushing Emily to ask for the sky-high price in the first place.

As they pulled into their driveway and headed inside, Hayley's mind was still swirling with possibilities. Bruce headed straight for the fridge to grab a cold beer, but before he could even pop the cap, the crackle of the police scanner sitting on top of the refrigerator stopped them both in their tracks.

"We've got a trespasser causing a disturbance at Tom Farley's farm," the voice of Sergeant Earl came through, garbled but unmistakable.

Hayley and Bruce exchanged a look. "That didn't take long," Hayley muttered.

"I bet it's Lester," Bruce said, already moving toward the door.

Hayley grabbed her jacket, adrenaline pumping. "Let's go."

By the time Hayley and Bruce arrived at Tom Farley's turkey farm, the scene was pure chaos. The sun was starting to set, casting long shadows over the sprawling property, but the bright headlights from Bruce's car illuminated the central area, where Lester Murdock was in full meltdown mode.

Lester, red-faced and screaming, was standing in the middle of the muddy yard, waving his arms wildly as he shouted at Emily and JD, who stood a few yards away. Emily looked shaken, but JD was wearing that same smug, self-satisfied smile that had always grated on Hayley.

"You greedy little brat!" Lester yelled, pointing an accusing finger at Emily. "You ruined everything! We could've all been rich, but you had to hold out like your worthless idiot uncle!"

Emily squared her shoulders, her voice shaking but firm. "I told you before, Mr. Murdock, I'm not selling. This is my decision, and you need to leave."

Lester was not having it. His fists were clenched, his whole body trembling with rage. "You think you can hold us all hostage? Well, you're going to pay for this!"

"Mr. Murdock, go home," Emily shouted back. "I've already called the police." She waved her phone at him, but it just seemed to make him madder.

Just as Hayley and Bruce were about to step in, JD added fuel to the fire. "Maybe if you hadn't blown all your money on that ridiculous new house you can't afford, you wouldn't be acting like such a—"

Before JD could finish his sentence, Lester lunged.

With a roar of fury, Lester charged at JD, tackling him to the ground. The two men hit the mud with a splat, rolling and wrestling as Emily screamed, and the turkeys—already unsettled—squawked and fluttered around them in a panicked frenzy. Wings flapped, feathers flew, and the sound of gobbling added to the chaos as Hayley and Bruce rushed forward.

"Lester, stop!" Bruce shouted, grabbing Lester's arm, but the older man was fueled by blind rage, his fists swinging wildly.

Hayley kept her distance, her heart racing, watching as JD, though younger, struggled to defend himself against Lester's sheer unbridled anger. JD's smug smile had disappeared, replaced with a look of alarm as he tried to push Lester off him. Mud streaked their clothes as they continued to grapple, their shouts drowned out by the cacophony of turkeys all around.

Bruce tried again to pull Lester back, but the man was relentless. "You think you can just waltz in here and take everything?" Lester bellowed, his voice raw. "You're nothing but a con artist, trying to gouge us all for more money!"

At that moment, the flashing blue lights of a squad car lit up the scene. The piercing wail of the siren cut through the din, and Police Chief Sergio and Lieutenant Donnie jumped out of the car, running toward the brawl.

"Sergio! Over here!" Hayley shouted, waving them over.

The officers reached the scuffle just as Bruce finally managed to pry Lester off JD. Both men were panting, their faces streaked with mud and sweat, but it was clear Lester had been the aggressor.

Sergio stepped between them, his voice firm. "That's enough! Lester, I need you to back off!"

Lester's chest heaved as he glared at JD, but the

fight seemed to drain out of him as Sergio took hold of his arm.

Lieutenant Donnie moved to restrain him, pulling his hands behind his back.

"That's assault, Lester," Sergio said, shaking his head. "You're under arrest."

Lester did not resist, but his eyes burned with rage as they locked onto Emily and JD. "This isn't over," he snarled. "You've destroyed everything, and I won't rest until you two—"

"I'd be careful about what you say next, Lester, you're already in enough trouble," Sergio warned.

Emily stood there, pale and shaken, her arms wrapped tightly around herself. JD, on the other hand, looked rattled but uninjured, his hands covered in mud as he wiped his face with a grimace.

"I'll confirm it," Hayley said quietly to Sergio, who had turned to her for clarification. "JD may have provoked him, but Lester was the one who attacked first."

Sergio nodded and motioned for Donnie to take Lester to the squad car. As they hauled him away, Lester's curses echoed in the evening air, carried away by the wind.

Once the scene had calmed down, Hayley turned to Bruce. "Well, that went about as well as expected."

Bruce sighed, wiping a speck of mud off his sleeve. "Sooner or later Lester Murdock is going to cause enough serious damage that he won't be able to buy his way out of it."

Hayley glanced over at Emily, who was now speaking quietly with JD. Something still did not sit right with Hayley. Lester's outburst was understandable given the circumstances, but Emily's decision to hold onto the land—and the way JD had handled everything—felt off.

"We need to keep an eye on those two," Hayley said, her voice low.

Bruce nodded. "Yeah. I have a feeling this is far from over."

Chapter 34

The familiar scent of stale coffee and cleaning supplies greeted Hayley as she entered the Bar Harbor police station, her heels clicking on the worn linoleum. The tension in the air was palpable, thick with the weight of a murder investigation that had finally taken a sharp turn.

Lester Murdock, the bombastic patriarch of the Murdock family, was inside, being held for assaulting JD, the boyfriend of Tom Farley's niece who seemed to rub everyone the wrong way. But it was not the assault that had Hayley rushing over—it was Lester's boozy wife Melody Murdock.

Bruce had stayed home, putting the finishing touches on his column for tomorrow's edition of the *Island Times*, but Hayley could not sit still. She had just received a call from Mona, who had been at the station picking up one of her grandkids who got caught shoplifting a bag of Skittles at the Big Apple convenience store but was being let off with a warning since he was a first-time offender. According to Mona, as they were leaving, they passed by Melody Murdock, who had just shown up at the station to bail Lester out, and Hayley knew the woman well enough to recognize an opportunity when she saw one.

Melody was always chatty after a few drinks, and Hayley had smelled the whiskey on her breath more than once.

The police station was quiet for the late morning, with the muted sounds of police chatter in the background. As Hayley approached the bench near the front desk, there was Melody, slouched over with her large handbag clutched tightly in her lap. Her makeup was smudged, her mascara streaking faintly under her eyes, and her bright pink lipstick was slightly smeared at the corners. Hayley could already catch a whiff of alcohol from where she stood.

"Melody," Hayley greeted, sitting down beside her. "Rough day?"

Melody looked up, blinking blearily before recognition dawned. "Hayley," she slurred, her voice thick with both alcohol and something else—guilt, perhaps. "You here to see the fireworks?"

Hayley smiled sympathetically. "I'm just here to check on you. It's been a rough time for everyone."

Melody let out a brittle laugh. "Rough? You have no idea. It's all just—too much." She waved her hand vaguely, knocking her handbag against the side of the bench.

Hayley leaned in slightly, lowering her voice. "I know

it's hard, especially with Lester getting arrested. But I couldn't help but notice something . . ."

Melody blinked at her. "Notice what?"

"You and Lester are always at Jordan's for breakfast on Tuesdays," Hayley said casually. "Blueberry pancakes, right? Same as me. It's like a tradition. That's why it stood out to me."

"What stood out to you?" Melody asked shakily.

"On the day Tom died, it just dawned on me, I didn't see you there."

The question landed like a stone between them.

Hayley was bluffing.

She did not recall whether or not she saw the Murdocks at Jordan's on that day or not, or if she even had stopped by for pancakes herself that particular Tuesday.

She just wanted to gauge Melody's reaction.

Melody's eyes flickered, her shoulders tensing. "We, uh, we stayed home that morning," she muttered, her voice wavering. "Just had breakfast at the house."

Hayley was not buying it. Melody was too loyal to her routine—and to Lester's. She pushed gently. "You're always at Jordan's. I thought maybe something came up?"

Melody was quiet for a long moment, her lower lip trembling. Then, as if a dam had burst, she let out a ragged sigh. "Lester told me to say we stayed home," she admitted, her voice barely above a whisper. "Told me it'd be easier that way. But we didn't stay home together. He didn't stay home. He left early that morning."

Hayley's pulse quickened. She knew Melody was

teetering on the edge of spilling something big. "Where did he go, Melody?"

"I saw him drive toward Tom's farm," she whispered. "He didn't tell me why. But when I heard about what happened to Tom . . . I can't stop thinking about it. I know Lester can be cruel, but—this? I'm scared, Hayley. I think he might have done something . . ." She then gasped, as if shocking herself by allowing those words to escape her lips.

Hayley's heart raced as the pieces began to fall into place. The Murdocks had not stayed home like they told the police, and Lester had gone straight toward Tom Farley's farm on the day he was murdered. Melody was admitting she had lied for him—and that she feared her husband was capable of killing Tom.

Just then, the door to the holding area burst open, and Lester Murdock appeared, his face flushed with anger. He stormed toward them, his eyes narrowing at the sight of Hayley sitting next to his wife.

"Melody, what the hell are you saying to that woman?" Lester demanded, his voice booming through the small waiting area.

Melody shrank back, her expression crumbling into guilt and fear. "I can't keep lying for you, Lester," she stammered, her voice trembling. "You weren't home that morning, and I know you went to see Tom!"

Lester's face turned a shade of deep red, his jaw clenching. "You're drunk, Melody. You don't know what you're talking about."

Hayley stood, her voice steady. "She knows exactly what she's talking about, Lester. She saw you drive toward Tom's farm. Your alibi is falling apart."

Lester's fists clenched at his sides, but before he could retort, Chief Sergio appeared from behind the desk. His eyes flicked between Hayley, Melody, and Lester, sensing the tension in the air. "What's going on here?"

"Melody just admitted that Lester wasn't home the morning Tom was killed," Hayley said, her voice firm. "She saw him drive toward Tom's farm."

Sergio's eyes narrowed as he turned his attention to Lester. "Is that true, Lester? You want to revise your statement?"

Lester's face twisted in frustration. "She's drunk, as usual," he repeated. "She's making this up! She's always desperate for some kind of attention!"

Sergio crossed his arms. "We've already got a boot print at the scene, Lester. But we just haven't been able to find the matching boots. Yet."

Lester opened his mouth to respond, but his words faltered. Melody's betrayal seemed to hit him harder than the accusation. He looked between his wife and the Chief, his bravado deflating.

"You can't arrest me based on a damn boot print and my drunk wife's ramblings," Lester spat, but his voice lacked its usual confidence.

Sergio took a step closer, his gaze hard. "You're under arrest for the murder of Tom Farley, Lester."

The color drained from Lester's face as Sergio cuffed him. "I didn't kill him!" Lester shouted, his voice cracking. "I swear, I went to talk to him that morning, sure! But I didn't kill him!"

Hayley crossed her arms, her eyes narrowing. "Then why lie about where you were?"

Lester's shoulders slumped as he was led toward the back of the station. "I didn't kill him. I went to try one last time—try to convince him to sell. He wouldn't do it. Said he couldn't leave the farm, that it was his home. We talked, that's all. When I left, he was still alive."

Sergio tightened his grip on Lester's arm. "Save it for the jury."

As they disappeared into the back, Melody broke into sobs, burying her face in her hands. Hayley felt a pang of sympathy for her. Melody had been dragged into this mess, forced to lie to cover for a husband who was not worthy of her loyalty.

Hayley stepped outside the station, her thoughts swirling. Lester's arrest felt like a victory, but something still gnawed at her. Lester insisted he did not kill Tom, and as much as Hayley wanted to believe Melody's confession, she could not shake the feeling that there was still more to uncover.

Tom Farley had been a stubborn, ornery man, but he had not deserved the brutal end he met. And if Lester was not the one who shoved him into that woodchipper, then the real killer was still out there.

She pulled out her phone and texted Bruce: **Lester's in custody, but I'm not convinced it's over yet. Something's still not sitting right with me.**

As she hit send, Hayley knew her instincts were telling her the truth. The mystery of Tom Farley's death was far from over.

And she was not done asking questions—not by a long shot.

ISLAND FOOD & SPIRITS
By
Hayley Powell

Hello, Bar Harbor! So, you know my BFF Mona, right? Calm as a cucumber and hard to ruffle—until last Thanksgiving. She called me up in a panic, voice shaking, talking about things mysteriously disappearing from her kitchen.

Now, I've known Mona a long time, so I fought back a laugh (barely) and asked her what was going on. Turns out, her Thanksgiving supplies were going missing right from under her nose. First, her favorite mixing spoon vanished. Then a bag of sweet potatoes, a stick of butter, cranberries, and an entire loaf of French bread pulled a disappearing act, one by one. And no, her grandkids weren't behind it—Mona had already threatened to take away every piece of technology they loved, and trust me, they weren't going to mess with her after that!

To catch the culprit, we set up a hidden camera in her kitchen. But as the days ticked down to Thanksgiving Day, we caught . . . absolutely nothing. The kids were off the hook, and we were left scratching our heads. Finally, Thanksgiving arrived, and Mona was busy prepping her glorious, golden turkey. Just as she set it down to rest, she suggested we have a pre-dinner cocktail (never a bad idea).

We were all set to eat, but when we returned to the kitchen, Mona's turkey had disappeared! The empty pan sat there as if mocking us. We searched high and low, but no sign of it. Then Mona, wild-eyed, remembered the camera. She pulled out her phone, watched the footage—and gasped.

We dashed outside to find her Golden Retriever, Sadie, lounging in the backyard, savoring every bite of Mona's beautiful turkey. Mona rushed to grab the turkey back, slipping in the mud and grabbing only a lone turkey leg. Sadie, thrilled by her newfound tug-of-war partner, pulled hard, leaving Mona in a muddy heap with a single turkey leg while Sadie pranced off with the rest.

Laughing through the mess, I glanced by the fence and found the motherload: Mona's spoon, a butter wrapper, an empty bread bag, and a pile of other random household items Sadie had apparently stashed away like some furry little thief. Mystery solved, and we all—except Sadie, who was quite full—settled for side dishes and desserts that day. Sometimes, the best memories aren't about what's on the table but the wild stories that come with them!

And speaking of stories, I recently found a cocktail that even my non-margarita-loving husband Bruce enjoys, so it's on our Thanksgiving menu this year.

Bruce's Beer Margarita

INGREDIENTS:
½ cup tequila
¼ cup fresh lime juice (about two limes)
¼ cup triple sec
Lime wedges for garnish
Ice
1 cup Mexican beer (Corona or Modelo works great)

Rub a lime wedge around the rim of your glass and dip it into margarita salt.

In a large pitcher, combine tequila, lime juice, and triple sec.

Slowly add the beer and stir gently to avoid too much foam. Pour over ice in your salt-rimmed glass, garnish with a lime wedge, and enjoy!

TURKEY NOODLE VEGETABLE SOUP

INGREDIENTS:
A great way to enjoy leftovers! Customize with your
   favorite veggies.
Leftover turkey, shredded or chopped (use as much or
   as little as you like)
4 cups chicken or turkey broth
2 cups of vegetables (I use carrots, celery, and peas)
1 onion, diced
2 cloves minced garlic
1 tsp ground thyme
Salt and pepper to taste
1½ cups egg noodles (or your favorite pasta)

In a large pot, sauté diced onion and garlic on medium
heat until softened. Add mixed vegetables and cook
for five minutes.

Pour in the broth, add turkey, thyme, salt, and pepper.
Bring to a boil, add noodles, and then reduce the heat
to simmer until everything is heated through and the
noodles are cooked—about 20 minutes. Serve hot
with leftover dinner rolls and enjoy.

   Here's to keeping your turkeys safe from thieving
paws and your holidays full of laughter. Cheers to a
memorable Thanksgiving!

Chapter 35

The morning sun barely broke through the gray skies over Hancock County as Hayley and Bruce made their way to the courthouse. It was the first day of Lester Murdock's murder trial, and the stakes could not be higher. With Lester arrested for Tom Farley's brutal death, the entire town had been buzzing with gossip, none more so than at Jordan's Restaurant, where Hayley had overheard all sorts of theories.

Bruce had pulled some strings to secure front-row seats in the courtroom for them both. As a crime reporter, Bruce had been itching to cover this trial, and his reputation had earned him access most journalists could only dream of having. As for Hayley, her involvement as an amateur sleuth—and her deep-seated curiosity—meant she was just as eager to be there. She still had her doubts about Lester's guilt, despite his wife, Melody, confessing that she had lied for him.

Hayley could not shake the feeling that something simply was still not adding up.

The courthouse loomed before them, a stately building of brick and stone, its columns standing like sentinels watching over the drama about to unfold inside. Hayley and Bruce walked past the throng of reporters and spectators, some holding up microphones and cameras, all hoping to catch a glimpse of the key players in this high-profile trial.

"Can't believe we actually made it to the front row," Hayley whispered as they entered the courtroom, sliding into their seats. "I feel like Dominick Dunne at the OJ trial."

The air was thick with tension, the kind that comes with a trial that had captured the attention of an entire town—and beyond. Wealthy landowners, backdoor deals, and a gruesome murder at the center of it all.

Bruce leaned closer, keeping his voice low. "It's going to be a circus. Lester fired his attorney Danny Maddox and decided to go for a defense team of top-notch, high-priced Boston lawyers. They're going to throw everything they have at this."

"Too bad all the money in the world might not save him," Hayley replied, glancing around. The gallery was packed with familiar faces—Tom Farley's neighbors, members of the press, and local business owners. People she had known for years. But one face was conspicuously absent—Melody Murdock. Only Lester's two sons, Alan and Bo, were seated in the gallery to represent the immediate family, looking tense and uncomfortable.

As if on cue, Lester was led into the courtroom by

his defense team. He looked haggard, his usual bravado deflated by the weight of the trial. The Murdocks' wealth and influence could not protect him here, not in the face of Melody's betrayal and the mounting evidence against him. The boot print found at the scene, the lies about his alibi—everything pointed to Lester as the man who had pushed Tom Farley into his woodchipper in a fit of rage.

The courtroom doors swung open, and in walked Assistant District Attorney Alley Roberts, her presence commanding the room. She was a force to be reckoned with—sharp, confident, and relentless. Hayley had seen her in action before, and she knew that if anyone could put Lester away, it was Alley.

"All rise for the Honorable Judge Amanda Parsons," the bailiff announced, and the courtroom stood as the judge, a stern-looking woman with a no-nonsense demeanor, took her seat at the bench.

"Let's get started," Judge Parsons said, her voice crisp and authoritative. "Counsel, are you ready?"

The prosecution and defense both stood to confirm. Alley Roberts wasted no time getting to her feet, her gaze sharp as a hawk as she addressed the court.

"Yes, Your Honor."

Alley gave a riveting opening statement explaining why Lester Murdock was guilty of Tom Farley's murder. She made eye contact with the jury of seven men and five women, detailing Lester's motive and opportunity. As Alley rattled off point by point why only Lester Murdock could have been the one to push Tom Farley into his woodchipper, Hayley tried to read the jury, but their expressions were inscrutable. They sat still, all twelve stone-faced, even a coughing fit from the gallery did not cause them to look away from the assistant DA.

When Alley concluded her remarks, she thanked the jury and sat down. Now it was the defense's turn. One of the highly paid suits with slicked back hair and a slight sneer, popped up and spent the next hour trying to poke holes in the prosecution's case with middling success. He threw everything but the kitchen sink at the jury, trying to cause reasonable doubt, but nothing seemed to stick, at least in Hayley's mind. By the time he was finished, the jury looked exhausted and slightly annoyed at the lawyer's bombastic rambling and verbose opening statement.

Hayley could only see the back of Lester's head but when he turned to whisper something to his lawyer seated next to him, she could tell from his expression that he was worried.

And he had every reason to be.

When the defense attorney finally sat back down at the table, the judge tried but failed to hide her irritation by how long he had droned on and on. "Okay. Thank you." She then glanced at the assistant DA. "The prosecution may call its first witness."

"Your Honor, the State would like to call—Alan Murdock," she announced.

The gallery rippled with whispers as Alan, the elder of Lester's sons, took the stand. His hands fidgeted nervously as he sat down, casting quick glances at his father, who sat nervously beside his defense team.

Hayley leaned in toward Bruce. "This is going to be interesting," she whispered.

Bruce nodded. "Alley Roberts doesn't play around. She knows Alan's not going to make this easy."

Alley approached the stand, her voice cool and calculated. "Alan, you were at the turkey shoot the day Tom Farley was shot, correct?"

Alan swallowed, his Adam's apple bobbing visibly. "Yes," he muttered, avoiding eye contact with his father.

"And you were aware that your father, Lester Murdock, was furious with Tom Farley for refusing to sell his land to Acadia Resorts, isn't that right?"

Alan shifted in his seat, clearly uncomfortable. "Yes," he admitted, his voice barely above a whisper.

The gallery stirred, and Alley pressed on, her tone taking on an edge. "How far would your family go to make sure that land deal went through, Alan? Far enough to kill Tom Farley?"

"I don't know!" Alan blurted, his voice cracking. "I can't tell you what anyone else would do!"

"But we know how far *you* would go, don't we, Alan? You took a rifle and shot Tom Farley that day, didn't you?"

Alan, face flushed, nodded.

"I need an answer, Alan."

He nodded again.

"I need you to say it."

"Yes!" he shouted in frustration.

The young defense lawyer popped to his feet. "Objection. Badgering the witness!"

"Overruled," the judge muttered, her eyes glued to some documents in front of her.

"In fact, you went to the turkey shoot specifically to

take out Tom Farley, to erase the problem that had been plaguing your family, Tom's utter refusal to sell his property to Acadia Resorts."

Alan shrugged.

Alley adopted a more gentle tone. "Alan, please answer the question."

He leaned forward and spoke into the mic in front of him. "Yes!"

There was ear-splitting feedback from the microphone.

"Mr. Murdock, please don't sit so close to the microphone. We've been having issues with it recently," the judge said.

"Okay," Alan mumbled as he sat back.

Hayley could feel the tension building, the air thick with anticipation. She glanced at Bruce, who was watching the proceedings with the intensity of a hawk, scribbling notes on his notepad.

"Alan," Alley continued, her voice growing sharper, "were you aware that after the shooting, when it became clear that Tom had survived the attempt on his life, that your father went over to his turkey farm on the day of his murder?"

"He didn't do it," Alan whispered.

"That's not what I asked you. I asked if you were aware that your father went over—"

"I heard you!" Alan snapped. "And I'm saying he didn't do it!"

"Did your father tell you that he didn't murder Tom Farley?"

"No, he didn't have to."

"Then how do you know for certain?"

The question hung in the air like a bomb waiting to explode. The gallery held its collective breath, waiting for Alan's response. For a moment, it seemed like he would remain silent, but then, to everyone's shock, he spoke.

"Because I did it!" Alan confessed, his voice shaky but clear. "I pushed him into the woodchipper."

Gasps erupted from the gallery, and even Hayley felt her breath catch. Bruce shot her a wide-eyed look, and the courtroom descended into chaos as murmurs and whispers filled the air.

Judge Parsons banged her gavel, calling for order. "Silence in the court!"

The defense team, visibly rattled by the confession, immediately jumped to their feet. "Your Honor, we request a recess," one of the Boston lawyers declared, his voice urgent.

The judge's eyes narrowed. "Granted. We'll reconvene in twenty minutes."

As the court recessed, Hayley and Bruce sat in stunned silence, the weight of Alan's sudden confession still hanging over them. Alan had admitted to the murder—something no one had anticipated.

And yet, despite the shocking twist, something did not sit right with Hayley.

"I don't believe him," Hayley said quietly, her mind racing. "That confession . . . it's too convenient."

Bruce raised an eyebrow. "You think he's lying?"

"I think he's trying to protect someone," Hayley said, her voice firm. "Maybe his father. Maybe someone else. But there's more to this than what we're seeing."

Bruce glanced over at Alan, who had slumped in his seat, looking as though the weight of the world had just crushed him. "If you're right, this trial just took a turn no one expected."

Hayley nodded, her eyes narrowing in thought. The Murdocks had always been a complicated family, driven by power, greed, and a desperate need for approval. Alan's confession might have been designed to save Lester, but Hayley was not ready to close the book on Tom Farley's murder just yet.

As the court reconvened twenty minutes later and the defense team huddled around Lester, frantically planning their next move, Hayley's mind was already turning over the possibilities. Alan's confession was a bombshell, but the truth still felt just out of reach.

This trial was far from over.

And neither was Hayley's investigation.

Chapter 36

The trial of Lester Murdock resumed after Alan's shocking confession in the previous session. Hayley sat next to Bruce, her hands clenched tightly in her lap, still trying to process the sudden turn of events. She glanced over at Lester, who sat impassively at the defense table, surrounded by his lawyers. His son Alan, who had just confessed to pushing Tom Farley into the woodchipper, had been led away by the bailiff after testifying.

Hayley suspected that Alan's confession was nothing more than a desperate attempt to win his father's approval. Lester had always favored Bo, the younger of the Murdock brothers. Alan had spent his life trying to earn his father's respect, and this seemed like just another tragic chapter in that sad story.

The defense attorney stood up and faced the judge.

"Your Honor, in light of this new evidence, we request an immediate dismissal of all charges against our client."

Alley sat back in chair and scoffed. "In your dreams."

The defense attorney ignored her. "Your Honor, our client has suffered enough from these baseless charges. We all heard with our own ears a full-throated confession from his son Alan."

Alley shook her head and rose to her feet. "Until we've seen enough evidence to convince us that Alan Murdock committed this crime, and we've seen nothing of the kind so far, just a desperate son trying to protect his father, in my humble opinion, we would like to proceed with the trial, Your Honor."

"I tend to agree," Judge Parsons said. "Motion denied."

The defense attorney grimaced but kept his cool. "Your Honor, we would like a brief recess to confer with our client."

"You just had one," she sighed. "But fine. The court will reconvene again in fifteen minutes."

"Thank you, Your Honor."

Everyone began filing out of the courtroom once more as Judge Parsons retired to her chambers.

As the court recessed for a second break, Hayley could not help but notice Lester quietly speaking with his lawyers in a corner of the room. Curious, she excused herself from Bruce and edged closer, trying to catch their conversation. Lester's voice was a low murmur, but in the near-empty courtroom, it carried.

"Should we let Alan take the fall?" Lester was asking, his tone completely devoid of concern for his son.

"Maybe it's the best way to get the charges against me dropped. We can worry about defending him later."

Hayley's stomach turned at the coldness in his words.

One of the older defense lawyers, a slick man with silver hair, leaned forward, his voice equally low. "The problem, Lester, is Alan's shoe size doesn't come close to matching the muddy footprint found at the scene. If we let him confess, it could unravel the entire case if they start focusing on the physical evidence."

Lester waved a hand dismissively. "My shoe size doesn't match perfectly either. It's close enough—a half-size off at most. But that's not a smoking gun, is it?"

The lawyer hesitated, clearly uncomfortable with the conversation. "It's a problem. If they push on this, we might lose control of the narrative."

Hayley's breath caught. Lester was actually considering letting his own son take the blame, despite knowing it was most likely not Alan who killed Tom. She did not even realize her hands were trembling until Bruce returned and squeezed her shoulder gently.

"Hayley?" Bruce asked, his brow furrowed. "You okay?"

"Yeah," she murmured. "I just . . . I need to check something."

She quickly excused herself and made her way to the hallway, where she spotted Alley Roberts going over some notes with one of her colleagues.

"Alley," Hayley called out, approaching her. "Can I ask you something?"

Alley raised an eyebrow, surprised to see Hayley outside the courtroom. "Sure, Hayley. What's on your mind?"

"The muddy footprint found at the scene," Hayley began, her voice hushed. "You said it came close to matching Lester's shoe size, but could it belong to someone else? Could it have belonged to someone else who was on the property that day?"

Alley frowned, clearly aware of the weight of the question. "It's possible, yes. We can't definitively say it was Lester's. There's enough reasonable doubt about the footprint. So yes, it could've belonged to anyone who was there."

Hayley nodded, her suspicions growing. "That means Alan's confession is probably a lie, right? Just a desperate ploy to protect Lester?"

Alley's lips tightened. "We're considering all possibilities. But I will say this. There's no direct evidence linking Alan to the murder scene."

Hayley thanked her and turned to head back into the courtroom when she nearly collided with Lester. His face was flushed, and his eyes glittered with anger.

"You just can't leave well enough alone, can you?" he hissed at her. "Why don't you mind your own business, Hayley?"

Hayley's temper flared. "You're seriously going to let your son go down for something he obviously didn't do? Everyone knows Alan's just trying to save your sorry behind, Lester. Why don't you grow a spine and finally face the consequences of your actions?"

Lester sneered at her, his voice dripping with disdain. "It's none of your business what happens between me and my family."

Hayley shook her head, disgusted. "You're a coward, Lester. A selfish coward."

With that, she marched back to her seat, her mind racing. The pieces were starting to come together, but she still did not have enough to nail Lester to the wall. And Alan's confession, if left unchecked, could throw everything off.

When the trial resumed, Alley Roberts called her next witness—Melody Murdock.

Melody stumbled up to the stand, clearly nervous. Her eyes darted around the room as she took the oath and settled into the witness box, her hands fidgeting in her lap. Hayley noticed that she avoided eye contact with Lester completely.

"Mrs. Murdock," Alley began, her tone firm but gentle. "Where was your son, Alan, on the morning of Tom Farley's murder?"

Melody's voice was barely audible as she spoke. "He was home. In his room. All morning."

Alley nodded and continued. "So Alan wasn't at Tom Farley's property that morning, was he?"

Melody shook her head. "No. He wasn't."

"Nothing further, your Honor," Alley said before returning to her chair.

In the gallery, Hayley could see Lester's jaw clench. Melody's testimony was damning for Lester's defense—and by extension, for Lester's attempt to let his son take the fall.

Judge Parsons gestured toward the defense table. "Your witness."

Another one of the team of defense attorneys, the older one with silver hair and an air of unshakable confidence, rose from his chair and approached the witness stand. His perfectly tailored suit seemed to gleam under the harsh courtroom lights as he glanced at Melody Murdock with a practiced, almost predatory smile.

"Mrs. Murdock," he began, his voice smooth and calculated. "You've had a rough time of it, haven't you?"

Melody shifted uncomfortably in her seat, her eyes darting briefly to the jury before looking down at her hands. "I suppose you could say that."

The attorney nodded sympathetically, as if he were on her side. "Yes, yes. It must be very hard, dealing with all this pressure. The trial, the accusations, your son . . . Not to mention, your husband." He allowed the last word to hang in the air, letting the jury fill in the blanks.

"I'm managing," Melody replied softly, though her voice wavered.

"Of course, of course. But wouldn't you say that stress can sometimes lead to . . . mistakes? A lapse in judgment, perhaps?"

His tone was deceptively kind, the kind of voice that seemed to offer comfort while subtly pushing someone toward the edge.

Alley Roberts, sitting at her table, tensed but stayed silent, watching the defense attorney with laser-sharp focus.

Melody hesitated. "I try not to let things get to me," she said, though her voice lacked conviction.

The attorney nodded, as if he understood her struggle perfectly. "I'm sure you do, Mrs. Murdock. But . . . let's be honest here. It's not uncommon for people under stress to seek out . . . relief. Isn't that true?"

Melody's brow furrowed, and she glanced up at him, uncertain where this was going. "What do you mean?"

The attorney turned to the jury, his voice dropping

to a lower, more intimate tone. "Relief, Mrs. Murdock. You know, a glass of wine at the end of a hard day? Or maybe two glasses? Perhaps even something stronger. You know, a little something to take the edge off?"

At this, Alley stood up. "Objection, Your Honor—"

"Overruled," Judge Parsons said with a wave of her hand, not even looking up from her notes. "I'll allow it."

The defense attorney smiled, knowing he had the floor. He turned back to Melody. "So, Mrs. Murdock, would you say that, from time to time, you've turned to alcohol to cope with the pressures in your life?"

Melody's eyes widened, panic flickering in them. "I—I have a drink now and then, like anyone else. But I'm not a . . ."

"Not a what, Mrs. Murdock?" The attorney's voice sharpened, like a wolf catching the scent of weakness. "Not someone who drinks excessively? Not someone who might—on occasion—have a bit too much and . . . well, lose track of time?"

Melody visibly stiffened. "I know exactly where I was, and I know where my son was," she said, though her voice faltered slightly.

The silver-haired defense attorney raised an eyebrow, as if her protest had only confirmed his suspicions. "Do you? Mrs. Murdock, were you under the influence of alcohol the morning Tom Farley was killed?"

"No!" Melody exclaimed, her voice a touch too loud.

The attorney's smile widened just a fraction. "You weren't? Are you absolutely sure about that? Because it seems to me that someone in your position—someone who has admitted to using alcohol to cope—might have a hard time keeping track of the events of that morning. Perhaps you were . . . mistaken when you said your son was at home."

Alley rose again, her voice cutting through the defense attorney's polished rhetoric. "Objection! This is pure speculation and an attempt to undermine the credibility of the witness without any evidence."

Judge Parsons looked up this time, her face impassive. "Sustained. Counselor, stick to the facts."

But the damage had already been done. Melody was visibly shaking now, and the defense attorney knew he had planted a seed of doubt. He took a step back, his hands up in a gesture of mock apology.

"Of course, Your Honor," he said smoothly, then turned back to Melody. "No more questions, Mrs. Murdock. You may step down."

Melody gripped the sides of the witness stand for a moment before shakily climbing to her feet. She looked like a woman who had just been dragged through a storm, her face pale and her movements unsteady. Hayley watched with a sinking feeling as Melody shuffled back to her seat, her gaze avoiding her husband's cold stare.

Alley Roberts, however, was not finished. As the defense attorney smugly returned to his seat, she stood and approached the bench with renewed determination.

"Your Honor, I'd like to introduce a piece of evidence that speaks to the credibility of the witness's testimony," she said, her voice firm.

The judge raised an eyebrow. "Go ahead."

Alley pulled out her laptop and connected it to the screen in the courtroom. "I have here a video posted by

Alan Murdock on social media, timestamped the morning of Tom Farley's murder. In it, Alan complains about being stuck at home with his mother, and how he couldn't wait to get away from her."

"Objection!" The silver-haired lawyer bellowed. "The defense was not given the evidence in discovery!"

"It was just obtained by my office and given to me during the recess, but it is extremely relevant to Mrs. Murdock's testimony before the court."

Judge Parsons took a few moments to mull over her decision. Then she spoke firmly. "I'll allow it."

"Your Honor!" the younger lawyer whined. "This is outrageous!"

"If you feel so strongly about the jury not seeing this evidence, you can bring it up on appeal, counselor, but if it's that relevant, let's see it and draw our own conclusions," Judge Parsons said acidly. "Play the video."

The bailiff rolled in a television set and Alley Roberts cast the video from her phone.

As the video played, Alan's voice echoed through the room: "Can't stand living with her anymore. Always nagging me about everything. I need to get out of here, get away from her. I'm done with this place. It feels like a prison."

The courtroom was still as the jury watched Alan's angry rant. Hayley glanced at Bruce, who gave her a knowing look. The video was proof that Alan was indeed at home with Melody that morning—and that he had lied about being the one who killed Tom.

Alley turned back to the courtroom, addressing the jury. "As you can see from the time stamp on the Instagram post, Alan recorded this in his bedroom on the morning of the murder. It's clear Alan wasn't at Tom Farley's property that morning, and despite the defense's attempts to paint her as unreliable, we have clear evidence that Melody Murdock's account of the day's events holds up. She knew exactly where her son was—at home, venting his frustrations on social media. Alan Murdock was not the one who pushed Tom Farley into that woodchipper. That man is sitting right there."

She pointed directly at Lester Murdock.

"Objection!" the defense team howled in unison.

Alley shrugged. "Withdrawn." She turned toward Murdock's team of lawyers, her eyes twinkling.

She had just scored a big win.

The defense looked rattled. The silver-haired attorney asked for yet another recess, but the damage had already been done. Alan's false confession had crumbled under the weight of the evidence, and Lester Murdock's fate was all but sealed.

By the end of the day, the prosecution rested, leaving the defense scrambling. As Hayley and Bruce left the courthouse, she could not help but feel a grim satisfaction. Lester Murdock had used everyone around him—his wife, his son, his neighbors—but now, the walls were closing in.

And this time, there was no one left to protect him.

Chapter 37

The atmosphere in the courtroom was taut as Hayley sat beside Bruce in the front row. Bruce was focused, scribbling in his notepad as he took lots of notes for his *Island Times* article. Hayley, however, was too caught up in the drama unfolding before her eyes to concentrate on anything else.

Lester Murdock sat rigidly at the defense table, his team of slick Boston lawyers whispering urgently to one another. Across the aisle, Assistant District Attorney Alley Roberts, in her signature no-nonsense stance, had her eyes locked on the defense's surprise move—a move Hayley had not seen coming.

Reid Norton.

Hayley's jaw clenched as she watched Reid take the stand.

He raised his hand as he was sworn in.

"Do you solemnly and sincerely and truly declare

and affirm that the evidence you shall give shall be the truth, the whole truth, and nothing but the truth?"

Reid nodded. "I do."

Reid, Tom Farley's prickly neighbor, who had always seemed to be hovering in the background of the case, had suddenly become the defense's star witness.

It felt like the earth had shifted under her feet.

"Please state your name for the court," one of the defense attorneys, the younger more nimble one, said, stepping in front of Reid with an air of rehearsed confidence.

Reid cleared his throat and adjusted his posture, clearly uncomfortable being the center of attention. "Reid Norton," he said, his voice gruff but steady.

Hayley leaned toward Bruce, whispering, "Why would they call Reid? I thought he hated the Murdocks."

Bruce glanced at her briefly, his pen pausing over the notepad. "They must think he can somehow exonerate Lester. Let's see where this goes."

The defense attorney smiled at Reid like a wolf about to pounce. "Is it true you are a veteran of our Armed Services, Mr. Norton?"

"Yup. Marine Corps. Twenty years. Two wars."

"Thank you for your service, sir."

Reid cracked a half smile and nodded his head slightly.

The defense attorney quickly moved on. "Mr. Norton, you've had some trouble with Tom Farley over the years, haven't you?"

Reid's lips tightened. "You could say that."

"Tell the court what kind of trouble."

Reid hesitated for a moment, his gaze flicking over

to Hayley as if he knew she was silently urging him to get to the point.

Then he turned back to the defense attorney.

"Tom's turkeys kept getting onto my property," Reid said. "I was sick of it. He wouldn't listen when I asked him to control them. We argued. A lot."

The defense attorney paced in front of Reid, his polished shoes clicking against the wooden floor. "So, you hated Tom Farley?"

Reid blinked. "I didn't hate him, hate's a mighty strong word, but I sure didn't like him very much."

"Noted," the attorney said, pausing to let the jury absorb the words. "Now, let's talk about the day Tom Farley was found in his woodchipper." The courtroom fell silent, the words hanging like a cloud of dread. "You were there, weren't you, Mr. Norton?"

The room felt like it collectively held its breath. Hayley leaned forward, her eyes narrowing as she waited for Reid to speak.

Reid straightened in the witness box, a defiant edge creeping into his voice. "Yeah. I was there."

The defense attorney's eyes glinted. "And did you leave a footprint at the scene?"

Hayley's pulse quickened.

This was the twist.

The footprint.

Reid looked straight ahead, his voice unwavering. "Yes. I believe I did."

A murmur rippled through the courtroom. Hayley exchanged a quick glance with Bruce, whose pen had stopped moving.

The defense attorney smiled like a cat who had just trapped its prey. "So you admit that the muddy footprint found at Tom Farley's farm belongs to you, not Lester Murdock?"

"I do," Reid said firmly. He shifted in his seat and reached under the bench beside him, pulling out a pair of worn, muddy boots. "These are the boots I was wearing that day. Size eleven, just like the footprint."

The defense attorney stepped back, dramatically raising an eyebrow. "Lester Murdock doesn't wear boots like that, does he?"

Reid shook his head. "No. I don't suppose so. Lester's a wealthy guy. He wears expensive shoes, not these. I got these on sale at Walmart."

Hayley could not believe what she was hearing. Reid was openly admitting to being at the scene of the crime and leaving behind the footprint that had been such a focal point of the case.

What was his game?

"And why were you at Tom Farley's farm that morning?" the attorney pressed.

Reid's jaw clenched. "I went to confront him about the turkeys again. Same old story. I wanted him to do something about it. We argued, but then I left."

"Did you see Lester Murdock while you were there?"

Hayley felt the courtroom shift, the tension spiking as Reid nodded slowly. "Yeah. I saw him."

The defense attorney turned to the jury, his hands spread wide. "Can you tell us what you saw, Mr. Norton?"

Reid sat forward, his eyes flicking toward the Murdocks before returning to the defense attorney. "When

I was approaching Tom's farm, I saw Lester getting into his car and driving away."

The defense attorney's tone shifted, softening as if he were coaxing the truth out of Reid. "What was Tom Farley doing when you saw this?"

"Still alive," Reid answered, his voice resolute. "Lester didn't kill him. Tom was alive when Lester left."

Hayley felt her stomach twist. Was Reid telling the truth, or was this just another twist in the defense's strategy to deflect blame?

The defense attorney turned to the jury. "You're telling this court that you saw Lester Murdock leave Tom Farley's property *before* Mr. Farley was killed?"

Reid nodded. "That's exactly what I'm telling you."

Hayley could see Alley's face tighten from across the courtroom. The defense had just given the jury an alternative version of events. One that did not place Lester at the scene of the crime at the time of Tom's death.

The defense attorney was building up to his next move. "But Mr. Norton, you and Tom didn't get along. In fact, you were furious with him, weren't you?"

Reid's brow furrowed. "Yeah, I was mad, but I sure as hell didn't kill him."

"Maybe not," the attorney said, his voice now laced with accusation, "but you were the last one to see him alive. And you admit you were angry with him. That's quite a coincidence, wouldn't you say?"

"You said you wouldn't do this if I testified. You promised not to make it look like a did it!" Reid protested.

The lawyer gave him a thin smile.

Reid sat up straighter, defiance burning in his eyes. "I'm not a killer," he growled. "I hated the way Tom ran things on his farm, but I'm telling you the truth. I saw Lester leave when Tom was still alive. After I spoke with Tom, I didn't stick around long enough to see what happened next."

The defense attorney sighed dramatically, his hands on his hips. "So we're supposed to believe that you—who have a history of bitter and at times violent conflict with Tom Farley—just left peacefully and someone else came along and killed him?"

"Exactly," Reid said firmly, his gaze not wavering.

The defense attorney raised his eyebrow, clearly unsatisfied with the answer but aware he was not going to break Reid's resolve. He glanced over at Alley, who was ready to strike back.

"Thank you, Mr. Norton. No further questions," he said, walking away from the witness stand.

As soon as the defense attorney sat down, Alley stood, her heels clicking as she approached the witness box with a calculated calm.

"Mr. Norton," she began, "just to be clear, you're admitting that the footprint at the scene belongs to you?"

Reid nodded. "That's right."

Alley smiled coolly. "So, if you hated Tom Farley so much, why didn't you kill him?"

Reid's voice was low but steady. "Because like I said, I'm not a killer."

"You're a military-trained sniper."

"Sure, but that was a long time ago. I don't do that

anymore. Look, I was mad, yeah, but I didn't want to see him . . . end up like that."

"And yet, the prosecution has shown that you were at Tom's property that morning. The same morning he was killed in his woodchipper."

"I left before anything happened," Reid repeated, his frustration clear. "I'm not lying."

Alley gave a small nod. "Okay, let's talk about Lester Murdock. You said you saw him leaving the property, correct?"

"Yes."

"And you assumed he had just been talking to Tom about the land deal, right?"

Reid hesitated for a split second before answering. "Yeah, I figured that's what he was doing."

"Isn't it possible that after you left, Lester Murdock came back? That maybe he wasn't done with his conversation with Tom?"

Reid blinked, caught off guard. "I guess . . . it's possible, but I didn't see him come back."

Alley's expression softened, but her eyes were still sharp. "Mr. Norton, the truth is, you didn't see what happened after you left. For all you know, Lester could have returned and confronted Tom again."

Reid opened his mouth, but nothing came out.

The silence in the courtroom was deafening.

Hayley glanced at Bruce, her mind racing. She did not know if Reid was telling the full truth, her gut was telling her he was, but one thing was certain—there were still too many unanswered questions.

Chapter 38

The courtroom was silent, thick with anticipation as Judge Amanda Parsons returned from her chambers. Her face was carefully neutral as she took her seat, rapping the gavel sharply to command the room's attention.

Alley Roberts, seated at the prosecution's table, looked poised and unyielding, while the defense team across the aisle had a barely suppressed air of triumph. The unexpected testimony from Reid Norton had sent shockwaves through the court, and now everyone waited to see what the judge would decide.

"Counselors, please approach the bench," Judge Parsons said.

The young defense attorney strode forward with confident steps, accompanied by Alley. Their quiet discussion with the judge was intense but inaudible to the rest of the court.

Hayley, sitting in the front row with Bruce, could only guess at the details. She felt her palms grow clammy, her breath shallow. Bruce's notepad was filled with scribbled notes, but for once, he seemed more absorbed in the drama in front of the judge than his work.

After what felt like an eternity, Judge Parsons leaned back in her chair and addressed the court. "The defense has argued that Mr. Norton's testimony raises significant doubt regarding the guilt of Mr. Lester Murdock. However, the prosecution has provided ample grounds to suggest that Mr. Murdock could have returned to the scene after Mr. Norton left."

The defense attorney's face tightened, but Judge Parsons continued, unfazed. "Therefore, I am denying the motion to dismiss. This case will continue, and the jury will hear all the evidence."

A wave of whispers swept through the gallery as the jury was led back into the courtroom.

Hayley released a breath she had not realized she was holding.

Alley's expression remained firm—her gamble had paid off, and the trial would go on.

The defense attorney rose, clearing his throat. "Your Honor, the defense would like to call its next witness. Daniel Sweet."

Daniel took the stand nervously, wiping his sweaty palms on his jeans. Once sworn in, he began recounting the night he and his wife, Hannah, were awakened by gunshots.

"We were sound asleep," he said, voice wavering. "Then we heard it—bang, bang—real close. We found out later it was Reid shooting at Tom's turkeys."

"And where were you when you heard these gunshots?" the defense attorney asked.

"In our trailer," Daniel said, shifting uneasily. "We live about a quarter of a mile from Tom's farm, but it was loud enough that it woke us up."

The defense attorney smiled thinly. "How did you know it was Reid Norton who was doing the shooting?"

Daniel's face flushed. "Oh, everybody knows Reid's always firing his guns, target practice, whatever, day or night."

"No further questions," the defense attorney said, turning toward the jury with a satisfied expression.

Alley stood up, her face impassive. "Mr. Sweet, you didn't actually see Reid with a gun that night, did you?"

"No," Daniel admitted.

"And your trailer is a considerable distance from Tom Farley's farm?"

"Yeah, but—"

"No more questions," Alley interrupted, her tone dismissive. She knew there was no point pressing further—Daniel's testimony had done little to sway the facts one way or another.

Next, the defense brought Melody Murdock back to the stand, hoping to shore up Daniel's claim. She took a deep breath as she was sworn in, her hands folded tightly in her lap.

"Mrs. Murdock," the defense attorney began, "you're familiar with the area around your home. On the night in question, did you hear gunshots?"

"Yes," Melody replied steadily. "I heard them clearly. And I called 911."

"So you can confirm that Mr. Sweet wasn't mistaken—there were gunshots?"

"Yes," she affirmed. "We live the same distance from Tom's farm as the Sweets."

"No further questions," the defense attorney said, clearly satisfied.

Alley rose, her expression calm but probing. "Mrs. Murdock, you heard the gunshots, but did you see Reid Norton firing them?"

"No," Melody admitted.

"So it could have been anyone, Lori Gunning, or even your own husband Lester . . ."

The defense lawyer shot to his feet. "Objection! Leading the witness!"

"Sustained."

"I have no further questions for this witness. Thank you, Mrs. Murdock," Alley said briskly, retaking her seat.

The defense continued their attack by calling Police Chief Sergio Alvares to the stand. His Brazilian accent was thick with nerves as he recounted various incidents involving Reid Norton over the years.

"Chief Alvares, how would you describe Mr. Norton's temper?" the defense attorney asked with an air of triumph.

"Hot," Sergio said, narrowing his eyes. "Like . . . very spicy pepper. He is a hot—"

"Hothead?" the attorney supplied.

"Yes, hothead," Sergio confirmed. "He can be a handful. Many calls. Many complaints. Trouble at Randy's bar, Drinks Like a Fish, trouble at the town pier, we even had to drag him out of a Bingo game after he accused a twelve-year-old kid of cheating, and he just went crazy."

"And has Mr. Norton ever been violent in these encounters?"

"Not really . . . no, I mean except for the incident with Tom Farley at the turkey shoot," Sergio said, a look of slight confusion crossing his face. "But he is always shouting and making noise."

The defense attorney pressed on, casting Reid as a volatile and dangerous man. He even highlighted the 911 call Melody had made, emphasizing the spent shells found on Tom's property. The defense's case seemed to be gaining traction, painting Reid as an angry man pushed to the edge.

Finally, it was time for the defense to call their surprise witness: Mona Barnes. Hayley's eyes widened in disbelief as she saw her friend stride confidently up to the stand. Mona had mentioned something about being subpoenaed, but Hayley had assumed she would not actually be called to testify, especially as a defense witness given her close relationship with Reid.

"Ms. Barnes," the defense attorney began, clearly expecting a favorable testimony, "you are a friend of Reid Norton's, is that correct?"

"Yup," Mona said bluntly, settling herself into the witness chair with a casual air.

"And you've witnessed his temper firsthand, haven't you?"

Mona's eyes twinkled with mischief. "Hoo boy, yes, old Reid's got a temper for sure," she said. The defense attorney's face brightened, sensing an opportunity. "But he's also one of the most loyal and kind-hearted people

I know," Mona added, her voice ringing out clear and strong. "Reid might yell and stomp around, but he'd never hurt a soul—especially not Tom Farley. He even rescued a neighbor's cat once that got stuck up in a tree."

The attorney's jaw dropped. "You're making that up."

Mona shook her head. "Nope. Edgar Allen Paw was up there nearly three hours. There was a car accident in the park and the police were occupied so Reid came along in his truck and climbed right up there to get him. Didn't even use a ladder. Just grabbed the lowest branch and hauled himself up. The cat panicked and scratched the hell out of Reid's hand," Mona chuckled. "Adelaide Smith was so grateful. You should ask her about it. She still tears up when she thinks about Reid saving her cat."

The attorney's mouth tightened, but Mona was not done. "You know what else? Reid's the first person to lend a hand when someone's in trouble. You ever see a man dive into icy water to save a drunk fisherman? I have. Reid Norton."

Hayley could see the defense attorney's irritation mounting. "Ms. Barnes," he said, struggling to regain control, "isn't it true that you described Reid's temper as dangerous during a pre-trial interview?"

Mona snorted. "Dangerous? Please. I said he had a temper, not that he was a killer. I bet half this courtroom has lost their temper over Tom Farley's ridiculous antics. Tom wasn't exactly Bar Harbor's favorite turkey."

A ripple of laughter spread through the jury box. Hayley caught a hint of a smile on Judge Parsons's lips before the gavel came down, calling for order. The defense attorney's face turned an interesting shade of red.

"Ms. Barnes, we're not here to entertain the court," he said sharply.

"Oh, I'm not trying to be funny," Mona replied innocently. "I'm just telling the truth. I'd think you'd want that."

Another chuckle escaped from the jury, and this time even the judge did not try to stop it.

"I believe you said *dangerous*," the attorney seethed.

"Did I? Well, I don't remember, but luckily when I talked to you I wasn't under oath like I am now, and now that I'm under oath, let me be perfectly clear. Reid Norton is not, and never was, a dangerous man."

The defense attorney, clearly flustered, quickly wrapped up his questioning and sat down, looking like he had just swallowed a lemon.

As Mona stepped down from the witness stand, she gave Hayley a quick, defiant wink. The tension that had gripped the courtroom lightened, if only for a moment. It was clear that, despite the defense's best efforts to paint Reid as the killer, Mona had done her part to undermine their strategy, and Hayley silently thanked her friend's quick wit and loyalty.

But the trial was not over yet. Hayley knew the defense still had more cards to play, and the next phase of the trial could be even more treacherous.

Chapter 39

Hayley Powell was wiping down the counters in Hayley's Kitchen when her phone buzzed with a message. She set down the damp cloth and picked up her cell, frowning as she read the short but urgent note from Lori Gunning.

Need to talk to you ASAP. It's important.

Hayley felt a flicker of curiosity. Lori, who rarely initiated contact, had been even more reclusive than usual since the disastrous reading of Tom Farley's will.

Hayley had convinced Lori to leave her house for that reading—her first time out in years—only to watch Lori's face crumble when she learned that Tom had left her nothing but his obnoxious, squawking turkeys. Hayley had felt guilty ever since. Lori had been devastated, retreating even further into her safe bubble at home.

Now, if she was reaching out, Hayley knew it had to be serious.

It did not take long for Hayley to close up the restaurant and head over to Lori's cottage. When she arrived, she took a deep breath before knocking, bracing herself. The door creaked open just enough for Hayley to catch sight of Lori's anxious face, pale and drawn.

"Thank you for coming," Lori said, opening the door wider to let Hayley inside. Her voice was shaky, and she looked as if she had not slept in days. They sat down in the cramped living room, and Hayley saw Lori's hands trembling as she poured them both a cup of chamomile tea.

"I've been keeping up with the trial," Lori began, her voice barely a whisper. "Everyone in town seems to be convinced that Reid did it. But they're wrong. Reid's innocent, and I have to set the record straight."

Hayley's brow furrowed. "What do you mean, Lori? What do you know?"

Lori took a deep breath, twisting her fingers together. "Reid and I . . . we've been seeing each other. Quietly, for a few months now. No one knows. We bonded over . . . well, both of us have our struggles. He's been kind to me, and I know he didn't kill Tom. He physically couldn't have. He has an injury from his military service—his shoulder. He can hold a gun, sure, but he can't lift his arms high enough to shove a grown man like Tom into a woodchipper."

Hayley's mind raced. "Have you told this to Alley Roberts? She needs to hear it if it could clear Reid."

"No. That's why I called you," Lori said, her voice

barely more than a croak. "I don't know how to reach her, and I'm scared . . . leaving my house after what happened with the will . . . I just can't."

Hayley reached across the table and took Lori's cold hand in hers. "I understand," she said gently. "I know that last time was hard. I never should have pushed you to go to that reading, and I'm sorry for what happened. But this is different. This could help Reid."

Lori's eyes filled with tears. "But what if it goes wrong again? What if they twist my words, or I make a mistake that could hurt Reid? I don't think I can handle another disaster, Hayley. I don't know if I can face those people."

"Listen to me, Lori," Hayley said, squeezing her hand. "I wouldn't ask if I didn't think it was important. Reid needs you. Lester's defense team are trying really hard to paint him as the killer. You know he's innocent, and right now, you might be the only one who can help him. It's worth it if he's special to you, isn't it?"

Lori looked down, silent for a long moment. Then, she nodded, her voice catching. "He is special to me. I just . . . I don't want to be the reason he's somehow down the line found guilty of a crime he didn't commit."

"You won't be," Hayley said firmly. "You'll be the reason he's cleared. I'll be with you every step of the way, just like before. And we'll make sure that this time, they can't hurt you."

Lori took a shuddering breath. "Okay," she said finally, her eyes meeting Hayley's. "Okay, I'll do it. I'll go. Just one more time."

The next morning, after a night of restless sleep and reassurance from Hayley, Lori emerged from her house, visibly shaking but determined. Hayley had spent hours helping her prepare, easing her anxieties, and walking her through what she might expect. They practiced what she would say, and how she could stay calm if things got difficult.

When they arrived at the courthouse, Lori hesitated on the steps, her face pale. "I can't," she gasped, starting to back away, but Hayley gently guided her forward, offering words of encouragement. "You've got this, Lori," she said. "Just one step at a time."

They walked through the metal detectors, Lori's face pasty and eyes wide with anxiety. Hayley kept a protective arm around Lori's shoulders as they made their way to the office of Assistant DA Alley Roberts.

When they reached the door, Hayley knocked, and Alley's assistant waved them in. Alley was sitting behind her desk, files spread out in front of her, but she looked up with interest when she saw Hayley. "What's this about?" she asked, curiosity mixing with suspicion.

"Alley, this is Lori Gunning," Hayley said, her tone serious. "She has information that could change everything about this case."

Alley's expression grew more intense as she leaned forward. "Is that so? What kind of information?"

Lori's hands were shaking, but she steadied herself. "It's about Reid Norton," she said quietly. "Everyone's saying he killed Tom, but he didn't. He couldn't have."

Alley's brow furrowed. "Why couldn't he have, Ms.

Gunning? The prosecution has already rested, and we've presented our case. I can't call new witnesses at this point."

Lori hesitated, and Hayley jumped in. "You have to listen, Alley. Lori and Reid have been seeing each other. She knows that Reid has a shoulder injury from his military service. He can't lift his arms high enough to throw a man like Tom Farley into that woodchipper. And I have a feeling that if you brought his doctor, Dr. Cormack, into court, he'd back her up."

Alley's eyes narrowed, calculating the potential impact of Lori's story. "This is all interesting, but it doesn't change the fact that the defense has already made their move. They've pinned their hopes on casting doubt on Reid, and like I said, it's too late for me to call any new witnesses."

Hayley bit her lip, her mind racing. Then, an idea struck her—a bold, risky move that just might work. "What if . . . what if you take a page from the Mona Barnes playbook?"

Alley cocked an eyebrow. "What are you talking about?"

"What if they were the ones who called Lori to the stand?"

Alley looked confused. "They would never do it, not in a million years, especially if Lori has exculpatory evidence that proves Reid's innocence."

"Yes, but what if we make them think the opposite, that Lori has dirt on Reid," Hayley said, a smile forming. "We tell them she has something that could ruin Reid's chances, something so damaging that they'll have no choice but to put her on the stand themselves. And we add a little detail about Reid's doctor giving him a clean bill of health at his last physical, just to make them think they've got this nailed."

Alley's eyes widened as the plan sank in. "You want to manipulate them into calling a witness who will actually clear Reid? That's . . . insane. But if it works, they won't be able to backtrack, and I'll have the chance to bring Dr. Cormack in to confirm Lori's story."

"Exactly," Hayley said, determination flashing in her eyes." They'll have no choice but to go through with it. And once they realize the truth, it'll be too late."

Alley leaned back in her chair, a slow smile spreading across her face. "I have to admit, it's a good play. I'll let you handle it. If they put her on the stand, I won't object—even if Lori's not on the witness list. And I'll make sure Dr. Cormack is on stand-by."

Hayley nodded, feeling a surge of excitement. She turned to Lori. "We can do this. I just need you to play along. You're going to be brilliant."

Hours later, Hayley sat in the bustling courthouse café with Bruce, waiting for Lester Murdock to show up. They had chosen a table near the back, hoping for just the right amount of privacy for their performance. When Lester arrived, clearly agitated from the day's trial, Hayley made sure to speak just loudly enough for him to overhear.

"I can't believe what Lori Gunning found out about

Reid," she said to Bruce, pretending to be engrossed in her coffee. "His doctor just gave him a clean bill of health, but this changes everything."

Bruce played his part perfectly, leaning back and crossing his arms with a skeptical look. "Do you think it's enough to sink Reid?"

"Definitely," Hayley said with confidence. "She's got evidence that could bury him. She came forward to tell Alley what she knew, and Alley swore her to secrecy and said not to say a word to anyone. If the defense got wind of what she knows . . . Oh, boy. Lester would get off scot-free in a heartbeat. Let's just be grateful they don't know any of this."

Hayley winked at her husband who suppressed a smirk.

Lester was pretending to ignore them, his face a mask of indifference, but Hayley caught the way his eyes narrowed at their words.

He was hooked.

Sure enough, it did not take long. The next day, when court was back in session, there was a murmur of surprise as the defense attorney announced a new, unplanned witness—Lori Gunning.

Alley Roberts barely blinked, making no objection. Hayley felt a thrill of triumph as Lori cautiously made her way to the stand, clearly nervous but holding her ground.

The young lead defense attorney, looking pleased with himself, began his questioning. "Ms. Gunning, thank you for coming forward today. I understand you have some information about Reid Norton?"

Lori swallowed hard, glancing at Hayley for reassurance.

Hayley gave her a small nod, and Lori took a deep breath.

"Yes," she said, her voice steady. "I do. I want to clear Reid's name because he didn't kill Tom Farley. He physically couldn't have."

The defense attorney's expression flickered with confusion. "What do you mean, Ms. Gunning?"

"Reid has a serious shoulder injury from his time in the military," Lori said, her voice gaining strength. "He can't lift his arms above shoulder height without significant pain. There's no way he could have done what you're trying to accuse him of. I've seen him struggle with the simplest tasks."

The attorney's confident demeanor faltered. He shot a panicked look at Lester Murdock, who was sitting rigidly in his seat, his eyes narrowing. "Ms. Gunning," the attorney said, clearly flustered, "are you aware that Reid's doctor recently gave him a clean bill of health?"

Lori's chin lifted. "If you're referring to Dr. Cormack, I think you should ask him about Reid's injury. He knows exactly what Reid's limitations are."

The courtroom was silent as the defense attorney tried to regain his footing. "Very well," he said tersely. "We'll bring Dr. Cormack in to clarify this."

Alley Roberts moved quickly. "Your Honor, if the defense wishes to call Dr. Cormack, I have no objection."

The judge nodded. "Okay, then. Let's bring in the doctor."

Minutes later, Dr. Cormack was escorted in, clearly annoyed at the abrupt summons. He took the stand, looking directly at the defense attorney.

"Dr. Cormack," the defense attorney began, "could you confirm whether or not Reid Norton's shoulder injury prevents him from performing certain physical tasks?"

"Yes, it absolutely does," Dr. Cormack replied without hesitation. "Reid has a permanent shoulder limitation that severely restricts his range of motion. There's no way he could perform an action like lifting and throwing a heavy object—certainly not something as large as a person."

The defense attorney's face drained of color. He had been played. Hayley watched with satisfaction as the realization spread across his features. Alley's trap had worked, and the defense had unwittingly provided the proof of Reid's innocence.

Lori was quickly dismissed, and Hayley rushed to meet her as she stepped down. "You did it," Hayley whispered, hugging her tightly. "You did exactly what needed to be done."

Lori nodded, her expression a mix of relief and exhaustion. "I just hope it's enough."

As they left the courtroom, the defense team's stunned expressions told Hayley that their last-minute gamble had worked. They had made their move, and now, the truth was out there—Reid Norton was innocent, and Lester Murdock's carefully orchestrated defense was unraveling before everyone's eyes.

Chapter 40

Hayley and Bruce left Hancock County Superior Court in Ellsworth, both excited and uneasy. Lori Gunning's testimony had thrown a wrench into the trial, but they both knew that Lester Murdock's defense team would come back with something new—anything to shift suspicion away from their client.

The midday sun was warm on their faces, and they decided to grab a quick lunch at a local diner on State Street before court resumed.

As they pushed open the door of Rosie's Diner, the familiar clang of the bell over the entrance greeted them. The place was packed with locals and out-of-towners, all of whom seemed to be chattering about the trial.

Hayley and Bruce slid into a booth near the window, glad to escape the intensity of the courtroom for a moment.

Lee Hollis

The smell of sizzling burgers and fresh coffee filled the air, and Hayley waved to Kelly Stevens, an old friend from high school who was working as a waitress. Kelly gave her a bright smile and held up a finger to signal she would be over in a minute.

Hayley's eyes wandered around the room, and she caught sight of Emily, Tom Farley's young niece, sitting in a back booth. She looked tense, her face flushed with anger as she argued with a young man across from her. Bruce followed her gaze. "Who's got your attention?"

"Emily, Tom's niece." Hayley said with a fixed stare.

"She's over there with her boyfriend JD. She looks pretty upset about something."

Emily's hands gesticulated as her voice rose in anger. JD quickly reached over and grabbed them, holding them in place and hissing something from across the table.

"Looks pretty heated," Hayley noted, as JD now tried bringing the temperature down by kissing Emily's hand. It was not working. She angrily wrenched her hand free. "She's mad as hell at him for something."

Before Bruce could reply, Kelly appeared at their table, order pad in hand. "Hey, Hayley! Bruce! Haven't seen you two in here in ages. What can I get you?"

"Just two coffees and whatever the lunch special is," Hayley said, her curiosity getting the better of her. "Say, Kelly, what's going on at that booth in the back? We know those two. Tom Farley's niece and her boyfriend? They look like they're about to come to blows."

Kelly glanced over her shoulder, lowering her voice conspiratorially. "Oh, you noticed, huh? I was wiping down the booth across from them when they came in. They've been at it for about fifteen minutes. From what I could overhear, Emily's accusing JD of fooling around with some other girl, and he's denying it like his life depends on it."

"Did you catch any names?" Hayley asked, leaning forward.

"Yeah," Kelly said, sliding into the seat across from Hayley forcing Bruce to move over to the corner. "Emily kept throwing the name 'Becca' at him. Said something about finding texts and that JD had been sneaking off to meet her all summer."

A chill ran down Hayley's spine.

Becca.

The name was familiar—too familiar.

Her daughter Gemma had a friend named Becca from high school, a girl who still worked in town.

"Becca? Did she say anything else?"

Kelly shook her head. "No, just that Emily's pretty sure JD was messing around with this Becca girl behind her back, and he was swearing up and down that it wasn't true. But in my experience, he's a man, so yeah, it's probably true. No offense, Bruce."

Bruce raised his hands. "Believe me, none taken."

Hayley exchanged a look with her husband. "Thanks, Kelly," she said, throwing a few bills on the table for the coffee they had not even had yet. "We'll be back for lunch another time."

Kelly's eyes widened in surprise. "Leaving already?"

"Yeah, I've got to follow up on something," Hayley said, grabbing her purse. She gave Bruce a meaningful nod, and he slid out of the booth after Kelly stood up, following his wife out the door.

The drive from Ellsworth to Bar Harbor took about twenty minutes, and Hayley's thoughts raced as she pulled into a parking space near Sherman's Bookstore, where she knew Becca had been working since last year. She and Bruce entered the cozy little shop, and Hayley spotted Becca right away, restocking a shelf near the back.

"Becca!" Hayley called out, walking briskly toward her.

The young woman looked up, her face brightening before clouding with uncertainty when she saw the serious expression on Hayley's face.

"Hey, Mrs. Powell," Becca said, nervously tucking a strand of hair behind her ear.

"You're an adult now Becca, you can call me Hayley."

"Okay, Hayley. Wow, that feels weird. Anyway, what's up?"

"I need to ask you something important," Hayley said. "It's about JD."

Becca's face paled. "JD?" She swallowed hard, her voice barely a whisper. "I—I don't know what you mean."

Hayley's voice softened, sensing the girl's discomfort. "Becca, I heard from a friend that JD was spending time with you last summer here in town while he was still with his girlfriend Emily. Is that true?"

Becca hesitated, glancing at Bruce who stood a few steps back, his arms crossed, a concerned expression on his face.

Finally, Becca let out a shaky sigh. "Yes," she admitted. "I didn't know about Emily when I first met him. He told me he was single, and we started hanging out. I didn't find out he had a girlfriend until later, and by then . . ." She trailed off, her eyes welling with tears. "By then, I was already . . . well, it was complicated. But I immediately broke it off when I found out. I swear."

Hayley's mind was spinning. "Where did you meet him?"

"He was working as a waiter at the Jordan Pond House last summer," Becca said. "We hit it off, and he kept coming by the bookstore to see me whenever he could. We'd spend our days off together."

Hayley felt her heart skip a beat. "But Emily told everyone that she'd only come to Bar Harbor once, to meet her uncle Tom for the first—and last—time. You're telling me JD was here before she ever mentioned her uncle?"

Becca nodded, wiping away a tear. "Yes. He knew the town pretty well, and he seemed really interested when I told him about all the Tom Farley drama with his land and everything. At the time, I thought it was just out of curiosity."

Hayley felt the pieces clicking into place, her instincts screaming that JD was not as innocent as he seemed. "Becca, do you have any idea why JD might have been so interested in Tom?"

Becca shook her head, confused. "No, but after Emily came into the picture, JD seemed to change. He got serious, and he started talking about a future together, about money and stability. I thought he meant us, but I was wrong. He quickly lost interest, and pretty soon I got the message. He had found someone better. Someone with money."

"Or someone who was about to come into some money," Hayley noted.

Hayley exchanged a glance with Bruce, who nodded subtly, sharing her suspicion. JD might have seen Emily as a ticket to something bigger, something that might involve Tom's potential inheritance. The motives were lining up like a row of ducks.

Back at the courthouse in Ellsworth, Hayley's mind was racing as she and Bruce walked back into the courtroom just before the afternoon session began. She had her phone out, furiously texting Alley Roberts about what she had learned. But Alley's one word response to Hayley's text spoke volumes.

Interesting.

She was in the middle of proving beyond a reasonable doubt that Lester Murdock was guilty of murdering Tom Farley. She was focused on a win. The last thing she wanted to hear was an alternative theory about the case. She wanted to nail Murdock for the crime.

JD knew Bar Harbor before Emily ever mentioned Tom Farley, Hayley typed. **He might have known about a possible inheritance. Could he have had his eye on it all along?**

As they took their seats, Alley shot her a quick glance, her brow furrowed with thought. It was too soon to say if they had enough to shift suspicion toward JD, so she was going to continue pressing her case in closing arguments when the defense rested.

Hayley, on the other hand, knew one thing for sure—they had a brand-new suspect, and JD's carefully crafted façade was starting to crack.

Throughout the afternoon, Hayley's eyes never left the defense table. Lester Murdock's unease was almost palpable, but now her attention had shifted to the back of the courtroom, where Emily and JD sat side by side. Emily's face was blank, her eyes fixed on the proceedings, but JD's eyes darted around the room, never settling on any one thing for too long.

Why were they even here?

Did they just want to see Lester Murdock go down?

Hayley's instincts told her that JD was hiding something—and that whatever it was, it was enough to drag him into the web of suspicion that surrounded Tom Farley's death. She just had to figure out how to untangle it before someone else got away with murder.

Chapter 41

As the courtroom recessed, Hayley slipped out, leaving Bruce behind to write a summary of today's events for his column. The latest twist in Tom Farley's murder case had her mind racing. The courtroom drama was heating up, but Hayley's instincts told her there was something more to JD's involvement. She needed to dig deeper into his past, so she pulled out her phone and called her old friend Stacy, the manager of the Jordan Pond House, who was now taking some time off since the restaurant had closed for the season.

The phone barely rang once before Stacy answered. "Hayley! Long time no see. What's up?"

"Hey, Stacy," Hayley said, trying to sound casual. "I need a favor. It's about a former employee of yours— JD. Remember him?"

Stacy snorted. "Oh, do I ever. That guy was a disaster. Charming, sure, but never met a rule he couldn't break or a shift he couldn't mess up. Honestly, I was thrilled when he quit. He was the type who made you wonder what kind of trouble he was getting into when he wasn't here."

Hayley felt a surge in her chest. "Did he have any close friends while he was working there? Someone who might know what he's been up to lately?"

"Yeah, there was this guy, Doug. They hung out a lot, always seemed to be up to something. Let me get you his number," Stacy said, sounding eager to help. Hayley scribbled down the number, thanked Stacy, and hung up.

Hayley dialed Doug's number as soon as she was back in her car, parked just outside the courthouse. The phone rang a few times before a gruff male voice answered.

"Doug speaking," he said.

"Hi, Doug, this is Hayley Powell," she said, explaining how she got his number from Stacy and dropping in that she was a local columnist. "I'm trying to get some information on your pal JD. I heard he was back in Bar Harbor recently."

Doug was silent for a moment before he spoke. "Yeah, JD came to town not too long ago. Crashed at my place."

"You mean the night before all that stuff happened with Tom Farley at his farm?"

There was a long pause on the other end of the line.

"Maybe, I don't know."

"When he was here, were you two together the whole time?"

"Pretty much." Another pause. "Wait, I remember I had a shift that morning. JD was still sleeping on the couch when I left. He was there when I got back around two, two-thirty."

Which was after the time someone pushed Tom into the woodchipper.

Hayley took a deep breath, choosing her words carefully. "I heard he was still seeing a girl named Becca back then."

Doug hesitated. "Yeah, he was. He never really stopped seeing her. He'd talk about her a lot, even when he and Emily first got together. He was always a smooth talker, making promises to both of them, I guess. What can I say, he's a popular guy with the ladies."

Hayley's heart sank. This confirmed it—JD had been two-timing Emily, stringing her along while still seeing Becca. This information added a whole new dimension to JD's motive. She thanked Doug, hung up, and pointed her car toward Tom Farley's farm.

It was time to confront JD and Emily.

Pulling up to the farmhouse, Hayley spotted Emily out in the distance, surrounded by a noisy flock of turkeys. They clucked and flapped their wings as Emily scattered feed from a rusted metal bucket. Hayley stepped out of her car and walked toward the house, where she saw JD sitting on the porch, nursing a can of beer.

"Hey," JD said, forcing a smile. "What brings you out here again?"

"I needed to clear up some things," she said evenly. "Where were you the day Tom died?"

"Why ask me?"

"I heard you have a history here in Bar Harbor that I didn't know about. You were a waiter last summer at the Jordan Pond House. You dated Becca who works at Sherman's Bookstore . . ."

JD suddenly sat up in a defensive posture. "So what?"

Then Hayley dropped the bomb. "I also heard you were in town on the day Tom Farley was killed."

JD's eyes flickered with panic momentarily, but then he quickly regained his composure. "I could've been. I came up here to hang out with my buddy Doug at some point. Can't remember an exact date."

"When you were here, did you spend the whole day with Doug?"

JD shrugged, not meeting her eyes. "Yeah, we hung out playing video games."

"Interesting. Because according to Doug, he had a shift that morning," Hayley said, crossing her arms. "Which means you were alone, with no one to back up your story."

JD's face reddened. "I don't have to explain myself to you."

"Not to me you don't. Chief Alvares is a different story."

Emily appeared from behind the barn, wiping her hands on her jeans. "What's going on?" she asked, her brow furrowed.

Hayley's heart pounded.

This was the moment.

"JD's been lying to you, Emily," she said gently. "He told you about dating a girl named Becca, right?"

Emily nodded. "Yes. He was honest about his past relationships."

"Well," Hayley said, her voice soft but firm, "he wasn't honest about when it ended. His friend Doug told me he was still seeing Becca when the two of you got together. JD's been playing you this whole time."

Emily's face went pale. She turned to JD, her eyes brimming with betrayal. "Is this true?" she demanded.

"Emily, it's not like that," JD said, panic flashing across his face. "It didn't mean anything with Becca. You're the one I care about. You're the one I want to be with."

Hayley crossed her arms. "Don't take my word for it. Talk to Doug. Talk to Becca. I can give you their numbers. They'll both confirm it."

"Don't listen to her, baby," JD pleaded. "She doesn't know what she's talking about!"

But Emily was already shaking her head, tears streaming down her face. Her gut was telling her that Hayley was not the one making up stories here. "You lied to me," she said, her voice cracking. "You were supposed to be different, but you're just like everyone else."

Before JD could respond, Emily turned and fled into the farmhouse, slamming the door behind her. Hayley watched her go, feeling a pang of sympathy for the young woman.

JD's expression darkened as he whipped his head back to Hayley. "Why are you so out to get me?" he hissed, his hands trembling with anger. "I didn't kill Tom, and now you've ruined everything with Emily."

"Then prove it," Hayley said calmly. "If you're innocent, you have nothing to worry about. But if you've been hiding something, it's going to come out sooner or later."

Without another word, she marched back toward her car, leaving JD standing on the porch, his face contorted with rage and frustration. Just as Hayley reached the driveway, she heard the farmhouse door creak open, and Emily's voice called out.

"Hayley, wait!" Emily hurried down the steps, past a stricken JD, her face streaked with tears but her eyes resolute. When she reached Hayley, she lowered her voice so JD could not hear. "I'm done with him. I don't need JD, and I don't need any of this mess. I'm selling Tom's farm. I want out."

Hayley paused, surprised by the sudden shift in Emily's tone. "What are you thinking?" she asked gently.

"I'm going to talk to a realtor," Emily said, determination replacing the sorrow in her expression. "I want to get a good price for the farm, sell it to Acadia Resorts, and leave Bar Harbor behind. Start over as a single woman . . . a *rich* single woman."

A smile tugged at Hayley's lips. "If you're serious about selling, I have the perfect realtor for you. My friend Liddy is the best in town. She'll make sure you get a fortune for this place."

Emily's eyes brightened a little. "Liddy? Yeah, I've heard of her. I think I'll give her a call."

"She'll take care of you," Hayley assured her. "You already have a very motivated buyer with Acadia Resorts. You'll get top dollar. You can get a fresh start, away from all of this."

Emily nodded, wiping away the last of her tears. "Thank you, Hayley. For everything."

"You're making the right choice," Hayley said, squeezing Emily's arm. "You deserve better than what JD was offering."

With one last look at JD, who was still fuming on the porch, Emily turned and went back inside the farmhouse, her posture more determined than before. Hayley's heart swelled with a mix of relief and hope for Emily's future.

Hayley's next stop was Sherman's bookstore on Main Street. She needed to update Becca about the confrontation with JD, and maybe get more information about his strange behavior. The bell above the door jingled as she stepped inside, and Becca looked up from behind the counter, curious but concerned.

"Hey, Hayley," Becca said, setting down a stack of books. "You look like you've got some news."

"Oh, I do," Hayley said, leaning against the counter. She quickly filled Becca in on her conversation with Doug and the confrontation with JD at the farm. Becca listened in stunned silence, her eyes widening as the story unfolded.

"So . . . he was still seeing me when he was with her?" Becca asked, her voice barely above a whisper. "I knew it."

"Emily dumped him as soon as she found out. He's lost his grip on her now, and he's desperate."

Becca's expression hardened, and she shook her head. "I can't believe I was such an idiot. He always had an excuse, always made me feel like I was the only one. And all this time, he was just using both of us."

At that moment, the bell over the door jingled again. Hayley and Becca both looked up to see JD storming into the bookstore, his face a mask of raw anger. His eyes locked onto Becca, and he seemed oblivious to Hayley standing nearby.

"Becca, please, I need to talk to you," JD pleaded, his voice breaking. "I know I messed up, but I don't have anyone else right now. Emily's gone, and I don't know what to do."

Becca's face remained impassive. "We're done, JD. Whatever you're going through now, you brought it on yourself. I don't want to hear any more of your lies."

JD took a step forward, his voice desperate. "Please, Becca, you don't understand—"

"No," she said sharply. "I understand perfectly. You're a chronic liar, and I'm done with you. Now, get out."

JD's face twisted with hurt and frustration. It was inexplicable to him that he had been dumped now twice.

In the same day.

He looked like he might say something more, but then he noticed Hayley standing off to the side behind Becca, watching the scene unfold with a keen, unflinching gaze. His eyes narrowed, and his mouth curled into a bitter smile.

"You're loving this, aren't you?" he said to Hayley, his voice dripping with venom. "Playing detective, screwing up my life. But I'm telling you—I didn't kill Tom. And if you keep digging, you're going to regret it."

"Then stop giving me reasons to suspect you," Hayley said coolly.

JD turned on his heel and stormed out of the bookstore, slamming the door behind him so hard that the bell rattled on its hook.

Becca let out a long, shaky breath, and Hayley placed a reassuring hand on her shoulder.

"Are you okay?" Hayley asked.

Becca nodded, though her eyes were glassy with unshed tears. "Yeah, I'm fine. Just . . . thank you, Hayley. For helping me see the truth."

"It's not over yet," Hayley said, a new resolve hardening in her chest. "But one thing's for sure—JD's running scared. If he's hiding something, we're going to find out what it is."

Chapter 42

Hayley tucked her coat around her shoulders as she made her way toward the courthouse steps the following afternoon. She was supposed to meet Bruce inside and watch more of Lester Murdock's trial for his alleged involvement in Tom Farley's death, though the case seemed murky at best at this point.

The recent investigation into JD had not led her any closer to finding Tom's killer, except that he lacked a solid alibi, but at least she felt relieved that Emily had dodged a bullet by dumping him.

As she approached the heavy wooden doors, her phone buzzed. She glanced down and saw a text from an unknown number:

I know what happened to Tom Farley.

A surge of curiosity swept over her, and she quickly typed back, **Who is this?**

The reply came almost instantly: **I heard you investigate stuff, and I don't want to go to the police.**

She hesitated, wondering who could be reaching out like this and why they were so hesitant to speak with law enforcement.

Where can we meet? she typed.

Town pier. In one hour.

After letting Bruce know she would be late via text, Hayley headed straight back to Bar Harbor and to the pier, the November air cold and damp. The scent of salt water mixed with the earthier smells of the wharf, where local fishermen were busy securing their boats after a day of lobstering and striper fishing. The clatter of traps, heavy with seaweed, echoed as the men stacked them on the pier, their hands moving with practiced ease. Lanterns hung from the boats, casting faint halos of light in the late afternoon gloom.

Hayley pulled her coat tighter around her shoulders, scanning the pier until she spotted Eben, a familiar face she had seen raiding Mona's snack cabinet on more than one occasion. Eben was a buddy of one of Mona's grandsons, there were so many she could hardly remember which one. But this kid, Eben, she had gotten to know him a little bit, and he was a boy with a reputation for being clever—and occasionally mischievous. Now, he looked out of place standing by himself, hands jammed into his pockets, gaze fixed on the ground.

"Hey, Eben," she greeted him gently, hoping to put him at ease.

He shifted nervously, glancing up. "Thanks for coming," he mumbled, his voice low. "I didn't want anyone else to know . . . especially not the police. My older brother has had enough trouble with the cops lately."

Hayley had heard about Eben's older brother Curtis, a rough around the edges troublemaker, who had been caught selling drugs recently.

Eben and Curtis had lost their parents six years ago in a tragic car crash in Tremont. Some drunken teenagers hit them head on. Their older sister had been doing her best to raise them, but Curtis had been a struggle, holding in a lot of rage, acting out, rebelling. Eben was easier to handle, but Hayley could not imagine the challenges their older sister who chose to look after them had to be going through.

"Why don't you tell me what's going on?" Hayley asked, keeping her tone light.

Eben took a deep breath, looking both guilty and embarrassed. "I, uh, skipped school the day Tom Farley died. My sister—she's been taking care of me and my brother since our parents passed, and . . . well, we don't have a lot of money. So, I thought maybe I could grab a turkey from Tom's place, you know, surprise her for Thanksgiving."

Hayley resisted the urge to smile at the innocence of his plan. "And?"

"Well, I was hiding by the trees near Tom's barn, just waiting for a chance to sneak in, when someone else showed up. I didn't mean to film it, but I had my phone out. Thought I'd record it, just in case." He rubbed the back of his neck, looking anywhere but at her. "Then, the next day, the Butlers—Bubba and Jane—they took Mona's kids and grandkids to Disney World, and they invited me to go, too."

"That must have been very exciting," Hayley said softly.

"It sure was. I've never been out of the state of Maine before. The plane ride was awesome and man, all those rides at Disney World, Space Mountain was sick!"

"I'm happy you had a good time."

"The Butlers are so nice. They paid for everything. That's the only reason I got to go."

So did you show anyone the video, your brother Curtis, your sister?"

"No, no one! If my sister found out I played hooky from school, she would've hit the roof! She keeps at me to finish high school, says it'll be easier to get a job."

"You should listen to your sister," Hayley said firmly. "Now about the video—?"

"I didn't even watch it until I got back from the trip. When I heard about Mr. Farley's murder, it's all anyone was talking about, I didn't dare come forward because I was so worried about getting into trouble, but then that rich guy got arrested and it looked like he might go to prison. He didn't do it, Mrs. Powell. He's an innocent man. I knew I had to say something to someone so . . . here." He handed her his phone, his hands shaking.

Hayley took the phone, scrolling through to find the video. The shaky footage came into focus, revealing Tom Farley's barn and the edge of the field, turkeys clucking about. Tom paced back and forth in front of the barn, looking agitated, and just beyond him was the hulking shape of the woodchipper rumbling in the distance.

Hayley's stomach turned as she thought about what had eventually happened to him.

She adjusted the screen's brightness, peering at the scene. Tom was speaking to someone just out of frame, someone who slowly stepped forward until his profile became visible. The figure was young, with a familiar way of standing, though his cap was pulled low.

As Tom spoke, Hayley felt her pulse quicken. The camera caught the young man's face in profile, and Hayley let out a soft gasp.

She recognized him immediately.

Tom's words were lost in the wind, but the two men seemed locked in some kind of intense exchange, and Hayley's heart pounded as she took in every detail.

In the background, the woodchipper loomed, a silent, ominous presence. She forced herself to keep watching, bracing herself for what might happen next.

Chapter 43

The Murdock trial at Hancock County Superior Court had wrapped up for the day so Hayley suspected the family would be home.

The sun had dipped behind a cluster of bare trees, casting long shadows across the uneven ground, and the silence felt heavy, broken only by the crunch of Hayley's boots against the gravel.

As Hayley approached, she could not help but note how big the house appeared. She knew that the Murdocks were planning to upgrade to an even grander estate by the sea in Northeast Harbor—a lavish piece of property they had set their sights on, that real estate maven Liddy Crawford had found for them. The whole town was aware of the impending sale, which further fueled suspicions about Lester Murdock's guilt. His blind ambition to be the most successful man in town, to trumpet such a show palace for everyone to admire and envy, had driven him to sell this huge house for one twice as big.

The door opened before she even had a chance to knock. Lester Murdock stood there, shotgun in hand, his piercing eyes cold with suspicion, his face twisted into a scowl. "What the hell do you want, Powell?" Lester barked. "Haven't you done enough damage to my family?"

He pointed the barrel of the shotgun toward the ground but still held it firmly in his grip.

"I need to talk to your son," Hayley said calmly.

Lester suddenly cocked his shotgun. "Over my dead body."

Before Hayley could respond, Melody Murdock appeared in the doorway behind him, her shoulders straight, eyes clear. She looked sober for once, and despite the tension in her expression, there was a calm determination there that Hayley had not seen before.

Melody's voice was surprisingly firm. "Let her in, Lester."

Lester looked at his wife in surprise, the corner of his mouth twitching in annoyance. "You're not seriously going to allow her in this house, are you? This isn't any of her damn business."

"It's all of our business now, Lester." Melody's eyes flicked over to Hayley, and she stepped back, gesturing her inside.

Grumbling under his breath, Lester reluctantly leaned the shotgun against the wall and stepped aside, his eyes never leaving Hayley as she stepped into the foyer. The tension in the room was palpable, and she could feel Lester's anger simmering just beneath the surface, but Melody's presence softened the edge of hostility.

Hayley turned to Melody, who looked at her with weary curiosity.

"This will just take a few minutes, I assure you," Hayley promised, one eye on the shotgun leaning against the wall in the entry hall.

"Is Alan home?" Melody turned and asked Lester, her voice strained.

"No, I sent him on some errands," Lester grumbled before turning and spitting out at Hayley, "He won't be back until after dark, so you wasted a trip out here."

Hayley shook her head. "Actually, I'm here to talk to your other son—Bo."

Lester's eyes narrowed, his jaw tightening. "What do you want with Bo? He's got nothing to do with any of this."

Melody's face shifted, worry flickering in her eyes as she glanced over at her husband. Bo was their golden child, the one who could do no wrong in their eyes. Hayley could sense the unspoken anxiety between them. They were wondering what evidence she had brought with her.

In the corner, Bo watched quietly, his shoulders tense, his gaze uncertain. Hayley walked over, her movements slow, giving him space to prepare himself.

"Bo," she said softly, "I think you know why I'm here."

Bo hesitated, his gaze dropping to the floor. "I don't . . . I don't know what you're talking about," he muttered, avoiding her eyes.

Hayley met his evasion with calm, pulling out her phone. "I think you do," she replied, then pressed play on the video Eben had handed over.

Bo's face paled as he watched the screen. His parents maneuvered their way behind him so they could see the video on the phone. There Bo was, standing near Tom Farley on the property, the two of them talking quietly as Tom leaned against his barn, looking weary. The rumbling woodchipper loomed ominously in the background, a detail that sent a chill through the room. Bo's hands clenched into fists as he watched the scene play out. Suddenly Bo could not watch anymore. He handed the phone back to Hayley who turned off the video but kept her phone ready in her hand.

Lester stepped forward, his voice a low growl. "Enough of this. Bo, don't say a damn word until I get our lawyer. You don't need to say anything."

But Bo raised his hand, cutting his father off, a look of defiance crossing his face. "I'm tired of keeping secrets, Dad," he said, his voice quivering with both frustration and relief. "Maybe if you'd been honest with people, we wouldn't be in this mess."

Lester's mouth tightened, but Bo ignored him, turning his attention back to Hayley. "I didn't tell anyone I was there because . . . well, I didn't want people thinking I had anything to do with it," he admitted. "I didn't want to be a suspect."

Hayley's gaze softened. "Then tell me what happened."

Bo took a deep breath, gathering his thoughts.

Hayley nodded encouragingly. "What were you doing there, Bo?"

He sighed and rubbed his temples. "I was trying to talk to Tom about Alan . . . about the trouble he'd gotten into after the shooting." He paused, swallowing hard. "Alan's not a bad guy, but . . . he's always trying to prove himself to Dad, and that means he doesn't always think things through. He went after Tom that day at the turkey shoot because . . . well, because Dad pushed him into it." His gaze slid over to his father, who stood rigid, fury smoldering in his eyes.

Lester snorted. "Don't put this on me, boy. Alan made his own choices."

"Maybe," Bo replied, his voice steady, "but you made it clear what you wanted him to do."

Lester's face twisted in anger, but Bo ignored him, turning his attention back to Hayley. "Anyway, after Alan shot Tom at the turkey shoot, he was . . . pretty shaken up. He's hot-headed but not a bad guy. Alan felt guilty, and he knew he had made a rash decision that could ruin his whole life trying to get on Dad's good side. So I thought maybe I could convince Tom to let him off the hook, maybe get him to drop any charges. I went over there, hoping that if I could just talk to him, maybe he'd come around."

Hayley leaned forward, listening intently. "And did he?"

Bo's face softened a little, and he nodded. "Yeah, actually, he did. At first, he was angry, understandably so. But after I explained, I guess he could tell I wasn't there to threaten him or anything. I just wanted to talk. Tom was drinking, and he looked . . . sad, honestly. I think he'd had a rough time with everyone around here wanting him to sell the farm, the whole community against him."

Bo paused, his eyes growing distant as he remembered. "I told him Alan was sorry, and he didn't want any trouble. And Tom kind of . . . well, he kind of relaxed. I think he was just tired of fighting everyone. He said he'd think about it, even told me to tell Alan he'd try and work something out." He looked at Hayley, his expression somber. "And that's when I left."

A heavy silence settled over the room, and Hayley could feel the weight of Bo's words.

Bo looked back at Hayley, his expression somber. "When I left, Tom was alive. He was fine. That's the truth." He turned to his parents. "You gotta believe me."

Melody walked over and hugged her son.

Lester stood silently, his mind reeling over this latest development. If Bo's story was true, then he had left Tom safe and sound—yet not long after, Tom had somehow ended up in the woodchipper.

Lester's expression softened, confusion clouding his face. "So . . . if Bo didn't kill him, then who the hell did?"

Without a word, Hayley lifted her phone, pressed play on the video, and handed it to Lester, letting the footage speak for itself. As he stared at the screen, the room held its breath, the answer lingering just beyond their reach.

Chapter 44

The courthouse echoed with the soft click of Hayley's heels as she strode through the dim, polished halls. Lester Murdock and his family trailed behind her, their expressions full of suspicion, hope, and exhaustion. Bo walked with his head down, avoiding his father's eyes, while Melody clutched her purse tightly, glancing between her son and Hayley. The events of the last twenty-four hours had left them all raw and weary, but Hayley was determined to see this through to the end.

She reached the judge's chambers and knocked firmly on the oak door. A few moments later, Judge Parsons's clerk opened it, regarding them all with a raised brow. "Yes?"

"We need a private audience with the judge," Hayley said, her voice steady. "It's about the death of Tom Farley. There's new evidence."

The clerk sized them up, her gaze lingering on Lester, and after a moment, she nodded. "Stay close by. I'll inform Judge Parsons."

After tracking down the judge who had a briefing on another case, there was a half hour delay before the prosecution and defense teams could be called and the judge was ready to receive them in her chambers. The clerk finally reappeared, waving for them all to come in. Hayley led the way into the judge's office, the Murdocks filing in behind her. ADA Alley Roberts and the defense attorneys were already there, their expressions sharpening with interest and skepticism as the group entered. Alley looked particularly displeased, her gaze narrowing as it settled on Hayley.

"Ms. Powell," the judge said, adjusting her reading glasses. "You've requested this meeting, so I trust it's important."

"It is, Your Honor." Hayley nodded, holding up her phone. "I have evidence that proves no one murdered Tom Farley. What happened to him was . . . an accident."

Alley raised an eyebrow. "An accident? That seems a bit convenient, doesn't it, given the circumstances?"

"Convenient or not, it's the truth," Hayley said, tapping her phone screen. "This video, recorded by a young witness on Tom's property the day he died, shows what really happened."

She pressed play, holding her phone up so everyone could see the screen. The video picked up just after Bo Murdock had left the property. Silence fell over the room as the video started, grainy and shaky but clear enough to make out Tom Farley, stumbling around his farm, a half-empty bottle in hand. His face was drawn, his movements slow, almost despondent.

In the video, Tom was muttering to himself as he wandered over to the woodchipper, oblivious to the watchful eyes of the turkeys clustered around him. They milled about, clucking and strutting, and as Tom stepped forward, one of them darted in front of him. He staggered and kicked at it, frustration flickering across his face.

"Get out of here!" Tom's slurred voice came through the audio, and he aimed another half-hearted kick at a bird that flapped away indignantly. His anger mounted as more turkeys pecked around him, their presence aggravating him further. He grabbed one of the turkeys by the wing, holding it up as it squawked and struggled in his grasp.

"Oh my God . . ." whispered Alley, her hand flying to her mouth.

Everyone in the room watched, mesmerized, as Tom climbed the small step next to the woodchipper, holding the squawking bird. It pecked him fiercely on the arm, and he jerked, releasing it. The bird flapped frantically, twisting out of his hands and flailing past his face.

Then, in a horrible instant, Tom lost his footing. His hand shot out, but there was nothing to grab. With a yell, he slipped backward, his body tipping over the edge of the woodchipper.

The screen went black, and the room fell into a shocked silence. Hayley turned off her phone, her gaze sweeping over the stunned faces around her.

Judge Parsons cleared her throat, her face ashen. "Well . . . I think that about settles it."

ADA Alley Roberts sat back, clearly struggling to compose herself. "Your Honor," she said, her voice measured, "in light of this new evidence, I recommend that all charges against Lester Murdock be dismissed."

Lester let out a heavy sigh of relief, a trace of satisfaction flitting across his face. He turned to Hayley, his gaze softening for the first time. "Hayley," he began, "I don't know how to thank you. You've cleared my name and my family's name."

Hayley held up a hand, stopping him. "Mr. Murdock, I didn't do this for you. I did it because the truth deserved to come out." She looked him squarely in the eye. "But if you really want to thank me, then start doing right by your family. Your sons, your wife . . . they need you to lead them with honesty, not fear or ambition."

Lester's gaze flickered with defensiveness. "I've done what I had to do for this family, Hayley."

"No," Hayley countered, her voice firm. "You've done what you wanted to do for yourself. You can't buy respect, Lester, not from your family. If you really want to be the father they look up to, then you need to work to bring them together, not push them apart."

He nodded, though his eyes were distant, his jaw tight as he absorbed her words. Hayley knew that look—she had seen it on people who did not fully grasp what they were hearing, who listened out of courtesy but refused to let the message penetrate.

Lester Murdock was already slipping back into his own reality.

Lester extended his hand, his grip firm and fleeting.

"I'll keep it in mind, thank you," he said, with a faint smile. He turned, guiding his family from the room.

As they filed out, Hayley stayed behind, feeling both relief and regret. She had exposed the truth, but part of her wondered if any of it would truly change the Murdocks.

Then she hurriedly speed-dialed her husband Bruce to let him know that she had finally solved the case.

Chapter 45

The Bar Harbor town council meeting was already underway by the time Hayley and Bruce slipped into the back row, the chatter of the townspeople a subdued hum punctuated by the tap of a gavel as recently installed town manager Seth Donnelly called for order.

Hayley scanned the crowd, noticing familiar faces—neighbors, shopkeepers, even the occasional out-of-town developer, like Tabitha Collins, who sat up front with a calculating expression. For weeks, Hayley had kept tabs on the twists and turns of the proposed Acadia Resorts development, and tonight, the council would make its final decision.

Beside her, Bruce nudged her gently. "If Acadia's proposal is approved, we'll be dealing with construction, traffic, new homebuyers being priced out of the market. Think you're ready for all that?"

Hayley gave him a wry smile. "I'll take that over another crime scene any day."

The council's agenda was relatively short, and soon, they reached the item everyone had been waiting for: the development proposal by Acadia Resorts, spearheaded by Tabitha and her company.

As the discussion began, a representative from an environmental group called Bar Harbor Green stood and presented a study on the ecological consequences of building on Tom Farley's property and the surrounding land. The potential pollution, disruption to wildlife, and strain on local resources painted a grim picture, prompting murmurs of disapproval from the crowd.

Tabitha Collins's gaze did not falter as the council reviewed the findings. When Donnelly called for a vote, the council members exchanged glances, some nodding to one another before delivering a decisive "No" on approving the proposal.

The majority of attendees erupted in spontaneous applause. Hayley felt a sense of relief wash over her as she met Bruce's gaze.

Tabitha's expression was unreadable as she turned to Liddy, who was seated beside her, and quietly informed her, "I'll be dropping out of escrow on the new property. There's no reason for me to stay in this town now. I'm a city gal at heart anyway."

"Are you sure?" Liddy whispered, though her disappointment was thinly veiled.

Tabitha nodded curtly, turning her head to address Hayley and Bruce as they approached. "Looks like I won't be coming back to Bar Harbor anytime soon."

Her tone held a forced politeness. "Goodbye, Hayley. Bruce."

They exchanged farewells, and Hayley watched as Tabitha exited the meeting room with her usual brisk efficiency. The sense of finality in her departure left Hayley feeling surprisingly light.

Liddy gave her a thumbs up. Although Tabitha's abrupt departure had cost her a healthy commission, she knew what it meant to her BFF.

With the meeting adjourned and the council having spoken, Hayley and Bruce took a slow stroll over to Randy's bar, Drinks Like A Fish. They found a booth near the back and ordered two beers and a heaping basket of Randy's famous onion rings.

As they waited, Hayley spotted Police Chief Sergio chatting with Randy near the bar, his face alight with relief as he leaned closer to his husband. A moment later, he joined them at their booth, sliding in with a smirk.

"Just heard some news that might interest you two," Sergio said, his tone carrying a note of satisfaction.

"Oh?" Hayley raised an eyebrow. "Do tell."

Sergio leaned in, lowering his voice. "Turns out Lester Murdock's murder charge getting dismissed only cleared the way for more troubles."

Hayley sat up straight, intrigued. "What do you mean?"

"The feds have been investigating him for massive financial fraud—embezzlement, money laundering, you name it. He was arrested earlier today and is looking at a long, long time behind bars."

Hayley exchanged a glance with Bruce, the irony hitting them both at once. After all of Lester's bluster and insistence on proving his innocence in Tom's death, he had walked into another trap of his own making.

"Justice always finds a way, doesn't it?" Bruce remarked, shaking his head.

"Sure does," Sergio replied, raising his beer with a grin. "And sometimes it even comes with a side of llama."

Bruce scrunched up his face. "Llama? As a side dish? I don't get it. What are you talking about?"

Hayley, who was more well versed in Sergio-speak, put a hand on Bruce's arm. "He meant to say karma. A big side of karma."

"Yes, that's what I meant. Karma. Actions have consecrations," Sergio said confidently.

Bruce shot his hand up in the air like a student eager to answer a teacher's question. "Wait, wait, wait! I know this one! He meant actions have consequences!"

Sergio sighed, annoyed. "Yes. Isn't that what I said?"

The following weekend, Hayley and Bruce drove up to the Murdock property after taking their dog Leroy for a walk in Acadia National Park. To their surprise, the once-quiet house was alive with activity. Cars lined the driveway, music drifted from the backyard, and the smell of charcoal hinted at a gathering. Hayley and Bruce exchanged curious glances before heading around back where they found Melody Murdock at the center of the action, flipping burgers over a grill, her face flushed and her laugh ringing out as she chatted with the neighbors.

Leroy took off running around, playing with anyone who would pay him any attention, including Melody who recognized him immediately. She spotted her new guests and broke into a broad smile.

"Hayley! Bruce!" she greeted them, setting down her spatula and waving them over. She looked different—lighter, almost carefree, her usual guarded expression replaced with something more open.

"Celebrating?" Hayley asked with a smile.

"Moving on," Melody replied, nodding. "Lester's . . . well, you know." Her voice softened. "It took me a while to see it, but it's time for a new beginning. I've saved up some of my own money, gave up drinking, and now my focus is on finding a more modest home and putting my boys through college. And who knows, maybe even a little vacation once in a while."

Hayley felt a warm surge of pride for her. "Good for you, Melody. I think you're going to be just fine."

Around them, the Murdock property was alive with activity. Neighbors exchanged stories, children darted across the lawn, and even Lori Gunning, who rarely ventured outside her tiny house, sat at a picnic table, laughing with a small group of women.

Melody caught Hayley's glance and grinned.

"Yes, Lori's been a bit more social lately. She and Reid have been going strong, and she even managed to find a buyer for most of Tom's turkeys. A turkey farm in Lewiston was happy to take them off her hands."

"Except one," Lori added, joining them with a grin. "I couldn't part with this guy." She gestured to a nearby turkey strutting around the yard, its feathers gleaming in the sunlight. Unlike the others, this one seemed almost friendly, sidling up to the picnic tables and pecking at crumbs left by the guests. "I named him Tom, as a tribute to his original owner. Tom Turkey. It was either that or Elvis but that just didn't seem to be a good fit."

"He's adorable," Hayley noted.

Lori sighed. "Unfortunately it turns out my cat is not a huge fan of turkeys flapping around the house and hasn't come out from under the couch since I adopted him so I'm in the process of trying to find him a welcoming forever home."

Hayley leaned down to study the bird, who met her gaze with an almost friendly, inquisitive glint. "Bruce," she said thoughtfully, "how do you feel about a new addition to the family?"

Bruce crossed his arms, studying the bird as if weighing its merits. "Long as Leroy's on board, I'm game."

As if on cue, Leroy trotted over, eyeing the turkey with a look that could only be described as suspicion.

Leroy gave a low, uncertain growl, but the turkey remained unbothered, fluffing its feathers and strutting closer.

"Looks like it'll take some adjustment," Hayley laughed, scratching Leroy's head. "But I think they'll be fine."

With that, Hayley and Bruce bid their farewells, carefully placing the turkey in a cage and setting it in the back of their car as they made their way home. The drive back was filled with laughter as they exchanged quips about their unlikely new pet, and by the time they pulled into their driveway, Hayley felt a deep sense of satisfaction.

That evening, she set up a small enclosure in the backyard for the turkey while Bruce tended to Leroy, who remained cautiously vigilant from the porch.

Hayley chuckled to herself, savoring the peacefulness that had returned to her life, knowing that even in the smallest, most unexpected ways, Bar Harbor always had a few surprises in store.

As the last rays of sun dipped below the horizon, Hayley settled onto the porch swing beside Bruce, holding hands, watching their new turkey explore the yard and Leroy's reluctant acceptance of his new feathered friend. Bruce slipped his arm around her, pulling her close.

"Here's to our very own Thanksgiving miracle," he murmured, pressing a kiss to her temple.

Hayley chuckled, leaning into him. "Here's to a little less excitement for a while."

But in her heart, she knew Bar Harbor would never stay quiet for long.

And that was just the way she liked it.

ISLAND FOOD & SPIRITS
By
Hayley Powell

Happy Thanksgiving! As I sit here penning my column, the quiet hum of our town feels comforting—especially after all the drama we've endured lately. Of course, I'm talking about the "murder" of Tom Farley. Now we know it was an accident, but for a hot minute, the whole town was whipped into a frenzy, debating guilt and innocence like we were starring in our own true-crime documentary.

Honestly, it reminded me of the great parking meter debacle. Who could forget Gary Rich's infamous tantrum at Drinks Like a Fish? Gary was furious that the town council had voted to install parking meters all over town to make more money during the bustling summer tourist season. Fueled by one too many beers, Gary decided to take justice into his own hands and rammed his shiny new Ford F-150 into one of those parking meters. Unfortunately, the meter won. Gary had to call his buddy Rodney for a tow, but before Rodney could arrive, Chief Alvarez spotted the scene, and Gary ended up in cuffs for destroying town property.

What followed was a showdown for the ages: pro-meter folks calling for Gary's head and anti-meter advocates hailing him as a local hero. Things reached a boiling point at Jordan's Restaurant when a breakfast debate turned into an all-out brawl, and the cops had to break it up. Chief Alvarez, bless his patience, finally declared, "Next time I'm called to deal with this nonsense, everyone involved is going to jail." That shut things down real fast.

And that's the thing about Bar Harbor. No matter how heated things get, we always bounce back. By the next week, folks were back to laughing over coffee, as if none of it ever happened. This Thanksgiving, I'm thankful to live in a community that knows how to move on and come together—even if it takes a few bruised egos and some fried eggs at Jordan's.

Now, let's talk turkey (or leftovers). I've got a drink and a dish that'll make your Thanksgiving—or the days after—even better.

HAYLEY'S SPICY BLOOD ORANGE MARGARITA

If you love spice and citrus like me, this one's for you.

INGREDIENTS:
Tajin (or salt, if you prefer)
4 ounces silver tequila
1 ounce simple syrup
2 ounces fresh-squeezed lime juice
2 ounces fresh-squeezed blood orange juice
2–4 fresh jalapeño slices (adjust to taste)
Extra blood orange slices for rimming glass
Ice

Wet the rim of your glass with a blood orange slice and dip it into Tajin.

In a shaker, combine tequila, lime juice, blood orange juice, simple syrup, and jalapeño slices. Shake well.

Pour into an ice-filled glass. This recipe makes two spicy, citrusy drinks. Cheers!

Recipe Index

THANKSGIVING LEFTOVER STUFFING WAFFLES

Because stuffing deserves to shine long after Thanksgiving dinner.

INGREDIENTS:
2–3 cups leftover stuffing
2 large eggs
½ cup broth
½ cup shredded cheddar cheese (or your favorite)
Salt and pepper to taste
Cooking spray for waffle maker
Optional toppings: gravy, cranberry sauce, turkey, veggies, fried egg—whatever you love.

Spray your waffle maker with cooking spray and preheat it.

In a large bowl, mix stuffing, eggs, broth, cheese, salt, and pepper. The mixture should be moist but not too wet.

Spoon the mixture into the waffle maker, close the lid, and cook until golden brown (about 5–7 minutes).

Remove, plate, and top with your favorite leftovers. Serve warm and enjoy!

Here's to a Thanksgiving full of laughs, love, and maybe a little less small-town drama. Now, if you'll excuse me, the police scanner is buzzing, and I'm half expecting Gary to try round two with the parking meters. Cheers!

lightly squeezed her hand, smiled knowingly, and mouthed, *"It'll be okay."*

Turning his attention back to Trevor, Noah ignored the man's comment and handed Trevor his bunched-up coat. "Here, put this under your foot."

"Really," said Trevor, shooing away the offered jacket, "I'm okay. I don't need an ambulance. I'm sure it's just sprained, and if I can get up, I can probably walk it off." He rolled on his side, shimmied up onto his elbow, then cried out and fell back down.

"That's what I thought," said Noah, adjusting Trevor's foot on top of the coat. "Addie, can you look around for something that would make a good splint? We're going to have to keep this immobilized until the medics get here."

"I'll go look in the kitchen," Addie said.

"The kitchen door is probably locked," groaned Trevor. "I think I knocked the brick away when I started back in."

Addie checked the door, and, sure enough, it had automatically locked. She flipped her flashlight on and quickly scanned around the back door for anything they could use to make a temporary splint. She spotted something with a flat side wedged behind the back left wheel of the garbage bin and snatched up a fist-sized chunk of slate and gave it a quick once-over. "Here, we can wrap my scarf around this to cover this sharp edge—" She gaped at the uneven edge on the corner of the step Trevor caught his foot on. The jagged edges on the step and the stone slab in her hand matched. "Trevor, did this just break off when you fell?"

"No," he groaned. "It broke off last spring. I knew it was an accident waiting to happen. We should have gotten it fixed back then, but it worked so well at keeping the bin from rolling backward onto the path and blocking the back door, so we just left it there." He laughed wryly. "I guess it's fitting that it was me and not one of the volunteers who paid the price for not looking after the maintenance issues of a two-hundred-year-old lighthouse."

Addie scanned the corner of the stone slab she held in her hand and the deformity now evident on Trevor's ankle just above the top of his shoe. While there was no blood on his leg, a rusty-brown color marred the ragged edge of the broken piece. A queasy sensation gurgled up from the pit of her stomach.

"Does that look like dried blood along the broken edge to you?" she whispered in Noah's ear as she knelt down and passed him the piece of slate.

Noah gingerly took it from her hand and studied it under the beam of her flashlight. He looked questioningly at Addie. She gestured to Trevor's sock, which was clearly free of blood.

His eyes widened. "I don't suppose you have an evidence bag on you, do you? Mine are in my coat pocket," he said, gesturing to his coat under Trevor's foot.

"I have a doggie doo-doo bag." Addie smiled grimly.

"Is it clean?"

"Yes!" She pulled a small plastic roll from her purse and tore off a small bag. "'Is it clean?' What kind of question is that?"

* * *

Hours later, after they had discharged Trevor to the care of the paramedics, Noah's comforting silhouette, outlined by the soft, flickering light of the fireplace, was enough to make Addie believe that dreams really did come true. She softly smiled and snuggled into the arm of her sofa, drew her knees up, and took a long, slow sip of sleepy-time tea. Like magic, the tension of the night and all thoughts of murder seeped from her body as Noah stoked the fire, keeping the room as cozy and warm as the tea made her feel.

With Nikki out for a few hours at Serena's to help settle the kids since Zach was working late and to, in her words, "get my mind off all this," Addie and Noah were alone. That comforted Addie more than she cared to admit, and she watched in fascination as Noah's shirt glided over his back every time he reached out to stoke the embers.

"I don't expect we'll get any results back from the lab until late tomorrow." Noah replaced the fireplace poker and brushed his hands together. "But if that is blood on the chunk of slate, and it's a match for the victim's, I believe you have discovered our murder weapon." He grabbed his teacup from the coffee table and raised a toast to her.

Just like that, her dream state dissolved, and reality set back in. She placed her own teacup on the table. "Can I see that picture of the wound site again?"

"Sure," said Noah, handing his phone to her. "But it's not going to have changed since you looked at it thirty minutes ago, or the three times before that."

"I know. I've been told many times that I'm like a dog—"

"With a bone. I know. I was one of the people who said that." Noah chuckled and gestured toward Pippi, asleep in her bed beside the fireplace. "But even dogs know when to take a break."

She smugly smiled before returning her attention to the image of the wound pattern. "I'm just trying to work out the exact angle the killer would have had to have been at in order to make this pattern at the base of Chad's skull. See this jagged edge?"

"Yes, I've seen it." He perched on the sofa beside her and looked at the picture again.

"I'm pretty sure the broken edge on the slate is a perfect match for the outer border of the wound here. What do you think?" She pointed to the image on his phone screen.

"Yes, and as we discussed earlier"—Noah circled his finger around the entirety of the image—"this bruise would have been caused by the full weight of the slate being brought down in a downward motion on the back of his head."

"That's the second time you've said '*brought down*' on his head, which means the killer would have been taller than Chad. Nikki would have to have been standing on a stool to swing it *down* on him, right? I'm not sure if you were aware, but the responding officers didn't put anything in their report about finding a stool anywhere near the cliff, and I highly doubt anyone, especially Nikki, would have hauled one over there and back again in a snowstorm just to kill Chad."

"Addie." Noah slipped his phone from her hand, turned it off, and set it back on the table. "I know you're hoping the detail about the angle of impact will take the heat off Nikki, but all it proves is that whoever killed Chad was positioned over him. For all we know, he could have been sitting on the cliff contemplating the error of his ways, and the killer came up behind him."

"I doubt Chad was the repenting type."

"My point is, we might never know everything that happened that night. All we can do is hope that the slate chunk you found will match the wound and proves to be the murder weapon, and the coroner will find something on it that leads us to the killer."

"Yes, but it also tells us a few other details, right?"

"It does, and as a police officer—"

She waved him off and walked over to the massive mahogany desk against the side wall. She ran her fingers over the ornate carvings on the front edge of the desk, then pressed a button. A hidden drawer opened with a *click*. She removed a folded-up piece of brown paper and laid it open on the desktop. "Come here and look at this."

"You didn't?"

"What?"

"Start a crime board."

"Yes, I did, and don't bother lecturing me. Marc already did. No one has seen it, and they won't."

"Then enough said on the topic"—surrendering, Noah threw his hands up—"but if I might add, that is an amazing desk. It looks really old."

"It is, and that drawer I opened is only one of many. This entire house has cubbies and hiding places that hold so many secrets. Even more than I've already found, I'm sure."

"I'd love a tour sometime," he said, his eyes seemingly devouring the room as he scanned it.

"As soon as we wrap up this murder investigation," she said, pointing to her makeshift crime board. "I haven't updated this in a while, so there's nothing about Peter Allen on it," she said, writing his name under *Suspects*.

"What makes you think Nikki's lawyer is a suspect?"

"What, did you leave your inspector hat in England?" Addie teased. "What makes you think he isn't?"

Noah opened his mouth, cocked his head, then snapped his mouth shut. He had the decency to look chagrined. "Fair point." He pulled out the desk chair and sat, gesturing to the board. "Walk me through your thoughts."

"Well, as you can see from the evidence under Nikki's name, we can keep *Nikki—phone calls to and from victim* and *Nikki—no alibi for time of death*. However, with Bin recanting her statement, we can remove *Nikki—seen at B&B night of murder* and *Nikki—seen leaving the B&B later going to lighthouse with victim*." Addie took a marker and made two neat lines through the two old facts, crossing them out.

"Ah, but you're forgetting something," said Noah. "*Stands to inherit millions from the victim* is still very relevant, wouldn't you say?"

At Addie's scowl, Noah stood, took her by the shoulders, gazing into her eyes. "I love the fact that you are defending your friend with all your heart, and while I'm not convinced she's guilty either, it's not me or you or even Marc who needs convincing. It's the DA—and perhaps a jury. And with the mayor breathing down our necks to find an easy target so he can potentially win his bid for reelection, even circumstantial evidence like what's on your board here is probably enough to see her at least go to trial. Don't you see, Addie? It's looking worse for her, not better, murder weapon or not."

She tilted her chin up and met Noah's gaze. "That's a fair point—so help me. Let's consider Peter for a moment, okay? There are things about him that tell me he's not all he appears to be."

Noah squeezed her shoulders, released her, and slipped his hands into his pockets. "Okay, I'll play along. We've checked Peter out. He seems legitimate, and he has a stellar reputation."

"Don't you find it weird he just happened to be here when Nikki suddenly needed legal representation for murder? The very same lawyer who represented her in her divorce? Who just so happened to be in town at the same time as Chad was killed, right when Nikki finds out about all this money she stands to inherit? None of that strikes you as way too coincidental?"

His eyes widened slightly, but he kept his blank cop expression. "That's a fair point. But let's go with his explanation for a bit, okay? He states that he was in town on another matter. When the murder happened, we contacted him with questions about the inheritance and why it wasn't mentioned in the divorce proceedings. He adamantly stated that he was only representing Nikki until he could find a criminal lawyer to act as her defense counsel in a murder case."

"And you believe him? Come on, Noah, I know you've got a cop gut like none other. You honestly can't tell me you believe *everything* he's said!"

"What could possibly be his motive? Cop gut or no

cop gut, there has to be means, motive, and opportunity. While Peter theoretically had means and opportunity, what on earth could his motive be?"

"Secrets he didn't want revealed?"

"Secrets? What secrets?"

"Deanna introduced him to me as a board member."

"There you go, the other matter he was in town for. How is this a secret?"

"Patience, Detective Inspector Parker." She grinned at his scowl. "Trevor told me tonight that Chad wasn't on the board, but was introduced to all of them as a friend of Deanna's. Like I said, she introduced Peter to me as a board member. And I tell you, there were some odd looks passing between the two of them when she said it."

"Well, that's interesting."

"I thought so too. People who lie about little things often lie about big things."

"Peter could simply argue that him being there and being friends with Deanna is a coincid—"

"Don't you dare say 'coincidence,'" Addie said. "I know everyone claims he's a well-respected lawyer, but he went right along with Deanna's lie about him being a board member. Besides, it's also weird that he showed up the day after the robbery and the murder. I'm positive he has to be linked to one of them, if not both." When Noah didn't argue with her, she continued. "Have you had a chance to interview Karl yet? Did he describe his assailant?"

"We talked to him briefly, but he has no memory of anything that happened that night. He sustained a traumatic brain injury, and the doctor said that some amnesia is not uncommon with the condition."

"Will he ever get his memory back?"

"Possibly, but they can't be certain. He might have a permanent hole in his memory for that night, or it could all come rushing back to him. The doctor hopes not, as that can re-traumatize a patient. Best-case scenario, the memories come back gradually, but so far there's nothing Karl can recall."

"That's too bad," said Addie thoughtfully. She closed her eyes and took in a deep breath, then let it out slowly. "The elf thief was roughly the same height as Peter . . . except the elf had a short beard. Peter is clean-shaven. Of course, the elf's beard could have been fake, part of his disguise." She closed her eyes tighter. "The eyes were different too." She opened her eyes and glanced at an amused-appearing Noah. "What?"

He waved her question away. "Nothing."

"Not gonna let you off that easy, Noah Parker. Are you laughing at me?"

"No." His cheeks turned red. "I simply enjoy watching you think."

Heat flooded Addie's inner core, and she turned to the board to hide what she knew was a blush mottling her entire face. "Anyway, I guess the difference in the eyes rules Peter out as the thief, and because of the angle of impact, that must mean—unless as you say, Chad was sitting on the ground—it excludes him from the murder too." She tapped Peter's name written on the crime board. "But I tell you, there's something fishy going on with Mr. Peter Allen. I feel it in my gut that he's guilty of something."

"Do you have a photographic memory?"

"No, but if I focus, I do have somewhat of an eidetic memory or recall, which is why I know the strange behaviors I saw in Peter mean something. I just can't quite figure out what it is yet."

"I agree, but if they were lying before the murder was discovered, they'll only double down on their lie now. Parsing out what is truth and untruth will not be easy."

"Are you giving up so easily, Noah Parker?" Addie challenged.

"No, just preparing you for a rocky road ahead, Addie Greyborne."

"Why do I get the sense that you and I will butt heads on that journey?" Addie chuckled and glanced down at the crime board. "Wait a minute. In all the commotion tonight, I completely forgot something else Trevor told me. He said that on the night of the robbery and murder, Deanna left the board meeting to retrieve some documents she'd left downstairs. He said she was gone so long they naturally assumed she was also making coffee. He got worried and thought she might need help bringing the coffee and cream and sugar upstairs, so he went downstairs to find her, but he found me instead, and then . . . we discovered the theft."

"And?" Noah's eyes snapped with interest, but he kept his body language loose, almost as if he was purposefully making her defend her ideas—treating her like a member of the team, not just throwing her a bone out of pity because she wanted to play cops and rob- bers.

"And . . . when Deanna appeared, she came from the kitchen area, but with no sign of coffee anywhere."

"Maybe she left it in the kitchen when she heard a commotion in the lobby?"

Oh, he was good at playing devil's advocate. Addie doubled down. "There was no commotion at that point. We didn't yet know Karl was missing and had only just discovered the theft."

Noah smiled, breaking his poker face façade. "While I think there's something there to look at, let's not put the horse before the cart. We still have to wait for the test results on the slate. Without any substantial evi- dence, like fingerprints or DNA, to counter the witch hunt the mayor and the DA are conducting with Nikki, we're no further along." He tapped Nikki's name on the paper. "I'll do my best, okay, Addie? Tomorrow, I'll pay Miss Deanna Jackson another visit."

"When you do, take note of her height, because I have to look up at her."

His grin slipped into a serious line. "You're really convinced the angle of impact is an important detail, aren't you?"

"Yes, and it's amazing how many cases can be solved by one seemingly incidental detail."

"Or blatant evidence." He grinned at her scowl. "So, until tomorrow . . ." His gaze held steady on hers while the tip of his tongue flickered over his opening lips. As his head dipped toward hers, Addie yearned for his lips to touch her own, but then he pulled his head back and smiled. "Goodnight, then." His lips briefly brushed her cheek. "I'll let you know the results of the test as soon as I hear back."

Addie walked him to the door, and after he'd left, she pressed her back against the closed door and slid down the length of it until she was seated on the floor. Pippi studied her from her bed by the fireplace, then tilted her head, trotted over to Addie, and licked her hand.

Addie reached over and ruffled the fur on the back of Pippi's head. "I don't get it, my friend. Why is it that every time I say goodbye to him, I feel like I've also said goodbye to part of me? It makes me feel so empty." She pulled the little dog onto her lap and snuggled her chin on the back of Pippi's neck.

Chapter Twenty-seven

Addie jerked and swatted her hand at the unrelenting, vibrating clunking sound in her ear. She cracked one eye open, caught sight of the bedside clock, and frowned.

"It's only seven?" She yanked the duvet over her head, but the incessant noise persisted. She tentatively peered over the top of the cover and scanned the room, looking for the source of the noise that had interrupted her dream of the English countryside and a certain handsome detective inspector.

The noise continued, and she finally saw her cell phone vibrating on her bedside table. She propped herself up on one elbow, and as it danced closer to the edge of the nightstand, she managed to save it from clattering onto the hardwood floor just in time.

"Hello?" Addie croaked and rubbed her eyes. "That's okay, Jerry, I was going to have to get up in an hour anyway . . ." She scoffed, trying to focus her dream-fogged mind on his words. "Yes." She pushed herself into an upright position and glanced over at the clock. "Yeah, I'll be there by then. Thanks for letting me know . . ." Addie clicked off and threw her duvet back, covering Pippi, who was curled up at her feet.

"Come on, sleepyhead, we have to be at the police station in an hour." Addie slid her feet into her fuzzy pink slippers and stumbled to the bathroom.

Addie shouldered Pippi's carrier case and grinned at Jerry when he gestured for her to hurry along. She smiled at the young officer at the desk, wishing she could recall his name as she skirted around the end of the reception counter, toward Jerry, who was waiting for her at the back stairwell.

"Jerry," she whispered, glancing back at the young officer, "can you give me some kind of a clue as to why you dragged me in here before the sun is even up?"

"You'll see," he said, descending the stairs to the lower level of the police station. "I think we finally have a lead on the robbery." At the bottom, he stopped, stood back, and motioned to the Evidence Room sign on the door.

Addie gasped. "You found the stolen property?"

"Yes, but according to the list we got from the museum, a few items still seem to be missing."

"Is the copy of *The Four Million* in there?"

He shook his head, pursing his lips tight, and gave a small shoulder shrug that was tinged with regret. "But that's only part of the reason I asked you to come in so early this morning. Since you have expertise in identifying some of the rarer or antique items that were on the list, I wanted you to see what we have before the museum sends someone to collect them at nine." Jerry unlocked the door, and they stepped into a large room filled with floor to ceiling shelves jam-packed with boxes and wire baskets. "All the donation stuff we uncovered is back here," he said, making his way toward the back wall. "I had the crime team lay it all out on a table after they finished scanning for evidence and fingerprints."

"And?"

"And, it was a dead end." He waved his hand toward the tables. "Whoever handled these wore gloves and left no trace fibers other than what we already determined came from the museum itself."

Addie quickly scanned the donation items spread across three tables at the back of the evidence room. "And you're releasing all this before you have even apprehended the thief? Isn't that unusual?"

"The mayor heard about the seizure and insisted—no, demanded—that the museum get it all back as soon as possible. When we let the museum know that we'd found it, they were most insistent they come and pick it all up this morning so they can salvage part of the fundraiser. The crime team had to work through the night, and there was no time to get an appraised value for any of it, so that's why I called you."

"I can't blame the museum for wanting it all back so soon. The loss of revenue from the raffle was a major blow to their program budgeting for the upcoming year." She walked the length of the tables, perusing each individual item. "Sure, I can get this done by nine."

"That's great, thanks."

"Where did you say these were found?"

"I didn't."

"Okay, fair enough." She looked at Jerry. "Can you at least tell me where they were found, or is it some kind of state secret?"

"I told the chief you'd try to wrangle that out of me," Jerry said with a hearty laugh.

"Marc's back to work?"

Jerry glanced around and lowered his voice. "No, but he is the one who strongly suggested I ask you to take a look before the museum came and took it all away. He feels the mayor is acting prematurely in releasing it, and he wants a professional opinion on its value before it leaves the station." He held out a clipboard to her.

"I'd better get to work, then." She took the list and made her way back down the table, checking off items as she mentally calculated what she thought the value of each might be. "You never did tell me how you happened to find all this," she said, ticking off the box of imported Canadian cabernet sauvignon from the Wine Shop on Main Street. Luckily it was Serena's favorite, and Addie had bought it often enough to know its sticker price. She jotted it down next to the wine's name. "Did you get a lead? Find a clue? How did you come to find all this?"

"Believe it or not, a lot of police work involves dumb luck, and this is one of those times."

"You're kidding?"

"Nope. One of the patrol officers was out making his rounds and came across a transport van stuck in the snow on a secondary road just off Home Road. He stopped to check it out, and"—Jerry waved his hand over the table—"this is what was inside."

"The thief just left all this?"

"Nah, it looked like he got stuck in the snowstorm, and by the faint ruts we found behind the van, it looks like another vehicle or a sled of some kind showed up. We couldn't tell which, but the ruts were a lot skinnier and narrower than the ones made by truck. My guess is they were changing vehicles, but either ran out of room in the new one or got spooked off before they could finish emptying the truck. It's hard to say, because the blowing snow the last couple of days has wreaked havoc with any other tracks."

Addie held up the clipboard with the inventory list. "From what I can determine by this, the *Four Million* book I donated, which sadly isn't here, is the highest-priced item not retrieved. Aside, of course, from the certificate for the all-inclusive, two-week vacation to Hawaii. There are actually only a few other items not here that are recorded on the list, but they aren't of a high monetary value."

"Such as?"

"Martha's hand-knit mittens, a handcrafted baby's patchwork quilt, a toy train set, two walking dolls, and a set of antique, hand-painted plaster owl bookends. Now, those might be worth a few dollars, but I'd have to go online in order to appraise them before I can give you a value amount."

"That means that aside from your book, these bookends you mentioned are the only items of any real value?"

"Yes and no. The trip tickets can be canceled so no one can claim them, or, if they try to redeem them, they'll be arrested. However, how much value can you place on handcrafted gifts? Or the expression on a child's face on Christmas morning when they receive a train set or a doll?"

Jerry shrugged.

"That's right, because monetary-wise, they don't seem to be items that someone would risk everything to steal—but, like so many things, they are priceless." She met Jerry's confused gaze. "My best guess is, you were right. The van simply got stuck, and either the thief had an accomplice who rescued him or they found another, smaller vehicle, but when they went back to transfer everything into the new getaway vehicle, they ran out of room or were scared off."

Jerry scratched his head. "I still don't see the purpose of ruining so many people's holidays if they ended up taking off with only a few items worth anything."

"Maybe making a large amount of money wasn't the motivating factor."

"Then what was it?" said Jerry. "In my experience, that's why most robberies occur. The thief pawns the stolen goods and gets the money for them, but like you said, there is no price you can place on a pair of hand-knit mittens. Why take such a risk?"

"I don't think you'll get the answer to that until you catch this elusive elf." Addie patted a sulking Jerry on the shoulder and handed him the clipboard, then checked the clock and hurried off to the bookstore.

* * *

"Paige, I insist you take the rest of the day off. You're getting married in a few days, and I know how many odds and ends there are to handle right before the big day. Go do what you have to do. I'll be fine here," said Addie, removing books from the counter and placing them onto a trolly.

"I told you, Mom's got it covered. There is nothing—and I mean *nothing*—for me to do. To be honest, I need a break from her hyper-energy and just need to chill. Besides, with Nikki off, I couldn't possibly leave you here on your own all day. And who would take my sweet little baby out for her walks?" Paige bent down and scratched behind Pippi's ear. "Isn't that right, girl?" she cooed.

"Look, before all this mess happened with Nikki, I told you I'd pay for the three of us to spend a day at that new spa in town. If your mom hasn't left any room for you in your wedding plans, how about I send you there today so you can get pampered—"

"I'm fine, really, and believe it or not, Mom has done a great job of looking after all the details. Of course, as you know, she tends to get herself in a frenzy over every little thing, which drives me nuts. But overall, I'm happy about it. It's been less stressful than it was with that wedding planner I hired." Paige grinned, but her smile didn't quite reach her eyes.

Addie paused her stacking, book in hand, and looked at Paige, waiting for the punch line. Paige shrugged and went back to restocking Christmas shopping bags from the bin on the floor to the shelf under the counter.

Addie gasped. "You're serious."

"Yes, she's actually been great lately."

Addie shook her head as she wheeled the squeaky cart away, wondering what Kool-Aid Martha had been giving to Paige. It seemed like just yesterday that Paige was in tears over her mother's interference, and now she was grateful? Addie didn't buy it. It seemed more like Paige had become disinterested and checked out of her own wedding when Martha took it over.

In moments like these, Addie missed Catherine Lewis. Catherine had played a motherly role in Addie's life when she moved to Greyborne Harbor all those years ago. Maybe Catherine could explain this relationship change between Paige and Martha, because Addie, whose own mother had passed when she was a toddler, sure couldn't figure it out.

"Say, Paige"—Addie placed a book on a sale shelf in front of the counter—"did Catherine and Felix respond to the wedding invitation?"

"You mean the jet-setting couple?" Paige laughed.

"Yes, they seem to have a new address every few weeks. I was just wondering if their invitation caught up with them."

"It did, finally, she said when she called—"

"She called you?"

"She did. I meant to tell you, but it's been crazy with the wedding and Nikki lately. I'm so sorry that it slipped my mind."

"That's okay. How did she sound? Are they coming back for the wedding? Is married life all she hoped it would be? Are her and Felix happy?"

"Slow down. Yes, to everything except them coming back for the wedding." Paige smiled sadly. "She didn't think they would be able to make it back. They're in Peru right now and had planned to go on a tour of Machu Picchu."

"Oh," said Addie, grabbing another book off the cart and placing it on the shelf. "That sounds nice." She fought to keep her voice even. "I hope they enjoy it."

Addie kicked the wheel brake off the cart and rolled it toward the back of the shop, biting her lip to stave off the tears that burned in her eyes. She'd thought for sure that even if Catherine didn't plan on being in Greyborne Harbor for Christmas, Paige's wedding would bring her back. Addie really needed to talk to her. Between Nikki and Noah, her head was spinning, and Catherine had always kept her grounded. Addie sniffed and wiped her eyes, then turned around and shrieked.

"Noah, what are you doing, sneaking up on me like that?" Addie thumped him on the chest with the book in her hand.

"I didn't realize I was sneaking. I believe you were just off in another world." He slipped the book from her fingers and set it on the cart.

"Yes, as a matter of fact, I was touring Machu Picchu."

"Oooh, do you have room in that fantasy for another person?"

"I think that could be managed." She laughed, stepped on the foot brake on the cart, and led him to the back room, keeping the door ajar behind her. "Did you need something, or did you just stop by to make sure your furnace handiwork survived this latest cold spell?"

He glanced over his shoulder at the half-closed door. "I'm here as a courtesy."

"And to what do I owe this show of gallantry?"

"I went to talk to Deanna Jackson again this morning, as you suggested, but she pretty much told me, word for word, what she'd told you about Peter." He leaned in and whispered, "However, something else came up that I thought I should tell you about."

"What's that?"

"The fingerprint analysis came back on the hunk of slate—"

"And whose prints are on it? Not Nikki's, I bet."

He shook his head. "There were multiple prints found. A lot of them were smeared, but there were numerous prints of one person."

"And?"

"And . . . I don't know how to tell you this." Noah placed his hands on Addie's shoulders. The look he gave her was so raw with emotion, she held her breath. "They were a perfect match for Nikki," he whispered.

Addie tore herself from Noah's touch and danced backward as far away from him as possible. "No." She veered from him as he approached her, then paced the back room. This just couldn't be true. There had to be an explanation.

"Addie?" Noah's voice softened.

She whirled and pointed at him, her finger digging into his chest. "You know perfectly well that she's a volunteer there. Those prints could have been made anytime. Trevor told us they've been using that piece of slate as a stopper on the bin for months. This doesn't mean she killed Chad."

"Listen. I know it's hard not to be emotional in situations like this, but Nikki needs you now more than ever. The DA now has exactly what he needs to put his 'witch' on trial. And I have to play by the rules, no matter how much they don't make sense at the time."

Addie refused to look at him. The truth was not something she wanted to hear.

With his finger, Noah tilted her face until their gazes locked. "Believe me, this hurts me just as much as it hurts you. But the DA could refuse to keep playing nicey-nice with me and kick me off the investigative team. We don't want that. I'm on my way to pick Nikki up again, and I'm afraid this time, she won't be released on bail."

Chapter Twenty-eight

An hour later, Addie looked up from the reports she'd run, scanned the bookshop, and frowned at Paige. "I think a lot of people are window-shopping today. With the number of times the doorbells have been tinkling, sales should be a lot higher than they are."

"I think that's my fault," said Paige.

"Why would it be your fault? Are you chasing them away for some reason? You do know that will cut into your Christmas bonus this year," said Addie, giving her a cheeky grin.

"Of course not, silly. However, it does seem as though lots of our regular customers are stopping by only to drop off a wedding gift."

"That's so sweet."

"You're not mad?"

"Why would I be mad? We have the best customers,

don't we? And you deserve to have them show you how important you are to them."

"But I feel bad that I can't invite each and every one of them to the wedding."

"Wouldn't your mother love that." Addie laughed and glanced around the shop again. "Since everyone is coming in to see you, anyway, would you mind if I went out for a few minutes?"

"Are you off to see Noah again? I know it's none of my business, but I saw how upset both he and you were when he left earlier." She leaned closer and dropped her voice. "Did you two have an argument or something?"

"Not exactly," said Addie, giving Pippi a quick scratch, and then she grabbed her handbag from under the counter. "It's just that more evidence came to light, and it's not looking good for Nikki. Noah's taking her in again."

"You're kidding!"

"I wish I was, because I feel it in every ounce of my being that she's innocent. Noah has his hands tied by the powers that be, and I don't envy him one bit. He went from being an excellent detective in his own right to playing the DA's stooge. I have no doubt that as soon as the DA gets his clutches on this new so-called evidence, he'll have the smoking gun he thinks it is, but if my hunch is right, Nikki will be out of jail before your wedding."

Addie pulled up to the museum and headed inside. She needed to ask Deanna if Nikki had ever taken out the trash, or in her volunteer duties had spent much time by the bin. Nikki wasn't a smoker, so there had to be another explanation as to why her prints were so predominant on the slab of slate—other than handling it while committing a murder.

"Deanna!" Addie spotted the woman across the lobby, stomped the snow off her boots, and walked as fast as she dared with wet boots across the tile. "It looks like I caught you just in time," Addie said, gesturing to the coat draped over Deanna's arm.

"Yes, I was just on my way to the hospital to check on Karl and Trevor."

"I can't imagine how hard this is on everyone here."

"The last two weeks have been a nightmare, but sadly, even with Trevor's surgery early this morning, business doesn't stop, and there are still some loose ends to tie up before the end of the year. So, if you'll excuse me, I had better get over there."

"Before you go, Deanna, I was hoping you could answer a few questions for me."

"I've already told you that the police took my statement the night of the robbery. They even interviewed me again this morning after they returned most of the donation items to us. For anything else, you'll have to speak to Trevor about it after he's out of the hospital," she said, shoving her arms into her coat sleeves. "Is it still as cold out there as it was earlier? I can't risk getting sick right now, since the gala is back on."

"The gala?" said Addie, distractedly staring at Deanna's coat.

"Yes, since we have most of the items returned, we're changing the format and holding the gala and silent auction on New Year's Eve. We need to try to make back some of the funds lost when we couldn't go ahead with the daily raffle."

"That sounds—"

"Are you okay, Addie? Your face went as white as snow. I do hope you aren't getting sick now and will miss the gala. We might not have the signed copy of *The Four Million* to auction off, but all the other books you donated are back."

"That's wonderful."

"I thought you'd be happier to hear that?"

"Yes, I am. Tell me something . . ." Addie's voice trailed off.

"Addie, are you sure you're okay?"

"Where was your coat the night of the robbery?"

"I beg your pardon. My coat?"

"Yes, your coat. Trevor said you arrived late for the board meeting, but then later you told the board members that the document they needed was downstairs in your coat pocket. I find that odd since I can see that your coat pockets are hardly large enough to hold a business document, or is this a different coat?"

"It is, but that doesn't matter. I'm sure you have more than one winter coat yourself."

"I do, but none that have document-sized pockets."

"It was folded," she snarled, then whisked a blue scarf out of her coat pocket and turned to walk away. "Now, if you'll excuse me, I really must be on my way."

Addie steadied herself, fighting to keep her voice even. "Yes, but the night you introduced me to Peter, you told me you had left the meeting and gone to the kitchen to make coffee. So, which was it, coffee or the document? Why did you really go downstairs, Deanna?" Addie grabbed Deanna's arm and spun her around to face her.

"I don't see how any of this is your business, Miss Snoopy-Pants." She shook Addie's hand off her arm. "Now, if you'll—"

"It's funny that when Trevor and I saw you coming from the kitchen, you didn't have your coat with you. Was that because it was covered in blood?"

"What are you talking about? I told you, while the coffee brewed, I cleaned the kitchen and took the trash out. I spilled something on my coat from the trash bag. It reeked, so I left it in the kitchen. That's all. Now, excuse me." She tried to shimmy around Addie, who kept up with her, and when Deanna was nearly to the exit, Addie circled around her, blocking her way out. Addie planted her feet firmly on the doormat.

"Was that trash named 'Chad Sanders'?" Addie asked.

"Do you mean the fellow who fell off the cliff? I didn't even know him." She straightened her back and sneered at Addie.

"You knew him well enough to visit him at the B&B, though, didn't you?"

"You're insane. Now. Get. Out. Of. My. Way," Deanna said through clenched teeth.

"Come on, Deanna, you were seen there, and Trevor said you were late for the board meeting that night. So, my guess is, you came rushing back in for the meeting. Dropped your coat in the kitchen and went up to join the board members. What happened when you went back to the kitchen to get the documents you forgot to take up? Had Chad followed you to the museum? Did he threaten you to get you to tell him where Nikki was? You said yourself you were afraid of getting sick, so having your coat handy to go out and confront him must have been a blessing, but after you hit him with the first thing you could get your hands on, your coat got blood on it. You couldn't take it back upstairs with you, could you? To cover your tracks, you made up the excuse of making coffee and tidying up after the volunteers."

"As fun as this little conversation has been, I really must be off now."

"Even if you say you didn't know Chad, I don't believe you, but Peter did, didn't he? He was Nikki's lawyer in Chicago." Addie kept her gaze fixed on Deanna, readying herself for the woman to run toward the kitchen exit. "Tell me something, Deanna. That night, when you ran into me and Trevor by the stairs, you didn't have your coat *or* the coffee with you. So, what had you really been doing?"

"This is ridiculous. I heard a commotion in the lobby and went to investigate."

"But Trevor and I were the only ones in the lobby," Addie said. "There was no commotion at that point. Tell me something else, Deanna. Detective Inspector Parker—"

"Who?"

"The English police officer you talked to."

"Right, he is easy on the eyes, isn't he?"

Addie rolled her eyes and shook her head. "Tell me why the story you told me the night I came and found you here with Peter matches, word for word, the same story you told Detective Inspector Parker? Did Peter tell you what to say? After all, he is a lawyer, and one of the best, I heard."

"Maybe my story sounded word for word the same because when you're telling the truth, it's easy to remember every detail."

"The truth is often not told in such well-rehearsed lines. In my experience, as time passes, people tend to recall details they missed the first time or they elaborate a bit, giving more information as the shock of the experience passes."

"This is crazy talk, Addie. Get out of my way." She pushed Addie back.

Addie stumbled and managed to catch her footing, but not before her arm slammed against the door, saving her head from striking it dead-on. She shored herself up and lunged forward, diving for Deanna's legs as she made a dash toward the kitchen.

"That scarf you're wearing." Addie tugged it from around Deanna's neck as they both hit the floor. "If I'm not mistaken, it's handcrafted and only sold in a boutique in Chicago, right? I know that because Marc bought Nikki a very similar one when he was there with his wife for a conference. I bet that was a gift from Peter, wasn't it?"

Deanna struggled to flip over onto her back and screamed at Addie, "The problem with you is you think you know everything, but you don't know *anything*!"

"Then fill me in. What am I missing?" Addie pinned Deanna face down on the floor.

"I don't need some man to buy me pretty things." Deanna bucked her back up, sending Addie scrambling to regain control. "I bought the scarf for myself when I was there visiting Peter."

"Then you *are* lovers?" Addie puffed and grabbed a writhing Deanna by the bun in her hair.

"We are very good friends, that's all." Deanna's garbled words were barely audible since her cheek was pressed against the floor.

"How good of friends? Good enough that you'd cover for each other in a murder?" Addie spread-eagled all her weight overtop the wriggling woman beneath her. "You were the blond woman at the B&B visiting Chad Sanders that night. That's why you were late returning for the meeting. Were you and Peter in on this together? After all, Peter knew Nikki was still Chad's beneficiary even though he'd told her everything had been dissolved in the divorce proceedings. What was your plan? Kill her after she received her inheritance, then ride off into the sunset with her estate manager *and* her millions?"

"No, Peter didn't kill anyone."

"What about you, then? You saw a chance to make millions, and you took it."

"It wasn't about the money."

"Come on, Deanna, you expect me to believe that? You're a smart woman. You know money is quite a motivator, and Nikki stood to inherit a fortune. Is that why you killed Chad?"

"It was an accident. Chad Sanders was a scum, the lowest of the low, but his death was an accident. You have to believe me, Addie."

"An accident?"

"Yes, I did go to the B&B that night to warn him to

stay away from Nikki. You see, Peter and I started dating when he was representing her in the divorce. Peter had been so torn up about the details of their horrible marriage. Peter told me Chad treated Nikki worse than an animal, even locked her up in the basement when he went out of town on weekends. It was one of those cases that haunted him, and it came to haunt me too."

"How did you even know Chad was in town?"

"Karl told me a fellow had been coming into the museum all week looking for a volunteer named Nikki. He didn't like the look of the man, so he told the stranger no one worked here by that name. When Karl came to me to report it, he described the man, and I knew right away it was Chad. I called Peter to tell him. He got worried and caught the next flight from Chicago to Boston."

"What did Chad do when you spoke to him?" Addie didn't bother asking why Deanna had confronted such a violent man in the first place. She clearly wasn't thinking at all.

"He laughed and told me Nikki couldn't hide behind me or our security guy at the museum. He'd find her one way or another. He . . . he . . . started to get violent, so I ran. I knew I had been gone from the meeting too long, so I went back to the museum. I wanted to be in a public place. I'd seen the monster in his eyes, and I wanted nothing to do with it. Everything after that is exactly as I told you and the police."

"Everything?"

"Yes."

"I can tell by your voice that there's something else to this story, am I right?"

"It was nothing really, Addie. Let me go. This is craziness." Deanna tried to lift her body up, but Addie counteracted her movements and managed to hold her on the floor.

"I can't let it—or you—go until the police get here."

"The police? How do they even know you're here?"

Addie fumbled in her coat pocket, managed to grab her cell phone, and pushed it in Deanna's face.

Deanna barked a laugh. "Then just you wait until I tell them how you attacked me and . . ."

"Tell them now. They've heard the whole thing. That's what happens to someone who tries to frame my friend for murder."

"I have no idea how Chad died or if Nikki had anything to do with it, but to be honest, I wouldn't blame her if she did. The man was a scumbag. Now, let me up before the police get here, so I can explain everything to them."

Addie let her body go limp, becoming deadweight on top of her catch. "No, I think we'll stay just as we are for a few more minutes."

Chapter Twenty-nine

Addie wasn't sure how she'd survived her brawl with Deanna, an hours-long police questioning, a splitting headache, and aching muscles from tackling a woman twice her size, but she had. Nearly twenty-four hours after the harrowing experience, Addie stood behind her sales counter, staring at the daily sales report. Not that she was seeing the numbers. They had blurred together long ago, and all she envisioned as she stared at the white paper in front of her was Deanna's tear-streaked face and wild hair, sobbing as police officers hauled her away from the museum. Addie wanted to cover her ears to drown out the reverberations of Deanna's repeated pleas that she hadn't meant it, that she'd been protecting Nikki, that it had been just an accident.

"It's funny how a whole case can be solved by one little detail, isn't it?" Noah's voice infiltrated her thoughts.

Addie jumped. The piece of paper slipped from her hands, and she scowled at the man standing innocently on the welcome mat below the tinkling bells. "I thought I locked the door."

He grinned and pointed up at the bells. "Nope, and you must have been in quite the trance to not hear these little jovial blokes."

"Either that, or you're a ninja."

"Wanted to be one when I was a boy, but sadly that never worked out, as you can see."

Yes, Addie did see. She didn't see a ninja, but she saw a man of integrity, one who, despite his penchant to follow a strict line to justice, had still wavered off the straight and narrow and followed Addie into her often color-outside-of-the-lines investigative style. Her eyes trailed from his glimmering eyes, over his sharp cheekbones, and down to his lips.

"What?" Noah wiped at his mouth. "Do I have the vestiges of a late-afternoon tea still on my face?"

Addie blinked and hated the heat flooding her cheeks. "No, although I've heard through the grapevine that the Thomas sisters are being extra-nice and treating their favorite customer"—she pointed at him—"with extra care."

Noah stomped the remaining snow off his boots, walked over to the sales counter, and took a seat at one of the stools. "I won't even ask how you know. I'm afraid small towns are the same everywhere: news travels faster than the victim of the gossip. But you're right. I've never been so well fed, and Bin didn't even try to cut my sausage for me this morning. She apologized profusely for not having black pudding, and I assured her, as I can't stand the stuff, that her apologies were a moot point anyway."

"I bet you a coffee that she still apologized during the whole meal." Addie grinned and walked over to the coffeemaker, knowing she'd made a sure bet.

"I like my coffee black, please." Noah's eyes sparkled, and there seemed to be new life to him, an energy Addie hadn't seen before.

Addie plopped a pod in, then sat next to him as the coffeemaker hissed to life. "Nikki was pretty quiet this morning, but she told me to tell you she owes you a debt of gratitude."

"Her gratitude is incorrectly placed. The only person she should be thanking is you." His gaze caught hers, and his voice dropped to a whisper. "Addie."

It was suddenly very hard to breathe, and Addie waved away his words. Anything to buy her more time to catch her breath. "Technically, we worked together."

"I think we work very well together, don't we?"

Addie hoped he meant more than just their working relationship. Her heart fluttered, and her mind raced with the possibilities his words held, and then she thanked her lucky stars when the coffeemaker finished brewing a cup. She scrambled from her stool, grabbed his coffee, and gingerly placed it in front of him.

"So, did Deanna or Peter say anything else?" She dipped her head and nonchalantly circled her spoon around the inside rim of her cup. "That is, if you want to tell me. I understand your hands might be tied and that—"

He laid his hand on top of hers. "I want to tell you, but . . ."

"That's okay. I get it. It's an ongoing case, and you—"

He suddenly turned to her and planted a soft kiss on her lips, then pulled back, avoiding her wide-eyed gape. His cheeks flooded crimson, and he played a finger between the collar of his sweater and neck. "Yeah, so the . . ."

"The case?" Addie stammered, fighting to hide the inner turmoil his kiss set off within her. His avoidance of her in this moment told her he had reverted just as quickly as the kiss had come, back to his British, stiff-upper-lip façade, and he wasn't going to say a word about what had just occurred. She touched her finger to her lips, where the taste of him still lingered. However, since the British upper crust weren't generally known for their spontaneity, she'd chalk his actions up to a fleeting celebratory gesture for them having closed the case.

"Yes, the case. Well, it turns out Deanna knew Chad from long ago. Apparently, Chad had dated Deanna's younger sister, Carolyn, when he first started playing college football. That relationship ended when Deanna's father sensed Chad was hurting Carolyn. He not only threatened to kill Chad but told him that if he ever tried to contact Carolyn again, he would destroy his football career by going public with everything."

"Wow!" Pity for Deanna unexpectedly washed over Addie. Now she felt bad about tackling the woman to the lobby floor of the museum. "Poor Deanna. Poor Carolyn."

"Yeah, her story was not easy to listen to, but Chad was never seen again by her sister or the family. That is, until the divorce proceedings started between Chad and Nikki. That's where Peter got involved."

"She told me as much when I was sprawled on top of her," Addie said.

"When I found you like that and knew you had put yourself in danger, my heart dropped." He rubbed the spot on his chest. "I still don't think it's quite back in its place." He held up a finger when Addie opened her mouth. "You don't have to like the fact that I feel protective toward you, but nothing you say will change my mind. I'm not saying you can't put yourself in danger or that you can't get yourself out of it. But when a man cherishes a woman, he would rather lose his life than see her in any kind of danger or pain."

Silence hovered between them. She'd seen the look in his eyes when he'd descended upon the museum with a team of officers and saw her bruised and battered. Addie blinked back the tears threatening to spill down her cheeks. "I'm sorry," she whispered.

He shook his head. "Don't ever apologize for doing what you think is right in the moment. There's a reason you're famous around here." His cheeky grin lightened the mood.

"More like infamous. Anyway, what else did Peter and Deanna confess to?"

Noah took a sip of his coffee and sighed. "Well, the museum guard, Karl, had informed Deanna of a strange man coming around, asking a lot of questions about one of the volunteers, Nikki. Karl said the man had also shown an interest in the fundraiser and the money collected."

"That's what Deanna told me, and she knew at once, by how Karl had described him, that it was none other than Chad Sanders."

"After that, things were foolishly set in motion. She called Peter and told him Chad was in town, and I'm afraid after that, things went all sixes and sevens," Noah said.

"Why on earth would she confront Chad, though? She had to have known that by her meeting with him, he'd know she knew where Nikki was. And especially she knew from past experience that Chad was a dangerous man." Addie shook her head. "Wow, seeing him on her own was a really risky, not-thought-out-at-all move, wasn't it?"

Noah grinned. "Isn't that your modus operandi?"

"We're not talking about me. We're talking about Deanna."

"Fair point. Well, in her confession, Deanna admitted to acting first and thinking second. She was just so afraid for Nikki and wanted to protect her. She'd seen what Chad had done to Carolyn, and she wanted to save another woman from his brutality."

"Even at the risk of losing her own life?"

"Bravery and stupidity often share a very thin line, but Deanna wanted to protect Nikki more than anything, so she went to the bed-and-breakfast, confronted Chad, and told him she'd tell the world all she knew about his past behavior if he didn't leave Nikki alone. Chad realized, there in his room, that her defending Nikki meant Deanna likely knew where she was, and he told her he'd beat Nikki's location out of her if he had to. That's when he made a grab for Deanna. She bolted and ran back to the museum, thinking there, at least, she'd be safe until she could figure out how to get out of this even-worse mess for Nikki she'd just created."

"He must have followed her back to the museum to finish the job he'd started at the bed-and-breakfast."

"Yes, Chad followed her back there, thinking Deanna would lead him to Nikki. When Deanna was in the kitchen, he banged on the window of the kitchen door, shouting for Nikki to come out. Deanna told him Nikki wasn't there and to leave or she'd call the police."

"But he didn't?" A sensation of nausea sloshed in Addie's gut. She knew where this was all going, and she didn't like it one bit.

"No, according to Deanna, she thought he'd left because it got quiet. She peered out the curtains covering the kitchen door window and saw Chad stepping off the step like he was going to leave. She figured that was too easy—that he would go around to the front doors and come in that way." Noah shook his head. "Here was the fatal mistake. She opened the kitchen door and shouted at him that he'd better leave because the police were on their way. I guess Chad turned and came at her, faster than she realized he would—which is odd, because he's an athlete—but be that as it may, Deanna saw the rock behind the bin wheel, grabbed it, raced back up the step, and when he lunged at her, laughing, she hit him."

"But he was struck on the back of the head. If he was facing her, that means someone else must have hit him from behind."

"She managed to catch him on the cheek. He yelled, turned, and stumbled back down the step. She hit him again on the back of his head. According to her, there was no one else there."

"And you believe her?"

Noah nodded. "Yes, I do."

"Come on. Deanna looks strong, but you can't think she dragged his body to the cliff top in that wicked storm and threw him over the edge all by herself. Are you sure Peter didn't help her?"

"She swears he didn't. According to her, the last time she saw Chad, he was stumbling off in the direction of the cliff. She admits she'd hoped he'd fall in a snowbank and lose some appendages to frostbite, but she swears she didn't push him or drag him anywhere."

Addie narrowed her eyes, studying Noah. "How does Peter fit into this?"

"According to Deanna, he's only a close friend. After Chad stumbled away, Deanna started feeling guilty that maybe he was lying somewhere out there, and contrary to her initial wish of him suffering from frostbite, she was concerned he'd freeze to death in the storm. She called Peter, and he came to look around for Chad to make sure he hadn't collapsed somewhere. When he couldn't find any trace of him, they both figured he had gone back to the B&B."

"But then, when a man's body was found—"

"Deanna says she was sick and hoped it wasn't Chad, but that hope didn't last long. When she heard it was Chad Sanders's body on the rocks . . ." Noah inhaled sharply. "I tell you, Addie, I've never seen a woman weep as violently as Deanna did when she told this part of her story. I don't think she ever meant to kill him. She only wanted him out of Nikki's life."

"Then why didn't she come forward when Nikki was arrested and under suspicion for murder? If she wanted to protect Nikki from Chad's violent nature, you'd think she'd want to protect her from going to prison for a crime she knew Nikki didn't commit."

"You'd have to ask her that, I guess. I never asked, and she didn't divulge that information. All I know is that panicked people rarely, if ever, do rational things. She was terrified."

As much as she resented Deanna hanging Nikki out to dry, Addie's heart broke for her, and she thought, too, about the lengths to which she would go to protect a loved one or the life of an innocent person. She shivered.

Noah slipped his coat off and placed it around her shoulders, giving her a half hug before taking his seat again.

Addie cuddled his coat around her and inhaled his scent. Comforted by his presence, his smell, and the residual body warmth of his coat, she sighed. In spite of all the mixed messages she was receiving from him—including the fleeting kiss, the thumb caressing her hand, and the gesture of wrapping her up in his coat—she knew she had to push all her fanciful thoughts from her mind. She sat up straight and brought herself back to the here and now. "Have you had any news about the stolen items that weren't returned, or anything about the thief? I guess my initial ideas about the theft and murder being connected were wrong."

"Welcome to police work." Noah grinned. "But, no, nothing else has been recovered. Sorry about your book. I know that was special to you."

"It's okay. It wasn't for me in the first place, but the loss of a book, no matter the value, always bothers me." She shrugged. "Maybe the missing items will still show up somehow."

"Miraculous things often happen when you least expect them," he said, his eyes glimmering with something that made Addie's heart race.

"Miracles?" She cleared her throat. "I'm not sure I believe in them, but enough about fantasy. What's the very real fall-out from everything?"

"Nikki is all free and clear." He ticked off his fingers as he spoke. "The DA and mayor, while they won't admit to their little witch hunt, at least looked humbled. I offered my sincerest apologies to Nikki on their behalf, and for my part in having to play their little game. There's nothing to hold Peter on, so he's free as well."

"And Deanna?" Addie clutched his coat tighter around her, chilled at the thought of Deanna's future.

"The official charge is manslaughter. I'm sure her lawyer, a bigwig whom Peter brought in, will plead it down so that her stint in prison will be negligible, but that's for the courts and a jury to decide." He clasped Addie's hand in his. "Our part is officially over." His voice took on a raspy quality.

Her stomach sank. This was it. His work here was done. This was where he'd walk out of her life, and she'd never see him again.

"Addie? You look as if you've seen a ghost. Are you okay?"

A ghost? If she considered the haunted past of her love life, he couldn't have spoken a greater truth.

"Yes." She forced a smile. "Just tired is all. It's been a long week."

His gaze tenderly moved over her face.

"I, ah, actually came by for two things, Addie. The first was to tell you how everything had settled, and the second . . ." He unexpectedly broke eye contact with her.

"And the second," Addie whispered, barely recognizing her own voice.

He reconnected his gaze with hers and took a breath. "I needed to tell you I'm leaving."

This was how she would die, Addie thought as she struggled to breathe under the enormity of his statement. An irrational fear seized her, and she knew right then that she didn't just like or respect Detective Inspector Noah Parker. She had fallen in love with him, and now he was going home to England. Just like she had once said her goodbyes to him to come home to Greyborne Harbor, a move she had come to regret. She had often wondered what would happen if they'd had more time together; now she knew, and it was all for nothing.

She knew she should fill the space between them with flippancy, meaningless phrases of the see-you-later-then variety, but if air couldn't pass through her windpipe, then words—especially words that meant nothing—wouldn't either. She blinked as the image of

Noah blurred through her tear-filled eyes. *Say something, Addie, anything.* "Safe travels," she squeaked. *Not that, Addie, anything but that!*

"'Safe travels'?" Noah repeated, his voice filled with confusion. "That's all you have to say? After all we've been through, after I thought . . ." His voice hitched. "Apparently, I was wrong. I won't take up any more of your time. I wish you all the happiness in the world, Addie."

Addie reached for him, staying him with her hand on his arm. "No, don't go. I . . . I . . ."

Noah tilted his head and studied her gently. "What, Addie? What do you want?"

Why on earth could she so freely hurl herself on top of someone she knew was a murderer, or repeatedly put herself in harm's way without a moment's hesitation, but when it came to professing her love for Noah, she couldn't find the words and turned pure coward?

The death of her beloved late fiancé, David, flashed before her eyes, and the sharp pain of that memory pierced her heart. Marc and Simon's faces also danced through her mental visions, and she recoiled at the pain of the premature love of one and the betrayal of the other. No wonder she was a coward when it came to love. Every time she risked her heart, she lost it.

However, looking at Noah, she knew he was different. She hadn't felt this way about any other man since David. Sure, there'd been Marc and Simon, and even though she'd fallen for them for different reasons, they'd each taught her different lessons about herself and her past self. But she was not her past self now. She was a new Addie. One who refused to sit in the passenger seat of her own life.

Addie reached out and cupped Noah's stubbly jaw. Through the education her messy life had provided, she'd learned what she wanted and needed in a man, and she wanted—and needed—Noah Parker.

"Addie?" Concern filled Noah's gruff voice.

"Ask me again."

"What?"

"Ask me again what I want," she whispered.

His eyes glimmered, and he leaned closer, his warm breath wafting over her cheek. "What do you want, Addie?"

"You."

Instead of kissing her as she'd hoped, Noah pulled back, his eyes filled with a mixture of emotions, but the only one that Addie latched on to was sadness. Great, she'd done it again. *So much for putting my heart on the line! When will I ever learn?*

"Will you wait for me, Addie?"

She blinked, trying to compute his question.

"I have something I need to take care of first." He pulled her closer and kissed her temple, staying there for blissful seconds before pulling away. "I need to go to New York City for Christmas. For . . . for my late wife, Julia. I must finish this for her . . . and for me . . . before I can . . . start again." His eyes searched hers as if pleading for her to understand.

Her heart skipped a beat. He wasn't leaving her; he was going to say his final goodbyes to his late wife. "Well, you'd better go then, before the weather changes its mind again." How she spoke around the rock-sized lump in her throat, she didn't know.

He smiled. "Happy Christmas, Addie, and don't forget that Christmas miracles sometimes do happen." He kissed her forehead, her right cheek, and her left cheek, and hovered over her lips, but then he eased away, took his coat from her shoulders, and walked out of her shop.

Chapter Thirty

Addie woke with a start to Pippi's frantic barking. Pippi often yipped, but rarely barked this loudly or for this long. Addie flung off her covers, jumped out of bed, tripped over her slippers, and ran from her room. She raced down the steps and snatched a yapping Pippi off the floor by the front door, cuddling the little dog to her chest.

"What's gotten into you? Is this how you wake your mama on Christmas morning?"

Pippi yipped and struggled in Addie's arms.

"Fine," said Addie, putting her down, "but what on earth are you barking at?"

Addie peeked around the window beside the front door. Nobody was there. She shook her head and was about to head back to bed, but Pippi yipped and pranced and yipped again.

Addie checked a second time out the window, pressing her face against the cold glass and peering down at the front step. She gasped. There was a beautifully wrapped present on the front porch.

"What in the world?" She opened the front door and glanced around. She couldn't make out any fresh tracks in the snow, but yet she swore she could hear the distant sound of jingle bells. A cold wind gust snaked its arms around her. She shivered and quickly brought the mysterious present inside setting it on the long table in the foyer.

It was a square box, neatly and expertly wrapped in sparkly red gift wrap and topped with a silver bow. On a tiny tag her name was scrawled in neat cursive letters. She eyed the package, thinking she should wait to open it until Nikki got up, but then her natural curiosity took over.

"Well, Pippi, here goes nothing." Addie tore into the packaging, lifted the cover, and gasped. Tucked neatly inside and resting on a blanket of white tissue paper were the red-and-white mittens she'd admired the night of the robbery at the museum. She put them on and held them under her chin, savoring the warmth.

She dashed to the front door, whipped it open, stepped out on the front porch, and craned her neck in all directions to see if she could catch sight of the elusive gift giver. Nothing but evergreens and a blanket of freshly fallen snow met her eye.

"Hmmm." Addie stepped back into the warmth of her house and rammed into Nikki.

"What on earth are you doing outside in your pajamas and"—she squinted at Addie's hands—"mittens?"

Addie held up her hands. "A mystery gift giver."

"But weren't those one of the stolen items from the raffle donations?"

"Yes. I suppose I'll have to give them over to Jerry." She tugged them off and shoved them back in the box.

"But who gave them to you?"

"No clue, and I don't have time to find out, as you and I have a very special place to be in"—she glanced at the clock above the mantel in the living room—"an hour. Yikes!"

Nikki waved away her concern. "You're always worried, Addie. Relax. What could possibly go wrong on Christmas morning—the morning of Paige's wedding?"

Addie ground her teeth as Nikki skipped off up the steps, humming the "Wedding March." "Now you jinxed us," Addie muttered as she ambled up the steps behind Nikki.

As soon as Addie got back to her room, Pippi at her heels, she closed the door and hurriedly pulled her bridesmaid's dress from her closet. She was about to head to the bathroom when her phone rang.

"It must be Paige, wondering if I can bring something she's forgotten." Addie laughed, gazing down at Pippi. "Yes, Paige, Nikki and I are coming. We've had quite the—"

"Addie?" A familiar male British accent sailed through the phone.

"Jasper?" Why on earth was Mr. Pressman's apprentice, Jasper Henderson, calling her on Christmas morning? Fearing the worst, she turned the phone's speaker on, and with trembling hands, set it on the bedside table.

"Addie, I'm so glad you answered this time."

Addie checked her missed calls. Five of them. "Jasper, what's wrong?"

"It's Mr. Pressman. He had a heart attack last night, and I . . . I thought you'd like to know."

"Oh my gosh." Addie smacked her hand over her heart. "Is Mr. Pressman okay?"

"The doctor thinks he'll make a full recovery, but he'll need to take some much-needed time off."

"Thank goodness," Addie said.

"My thoughts exactly. While Mr. Pressman is recuperating, I'm taking over the shop, Addie."

Addie smiled at the self-important tone seeping into Jasper's voice. Of course, Mr. Pressman's apprentice would love nothing more than to pretend to be in charge for a while.

"I mean, how hard can running a business be?"

Addie's smile disappeared, and she hoped Jasper hadn't noticed her gasp of shock.

With Jasper's blasé attitude about everything, having him at the helm could very likely bring about an end to Mr. Pressman's centuries-old family business.

"Jasper, if you do anything to ruin Mr. Pressman's business, I'll fly across the pond and—"

"I figured you say that. I'm hoping you'd do just that, actually."

"Oh, Jasper." Addie chuckled. "I would if I could, you know that, but this isn't a very good time for me. But please know I'm happy to help in any way I can. There's a lot I can still do to help, even from this distance. I'm here for you, anytime, so call me whenever you need to, even if it's just for a few words of encouragement, promise?"

"Promise, and thanks, Addie."

"Thank you for letting me know, and please keep me in the loop, but if anything changes, let me know right away. Then I'll do whatever I have to do so I can come back."

"Thanks for that. But don't worry. He's fine, and we'll be fine. Happy Christmas."

"Merry Christmas, to you, too, Jasper. Remember, call whenever you need to." Addie clicked off the call and sank onto her bed, her mind spinning.

Between the mystery mittens and Jasper's phone call, Addie wasn't sure she could concentrate on the task of the day: getting her friend down the aisle and happily wed.

Nikki burst through the door. "Addison Greyborne, you're not even dressed. Come on, the one person who cannot be late to a wedding is the maid of honor." Nikki tossed Addie's dress at her. "Hustle, my friend."

An hour later, Addie, showered and all dressed up, pulled her MINI into the back parking lot of Mario's; dug out her wedding emergency kit from the trunk; lifted the hem of her burgundy, floor-length velvet dress; and walked gingerly in her high heels down a narrow, shoveled path to the back door, Nikki hot on her heels.

Addie stashed her coat and wedding-emergency kit in the back room, then entered the main restaurant and stood in awe. Mario's restaurant had been transformed into a magical winter wonderland, complete with flocked Christmas trees glistening with white lights and silver and gold ornaments. Fairy lights dripped from the ceiling, and Addie pinched herself to make sure she hadn't been sucked into a fairy world.

"Rumor has it that if you stare too long at fairy lights, you become a fairy yourself."

Addie spun around at an all-too-familiar voice, squealed, "Catherine!" and squeezed the woman's slender body in a hug so tight she was afraid she might break her.

Catherine embraced her just as hard back and chuckled. "You're a sight for sore eyes, Addie." She eased out of the embrace and held Addie at arm's length. "You look stunning."

Addie swiped a tear from her cheek. "Careful or I'll mess up the makeup I worked very hard to apply so I wouldn't look like a painted lady." She squeezed Catherine's slender hand, then led her through the crowd of wedding guests awaiting the start of the ceremony. They found two chairs tucked away in a corner. "When did you get here?"

"Last night. I was going to drop by, but both Felix and I were so tired from our journey we even contemplated sleeping in the car instead of walking to our hotel room." She clasped Addie's hand. "It's so good to be home. To see you." She released Addie's hands and placed her warm palm against Addie's cheek. "Something's eating you, though, dear. What is it?"

Addie cast her gaze down; the tips of her shoes were suddenly easier to face than her dear friend, who always could see right into her soul. After all that had happened with Marc and Simon, Catherine had always been there to help pick up the pieces of Addie's shattered heart. How could she tell Catherine now that ever since Noah had left her with a promise to return, she'd felt unsettled and powerless?

At times, she'd even debated going to New York to find him, just to be sure he hadn't vanished. Other times, she'd been tempted to text him or call him, but she knew he needed his space to say goodbye to a woman he'd loved and probably always would in his heart, just as she'd done with David. There was something about first loves and loss that never did actually leave you and Addie knew that's what Catherine felt about Addie's father when she was forced to give him up by Hattie, so she might understand. On the other hand, what would Catherine say about this seeming whirlwind state of anxiety and love Addie found herself in today?

But Addie was saved from having to open her soul for inspection when Nikki waltzed over and grabbed her arm.

"We're up, maid of honor. It's time for some wedding bells," Nikki sing-songed and led Addie away.

Addie waved helplessly at Catherine, who chuckled, waved back, and mouthed, *"We'll talk later."*

Addie grinned in response, and for the next hour, she stayed busy orchestrating, managing, and dabbing away tears—hers and Paige's—brought on by witnessing and then celebrating the wedding of her friend, Paige, to the love of her life, Logan.

In one final moment, the officiant declared them husband and wife, and just like that, the final page of Addie's old life turned, revealing no new pages. This was it. This was final. All ties to the old Addie were gone, and for the first time since realizing her life was changing, Addie had no remorse. Everyone was moving on—and so was she.

She snatched a post-ceremony drink from a serving tray that passed by her, slid up to the newly wedded Paige, and gave her a hug. "I'm so happy for you! You're going to be the happiest woman in the world."

Serena, who looked gorgeous in a teal-green wraparound dress, gushed, "Especially since a surprise showed up at Paige's door this morning."

"Oh, was Logan being super romantic?" Addie grinned.

"If it was him, he's denying any involvement," Paige said. "On the doorstep were two wrapped packages. One had a pair of antique plaster owl bookends, and the other was a doll for Emma."

Addie sucked in a breath. "You're kidding!"

"No, and the funny thing was Emma swore she heard jingle bells just before the doorbell rang. I told her it must have been Logan playing a Christmas trick on us, but he says it wasn't him. Why do you ask? Did you leave them?" asked Paige.

"No, but those are some of the still-missing donated items for the Twelve Days of Christmas raffle." Addie filled them in on what Jerry had told her about the still-unaccounted-for donation items—and the pair of mittens she'd found on her doorstep that morning. She mentioned she'd heard what she thought were jingle bells too.

"You're telling me that the doll, a train set, and the handmade baby blanket on my doorstep this morning are *also* stolen goods?" Serena asked, a slight pout on her lips. "The twins will be heartbroken because they said they heard bells too and got so excited about it being Santa."

"I'd say it's more like an elusive, jingle bell–toed elf thief who suddenly had a guilty conscious and found a way to return stolen property while still managing to remain anonymous." Addie shook her head.

"What's this about stolen property?" Jerry asked, a grin on his face. "Is one of you the elf thief I've been looking for?"

"If we were, we wouldn't make it nearly this easy for you to find us out. Besides"—Addie threw her arm around the new bride, swathed in a princess-cut ivory wedding dress—"you can't arrest a bride on her wedding day."

Jerry chuckled. "I know for a fact you three didn't do it, because I'm not sure you could act normally if you'd committed a crime. You'd probably break down in a fit of giggles just from me looking at you sideways."

Addie quickly filled him in on their morning surprises. "So, what would you like us to do with the contraband?" she asked.

"Well, the gala is now being held on New Year's Eve, and my understanding is they're going to hold a silent auction then of the donations recovered so as to try to raise the needed funds they lost on the raffle. I suppose you'd better give the items back to the museum. Although I know Trevor isn't heartless. Since most were for the kids, maybe he'll let you keep the toys. I'm not sure about the mittens, though, Addie"— he chuckled—"but if the chief says it's okay, I don't see why you couldn't." Jerry saluted them with his champagne glass and disappeared into the crowd.

"Here's hoping they don't want Martha's hand-knit mittens back." Addie grinned.

"If they do, your chances are pretty high that if you ask her, Mom would be more than happy to knit you another pair. She's never been in a better mood." Paige gestured with her champagne flute to a dazzling Martha decked out in an emerald-green, sequined mother-of-the-bride dress and smiling as she'd never smiled before.

"Well, well, well," Addie said. "It looks like weddings agree with everyone."

The DJ cued up the bride and groom's song, and a dapper, tuxedo-clad Logan walked over to them and slid his arm around his new wife. "Will you do me the honor of dancing with me, my lovely bride?"

Paige looked at him with such love that Addie had to look away from the pain it caused her. Not that she wasn't happy for her friend, but her own love ghosts threatened to overtake her, and she willed herself not to cry. She'd already cried enough during the ceremony, so much so that her purse was stuffed with used tissues.

As soon as Paige and Logan waltzed off to the middle of the dance floor, Zach came up, smiled at Addie and apologized, and apologized for whisking his wife away. Before she knew it, Addie was alone on the outskirt of the dance floor, witnessing true love's first dance.

A familiar musky, amber scent tickled Addie's nose, and her heart thudded so hard she lost her breath. It was unfair that she couldn't even get Noah's scent out of her mind. That, or she needed to talk to him about wearing so much cologne that she could smell it from New York. Despite the heat of the crowded restaurant, she curled her faux-fur wrap tighter around her shoulders, imagining for a second that the arms of her wrap were Noah's.

"Why such a long face, Addie? Don't you believe in Christmas miracles?" Noah's voice came from behind her.

Addie whirled around, squealed in delight, and threw herself in his arms. His arms tightened around her, and for the first time in a long time, Addie felt whole.

After several moments spent clinging to each other, Noah eased out of her embrace and cupped her cheek with his hand. "I thought the maid of honor was supposed to smile at her friend's wedding?"

Past Addie would have hedged the question, come up with something that diminished her feelings instead of being honest with herself or him. New Addie was fully here to stay. "I missed you, and I couldn't bear it."

His gaze was tender, and he moved to draw her in, but a throat clearing behind them stilled his hands.

Addie blushed and dipped her head as Catherine openly perused Noah. "I see I've interrupted a moment. I do hope you'll forgive me, Addie, from ripping you away from this gentleman here."

"Catherine, let me introduce you." Addie motioned to Noah. "This is Noah Parker, a detective inspector from the UK." She gestured to Catherine. "Noah, this is Catherine Lewis, a dear friend of mine."

Catherine shook Noah's extended hand. "Pleased to meet you. Do you mind if I steal Addie away for a moment?"

"Of course not," Noah smiled at Catherine, then dropped his head and whispered in Addie's ear, "Meet me outside when you're done?"

Addie nodded, relishing in the kiss he left on her cheek. She knew the goofy grin she had on her face made her look like a fool in love, but she didn't care.

"So," Catherine drawled as she unceremoniously dragged Addie to a corner of the room and sat her down on one of the two open chairs. "I see a lot has happened since I left you to your own devices." Catherine settled herself in a chair, clasped her hands together in her lap, and grinned like a child preparing to listen to an epic fairy tale. "Do share."

Addie all but bounced out of her chair, but she gathered her thoughts and dove in, regaling Catherine with the details of the theft, the murder, the investigation, and the fallout from all of it.

When Catherine sat quietly, her head tilted at Addie as if she expected more, Addie asked, "What else do you want to know?"

"You know exactly what I want to know. While I appreciate the saga of your crime-solving adventure, I want to know who that tall drink of British water is, and I want to know all about him." A twinkle in Catherine's eye warned Addie that nothing but the truth and the whole truth was going to satisfy her friend.

"It's a long story," Addie said, eyeing the dancing couples who were now on to song number three. She wasn't sure whether Noah was waiting for her outside, but from the way Catherine was eyeing her, there was no way she was going to get out of this one. Poor Noah. She hoped that if he was, he was at least wearing warm outer clothes and wool socks. He was British—of course he was. What was she thinking? Those English were always grumbling on about the weather.

"Then you'd better start telling it, so your man doesn't turn into an icicle out there." Catherine grinned and gestured with her hand toward the window and the man standing outside, briskly rubbing his arms and stamping his feet.

Addie took a deep breath and then dove into her storied history with Noah—their initial meeting, their first impressions of each other, the eventual softening, and ending with, "And now I love him, Catherine. I really do."

Catherine clasped Addie's hands in hers. Tears swam in her eyes. "I'm so happy for you, Addie. I knew this day would come for you, and I feel as if my heart couldn't fill with any more joy without exploding."

"I feel the same," Addie said, but she couldn't fight the frown that threatened to kill her smile. "I just . . . What do I do? Loving someone is the easy part. Making sacrifices and changes to one's normal life, that is the hard part."

"Ah, so he either needs to leave everything in England and move here, or you have to leave your life and friends here in Greyborne Harbor and move across the pond?"

Hearing the stark truth from Catherine caused a

dark rain cloud to settle upon Addie's earlier sunny mood. Basking in Noah's arms was the easy part. Choosing where she'd be while in his arms was the hardest. "I don't know what to do," Addie whispered.

She knew from her experience with David when she spent six months on a work exchange in England that long-distance romances were hard. She wasn't sure she could bear the long periods of separation from Noah too. Leaving Greyborne Harbor would be difficult, but she'd already come to terms with and accepted her present self—and the different future she'd have from her dear friends, who'd found futures of their own.

What on earth was she thinking? It was time she found hers as well.

Addie wanted Noah for her future, and if that meant moving back to England to see what the future held for their newfound love, she would. Besides, with Mr. Pressman recuperating from his medical emergency, Jasper could use a helping hand. Was this fate's way of pushing her in the direction it wanted her to go?

Catherine took Addie's hands in hers and squeezed them. "I know you'll make the right decision. You just need to give yourself permission to take the risk. Don't be too hard on yourself and always remember that the road to so-called perfection is filled with disappointment. The truth is, my dear child, things like family and love are messy. There is no perfect in life. You just have to enjoy the beauty in the mess."

"And what a mess I'm in." Addie smiled through her tears.

"There's only one person right now who can help

you with that mess, and I think he's still standing out-side waiting for you." Catherine winked. "I believe that's your cue to start the rest of your life, Addie."

Addie embraced Catherine. "Thank you," she whis-pered and skirted the outside of the dance floor toward the front door and her future.

Chapter Thirty-one

Addie stepped out into the frosty, clear Christmas Day and right into Noah's welcoming arms.

He pressed a quick kiss on the top of her head. "Let's get out of this cold." He grabbed her hand and tugged her down the street, around the corner, and past her bookshop, with the Closed sign clearly hanging on the door, all the while ignoring her pleas and questions about where he was taking her until he finally stopped.

"Serena's tea shop?" Addie asked. "But it's closed. Elle and Serena are at the wedding, and besides, it's Christmas Day?"

"It's someplace to keep warm while we talk, and Serena was kind enough to lend me her shop keys." Noah dangled them in his hand, unlocked the front door, and ushered Addie inside.

The comforting scent of the familiar herbs and spices Serena used in her tea blends calmed Addie, and she settled into a chair at a table away from the large picture window facing the street. There was no need for passersby to think the tea shop was open, only to be disappointed when they were refused entrance.

Noah settled in across from her, joined his hands with hers in the center of the table, and ran his thumbs over the back of her hands. He studied her face as if he wanted to memorize it for eternity.

Her heart dipped, and an uneasy sensation swirled in her stomach. Had he decided while on his New York venture that he couldn't leave the memory of his late wife and move forward with Addie? Was he leaving for good, with no intention of seeing where their relationship could go?

"Stop it, Addie," Noah said, his hands squeezing hers.

"Stop what?" Addie said, her voice hardly recognizable to her own ears.

"Stop thinking the worst." He smiled gently and smoothed his finger down her scrunched-up nose. "You're already thinking the worst-case scenario, and I haven't even spoken yet."

How did he know? It was as though he were inside her head. Addie couldn't speak around the lump in her throat. She swallowed hard and took a deep breath. "Got me there. What is it you want to say?"

He chuckled. "Why do I get the sense that this is exactly how you are when you have to go to the dentist?"

"Because this is exactly how I feel going to the dentist. Filled with dread." She nervously chuckled.

"Dread?" Noah shuffled around the table, sat next to

her, and pulled her to him. "Why dread? What's wrong? Has something changed between us, because I—"

Addie rested her hand on his cheek. "No. I'm afraid I've chosen you, Noah Parker, and there's nothing you can do about it."

"And this causes dread?" he asked, his voice teetering on concern.

"It's just that . . ."

"It's just that what? I thought you felt this"—he squeezed her shoulder—"whatever this is, the same as I do?"

"It's just that I've been thinking, and realistically, I can't be at two places at once. And I'm torn, Noah. I don't know what to do. Could we . . . can we do a long-distance relationship? Will that work? So many couples think they can, but then time eventually takes its toll, and . . . and now that I've found you, I don't want to risk losing you."

"You won't ever lose me, Addie. At least not because of the distance between us. On that, I swear, but I do have a confession to make." His hand tightened on hers.

Panic sent icy fingers across her skin, and she shivered.

"I didn't just go to New York to say my final good-byes to Julia." His voice wavered, and he closed his eyes and rested his forehead against hers. "I needed to leave to gather my courage, but when I got there, I realized two things. I'd already said my goodbyes to Julia, and she'd want me to find joy and happiness wherever I was, bucket list or no bucket list."

After a beat of silence, Addie asked, "And the second?"

"My future is here with you, not all alone in a crowded city, where nobody cares who I am or about the ache I carry in my heart."

"And what ache do you carry in your heart, Noah?"

He leaned back and stared up at the ceiling. "Remember that judge I mentioned, the one who gave me the wise advice?"

Addie blinked at the sudden change in topic. "Yes?"

"That judge was my father," Noah said, his tone flat and dead.

"Your father? You refer to him in the past tense. Has he passed?"

"No, he's still very much alive."

"I see," said Addie, furrowing her forehead at Noah's vicious tone.

"He and I are, shall we say, estranged."

"I'm sorry," Addie whispered and clutched his hand. "Why are you estranged from him?"

Instead of answering her question, Noah smiled sadly at her. "Can I tell you about Julia?"

Addie's toes curled in her high heels. She wasn't sure she wanted to hear about Noah's late wife, but from the glimmer in Noah's eyes, she knew he needed to share. "Of course."

"Julia was one of the finest women I knew, and the worst day of my life was when I got the call that someone had ripped her life away from her . . . away from me . . . away from . . ." He closed his eyes and took a few deep breaths. "Our daughter."

Addie gasped. "You have a daughter?" she whispered.

"Yes."

"How old is she?"

"She just turned ten." Noah shifted in his chair until they were facing each other and drew Addie's hands to his chest. "I need to tell you about her before we go any further with us. I need to know that you'll love her as I do, Addie. She's the most precious person on earth to me, and I . . . I . . . ." Tears shimmered in his eyes.

Addie's heart raced with a warm sensation she never knew she could experience. "How could I not love her? I love you, Noah Parker, and she is part of you."

He gave her a cheeky grin. "Did you just admit that you love me, Addie Greyborne?"

"Perhaps. But those words don't come easy for me, so if you weren't listening the first time, I'm afraid you've missed your—"

"Oh, how I love you." Noah's lips descended on hers and kissed her until Addie felt like she'd never be able to think again. Not that she wanted to think, because being in his arms, his lips on hers, was what her dreams of the past year were made of.

He broke off the kiss and nuzzled her ear. "You're thinking again."

"How'd you know?"

"Your nose. It scrunches in a rather adorable manner when you think."

"I guess I do have a tell." She giggled and cuddled into his chest. "So, when do I get to meet your daughter? What's her name?"

"Hannah. Her name is Hannah, and I don't get to see her as often as I want to."

Addie's heart broke at the anguish in his voice. "You don't? Why? Where is she? Why isn't she on this trip with you?"

"Always with the rapid-fire questions, aren't you?" He sat forward and smoothed his hand down her back. "Hannah is with my parents now, on the family estate outside of London."

"And you still don't get to see her?"

"You see, my father, the judge, works for the Ministry of Justice." Noah shifted in his seat.

"It was his office overseeing the case against the man who'd killed my wife."

Addie cringed. She could sense she'd soon find out why Noah's voice was filled with bitterness when speaking of his father. "What happened?"

"The man was guilty as sin, but due to a technicality with how some of the evidence was collected, every other piece of evidence was thrown under scrutiny, and in the end, my father's office ruled for the case to be dismissed and a new trial was ordered. That, of course, gave the criminal time to assemble one of the best defense teams in the UK—and ultimately he was found not guilty."

Anger flooded Addie, heating her from the inside out. "How dare he!"

"I thought that same thing," Noah said. "I had a nervous breakdown, actually, and Hannah and I went to live in Mayfair with Julia's parents for a while until I could get my bearings straight."

"What happened then?" She tilted her head and looked up at him.

"My father resented that I'd questioned his office's authority in a televised interview about the case, and shortly after that, he became the driving force behind my sudden transfer from the Met Police to the West Yorkshire Police Department. He even claimed that I was an unfit father, using my recent breakdown as a perfect example, and stated that Hannah would be better off living with them, so that she wouldn't be taken out of her private school in London."

"I take it he lied?"

"Yes. In order to save face, he took my rights as Hannah's father away, and to make it worse, Hannah *didn't* get to stay in her school with all her friends, at a time when she needed them most. Instead, he sent her away to boarding school. Just like my brother and I were sent away when we were kids. All because he and my mother are far too busy, socially, to look after a child, and being who my father was, a sitting lord at the time, I bet you can guess whom the courts sided with."

"And your daughter? How is she dealing with all of this?"

"I think she's stronger than I am." He chuckled and shook his head. "Always a little firecracker."

"When do you get to see her?"

"I'm allowed to see her at the school once a month, supervised, of course."

With his words, Addie's heart crushed against her chest wall, and she wrapped her arms around him, holding him tight.

He eased from her arms and ran his finger down her cheek. "So, Addie"—his gaze searched hers—"with all of my skeletons out of the closet, are you sure you still love me?"

"I love you even more, if that's possible," Addie said, her heart so full in the moment she feared it would burst. "But I've been thinking—"

"Uh-oh." Noah grinned and evaded her playful swat.

"You're incorrigible." Her smile slipped, knowing what she was about to say, but she forged ahead. "Noah, I don't want to do a long-distance relationship. Not that I think we couldn't do it. I just don't want to be far away from you, like across-the-pond far."

"I agree." Noah's eyes were twinkling.

Addie cocked her head and studied him, unsure why he found her confession so humorous. "Well, I don't know if you've heard, but Jasper called me this morning and told me Mr. Pressman had a heart attack."

Noah nodded. "He called me, too. I didn't want to ruin your special day with Paige, so I figured I'd tell you the news later. But what does this have to do with your no-long-distance-relationship proposal?"

"My life here"—Addie paused, took a deep breath, and grasped Noah's hand—"has changed. You could even say it's nonexistent. All my friends have moved on to the next chapters of their lives, and I'm tired of clutching onto a book that's been closed for a long time now. I've been thinking that I could go back to Moorscrag for a while, help Jasper so he doesn't run Mr. Pressman's business into the ground, and you and I could start building a life together there in England. And now that I know about Hannah, it sounds even more perfect. Until we can get the legalities around her custody sorted out, you'd still be able to see her."

"You'd be willing to give up all this?" Noah gestured out the window, where a light snow had started to fall. Across the street, in the park entrance, a few wedding guests, including Serena and Zach, Paige and Logan, and Marc and Whitney, milled around as a man carrying a camera case slipped and skidded across the street toward them. Marc bent over and kissed the top of Whitney's head, and Zach and Logan laughed at something Serena and Paige were animatedly talking about.

Addie swallowed around the lump that had grown in her throat. The idea of her friends moving on without her had once terrified her, making her feel insignificant. But now, with her hand in Noah's and the idea of an adventure with him, she didn't feel lonely anymore. Her friends would always be with her. They were all simply on separate paths to their own happiness.

"Bad timing for that question, I suppose?" There was doubt in Noah's voice.

Time to squash his and her doubts for good. "No." Addie tore her gaze from her friends and turned her attention to Noah. "There is no such thing as bad timing. Everything happens for a reason when the time is right. And all the roads I've traveled have led me straight to you."

"How so?"

"Take Marc and me, for instance," she said, gesturing to him across the street. "He came along at a time in my life when I had experienced a horrific loss and thought I'd never be able to love again. He showed me I could, even though it turned out not to be him, and that was for the better, because look at him now. He's found his true love match. Then there's Simon. He helped me to open up my whole heart, with no reservations like I'd had with Marc, and for the first time, I walked down the aisle as a bride-to-be." She lowered her gaze. "Then a few words changed everything, and I was on my own again. Then something else happened, and I discovered I had some self-reflection to do about who I really was, and through that, my heart began to heal again."

She squeezed his hands and met his steady gaze. "Then I met you. It's been slow, painfully slow, to get to this point, but I feel totally free now, not hindered by my past self. The old Addie doesn't exist anymore—no baggage, no ghosts. So, to answer your question"—Addie cupped his cheek—"I don't consider myself to be giving up anything. I consider myself to be gaining everything."

"Have I mentioned that I love you?"

"Only once, which I'm sure is an oversight on your part." Addie grinned.

"An oversight I plan to rectify as soon as I can, but I fear poor Jasper will have to manage on his own for a while."

"And just how does Jasper again sneak his way into our conversation?"

"Because I didn't just go say my final goodbyes to Julia. I made a pit stop on my way upstate."

"And where did you go?"

"A little town called Pen Hollow."

Addie's mind whirled with memories of her stint there and the crime she'd helped solve. "What on earth were you doing there?"

"It seems a certain police chief has fallen out of grace with his community, and he retired. The town council is looking to reform their entire police department—and so you're now looking at the new police chief of Pen Hollow."

Addie gaped at him. "When? How?" She shook her head. "When?"

"That's part of the reason I got a hire car. Obviously, then I didn't know I'd get the job, but I thought if I had my own transportation, I could bring you the book, see you, and try to gauge where we stood after England last year. Then, of course, I got waylaid here and more time passed before I could drive back to Boston to get a flight to New York City to say goodbye to Julia as planned. Then fly back to Boston, drive up the coast for my interview, and then hopefully"—he took a breath—"should things work out between us as I'd hoped they would after this time together—I'd surprise you with the news of the position offer. As I am now."

Addie's heart flip-flopped in her chest, and she flung herself into his arms and squeezed him until he patted her on the back.

"I can't breathe, love."

"Sorry." Addie let up some pressure but didn't let go. "You know what this means, right?" Addie whispered into his neck.

"Yes." He withdrew from her embrace, cupped her

face in his hands, and kissed her. "I'll only be fifteen minutes away, and you don't have to give up your life here to be with me. You can also—"

"Shhhh." Addie placed her finger against his lips. "Just kiss me."

Noah grinned, dipped his head, and did just as she ordered.

And while she was still able to think with his lips on hers, she realized that Christmas miracles did come true.

Visit our website at
KensingtonBooks.com
to sign up for our newsletters, read
more from your favorite authors, see
books by series, view reading group
guides, and more!

BOOK **CLUB**
BETWEEN **THE** **CHAPTERS**

Become a Part of Our
Between the Chapters Book Club
Community and Join the Conversation

Betweenthechapters.net